SUNSET CHASING

by
Jack Graham

Published in 2013 by FeedARead.com Publishing –
Arts Council funded

This book is dedicated to Lurline Soignet, one of the 'neighbourhood nuts' and our first friend in New Orleans.

Look for Jack Graham on
www.schemingpen.com

1.

New Jersey. USA. April 4th 2001.

'Follow the red line,' was all the man in the dinner jacket said.

Lewis Barasitch tugged his step-daughter along dimly lit corridors. In front of them, the murmur of young voices grew louder, until they finally entered a large room. It was the original, now-emptied kitchen of the old mansion house – it had an old-fashioned range at the far end. The centre was filled with thirty or so children of both sexes, some as young as eight; none older than fourteen. Around the walls stood men, some leaning back watching their charges. Lewis stepped away from Alice and joined them.

The selection was made by a glamorous woman, younger than Alice's mother, dressed in a low-cut gown. It took less than five minutes. Only half the children were chosen, Alice amongst them. Those rejected, shuffled out with bowed heads, leaving the 'selected' few huddled together in the centre of the room. They moved fretfully; a small flock of timorous chicks who'd lost their mother hen. The hostess faced the children.

'You will follow me,' she said sternly. 'You will not speak, and at all times you will smile. If a guest chooses you, you will go with them without protest. If a guest asks you to do something you will obey. No argument. Is that clear?'

There were fragmented murmurs amongst the children.

'Is that *clear*?' repeated the woman sharply, like an old-fashioned schoolmistress.

'Yes.' A ragged chorus.

'If you disobey or misbehave in any way you will be punished, and I expect that whoever you belong to will punish you as well, because they won't get paid. Do you understand?'

There was another uneven chorus of assent.

'Good. Now follow me.'

The children filed out after her. As the last one passed through, the door closed and the lock was heard to turn. The men visibly relaxed and started chatting. It was obvious that some had met before.

Five hours passed before the door was opened again. Two of the youngest children were brought in. This time the door was left unlocked. Lewis eased it open; no one was guarding it. This had happened the last time. Things were coming to a close and security had become lax. He slid out and disappeared down the corridor into the house.

He found a servants' staircase. The last time he'd gone no further, but now he took his chance, climbed up and entered a dimly-lit corridor that ran from the head of the stairs. At the far end he chose the right-hand passage, deeply carpeted and lined on both sides with doors, presumably to bedrooms. He put his ear to the first and listened, heard a radio playing, and went on to the next. No sound. He opened it cautiously; the wash of light from the passage showed a large bed in the centre. Outside the opposite room he grinned at sounds of whimpering and heavy breathing. Behind him a door opened noisily. He dodged back into the empty room. A security guard emerged into the corridor, locked the door, and hurried off down the backstairs.

Alone again, he padded back, took thin wires from his pocket and with several sharp twists of his wrist, opened that door. The room was lit by a bank of monitors. Each of the screens was connected to a DVD recorder. It was what he'd suspected all along; it was a high class honey trap.

One screen registered a limousine as it rolled up to a portico to collect its owner. Six more showed views of two bars and a large lounge with several guests sitting on plush sofas and deep, soft chairs. Naked boys and girls served the men drinks. He peered hard at the screens and found Alice. She sat stoically on a fat man's knees while he guzzled greedily from a brandy balloon. His free hand was between her legs. From grilling Alice, Lewis knew that the guests were important people. Some of the men (it was mostly men) could not speak English. The hostess entered the lounge and started rounding up the children. The party was ending.

The last two rows of monitors were of bedrooms. All but one was empty. The screen showed a naked boy, no more than twelve years old, kneeling on a bed facing the camera. His eyes screwed up in pain, tears running down freely. Every second or so he was jolted forward by the naked man behind him, whose fat face dripped sweat, eyes screwed up with effort. He had a middle-eastern look.

Lewis felt sure he'd seen his face on television the night before. He searched and found the machine and ejected the disk, then disconnected the feed cable. On a shelf were more blank disks. He inserted one and pressed the play and record button. If he was lucky, it might trick them into thinking that they had not connected the machine properly.

He glanced again at the banqueting-hall monitor. The last of the children, including Alice, were being herded out of the room. He needed to go or he would be missed. He also had a thousand bucks to collect.

2.

Cornwall, Britain. 6th. April 2001:

The hectoring ring of the telephone woke Molly Banks. She broke through the gauzy layers of sleep, floundered in a tangle of bedclothes, finally freed herself and dragged the phone to her ear.

'Hello,' she mumbled.

'Nan?' It came in a little whisper.

Molly blinked, and miraculously was fully awake. A groan from the other side of the bed announced that Bert was disturbed by her struggle with the sheets.

'Alice? It is you, isn't it?'

She peered myopically at the bedside clock; its hands glowed in the dark. Alice was the only grandchild she would ever have, yet she had not seen or heard from the girl in four years.

'Yeah, Nan.'

'How are you? Are you alright, dear?'

'Who the hell is it?' mumbled the bundle of joy beside her. 'Tell the silly buggers to call back.'

'Shh, Bert, stop your swearing. Alice?' She waited expectantly.

'Nan, help me...' The voice trailed off into a bout of sobbing.

Molly slapped Bert to rouse him. He emitted an angry growl, turned his back and pulled the duvet over his head.

'Bert, wake up. Bert - *wake up*.'

In desperation she dug her elbow sharply into him.

'What the hell?' he shouted, jerking up in the bed.

'Bert, it's Alice,' she almost screamed, then shushed him and held the phone closer to her mouth. 'It's alright dear; I was talking to your Granddad. Now; calm down. Tell me - what's the matter?'

She let Alice sob on about her mother and stepfather. Molly stayed silent, collecting her wits while listening as the twelve-year-old vented anger at her parents.

She cupped a hand over the mouthpiece. 'Put the light on, Bert.'

Light exploded around them.

Bert groaned. 'It's 3.30 in the morning.'

She ignored him. He watched Molly nod and shake her head, then tut at an incomprehensible string of mutters from the handset. There was no point arguing with her while she was on the phone. He got out of bed. She smiled to herself; he'd make a cuppa after using the loo. She carried on listening, her brow stitched with concentration to catch each word.

'Alice, dear,' Molly interrupted, 'are you sure? What you're saying is very serious.'

'He hurts me, Nan. Don't you believe me?' Alice whined.

'I don't know what to think, dear. After your father died, your mother got very difficult.'

'Mum said you never liked her,' Alice grumbled, as if to defend her mother.

'That's not true, Alice,' Molly lied. 'I didn't know you were going to America until you sent that card.' She hastened to add 'since then I haven't heard a thing.' She paused and listened as Alice's anger grew.

'Alice; I expect that's right,' she said, to placate the child, 'but I've written every month and sent you presents and things.'

'I never got them.' Alice grumbled.

'I'm not surprised. Listen, dear; if everything you say is true, we'll do something. I want you to write down what you've told me and send it to us. I don't suppose you still live at the same address? - I thought not; let me have that now.' Molly leant sideways. 'Wait, dear.' She dragged her night-time read off the bedside table and opened it to the flyleaf, her pen poised. 'Go ahead.' She had just finished scribbling down the address when the phone went dead.

3.

Five thousand miles away Tracey Barasitch had had a bad night; it had rained hard all evening. None of her regular tricks were out on the streets. She'd come home early, dispirited and penniless, knowing Lewis would give her hell. The apartment was in darkness; Lewis was out, so she relaxed a little. As she walked to the bathroom she heard Alice whispering to someone in her room. Tracey opened the door a crack.

The child had her back to her, cradling the cordless phone. Her skinny arms and legs poked out from a tatty nightdress, and in one or two places there were scars and recent bruising.

'Who you talking to?' Tracey demanded, hard-faced, hands on hips.

Alice turned, fear in her eyes as she disconnected the call.

'No-one.'

'Don't lie.'

Tracey crossed the room, grabbed the phone and pressed the redial button. The number was not one she recognised. It was answered in a breathless voice.

'Alice?..'

'Who is this?' Tracey demanded.

Molly stayed silent. Her hands went quivery and her breathing started to go into spasm; she reached out to the bedside table and felt for her inhaler.

'I know that wheeze,' snapped Tracey.

The phone was dropped with a clunk; from a distance Molly heard Tracey yell 'You stupid little bitch!' There was a sharp slap, a scream, then more. All Molly could do was listen. Tears streamed down her face as the beating continued.

'Stop,' she begged. 'Please, stop.'

Except for Alice's crying, the noise ceased, and the phone was picked up.

'You still there? You interfering old bag, I hope you suffocate!' It went dead.

Molly pushed the inhaler into her mouth, and squeezed.

Tracey's anger and fear uncoiled in her as she jumped at Alice.

'You stupid little bitch.'

Alice tried to escape, but Tracey caught and laid into her once more. All she could do was curl up and shield her face.

'No, don't Mom. Please, Mom, stop.' But Tracey didn't stop, couldn't stop; she was beside herself. 'Don't mark me!' Alice screamed in desperation.

Tracey abruptly halted and slumped back onto the bed, breathing in gasps. 'Don't ever do that again. If Lewis finds out he'll kill you,' she said breathlessly. Her hand shook as she tried to light a cigarette. She cut her eyes to Alice once it was lit. 'What did you tell her?'

'Nothing Mom, but Mom - I don't want to go to any more of those parties.'

Tracey gripped hold of her daughter's hair and pulled her face up close.

'Listen, and listen good, you silly bitch. Never cross Lewis. Do what he wants. Get it?'

'But Mom…'

Tracey pushed Alice to the floor before her temper got the better of her and she did the girl an injury. Alice gazed up at her mother as she sat on the bed and cradled her head in her hands. Tracey started to weep.

'Oh, Alice. Do as you're fucking told.'

She got on the bed and tried to comfort her mother.

'Mom, Mom, I promise. Please, stop crying.'

Tracey gave a noisy snort, sniffed back her tears and gave the girl a fragile smile. She gazed at her own hands. They were still trembling. She needed a fix.

4.

Molly said nothing as Bert came back into the bedroom carrying a tray. She felt drained from the encounter with Tracey and what Alice had told her – and the beating she'd heard.

'That was a short call,' he said, trying to make light of it.

He placed a mug on the bedside table and picked the atomiser off the bedcover. Molly's face was pinched and drained of colour.

'You've had another attack.'

Her lips quivered. 'Yes, Tracey came on the phone.'

'Oh, and what did she have to say for herself?'

'She was awful. She must've caught Alice talking to me. She started hitting her. I think she meant me to hear.'

'Oh, dear.' Bert sat down on the edge of the bed and took her hand. 'Take a sip of tea.'

'Your answer to everything,' she snapped.

Bert ignored her and took a swig of his, as if to encourage. Studying Molly over the rim of his cup, he waited until she started to drink.

'So; how is Alice? How bad is it?'

'Bad enough.'

'How old is she now? Twelve, thirteen?'

'Just twelve. You didn't really know her, did you?'

'Not really. I came on the scene months before your son died. I recall her being a timid little thing.'

'Yes. Tracey was always hard on the girl, in fact with everyone, and Brian was never one to stand his ground.' Molly looked at Bert, her eyes watering up. 'He used to work so hard to give that woman everything. It killed him in the end.'

'You can't say that, Moll. It was a road accident.'

'It happened because that bitch demanded he get back instead of stopping overnight, so she could go out with her friends.' Her voice was full of bitterness. Bert patted her hand, trying to soothe her. 'No sooner had she buried him than she was off with that awful Yank, dragging Alice with her.' Her eyes glittered with anger. 'She didn't have the decency to tell me her plans. I only found out because Alice sent that card.'

He remembered. It was an old conversation that would never go away. They had tried everything; Social Services, the lot, but being a grandparent gave them very few rights.

'Come here.'

He opened his arms and pulled her into his embrace. Lightly, he stroked her back.

'It's been four years and not a word,' she muttered into his dressing gown.

'I know. So what did Alice have to say?'

'That she's being mistreated. You know the mother's married that Yank.'

'No, I didn't.'

'Well, it seems he's particularly nasty with her; hits her and things.'

He stiffened. 'What things?'

'You know, severe with her, I suppose. Anyway, I've asked her to write it all down and send it to me.'

Bert shivered. He should've got back into bed, but with Molly still desperately clinging to him he was loath to move.

'So, all Alice really went on about was that she's being mistreated.' He touched a finger to her lips. 'Shush - though she wasn't specific,' Molly gave an imperceptible nod. 'and that she hates her mother, and her stepfather most of all. Is that right?'

'Yes.'

'Well, that isn't much to go on, Moll. The girl's twelve; her hormones must be racing round her system. Tomorrow she'll be loving the whole world.'

'But I heard that woman lay into her,' Molly protested.

'Admittedly there's that, but God knows what a merry dance Alice may be giving them. Now, be fair. Teenagers can try the patience of a saint.'

'Oh, Bert - what should I do?'

'Now you've got their address we'll sit down sometime today and write a letter to Alice - and one to her mother. Tracey, isn't it?'

'Yes,' Molly smiled at him. She stroked his bristled cheek with the back of her fingers. 'You're so good, Bert. I don't know what I'd do without you.'

'Nor do I,' he gave her a quirky grin. 'It's a good job you married me. Isn't it?' He got stiffly off the bed. 'Want another cup?'

'No; I'll try and catch some sleep. I feel that wrung out. What about you?'

'No, I'm as lively as a cricket. I won't get back to sleep.' He stared at the open book beside her, then squinted as he noticed the writing. 'Is that her address?'

Molly picked the book up and passed it to him.

'Newark, New Jersey,' he remarked. 'That's near New York isn't it?'

'Couldn't tell you.'

'And this website; what's that?'

'Something Alice had me write down.'

'-www.sunsetchasing.py- sounds a bit strange, don't you think?'

'I wouldn't know; I'm not the computer geek in this house.'

Bert straightened himself. She gazed up at him. She loved tall men; most small women did, she thought idly, though he was all skin and bones.

'I think I'll go and see what's on this website Alice gave you.'

'You and that flipping computer.'

5.

Before tapping into the site Alice had given Molly, Bert googled the 'py' on the end of the address, because it seemed somehow strange and unfamiliar. It was a Paraguayan site; he wondered how on earth she had got hold of it. He surfed it more out of curiosity, not thinking he'd find anything scintillating in a twelve year old's blog.

Tears came unheeded to Bert's eyes, bitter and sour. He leaned across the computer and tugged out the plug. There was something final about how the screen went blank after what he had witnessed. No clicking of the mouse to log off, no dying glimmer as the picture dissolved. When he re-booted there would be a message telling him the computer had not been closed properly and that there might be corrupted files: whatever; he didn't care. He sat back, shocked, pondering over the images that seared his mind, and wondered how he was going to explain it all to Molly. Alice's naked body stretched out for sickos to gloat over.

'Bugger,' he muttered to himself, pushed back his seat and left his office, now too small and cramped to contain his anger and shock.

Molly found him in the garden, digging furiously. She was almost at his side before he realised she was there. He couldn't look her in the eye.

'I thought you'd dug this bit already.'

'Felt like doing it again.'

She gave a shrug. Married twice, she still couldn't fathom men out.

'Why don't you come on in and tell me what you've found on that blessed computer of yours. I've brewed a pot.'

It was gone ten when Bert found a space in the small car park off St Clement's roundabout. Truro's Tregolls Road police station was a 'seventies boxy build; four floors of grey, featureless concrete peppered with large windows. He was always surprised how large it was for a sub-station. It was only staffed from eight in the morning till six at night.

At the front desk a constable worked at a computer. He's hardly started shaving, thought Bert. The officer raised his head and smiled. Molly and Bert stepped up to the desk.

'Good morning, Madam. How can I help?'

Molly glanced around the crowded lobby. The place was full of people she would rather not hear her business. She leaned nervously forward, still ashen-faced from the shock. It didn't feel right to talk about Alice in front of a crowd.

'We've come to report a crime,' she whispered.

The officer picked up a pen. 'Your names, please?'

'Bert and Molly Banks,' she said timorously. He scribbled it down.

'So, Mrs Banks, what's this about?' he asked softly.

'Me grandchild is being abused - and worse. She's only twelve.'

'Can we start with her name and address?' he asked.

'Alice Jones. She lives in Newark, New Jersey, America, with her mother and stepfather. Her father, my son, died four years back.'

He laid down his pen and gazed at Molly.

'And how do you know she's being abused?'

'She called me up early this morning.'

'*She* told you?' the constable asked slowly.

'Of course she did. About three-thirty this morning.'

'This is really a welfare case. If you would hold on I'll see if the Family Liaison officer is available.'

'But I'm reporting a crime.'

'No doubt, Madam. Let's see if the relevant officer is available. If you'll take a seat, I'll see what I can do.'

Bert pulled Molly away from the desk. They stood with their backs to the wall and waited; there were no seats. They watched the officer speaking on the phone; he kept glancing over. Finally he lowered it and beckoned to them.

'I'm afraid the officer is busy at the moment. You could wait, but I don't know how long she'll be. My advice is for you to go home and we'll be in touch.'

'Home?' Molly, squared her shoulders, 'I don't think you understand young man, we've come to report a *crime*. Isn't there a detective we can speak to?'

'It's not really the sort of thing CID gets involved with.'

'Then what do they involve themselves with?' asked Bert, losing patience. 'This?'

He slapped several sheets of printouts on the counter. From each picture Alice stared up at the officer. She was naked in every one.

'Why didn't you show me these in the first place?' The policeman reappraised Molly, who was shaking violently. Her eyes glazed with unshed tears.

'Because Moll was embarrassed.' Bert looked around him to emphasise the point. A drunk further along the desk was trying to peer over Molly's shoulder. 'Now can we see someone, please?'

The rest of the day was taken up with interviews spaced out between long waits. An officer in the Child Protection Unit arrived from Bodmin. After another lengthy interview they were told that a special Child Abuse Investigation Team set up by the government in London would take the case forward. This unit had the power to close down websites in Britain. It would have taken a few hours, but as the designated site was in Paraguay it would be far more complicated. Interpol in Paris would be informed and officers from there would work with the Paraguayan authorities to shut it down, though it would be difficult. Maybe a day or two - no one was quite sure.

'What about Alice, my granddaughter?' asked Molly.

There didn't seem to be any firm opinion about what the authorities in the States would do. She was a British citizen, so it would go through the Foreign Office. 'It would take time' was all they kept cautioning, but something would be done. Officers involved with the case would be in touch. Bert drove home in silence.

6.

The day after the party Lewis was up unusually early. The place he was visiting was eight blocks away, in the seediest part of the city. He decided to walk. It would be a bitch to park the car and even his old Cutlass wouldn't be safe. More likely some kids would crash it after a joy-ride.

The place was a rundown office block, at the dock end. The top floor was rented out to a guy he knew who ran his own internet servers; it was where he'd posted Alice on the net. Ben Meyerson didn't know much, but what he did know was computers and anything to do with them. He'd chopped his office up into several sound-proof cubicles. Each held their own computer wired to the net; copiers, printers, the lot. For twenty bucks an hour anyone could hire a mini-office with the knowledge of complete privacy.

Lewis was on the doorstep when Ben turned up. He followed him up the stairs. Once in a cubicle, he booted up the machine and inserted the disk he'd stolen the night before - and sat back and watched it from beginning to end. The disk was almost full; it took three hours. The camera had captured eight nonces in all. He made copies onto memory sticks and printouts of all the faces. The last one was the Middle-Eastern with the boy; and yes, he'd been right about the newscast the night before the party.

He fired up the internet and got on to the TV sites for that evening. It didn't take long before he found his quarry. A Mr Mohammed Assaf was with the Saudi delegation attending a conference at the UN, discussing the world water shortage. Lewis had a thought, and scrolled through all the delegates at the conference. He found the other seven nonces there, too. Life had been made a little easier. He left the booth pleased with his day's work. It surprised him to see that the sun was going down. Now he was hungry. He'd send Tracey off to work the streets and have some quality time with Alice.

Washington, DC.

Karl D Brevison, Jnr. stared down from his office onto the street below. Dusk was falling, it was raining hard and the traffic was nose to tail. All he could see were bobbing umbrellas as everyone scurried to get out of the downpour. He hated Washington when the weather was like this, though his mood was no fault of the rain. It had changed moments before.

A cough brought him back to the present. His eyes moved from the street and focused on the reflection in the window. Simon Fenwick was in his late forties, and smartly tailored.

'Well, Fenwick? When did you find out?' Brevison asked, waving the picture of Alice taken off the website.

'An hour ago. It came over from Interpol. It was sent to the FBI, but one of our people fielded it.' He paused for a second. 'Unfortunately, we can't stop it going into the system; otherwise someone will start asking questions.'

'You said it was a Paraguayan site.'

'Yes, but sourced from New Jersey.'

'Is that how they knew she lived there?'

'No; it was picked up in England by the girl's grandparents.'

'So, the kid's British. Shit.' It was the most heated Fenwick had seen Brevison.

'Yes, Sir. But as I've mentioned it came through Interpol, not the British. That's why there's no address or contact number.' He studied his boss, wondering how much more to tell him. It was always wise to hold something back. He didn't trust him not to shoot the messenger. 'The British may have it, but they're keeping that quiet for the moment. Presumably they'll use that card in any kind of repatriation deal they may be seeking.'

Brevison walked back to his desk. 'How long will that take?'

Fenwick shrugged. 'Could be weeks, if not months away. By then, our little problem will have disappeared.'

'And you're sure she's one of ours?'

19

'Yes, Sir.'

'And the sponsor?'

'A lowlife called Lewis Barasitch. That's how we came to use her. She was on his website.'

'Wasn't he told to take her off if she worked for us?'

'Yes, Sir.'

'So why didn't you check?'

'We did, Sir. He closed that site. What we didn't expect was that he would find an obscure one coming out of Paraguay.'

'How the hell did he get down there? I thought he was a petty criminal.'

'He is, Sir. You don't have to go to the country; there are people who can feed it through into there, but it starts here.'

'Where?'

'We're looking, Sir.'

'Have you talked to Barasitch?'

Fenwick reddened; he found something interesting on the toe of his left shoe. 'Well... All we have is a mobile number.'

'What, no address?'

'Not a correct one; no, Sir.'

'So how are we going to find him without ringing up and asking him where he is?'

'When we've traced the server that should get us an address. Don't worry, Sir. We'll find him.'

'You'd better - and fast.'

'Yes, Sir.' Fenwick started for the door.

'Oh, one more thing. Once you've found the server, use the Dancers. If anything goes wrong, I don't want it leading back to this department. We've spent too much time and money to have it screwed. Is that clear?'

7.

Cornwall.

It was two days before the police got back in touch with Molly and Bert and then it was merely the Family Liaison officer from Truro. She introduced herself as Constable Annie Perkins, and for the next hour questioned them about everything they had been asked before. They tolerated her intrusion with mounting anger. Finally, Molly leaned forward and touched the younger woman's hand.

'Tell me, me dear, when will Alice be coming home?'

The officer bit her lip.

'You don't have a clue, do you love?' said Bert, gazing at her. He shook his head.

'It's not quite that simple, Mr Banks.'

'I see. Tell me, what is the timeline with this thing? That is the phrase you lot use nowadays, isn't it?'

The officer reddened. 'Well; first I have to make a report for the Child Protection unit in Bodmin; this will be attached to their own report and sent to the CAIT London.'

'The what?'

'The Child Abuse Investigation Team.' She took a breath. 'In turn, the two reports will be attached to their analysis and sent to the Foreign Office with a submission to extradite the mother and child. An officer from the FO will contact his counterpart at the US embassy.' She gave a weak smile.

Bert sighed. 'And you don't know how long the Yanks are going to take, do you?'

'Mr Banks, you have to understand; these things take time.'

'And while you lot are do-addling around with paper, God knows what dangers Alice is facing,' piped in Molly.

'Mrs Banks; there are certain procedures to follow. I'm sure everyone will do their best to expedite things.'

'What, d'reckly?' asked Bert, wryly.

Annie Perkins gave a wince. She'd heard the joke: "What's the difference between the Spanish Manâna and the Cornish D'reckly? – D'reckly's not so hasty."

Bert continued. 'It took you two days to come and see us and ask the same fool questions that were asked when we reported this.' His lip lifted in disgust. 'Well, let's see...' He raised his hand. 'Two days for you to check that our story is straight.' He ticked off two fingers. 'Let's be generous and say it takes another day for you to write and send your report.' Another finger dropped. 'Are you sending it by post or email?'

'By post,' she admitted, knowing it sounded laughable.

'Well; there's another day, and it isn't out of the county yet,' said Molly heatedly. 'And then there's the weekend. I doubt those people up at Bodmin and in London, let alone the Foreign Office, work over the weekend, do they?'

Constable Perkins opened her mouth to protest, but closed it again. She knew the Banks were closer to the truth than she cared to admit.

'So it could take as long as a month before anyone in America knocks on Alice's door,' said Bert. He got up and walked over to the window.

'I doubt if it would take that long, Mr Banks,' she said hopelessly.

'But you can't guarantee it.'

She swivelled her head back to Molly. Between them they were making her feel dizzy.

'Of course I can't,' she snapped, in frustration.

'There's no need to bark at me, girl,' Molly said softly. She squeezed out an apologetic little smile as if to mollify her, but it irritated the officer further.

'You have to understand. I'm one little cog in the works. I will do my job as quickly and efficiently as I can, but that is all I can do.'

'We do understand, love, and we realise you'll do your best, but that doesn't help Alice, does it? She needs help *now*.' Molly stared down at the table top and started to knit her fingers together.

WPC Perkins was crestfallen. 'I don't see what else I can do.'

She stared at Bert's back; he was still gazing out of the window. He jiggled the change in his pocket and turned abruptly.

'Sorry, me love, it's unfair of us to take it out on you. It's our responsibility when all's said and done. Molly and me should pack our bags and go over there and bring her back.'

'You can't be serious.'

'Of course not, girl. I doubt whether the mother would give her up without a fight, even if we went.'

'Maybe that's what we should do; go over there and kidnap Alice.' Molly gave the officer a quick, sly glance before fixing her eyes back on the table again.

The constable stiffened. 'That would be illegal.'

'No more than what's happening to her now,' Molly snapped back, not even raising her head.

Bert came back to the table and sat heavily. He laid a gentle hand on Molly's shoulder.

'Com'on Moll; t'ain't the girl's fault. Tell me, me love. Could you find out the names of the people up at Bodmin and London who we should be talking to?'

'Of course I can.' A thought occurred to her. 'You should also go and see your MP. Do you have some more of those photos of Alice you could show him? Just the face.'

'No; but I could print more off.'

'I didn't hear that, Sir. Do the prints, then delete the file from your computer. It's an offence to have them. No one's going to do anything about it now, but suppose you forgot and a couple of years later they were found. You'd be in big trouble.'

'Thanks.'

'Not at all.' She gathered up her pad and bag and stood up. 'I'll do my best for you.'

She gave an encouraging smile; what else could she do? She knew it wouldn't be enough. It just took someone to go off sick with it in their in-tray and the file could get log-jammed. A week of inaction could pass with no repercussions.

Bert struggled to his feet again. 'I'll see you out, love.' Molly hadn't lifted her head.

When they got to the front door the policewoman stopped and faced him. 'Please, put any thought out of your mind about going over there and snatching Alice.'

Bert chuckled. 'Don't take any mind of Moll; she was venting her frustration. We've been across the channel a few times, that's all. Nowhere far away - and certainly not flying. We're too old to start that kind of malarkey.'

8.

Molly was still staring down at the table-top when Bert came back into the kitchen. He glanced at her, but said nothing and got on with clearing the tea cups.

'Bert - do you think we should get hold of old Prudhoe?'

'Not that 'e's much use, but yes, the girl had the right idea.'

He went over to the cupboard where they kept bills and letters, pulled open a drawer and riffled through papers bunged out of sight.

'I can't find his blurb.'

Molly gave an irritated sigh, scraped the chair back and bustled over to him.

''ere, let the dog see the rabbit; you can never find nothin'.' She nudged him out of the way and shuffled through the drawer, finally bringing out an envelope. 'Knew it were there. You men, you couldn't find your breakfast if it weren't put in front of you.'

She slipped the letter out of the envelope and handed it to him.

'You want me to phone?'

She glanced at him with veiled annoyance. 'Of course. Get on with it.'

Bert picked up the phone and pressed out the number that was at the bottom of the letter. He waited while it rang. Molly had sat back down and was staring at the table top again. The phone was answered by a woman.

'Peter Prudhoe's constituency office. How can I help?'

'Ah, yes, me name's Bert Banks, I need to speak with Mr Prudhoe urgently.'

'Please hold while I check his diary.' She came back on the line after a moment. 'I'm afraid the earliest is Friday week.'

'Nothing earlier?'

'Sorry, no.'

Bert hated dealing with these women with their emphatic answers. In his day they were called dragons. He wondered if people still called them that.

'This is very urgent, you know; it needs to be sorted right away.'

'I'm sorry; that's the earliest.'

He was tempted to make a comment about the woman's take-it-or-leave-it attitude, but decided on a more direct approach.

'I'll go and see Garvney then,' he threatened. 'I'm sure he'll make some political capital out of it.'

'That won't do you any good, Mr Banks,' she said smugly. 'All five MPs from this area are on a fact-finding tour in the South of France.' He now realised why she sounded so stroppy. She was feeling left out; probably felt she should've gone too, instead of holding the fort against people like him. 'They won't be back until next week. Thursday at the earliest,' she added smartly.

'Sunning their buns, are they?' He slammed the phone down in disgust. Molly peered up at him. 'Bloody MPs, like the police. Never about when you want 'em.'

'Still, you shouldn't have been so rude, and stop that swearing.'

'I felt like it.' He said, unchastened.

'I gather from your belligerent tone that you think they'll be a fat lot of use.'

'You gathered right.' He pulled his jacket from the door peg. 'I'm out to do a spot of digging before I ring the whole damn lot and make a fool of meself.'

'Maybe you had the right of it, Bert,' she said.

He stopped in his tracks, his jacket half on.

'What's that s'posed to mean?'

'Maybe we should go over and fetch Alice back.'

''nd pigs might fly. Don't be mad, woman. I was jesting.'

'I'm not.'

'I know. It's written all over your face. I knew I'd pay for that bit of silliness.' He pulled his jacket right on with a snap and walked out of the door. 'You can forget that nonsense as soon as you like. We're going nowhere,' he shouted over his shoulder.

Molly waited five minutes before she got up and lifted the phone. While she waited for it to be answered she scrawled on a scrap of paper: *Bert, I've gone out to do a bit of shopping. Moll.*

9.

Newark New Jersey.

It took Brevison's people the rest of that night and part of
next morning to find the source location of the internet site
www.sunset-chasing.py. The Dancer twins arrived at the
office a little after ten. Ben Meyerson was settled behind his
desk, monitoring some of the hits on that and the other sites
he managed. It was a slow start to the day. No-one else was
using the cubicles; a 'nothing out of the ordinary' day. He
had a mug of coffee at his elbow when they kicked open the
door and strode in.

Harry, the thinner of the two, sat on the corner of the desk
and greeted an open-mouthed Ben with a wolfish grin. The
other brother, Harvey, the more sombre, stood back
watching, hands held in front of him. They were twins, but
apart from being the same height and colouring the similarity
stopped there. They were the different sides of a bad coin.

'Hello, Benny,' said Harry, bringing out a knife, flicking
it open and ostentatiously cleaning his nails with the tip.

'Hello, Mr Stenato.' Ben's eyes cut over the top of his
glasses nervously; they flitted between the twins, not
knowing where to come to rest. 'What can I do for you?'

Harry smiled and glanced at his brother. 'Isn't that nice,
Harvey? I like a show of respect, don't you?' Harvey lifted
his shoulders fractionally in a little shrug, but his cold eyes
never left Ben.

'Haven't seen you for some time, Mr Stenato. Is there
anything special you want?' His voice quavered a little.

Harry got up and sauntered behind Ben, who turned to
follow his movements, but felt a sharp tug as Harvey
grabbed his tie and pulled him over the desk. Harry stopped,
placed his hands on Ben's chair, and gave it a shove. It
rolled forward, jamming him hard against the edge of the
desk. His glasses fell from his nose. Bringing his face down
to the level of Ben's head, Harry whispered:

'We need a little information, Benny.' He glanced up at
his brother. 'Is it hot in here, Harvey?' The twin grunted

what could have been a 'no'. 'Why you sweatin', Benny?' He took his hands off the chair, but kept his hip hard against the back. 'That's a nice tie you're wearing.' He leaned over and stabbed his knife through it and into the desk. Harvey let go and stepped back, taking up his former position.

'About this help, Benny.'

'Yes, Mr Stenato. If I can.'

'Oh, you will.' There was a dreadful certainty in Harry's voice. He pulled a slip of paper from his pocket and waved it under Ben's nose. 'Recognise this site, Benny?'

Ben tried to focus on the slip of paper.

'I 'm not sure, Mr Stenato.'

'What do you mean, not sure?' screamed Harry. 'It came from this office, from your server.'

'I, I mean, I can't see without my glasses.' His voice was trembling badly.

Harry grabbed the tie and pulled it. There was a shiver of sound as it was drawn past the knife-blade and came free. He let go and Ben slumped back into his chair. Harry crouched and whispered into his ear again.

'You'd better take another look, Benny.'

Ben hastily donned his glasses and picked the slip of paper from the desk, while Harry pulled the knife free. He leant back over Ben's shoulder.

'Well?'

'It's Lewis Barasitch' site, his girl.'

'We know that, Benny. Where does he live?'

'I don't know, Mr Stenato.'

Harry glanced at his brother again. 'Do we believe him, Harvey?'

Harvey gave a grunt.

Ben gazed anxiously, waiting for the verdict. Harry tutted and shook his head. 'We don't believe you, Benny.'

'Please Mr Stenato, I'm telling you the tru...'

Ben let out a scream as the point of Harry's knife slid down his cheek leaving a bright wound. Blood ran down onto his chin and neck, the grubby white collar of his shirt turning red.

'He lives close, but I don't know where.'

Harry stood up and moved to Ben's other side, and crouched down again. He placed the tip of the knife on his other cheek, and a spot of blood blossomed around it.

'I'm going to count to three, Benny.'

Please Mr Stenato, I don...'

'One.'

'Anything else?'

'Two.'

'Please, I...' Ben screwed his eyes up waiting for the pain.

'Three.'

'He was here a few days ago,' he gabbled out.

'And?'

'He used one of the cubicles.'

'What for?'

'It's in the drawer.'

Ben started to open it and froze. Quick as a snake, Harvey had the silenced muzzle of a gun an inch away from the bridge of his nose.

'I should open it very carefully; otherwise Harvey might make a regrettable hole.'

Gingerly he opened it and lifted out eight sheets of paper and handed them to Harry.

'What are these?'

'Don't know. It was what Lewis was working on; took him all day.'

'Got anything else?'

'No, Lewis was very careful; I got these off the printer memory.'

Harry folded the papers and tucked them into his pocket.

'Which cubicle did he use?'

'The middle one.'

'When do you expect him back?'

Ben gave a shrug. 'Could be anytime; today, tomorrow, maybe next week. There's no telling with Lewis.'

'You did well, Benny.' He patted him on the shoulder and stood up. 'You won't be telling Lewis any of this, will you?'

Benny looked up and tried to smile. 'Of course no...'

The knife sliced cleanly across his throat; Harry gave him a shove. Ben toppled forward onto the desktop. Blood gushed out and pooled around him.

'Shit, Harry. How the hell are we s'posed to get the address now?'

'He didn't know.'

Without another word, the twins started to pull the office apart. They found nothing else that would help.

'We'll have to wait for Barasitch,'

Harvey gave a grunt.

'We'll take these.' He nodded at the computer and server-bank, 'and the one from the cubicle - see what Jake can find.'

10.

Lewis's second visit to Ben's office was much later. Luck was on his side. He was in the store across from Meyerson's building buying cigarettes, and on the verge of leaving when he glanced across the street. The Dancer twins came out of the office building, carrying two computers. He'd never met them, but their reputation was well known in the city. He pulled back into the shadows of the store and watched. They packed the computers into a car; Harry got into it and sped away. Harvey stayed, tucked inconspicuously into a doorway several buildings down the street. So - the twins were casing the place. He didn't know why, but it wasn't a good sign.

After some time hanging around waiting for Harvey to leave, Lewis lost patience. The sister building to Meyerson's was separated by a narrow alleyway. He entered it from the back, climbed up to the roof and jumped over to the other. Once through the fire escape he crept down to Ben's office. No sound from inside. The door was ajar. He gave it a push, and it slowly swung open. Strewn across the floor were paper, computer disks and the emptied drawers of Ben's desk. Touching nothing, he slipped into the room.

Ben was lying face down on his desk, waiting for no-one. Blood haloed his head in a dark pool and dripped onto the floor. He was clutching a slip of paper. Lewis gently prised the fingers apart and removed it. The Sunset Chasing website was written on it. Without another thought, he left. The only thing on his mind was to get out and lie low. He wasn't sure of the connection, but he knew for certain he would be on their visiting list.

Lewis was so shaken by the scene at Ben's place that he hit the bars before going back to the apartment. He came through the door shouting and a little the worse for wear, totally unprepared to find Captain Sean Murphy, a large cop with a florid face, sitting on their worn-out sofa. Lewis stopped dead in his tracks.

'What'd you want?' growled Lewis.

'A bit of ass, for some information.'

'You can pay, like the rest.'

'Like hell, I will.' Murphy got to his feet and went over to him. He studied Lewis fleetingly. 'What's wrong? Looks like you're ready to piss your pants.' He gave a sneer, brushed past him and opened the door. 'Who d'you want to come visiting first?' he asked over his shoulder. 'Us, or the others?'

'Don't know what you mean. What others?'

'That's why I'm offering you a chance to find out.' He started to move through the doorway.

'Okay, okay. Tell me what you know and if it's worth...' Lewis gave a shrug.

'Oh, it's worth it, but the ass first.'

Lewis glowered at the cop, wondering how much he knew. The sight of Ben lying in his own blood had weakened his resolve.

'Sure; why not?' He jerked his head towards Tracey. 'Use the room in the back.'

'Na. I want the kid.'

'No, you bastard!' screamed Tracey, and launched herself towards him, but she met Lewis's fist before she was halfway across the room. She crumpled to the ground.

'If you want the kid, I want the news first.'

'You'd better disappear, Lewis. The word on the street is that the Dancer Twins are trying to trace you.'

'I know that already.'

'Bullshit.'

'If you think I'm shitting you - go along to Ben Meyerson's place. Take a bucket and swab to clean up the mess.'

Murphy gazed at Lewis and knew he was telling the truth. He gave a shrug.

'Something heavy is going down. Someone in England recognised the kid on that site of yours. The FBI's involved. It came through from our embassy liaison officer with your address on; mid-morning.' Lewis gave a grunt. 'Leave town and take them with you. Now, do I get my tail?'

Lewis gave a slight movement of his head. Tracey was not there when Murphy came back zipping up his flies. As he went out through the door he shouted over his shoulder.

'Lewis, do yerself a favour. Get rid of that kid.'

'How long have I got?'

'I can hold it up for two days.'

It took Lewis three hours to dump his old Cutlass, steal another car and pack. Tracey sat quietly in the passenger seat of the Ford station wagon Lewis had stolen. She was nursing a black eye. Alice was squashed in amongst their belongings in the back as the Newark skyline got smaller in his rear mirror. As soon as he could, Lewis would get off the Interstate and use the minor roads. They would be virtually impossible to trace.

Brevison was too angry to get up from his desk and stare out of his window. Moments before, Fenwick had laid the eight sheets of paper taken from Meyerson. He glanced up from the pictures to Fenwick, who stood silently on the other side of the desk.

'And these came from Barasitch?' Fenwick nodded. 'How the hell did he get hold of them?'

'You remember I told you one of the machines hadn't been connected properly?'

'Yeah.'

'That machine covered the bedroom used by those guys. Before coming to you I asked for the security tapes. We knew Assaf was the last one in that room.'

'And?' Brevison asked impatiently.

'We found footage of Barasitch entering the secure room and minutes later coming out with a disk in his hand.'

'The rules were to be strictly enforced. That room was never to be left unguarded, and the escorts locked in theirs until they left with their kids.'

'I don't have the answer to either of those questions. I felt you needed to know about this and what we're dealing with.'

'You did right.' There was no smile with the acceptance. 'So, have the twins found Barasitch yet?'

'No, but I told them it's important.' Fenwick took a deep breath. 'I also said the whole family needs to disappear without trace. No comebacks on anyone, especially the department.'

'Good. Now get out of here before I start throwing things.'

'Sir.' Fenwick hesitated.

'What?'

'The operation: what do you want to do?'

'We'll mothball it until all this blows over. Then we'll rethink about what we do next.'

'That's going to be expensive, isn't it?'

'Not my problem, thank God. The politicians can worry about that.'

11.

Cornwall

Bert woke to a loud bump outside the bedroom. He slid his hand over to Molly's side of the bed and found it empty.

'Damn and blast, what's going on?' he muttered, switching on the light as he swung his legs out of the bed.

More bumps came from the landing. By the time he got to the head of the stairs Molly was near the bottom, fully dressed with hat and coat, dragging down a large suitcase a step at a time. She reached the hall, staggered, tried to lift the case, then collapsed over it, wheezing.

'Oh, bugger.' He ran down. 'Are you out of your mind, woman?' She stayed bowed over the case, gasping. 'Where's your inhaler?'

Molly pointed to the far corner of the hallway where her handbag lay. He picked it up and crouched down beside her, placed the inhaler in her outstretched hand and waited for her to recover.

'Oh, Bert.'

He opened his arms and she fell against his chest and clasped him. His arms closed about her round body.

'I must go. I can't fail Alice.' Sobs racked her body.

'You're not failing her, love. You can't go like this.'

'I know, but I've got to, even if it kills me.'

'And what would happen to Alice?'

'*I've got to go*,' she insisted, clutching him even tighter.

Bert winced. 'Moll, you're breaking me ribs.'

'That's 'cause you're all skin and bones.'

'We're a fine pair.' He shook his head and chuckled. 'What am I going to do with you?'

'Come with me?' she asked hopefully.

'I don't know where my passport is. Haven't needed it since our honeymoon.'

'I found it this afternoon.'

He gave her a smile. 'I don't have a ticket.'

'I got one for you as well.'

'You've planned for every contingency, haven't you? You must think you're very clever.'

Molly dropped her head guiltily and kicked out her foot in a child-like gesture. It hit his shin.

'Ow! What the bloody hell was that for?'

'Don't swear, Bert Banks. Sorry. Didn't mean to kick you.'

Bert bent down and rubbed his leg. Molly giggled.

'It's not funny.'

'I'm still going.'

'Not without me, you're not.' He gave a sigh and muttered. 'Damn women. Now leave that case there and make me a cuppa, while I get a gown on. It's a bit parky down 'ere.'

12.

The flight had been long and arduous. They had not returned to bed after her demonstration of stubbornness. Instead, he had made lists of things to do whilst she re-packed and sorted out the house. The last thing he did was go to the bank. Molly had planned to be away for no more than a week. The morning had been a whirlwind; they'd left their house in the early afternoon. Bert had put his foot down about 'saving money' and had hired a taxi all the way to Newquay airport. Now, Molly was grateful.

Crossing from Gatwick to Heathrow to catch the eight twenty-five to Newark Liberty International had been fraught with delays. Now the anxious pair fidgeted throughout the long flight. They landed after eleven US time, and took a cab to the Renaissance Hotel on Spring Street (the shortest part of their journey), entering the hotel after midnight. It was a struggle for both of them to stay awake. Over twenty-four hours had passed since Bert's sleep had been interrupted. The next day they missed breakfast, not waking till noon, feeling exhausted.

'Can't see why people go abroad on holiday, if flying is so wearying,' grumbled Bert as he left the room.

It was pointless arguing with him when he was tired; he only became grumpier. She waited for his return. It should have been a matter of minutes to deposit his money belt in the hotel safe, but he got lost. Losing patience waiting for him, she had him paged.

'Damn place is so big, it's a wonder anyone finds anyone,' he said, as they sat down to a late lunch.

'Stop your swearing, Bert Banks. You're miserable because you're tired.'

He glanced at his watch. 'No wonder; I should have me feet up and listening to the Archers, not sitting down to lunch.'

In the end neither ate much. They decided it was pointless trying to find Alice until they were more rested.

Instead, they took a short coach tour around Newark before coming back for an early night.

''S 'Nothing like the movies,' Molly had commented as she'd stared out of the coach.

'If you ask me, they've used concrete like they thought it were going out of fashion.'

Before retreating to their room they showed the young man at the reception desk the address Alice had given Molly. He stood gazing at it for several moments, a frown creasing his forehead.

'Is there something wrong?' asked Bert.

The receptionist studied him candidly.

'Are you sure of this address?'

'As sure as we can be. Alice, me granddaughter, gave it me.'

'Wrong side of the tracks, lad?' asked Bert, discerning the receptionist's unease.

His eyes moved from Molly back to Bert. 'You could say that, Sir. Not a place I'd recommend you go sight-seeing.'

'How far is it from here?' asked Molly, trying to make some sense of the conversation.

'Not so far; maybe twenty minutes in light traffic, a lot more at peak. And you're sure your granddaughter said 353 Avon Avenue and South Eleven Street?'

'Yes,' Molly said in a whisper, her eyes not leaving his.

'Is she black?'

'No. Why do you ask?'

'That area's mainly black. It's also run-down.' He gazed at them thoughtfully, then said in a low voice. 'We don't advertise it, but Newark can be dangerous; there's a lot of crime. I have to warn a lot of overseas visitors to avoid certain parts of the city. You could find y'selves in a whole mess of trouble.'

'So whereabouts is it?'

He opened out a map and spread it on the desk; his finger came to bear on a road south of the airport.

'We're here.' His finger slid along the road past the airport and stopped where it became a tangle of roads. A large road cut across. 'This here's the Interstate. We call this part the Pulaski Skyway. It goes right through to New York.' His finger moved past it and threaded through a maze of roads blocked out in squares. 'Your granddaughter lives about here.'

'Can we catch a bus?' asked Molly.

'I wouldn't advise it. Have you a phone number? Maybe she could come visit you here.'

'No, we haven't,' Bert lied. 'We wanted it to be a surprise. What about a taxi?'

'Sure; but most won't want to hang around.' He paused, and considered for a moment. 'Can I make a suggestion?'

Bert glanced at Molly. 'We're listening.'

'The hotel has dealings with several limo companies. You can hire by the hour and if you get the right guy he'll be able to take you there and look out for you as well.'

'But that will cost...'

'You think that's the best?' asked Bert, overriding Molly.

'Matter of fact, I do. I also think I know the right guy for the job. You off to catch an early night?'

'We were.'

'Leave this with me and I'll organise things for the morning. What kind of start do you want to make?'

They glanced at each other and shrugged.

'Is ten-thirty too early?' Molly asked.

'No. I'll make it for then. You have a good night, Ma'am, Sir.'

With a bemused smile on his lips he watched as they crossed the foyer to the lifts, then he picked up the phone.

13.

Calvin Croft was a large man by anybody's standard. As he got out of the limo it seemed to rise with relief. It was a long, sleek black job. Molly and Bert, who stood under the hotel canopy, glanced at each other and wondered what they'd let themselves in for. All Calvin knew was that his clients were British, and from their clothes this couple in their late sixties (or probably older, looking at their clothes) were unmistakeable. They wore an air of bewilderment as their gaze settled on him. Bert held a screwed-up flat cap in his hands, while Molly clutched her purse as if someone was about to snatch it. They fitted the receptionist's description - she short and wide; he tall and thin. Calvin gave a broad grin, showing off a mouthful of large white teeth; one glinted gold. He removed his chauffeur's hat.

'Mr 'n Mrs Banks?' Their faces showed caution. 'The name's Calvin Croft. My friends call me Calvin.'

Bert held out his hand. It was enthusiastically grasped and he was rewarded with a generous smile.

'This is Moll and I'm Bert.'

'You can call 'im whatever you like, but don't you dare call me Moll.' She gave Bert a withering glare. 'The name's Molly.'

'Sure, Ma'am.'

Calvin opened the back passenger door of the car and swept out a hand, inviting her to step in. She settled herself and looked out at the tightly curled hair that was dusted with white and topped the blackest face she had ever set eyes on.

'Thank you, Calvin. Molly will do fine.'

As Bert made to step in after her, he laid a hand on Calvin's arm.

'You'll find we don't stand on ceremony, 'specially Moll.'

As he sat back heavily next to Molly, the door closed with a soft click. She elbowed him.

'I wish you wouldn't introduce me as Moll, it makes me sound like a gangster's squeeze. 'Specially over 'ere.'

41

'You don't mind me calling you Moll.'

'That's different. We're married.'

'I called you that before we were.'

'Oh, stop your arguing, you've always got to have the last word.'

He opened his mouth to say 'that's grand, coming from you,' but thought better of it. The driver's door opened and Calvin slid into his seat. The limo sank a little on his side. The glass panel that separated him from the back slid down. He swivelled in his seat and beamed.

'You folks comfortable?'

'Yes, thank you.'

'Do you know where we want to go?' asked Bert.

'Jerry gave it to me yesterday evening, but let's check it's right.'

He pulled a crumpled bit of paper from his breast pocket.

'Who's Jerry?' Molly whispered to Bert.

'The receptionist. Didn't you notice his name tag?'

'That's right, Sir.'

'Bert will do, Calvin.'

''Fraid it's against company rules, Sir.'

'So who's to tell, Mr Croft? We're not.'

Calvin tapped a small black cylinder on the dash.

'They can listen in, Ma'am. It's for security.'

'Damn spies everywhere, these days,' Molly tutted.

'Ain't that a fact. Let's check this address.' Bert read it out to him. 'You sure it's right? 'Cus that's a bad neighbourhood.'

'Yes, your friend Jerry said. Are you willing to take us?'

'Sure, but you ain't getting out unless I think it's safe. Deal?'

'But...'

Bert touched Molly's leg.

'It's a deal.'

'Righty'o, let's get moving. You folks want the screen up?'

'No thank you.'

'Thought not. Best fasten your seat belts; there're some crazy drivers in this city.'

Jerry had been a little optimistic about how long it would take to get to Avon Street. They entered it at the Jesse Allen Park end and crept along at a snail's pace through unremitting drear. The closer they got to their destination the more down at heel the neighbourhood became. Finally, Calvin pulled in outside a redbrick Church that had seen better days. The next block on was a row of shuttered shops, and above, apartments.

Bert leaned forward over the front passenger seat.

'This it?'

'Yeah, about the middle of that block.' He gestured with his head. 'Where they're moving some furniture.'

A couple of black men were struggling to get a large sofa off a shabby box van. Around it and on the sidewalk up to the building, boxes and tables were stacked. He glanced behind him.

'If you'll sit back, I'll see about gettin' us closer. There's a gap on the opposite side. You'll get a better view.'

He waited for a line of cars to pass and eased the limo back into the traffic and crawled along until he was adjacent to a gap. He pulled across and parked. Immediately across from them a pharmacy was open, though there was a thick mesh over the windows and nothing much could be seen of the interior. Each side of it the shops appeared to be closed. The windows above most of the row were boarded up, except for the one where the furniture was being moved in. Roughly painted white on a pillar by the open doorway was the number 353.

Calvin laid his arm across the top of the passenger seat and turned. 'Who should I ask for?'

Bert and Molly glanced at each other.

'We can't remember their surname; Moll's daughter-in-law got remarried,' said Bert.

Calvin thought for a moment.

'They're white ain't they?'

43

'Yes.'

'And the guy?'

'Not sure.'

'That shouldn't be too difficult. So it's your daughter-in-law and your grandchild. How old's the kid?'

'Twelve.'

'I'm going to lock you in. If anything happens to me don't get out of the car, just scream police. The office will pick it up.'

'But...'

'No buts, ma'am. We play it my way or we leave now. No windows open; nothing.' His eyes flitted to Bert. 'How much you willin' to spend?'

'What do you mean, spend?'

'Jeezus; Jerry warned me you were innocent. They see this car, they'll want paying for any information. That's how it works.'

Bert nudged Molly, who gave a shrug. 'I don't know. It's important, so we'll leave it to you.'

Calvin got halfway out, stopped, and ducked his head back into the car. 'You got any pictures?'

Molly rummaged in her bag and brought out one of Alice and another of Tracey, taken six years before. He took them, gave a wink and closed the door. There was a clunk as the remote triggered the lock.

14.

Calvin waited for the traffic to ease. The men hauling the furniture saw him cross and stopped to take a breather. They could recognise a paycheck when it arrived. He got to the corner of the van and stopped. They both looked him up and down, but said nothing.

'Hi, man,' he said. 'I'm trying to find some white folks who live here.' His eyes flitted to the open door.

'Not any longer.'

'I can see that. Know where they've gone?'

'Maybe.'

Calvin chewed it over for a few moments, then dipped his hand into his pocket and drew out a couple of tens. He held the notes up to flutter in the air.

'When did they leave?' He held one note out.

The one wearing a bandanna snatched it out of his fingers.

'Two nights ago.'

He waited, but nothing else was forthcoming. This was going to be like coaxing a turtle out of its shell, he thought. He pulled out the two photos and passed them over. 'Was this the woman and girl who lived here?'

'Could be.' He handed over the other note. 'Yup.'

This was getting trying. 'Give me everything you got, and there's another thirty bucks in it.'

'Let's see it.'

'Hey man, I'm cool for it.'

The two cut a glance at each other.

'They going out of town, driving a white Ford station wagon, loaded right up. The 'ho had a black eye and the kid was in the back. Left some mail. Do you want it?'

'Sure.'

'That's extra.'

'That's not what we agreed. Anything else?'

'Yeah; two white guys come asking for them yesterday; could have been brothers. They looked mean.'

'That it?' Bandanna-man gave a nod. 'Okay. Get the mail and you get your thirty.'

The other guy slouched off and was back in no time with a grocery bag. Calvin handed over the money and turned back. He swung into his seat and started the car.

'What say we get out of here and take a coffee break?'

He drove to University Heights and stopped at a small sidewalk café.

'Right,' said Calvin once they were sitting round a table with cups of coffee. 'Your people definitely lived there until two nights ago. They left in a hurry, said to be driving a white Ford station wagon crammed with gear.' He decided to leave the mysterious visitors until last. He emptied the bag of mail onto the table and they all sorted through it. Everything except one envelope was junk, which he shoved back in the bag. The envelope contained a bill for unpaid utilities. It was made out to a Lewis Barasitch. 'Does that ring a bell; Molly, Bert?'

'I thought it was company policy to use Sir or Ma'am?' Molly said with a smirk.

He waved a hand as if to say "forget it".

'That's in the car.' His mouth cracked open in a broad grin, showing off his gold tooth. 'So?'

'I think it might be him. It was over four years ago. It sounded foreign. Anything else?'

'Yes. Yesterday two men were asking about them. The guys said they could've been brothers and they looked *mee-ean.*'

Bert nudged his arm. 'How much do we owe you?'

''Fraid it's more than the information is worth. Fifty bucks.'

'That's dollars, isn't it?'

'Yeah. Sorry. They strung me along, but I think I got the truth.'

'Don't worry; at least we're one step closer.' Bert mulled over what Calvin had said. 'What do we do now?'

Calvin gave a shrug. 'It depends on how important it is to you.' Bert and Molly gave each other a surreptitious

46

glance. 'It's none of my business and you can tell me to butt out, but if I knew a little more, maybe I could help.'

'The girl in that photo is Moll's granddaughter and the mother was married to her son.'

'We hadn't heard from Alice for over four years, then we got a call a few days ago,' Molly gabbled out.

'Alice is the child.' Bert explained. 'She's in trouble. That's why she called.'

'What kind of trouble?' he asked slowly. He had a premonition that it was serious, and Bert and Molly's faces reinforced it. 'As I said, it's none of my business, but the more you can tell me, the better I can help. You ain't gone to the cops, so it's something real bad.'

'We've been to the police back home, but it seems it's going to take weeks and we felt Alice was in too much danger and as it happens we were right, otherwise why did they disappear? Do you think those men were police?'

'Na, those guys back there would have said. I don't want to frighten you, but when they said mean they meant killers.'

Molly clutched Bert's hand. 'Tell him,' she whispered.

Calvin called for a refill before Bert had stumbled his way through the whole story. He felt exhausted by the time he'd finished and was grateful for the extra coffee. Molly nudged him.

'You haven't told him everything.'

'Alright, woman; give me a chance.'

'What else?'

'Two days ago, before we left, I tried Alice's site again, but it was gone.'

Calvin nodded his head. 'That makes sense; this Lewis is covering his tracks.'

'So what do we do, go to the police here?'

'You could file a missing person, but I 'spect the cops will think the parents forgot to inform you they were moving. Do you have any proof of the website, Bert?'

'No. It would have been illegal to carry such pictures.'

'That's what I thought.' He rubbed his chin. 'I have a friend who works for a bond agent. He's an ex-cop, but he won't be cheap.'

'What - a private detective?'

'Well, not quite. A bit closer to the edge, so to speak. He's a bounty hunter.'

'Do you think he could help?'

'It's worth talking to him; won't cost a dime. Shall I give him a call?'

15.

They met in a dingy bar. After the bright mid-afternoon
sunshine it took a few moments before Molly and Bert could
make out anyone there, apart from the barman. A man
wearing black wrap-around shades sat in a stall near the back
of the room, hunched over a bottle of beer. He didn't bother
to stand when they got to his table, but nodded at the bench
opposite. They shuffled along it and waited for someone to
say something. In the end, Calvin broke the silence.

'Bert, Molly, this is Arran Marx.' Marx gave a slight
incline of his head.

'What you drinking?' Molly and Bert declined. 'If we
don't drink Dappy over there is liable to throw us out.' He
noticed they frowned at the name. 'He's Vietnamese. His
name's Duc – something.'

'I'll have a beer, then, and Moll will have an orange
juice.'

'And you, Calvin.'

'Beer'll be fine.'

'Hey, Dappy,' shouted Marx. 'We'll have three more
beers and an orange juice.'

His head moved to take in Molly and Bert who were
sitting nervously on the edge of the bench, not knowing what
to expect. The corner of his lip curled at their apprehension.
Most of his clients got nervous at one time or another, while
dealing with him. He pulled off his shades. His eyes were a
cold, pale blue that did nothing to ease their feeling of panic.

'Calvin says you have a problem.'

Bert opened his mouth to say something.

'It was rhetorical, mister; no one comes to me unless they
have a problem. The point is, can the cops solve your
problem or is it of the untidy kind?' He stopped as Dappy
came and plonked down the drinks. He lifted two fingers to
thank the barman and cut his eyes to Calvin. 'What's it
about, Cal?'

Calvin laid it down straight about Alice, and what he'd
found out from the black brothers moving the furniture. The

information that Tracey was an 'ho' - although they needed it explained, shook Molly and Bert. Marx fingered the photos and utility bill.

'It seems your daughter-in-law and kid got themselves mixed up with the wrong sort of person. You said she met him in England.'

'Yes,' said Bert.

'Oldest scam in the book. Bring a woman with a kid into the States, show them a good time, marry her so she can stay and then put her on the game. She's most likely a druggy; possibly the kid, too.' His eyes flitted to Calvin. 'And the two men - probably brothers, you say. Both tall and slender, one silent the other chippy but menacing.'

'Yeah, that's what the guys said. Know 'em?'

'Maybe.' His gaze reverted back to Bert and Molly. 'Three mee-ean men.' He shook his head and grinned. 'The reason why Calvin brought you to me is that he knows no one meaner than me.' He gave a chuckle. 'Now this is how it works. I charge five hundred bucks a day, and I don't do half-days. There is an advance of a thousand bucks and any outstanding bill is paid before any information is released. Further to that, I don't do receipts. Then there's expenses. These can be considerable. Information don't come cheap, as you've already found out.' He raised a hand to stop any interruptions.

'This Barasitch fella' has done a runner; most probably out of State and more than likely across quite a few. I work as far as the Mason Dixie line going south and the Continental Divide going west. I have associates who pick up from me if the chase continues into their territory. They charge the same as me. Any questions?'

'How long?' asked Molly.

'My guess is he's got no real plan, simply a destination, so he'll make mistakes which will be easy to pick up. He's already made one by leaving his mail. The problem is - those who are chasing him will have an easy time too. I should have a good idea what's going on in a day or so.'

'How about you get back after two days and they can decide where to go from there,' put in Calvin. 'These folks ain't rich, Arran.'

'Yeah, I can see that. So; what's it to be?'

'Mr Marx: can you excuse us while we talk?' asked Molly.

'Sure.'

He started to rise from his seat, but Bert stretched across and placed a hand on his arm.

'There's no need, Mr Marx. You want a thousand dollars now?'

'Yep.'

Bert unzipped his belly pouch and drew out a thin sheaf of notes bound with a paper band. He pushed it across the table.

'It should be correct, but please check.'

Marx picked it up and flicked his finger over the edge of the notes.

'I'll call you at your hotel.' He stood up to go. 'And a word of advice: Get rid of that pouch; it tells people you're carrying a lot of money. Use a proper belt if you're carrying a lot, and stash your money in all your pockets, not one. And that handbag, lady; get one with a shoulder strap and put it over your head like a satchel.' As he stepped away from the table another thought came to him. 'Make sure you pay the barman.'

16.

As Marx was pocketing Tracey's picture she was emptying a box of clothes into a rickety chest of drawers. Alice sat on a bed, snivelling. Lewis had gone out to get rid of the car. He hadn't said how long he'd be, but Tracey presumed it would be all day.

'For Christ sake, shut it!' Tracey shouted, weary of the girl's whining. 'Count yourself lucky. If Lewis had his way, you would've been dumped.' She leaned into Alice's face. 'And you know what that means!' Alice cringed.

Two nights before at a Godforsaken motel Tracey had fought Lewis off the child. Fear had driven her to it. She knew what he was capable of.

Marx had been right. Tracey had met Lewis while he'd been on a visit to England. He had enticed her to move back with him and within six months they'd married, because she needed papers. Within a year she was drinking heavily, and on drugs. Lewis introduced her to the streets as a way to feed her habit. Tracey had always dealt severely with Alice; now Lewis compounded this by taking a delight in hurting the girl. They moved around, keeping one step ahead of trouble. This life meant that Alice slipped through the welfare net, becoming one of the lost ones.

The child was ten when things took a turn for the worse. Tracey was out doing tricks one night when Lewis was in one of his soberer moods. He was watching a video, and glimpsed Alice flitting to the bathroom in ragged knickers. When she came out - he was waiting. When Tracey found out she threatened to leave. Lewis beat her. She was off the street for a week.

Drink, drugs and the streetlife were showing on Tracey. The money she brought home was not as much as when she'd first entered the game. She knew that once she stopped earning he would kick her out. Her hope was that Alice's usefulness would save them both. That was one reason she'd fought to save her daughter.

When he finally returned home Lewis pushed Tracey out to find a pitch in the strange city. He'd brought a friend back with him. It wasn't long before money changed hands and the man entered Alice's bedroom. Lewis had a new earner; he wondered why he hadn't thought of it before. Murphy had pointed the way; some ordinary Joes would pay a lot for fifteen minutes with a young girl. In another couple of days he would find a new website. Things were going right for a change and even better, he felt confident that he'd covered his tracks well. He was feeling lucky.

It took Arran Marx twenty-four hours to pull things together. A contact in the police department warned him about Lewis, giving him the details - for some bucks. Another contact at Motor Licences passed on the vehicle number and driver's details, including a photo. More eagles flew. The car details were different from the station wagon, so Lewis had changed vehicles. A street boy found the old one four blocks away in a car lot. That cost another twenty bucks.

Again, Motor Licences obliged with a list of vehicles stolen in the area. All but two had been recovered. One - a white Ford station wagon stolen close to where the old car had been found. Two nights before it had been spotted in Holly Springs, Mississippi, a small town south of Memphis. It had been parked up on the wrong side of the tracks. Because it had an Out-of -State licence plate the highway patrol had sent in a report. Later, the officer had checked back to find it gone. The contact could add nothing more.

Marx sat in his office checking through everything he had so far. This included a dossier he'd built on Lewis Barasitch. He studied the route they'd taken, and felt certain of where they were heading. He called the Banks' after they'd finished their evening meal.

'Mr Banks? Arran Marx here. I have a dossier on your daughter-in-law and Barasitch.'

'Has he found them yet?' asked Molly urgently, but Bert waved the question away.

'I'm listening, Mr Marx.'

'I'll leave everything I've pulled together at the hotel reception for you sometime tonight. It'll be there for you in the morning.'

'Can you give me a brief outline of it now?'

'Sure; but first, there's a curious thing I've learned from the neighbours. We know the family left in a hurry after a cop visited. No ordinary cop, though. He was a captain from Juvenile Section. Does that make any sense?'

'Possibly the British Foreign Office got their act together quicker than we thought.'

'Maybe - and then there were the two men who came asking around a day after the family left.'

'Are they significant?'

'You bet. They fit the description of a couple hit men known locally as the Dancer Twins.'

'The what?'

'Never mind - it's all in the dossier. These guys have heavy Mob connections. It's safe to assume Barasitch was tipped off by that cop; for what reason, I can't tell you.'

'Have you any idea where they've gone?' Bert knew he wouldn't be able to stall Molly from grabbing the phone much longer.

'I reckon, from their route, they've probably gone to N'Yawlins.'

'Where?'

'New Orleans,' Marx enunciated slowly. 'I come from down that way. They call the city the Big Easy; a lot of corruption down there.'

'That's some way from here, isn't it?'

'Yeah, it sure is. Deep South. Doesn't get any deeper.' Arran told Bert why he thought the trio were heading there.

'So what now?'

'My associate down there: He's good; good as me.' He gave a deep-throated chuckle. 'I've already faxed him all the details to get the ball rolling. His name is Danny Generve. A Coon-ass.'

'What?'

'Cajun: All I need is your okay.'

'How much have we spent so far?' Bert asked, feeling out of his depth. He heard the rustle of paper.

'Twelve hundred bucks; that covers everything. If it's any consolation, what's in that dossier didn't come cheap. At least you won't have that expense again.'

'So we owe you two hundred. We might as well go with it; we knew it was going to cost. Tell him to be careful how he spends it. There's not much left. How do we get the money to him?'

'I'll drop by tomorrow evening about this time. Let me have it and I'll get it to him.'

'Shouldn't we go on down there?'

'If I were you I'd stay put. We don't know what Danny might find and there's a possibility they might move on. See you tomorrow.'

'Thanks, Mr Marx. We'll wait and see what Mr Generve digs up.'

17.

Danny Generve was a laconic man, skinny and slight. Lank hair hung over deep-set, penetrating chocolate brown eyes and a large nose. He had been in the business five years and knew how sleazy New Orleans could be. Arran and he had grown up there and in the bayous. They had served on the Force together for fifteen years, before leaving. Nothing had been pinned on either of them, but it became too hot for comfort.

Arran had gone to his sister in Newark, but Danny had decided to stay. Both had started up bounty hunting within months of each other and had handed work back and forth. The business mostly involved missing spouses and bail-bond work. Arran covered the Northern States while Danny worked up as far as North Carolina.

He was reading the dossier when Arran called to give him the okay. Until he knew it inside out he wouldn't start asking questions. The wrong word in the wrong place could screw everything. It took him an hour or so to get himself acquainted with his quarry. What he read made him realise how careful he needed to be. Lewis's record spoke volumes. A violent sonofabitch.

Danny started asking questions that night. He reckoned they must have now been in the city for at least two days. The dossier showed Lewis had no bank account. If he had any money it would be a stash, and was sure to be dwindling. The kind of low-life Lewis was he probably lived from hand to mouth, grabbing whatever he could and not planning too far into the future.

He felt sure it wouldn't be long before he pushed Tracey out to sell her tush. The French Quarter would be the obvious place. Bourbon Street was crowded with tourists gawking at sex-shops and grazing on the pictures outside the strip clubs. A whore in a strange city would go for the tourists, and stand out like a bible-puncher in a brothel. He talked to some of the girls and gave copies of Tracey's photo. They knew he was good for a few bucks if they came through.

The next night he was waiting for Tracey, his motorbike parked round the corner. She didn't do her picture justice. Gone was her youth. By midnight she had turned a few tricks, but they were mostly short blow jobs in dark alleys.

At three she called a taxi. If she'd made a hundred and fifty bucks he would be surprised. Danny ran to his bike and was soon following. The traffic thinned as they went uptown. He had to distance himself as they rode up Tchoupatoulis, a dismal stretch of road that ran by the levee and the railroad tracks.

Between Jackson and Louisiana Avenue intersections, three miles from the Quarter, the taxi turned right, into an area called the Irish Channel. It was an old neighbourhood with a lot of run-down property. Two blocks further on it stopped outside a cheap, rundown rental.

Parked outside were a beaten-up twenty-year-old silver Buick Riviera and a slightly newer green Chevi. Danny took the numbers of both cars as he watched her go in. The top bedroom had a light on, which blinked out after ten minutes. Moments later, the front door opened and a small, late-middle-aged man came out. So Alice was on the game as well. He got into the Chevi and drove away.

18.

Danny followed the Chevi's zigzag progress uptown. After ten blocks it drew up outside a bar. The neon light above the door flashed 'The 901 Club'. His quarry banged on the door, then disappeared inside. Danny waited several minutes before knocking. He knew the drill with these local bars. A spy hole slid open and an eye regarded him. A latch clicked, and he entered. The security was not to keep out robbers, but blacks. This was a 'white bar' - a members-only club. He signed a book, threw five dollars on the counter, ordered a beer, settled himself on a bar stool, and glanced around. All the clientele were white, even the barman.

Danny's mark, two stools away, was older than he had first thought - in his sixties. He was scribbling on a betting slip, his tongue poking out in concentration.

'Doing the dogs?'

The nonce jerked his head up. Danny smiled.

'I've come in from Lafayette this evening. What's the racing like around here?'

'Not bad,' he muttered.

'Andy French,' Danny said, holding out his hand. 'Friends call me Andy.'

He took it nervously. 'Jed.'

'Sorry, man, I don't mean to intrude.'

'That's okay; Andy. You startled the shit out of me, that's all,' said Jed weakly.

Danny supped his beer, eyeing the nonce over the rim of his beer can. Two rounds later they had become great buddies. They moved from the bar and huddled in a darkened booth. Jed was giving Danny the lowdown on racing, New Orleans style. Another round of beers and Danny came to the subject on his mind.

'Jed, d'ya know of any pussy around here?'

Jed gazed steadily into Danny's eyes.

'Wotcha mean, a guy like you?

Clapping Jed on the back, Danny laughed. 'The kind of pussy I like don't always come free.'

'You like it kinky, do ya?' Jed sniggered into his beer.

'Come on man, be real. Ever know a guy who don't?' Jed nodded in agreement. 'Tried most things, man. I'm up for anythin' this wicked ol' town can throw my way.' Danny laughed. 'Well, nearly anythin'.' Jed giggled again

'Still don't see why you would have to pay to give a girl a good time,' he said.

'That's the world, man.' Danny gave a sigh. 'You gonna tell me what *you* like?' he asked, changing tack.

Jed hesitated.

'Shit; don't be shy, man. You ain't going to shock me; everyone has a turn-on.' Danny eyed Jed speculatively, leaned forward, and whispered. When he'd finished he sat back, crossed his arms and gave a smug smile. 'It was real wicked. Bet you can't beat that.'

'I can,' muttered Jed, and giggled.

'Shi-it,' said Danny admiringly, 'you been holding out on me.'

'It's not the kind of thing you spread around.'

'Sure. Sorry, man,' he whispered.

'That's okay; but keep it quiet.'

'You going to tell me what you did?' Danny could see that Jed wanted to boast, so he pushed some more. 'I believe you're pullin' my dick.'

'That I ain't.' His eyes darted nervously around the bar, then he leant forward and with stabs of his forefinger, proceeded on the enjoyable task of shocking his new friend.

'Shit man, that's something else!' whistled an astonished Danny. 'I gotta get some of that pussy.'

'Going to cost you for an introduction.'

'Sure; how much?'

'Twenty bucks.'

'When?'

'Too late now. Tomorrow.'

They went on talking for some time, then Jed got up and left. Danny waited another ten minutes before following him out.

19.

The early evening sun slanted through the grubby window in one piercing beam, highlighting a litter-strewn floor. The room was shabby. Cobwebs fluttered in the wash from a ceiling fan revolving lazily above Danny's head. He was relaxing in a well-worn office chair, feet on his desk, waiting. When the phone finally rang he swooped on it like a dog on a bone.

'Mr Generve? It's Bert Banks. Your associate Mr Marx asked me to call you.'

'Yeah. I've found your people.'

'You have?'

'Yeah. I've faxed a whole lot of stuff to Arran. He'll drop it over to you.' He paused for a moment. 'The reason I wanted you to call is - we need to make some decisions.'

'About what?'

'I don't think asking for the girl is going to work.'

'No?'

'Not if I read Lewis right.'

'What about the mother?'

'She won't have any say in the matter. He's pimping the girl too, and pimps don't let go easy.'

'So what do you suggest?'

'We snatch her.'

'Would you do it?'

'No; it's illegal as hell, but there are some groups around, mainly religious, who might. We keep this at arm's length.'

'And that will cost?'

'Sure it will. Before we approach these people I'll watch the house for a few days. What I need to know is this; in principle, are you willing?'

'Yes, but don't you have any idea of the cost?'

'No. What's your ceiling?'

'Thirty thousand.'

'That should more than cover it.'

'When you say a few days, how many precisely?'

'This business doesn't use the word 'precise', Mr Banks. By the end of the week I'll have a better picture.'

'Very well,' Bert gave a deep sigh. 'So we should have something to go on by then?'

'Hope so, but I warn you - it's all in the laps of the gods. It's not like they'll advertise themselves. It's illegal. *Some* have been sued and put in jail.'

'Can you suggest another way, apart from the police?'

'Apart from you knocking on their door, no. We're wasting time. I'll get Arran to ask around as well, but a home-grown group will be a deal cheaper.'

'There is one other thing.'

'Shoot.'

'What? Oh. Right. You said he's pimping Alice. Could you get in and see her? Let her know what's happening.'

'I'll think about that one. I wouldn't be able to do anything before, say, eleven tonight.'

'That's alright. We can wait three hours.'

'Mr Banks; you're an hour ahead of me. As I said, I'll think about it. I'll try; but no promises, okay?'

'Yes.'

'I doubt I'll call you for at least three days. Don't worry.'

Molly was in bed re-reading the report Arran Marx had left a few hours after his conversation with Danny. It was up to date on all the information that had been gathered.

'Bert?'

'Molly. Switch your damn light out and go to sleep.'

'No; and don't swear! Now, listen.'

Bert sighed.

'I can listen just as well with the light out.'

She switched off and snuggled into Bert's back.

'Bert?' This drew another sigh from him.

'I'm listening.'

'I've been thinking.'

'You haven't stopped since he called,' said Bert bluntly.

She pressed a balled fist between his shoulder blades. 'Oh, stop your grumbling. We don't know what these people are like who might rescue Alice, even if this Mr Generve can find any. We should go ourselves and talk to Tracey. We could offer her the money.'

Bert switched on the light and sat up.

'Are you daft, woman?'

Molly rolled over onto her back and crossed her arms.

'Give me ten good reasons why not,' she said stubbornly.

'I'll give you one. It's crazy, and so are you.'

'That's two. I want ten.'

'We don't know where they live.'

'We do. We also know the name and address of this Danny Generve person down there. It's all in the file.'

'I can imagine what the papers would say: 'Two Geriatrics Snatch Child from under the Noses of Desperate Criminals.''

'So?'

'I forgot to add - 'Two Geriatrics Found Floating Upside Down in - what's the name of that river?''

'Mississippi.'

'Upside down in the Mississippi.'

'Alice knows us. She would be terrified of strangers.'

'You're talking daft.'

'We should have gone the day Alice first phoned us; then all this would never have happened.'

'We don't know that.' He switched off the light. 'Now go to sleep.'

Danny worked through the evening following up ghost leads of nonexistent kidnapping groups – but with no success. In New York Arran was having similar problems. Their conversation ended on a flat note. With nothing to do until later that night, Danny decided to research child sex in the city. He still had contacts in the precinct.

A few minutes past eleven he went back to the 901 Club. He was talking to the barman when Jed strolled in.

'Hi, Jed. Give me two beers,' he told the barman. 'How you doing, man?' He passed one to Jed, then placed a hand on his shoulder and guided him to a table at the far end of the room, away from everybody.

'You still want that pussy, Andy?'

'Do fish swim?'

'You got the money, plus my commission?'

'Sure. Drink your beer and let's go.'

'Not so fast. Got a dime?'

Danny pulled out some money and tossed a dime on the table. Jed picked it up and went to the phone at the end of the bar. When he came back he swigged his beer down, burped, slammed the bottle on the table and started for the door. Danny followed. Outside, Jed stopped abruptly and held out his hand.

'Give me my twenty bucks.'

Bert woke in the middle of the night. He could hear Molly whispering.

'Is that you, Molly?'

'Shh. Go back to sleep.'

'Come back to bed.'

'In a minute.'

Bert turned over and switched on the light. Molly was on the phone.

'What the hell are you doing?'

She said 'thank you' and put down the phone, looking pleased with herself. Bert got up on his elbows and glared at her.

'Are you going tell me what's going on?'

'Yes, we're booked on a plane to New Orleans tomorrow morning.' She glanced at her watch on the bedside table. 'Correction; later this morning.'

'And what do we do when we get there, twiddle our thumbs?'

'Well, that's what we're doing here. At least we'll be at hand when he needs us. You know it makes sense.'

She leaned across and gave him a kiss on the cheek and then dropped her head on the pillow. 'Good night, dear. Get some sleep; we've got a long day ahead of us.'

20.

Jed left Danny on the doorstep. He entered a room as dingy and depressing as the exterior of the house, empty cans of beer strewn everywhere, and a half-eaten carton of food spilled over the table. Lewis held out his hand.

'A hundred 'n' fifty bucks.'

'It was a hundred n' twenty last night.'

'That was last night. It's gone up.'

'Shit, man. I want to rent pussy, not keep it.'

'Fucking comedian. It's up to you, buddy. No bucks, no fucks.'

Danny shrugged, brought out a wad of notes and counted off the money into Lewis's hand.

'You got twenty minutes.'

'The fuck I have. Hundred and fifty buys me half-an-hour.'

'Okay,' said Lewis begrudgingly. 'Lolita's up the stairs. Make sure you don't mark her.'

'Sure, man.'

Danny climbed narrow stairs and opened the door at the top. The room was dimly lit. Attempts had been made to make it enticing. Strips of gauzy cloth hung from the ceiling over a low bed. Alice lay on a pile of cushions against the wall, wearing a scanty basque which was far too large for her. Her scared face was heavily made up; the mascara had run. Danny hung onto the door, and looked in.

'Hello, honey chile'.'

She flinched, and attempted to smile. Danny closed the door behind him and pushed the bolt closed, then put a finger to his lips, bringing a surprised frown to Alice's face. He pulled a pad from his pocket and wrote on it, chattering all the while. When he'd finished he handed the pad to Alice. She read 'Keep quiet. I'm sent by friends in England.' Her eyes widened with astonishment.

Danny kept on talking as he silently searched the room. He went back and put his ear to the door. Once satisfied that

Lewis wasn't outside, he crossed and sat close to Alice. Suspicious, she shrank away from him.

'It's okay, Alice. I'm not going to touch you,' he whispered.

'Who are you? How do you know my name?' she asked quietly.

'From your folks in England. That's all I know.' He bounced up and down on the mattress, making it squeak. 'We've gotta make some noise like we're screwing; otherwise he might come to find out why we're silent.'

Alice stared with shock at him, then started to get up. He grabbed her arm and stopped her from rising.

'Bounce up and down.'

'Who are you?' she asked with hoarse urgency.

'Danny.'

With that he groaned. Her eyes widened with surprise, she grinned and started rocking the bed, making it squeak. Suddenly, she too let out a long groan. He winked at her. Shit, he thought, she catches on quick. Both of them kept up a rocking rhythm, but slowly eased off on the moaning. He bent close to her, and could taste the cheap perfume that clung to her.

'Keep rocking.'

Getting off the bed he went over and put his ear to the door, then knelt down and peered under the gap. He'd thought he'd heard a noise on the stairs, but no one was there.

'Have you come to get me?' Still she rocked the bed.

'Not so fast, Alice.' She stopped rocking. 'Keep rocking.'

She started again. Danny went over to the window, pulled out a clasp-knife and slipped it under an edge of the wallpaper close to the skirting board, behind one of the drapes. He took a card from his pocket and held it up for her to see, before slipping it behind the loosened paper. He sat back down on the bed, keeping in rhythm with her, letting out little gasps and groans. She followed suit.

'I can't take you now,' he whispered.

'Oh, please!' She started to sob.

'Cut it out,' he said sharply. 'That won't get us anywhere. Have you a place to stash things?' She nodded. 'Show me.'

Alice went to the corner of the room and pulled back a small piece of skirting board.

'Here.' He threw her the knife. 'Only use it in an emergency.'

She stashed the knife and came back onto the bed and started rocking again. He smiled and increased the tempo, then let out a loud moan that faded away and she whimpered. The rocking stopped.

'Okay we don't have much time left. If you escape you'll find my address behind the wall covering. Make sure you don't leave it about. And if you have to use the knife you'll get one chance, so either go for the eyes or crotch.' He touched the wall behind him. 'This wall is thin and lets out onto the roof. If you can dig through, this is the way to go. Once through the plaster, kick yourself out, but it'll make a noise, so jam up the door.' He got up from the bed.

'Don't leave me,' she whined.

'Hush now, child.' He bent over her and held her chin and kissed her on the forehead. 'I will be back, when everything is ready.' Tears trickled down her face.

'Shh! When you're free I'll take you far away from this on my big black motor bike,' he said gently. 'Now take off your clothes.'

'What?'

'Take them off. You're never dressed when the men leave you, are you?' She shook her head.

Danny went to the door, gave her a little wave, unbolted the door and was gone. The sound of his feet on the stairs was the only memory left to her. She buried her head in the bedclothes and wept.

21.

Alice was not disturbed again for the rest of the night. After Danny left Lewis checked on her, saying he was pleased, and was going out. He switched the light off and bolted the door behind him. The front door slammed, and the throaty roar of Lewis's car revved up and dwindled into the distance.

Now, she was alone in the house for the first time in days. Her mother would not be back until the early hours of the morning. She hoped she was having a successful night and would be back before Lewis. When he came home he would be drunk and mean as hell. If her mother had a large wad of notes to hand him it might fend off violence.

Thanks to Danny, she had not been used this night, but she knew it wouldn't last. Her sobbing meandered through a miasma of self-pity. One minute she adored the stranger who'd brought a ray of hope to her fear and loneliness, the next moment she hated him for leaving her there, not understanding why he couldn't have carried her off.

She slowly pulled herself out of her despondency, rose and switched on the light. The neighbourhood was silent, save for the intermittent howling of a lone dog. She pulled away a drape. Bars criss-crossed the window. Without them it would still have been a long drop, too high for her courage. Her hand slid down the wall until she felt unevenness in the wallpaper. With care, she eased out the card Danny had hidden. A piece of paper fluttered to the floor. Reading the card left her no wiser as to how to find him in this strange city. She crouched down and slipping it back noticed the twenty-dollar bill. She picked it up, kissed it, and slipped it back behind the loosened wallpaper.

Dropping the drape she went to her secret hidey-hole and lifted out the knife. It felt heavy in her hand. It was a type that fishermen used, with several blades and other attachments. One of these had a saw-tooth edge to it.

The low bed with its solid headboard was hard up against the wall that backed onto the roof. It took some tugging to drag it away. From one of the long drapes, she tore off a length and laid it on the floor against the wall. The old wallpaper came off with her nails; a patch large enough for her body. Opening the smallest blade, she stabbed at the bare plaster. It was soft and crumbly and the blade penetrated it up to the hilt. Once there was a hole the size of her large finger she closed the knife blade, and opened the saw-toothed one.

After several hours the hole had become the size of a football. It was with satisfaction that she watched it grow. Instead of a large pile of debris mounting on the cloth, the bits of plaster had started to fall back in and down between the inner and outer walls with a rattling clatter. The outside boards were cracked and split and moved at the slightest touch. When the hole was large enough, a kick or two would knock the boards away.

As time went on she became tired. Her assault on the wall slowed, until she found her head drooping. On the third occasion, the sound of a door slamming and a car driving away woke her with a jerk. Quickly rubbing her hands on the cloth, she stuffed it into her hidey-hole with the knife. She'd manoeuvred the bed back in place as the front door banged. Hearing the tired clack of heeled shoes on the stairs she switched off the light and got under the sheets.

Tracey checked on her daughter, found her asleep, went back down and gave herself a fix. She had fallen asleep in a drugged stupor when Lewis finally got back. The sun had already risen, heating up the day. He staggered in drunk, but for once he seemed to be in a good mood. Shoving her over, he lay on the bed and was soon asleep.

24

Bert and Molly were a little sweaty and travel-weary after sitting for so long. They showered, changed their clothes, and went down for something called 'brunch', feeling fresher.

'What should we do first?' asked Bert, as he crumpled his napkin and dropped it onto his side plate.

'I'd like to locate Alice, if we can.'

'Good Lord; you're not proposing to go and visit her?'

'Don't be silly, Bert. We'll locate the street and take a peep at the house. We might even see her,' she said hopefully.

Bert pushed his chair back. 'I'll see if I can get rid of this belt.' He patted his stomach. 'Maybe reception will have a map.'

He strolled out to the lobby and went over to the desk, where a young man sat tapping something into a computer. He gave a little cough.

'Yes, Sir. Is everything okay?'

'Oh, yes.' Bert bent forward over the desk, and beckoned to him. 'I was wondering - do you have a safe?' he whispered

'Yes, Sir. Is there something you would like us to hold for you?'

'Yes; some money I changed in England. I don't like to carry so much with me.'

Bert looked around; the lobby was empty. He opened his jacket and unbuttoned his shirt and after some fumbling, withdrew the money-belt. There were six pockets, each tightly packed. He laid it out in front of the clerk and opened the pockets, withdrawing neatly folded wads of dollar bills.

'There should be $12,000 dollars.' He counted each wad. 'Do you mind storing the belt, too? It's so uncomfortable to wear.'

'Not at all. I'll put the money back in the pockets. I think you're very wise. This is not the safest city.' The clerk wrote something in a book. 'Can you sign here, please?' He tore out a flimsy and gave it to Bert. 'Your receipt, Sir.'

'Thank you.'

'Not at all.' Bert stood watching him write something down before the belt was put in the safe. The receptionist turned back to the counter, surprised to see Bert still standing there.

'I'm sorry, is there anything else, Sir?'

'Do you sell maps of the city?'

'We have some free tourist ones.' He passed two thin brochures to him. 'This one is of the French Quarter, and this of most of the city, and everything y'all will want to see is there.' He opened out the map and laid it flat on the desk. 'Here's where the hotel is.' He put a cross on the map, and then flicked it over. St Charles Avenue was enlarged on the back. 'Now see these marks here? They indicate where the streetcars stop, and the number here tells you what block it is. That's the same from the river to Clairborne.' He folded the map again and gave it to Bert.

'Thank you.'

'My pleasure, Sir. Y'all have a good day, now.'

He shook his head as he watched Bert walk back to the restaurant.

'You took your time,' said Molly, as Bert sat down.

'Give over, woman. I put the belt in the safe. Here; move your stuff.' Bert started to unfold the map. 'What's the name of the street?' She rummaged in her bag. 'C'm on.'

'Give me a chance.'

'I'd've thought you'd sort that thing out before coming here. You've got everything bar the kitchen sink.'

'Oh, stop your grumbling. It's here somewhere. Got it!' She triumphantly held up her little address book.

'So what's the name?' Bert could not conceal his excitement.

'Hold your horses, will you? 2451 St Thomas, then it's got 'division' next to it. A street or two off Tchoo -pi-too - lass Street," she read with difficulty. 'I s'pose that's a main 'road.' Molly leant over the map. Bert pointed out the hotel. She traced her finger back towards the river.

'Found it. It's a funny word to say. There's a number 36, must be in the thousands. The next one down is 35.' She checked the address, her finger following the road. '26,25,24. Between First and Second. It's close to the river, and a railway line.'

'They're called railroads. I bet it's rough. No better than Newark. Maybe we should get a taxi.'

'What, after what we spent on the limo? We know what to look out for now.' Bert eyed her, unconvinced. 'If it starts to get bad we'll come back. Anyway, I want to go on one of those street cars.'

Bert studied the map again. 'We'll have to get off at stop fourteen, and walk the rest of the way.'

'See what it says there.' Her finger circled the area they would have to walk through. 'This part's called the Garden District. If St Charles Avenue is anything to go by, it won't be too bad,' Molly said optimistically. 'Can you mark it, Bert?'

He picked up a pen and put a cross. A waiter came in with a tray.

'Y'all planning your afternoon?'

'Yes, we're going to visit the Garden District. Molly likes her flowers.'

25.

They left, map in hand, took the streetcar to stop fourteen and walked into the Garden District, along a road lined with trees. Pretty wooden houses with carved porches and wrought-iron balconies had gardens bursting with azaleas, camellias and magnolia trees. The sight was colourful and the scent heavy on the humid air. Once past Chestnut Street the surroundings started to get a little scruffy. It was after crossing Magazine Street that things went downhill.

They had left Annunciation Avenue a couple of streets back. Bert was becoming worried and on the point of turning them round. Dead vehicles with no wheels and smashed windscreens sagged in the gutters. There was no division between road and sidewalk. Litter and junk lay everywhere, and many of the squat houses, built on pillars of brick, stared unwelcomingly - with blank windows.

A police car trundled along the road towards them. It slowed as it passed, then stopped and reversed back until it came level. The passenger's window slid down, and a cop in dark shades leant across the seat.

'Hi, Folks. Y'all lost or something?'

'No, officer. We're sight-seeing.'

Gene MacIntyre frowned. Damn Limeys, he thought. Some people had no sense. He lived much further up, close to the Nashville Avenue intersection, right in the heart of the Irish Channel. Down this far and close to the river it wasn't safe to go walking, especially for tourists.

'Are we doing anything wrong, officer?' asked Molly.

'No, Ma'am, but you're in the wrong part of town. It's not safe to go wandering round down here.' He got out of the patrol car and pointed back the way he had come. 'There's nothing down there; low neighbourhood is all you'll find. The railroad and the levee: Thought you folks would realise. Are you looking for something particular?'

'Some friends of ours from Britain moved to New Orleans many years ago. Their last address was from around here.' Molly had to shout, as first a noisy car, then a battered blue truck swept past leaving a cloud of dust in their wake. 'A street called St Thomas - Division.'

'You're on First, so you're going in the right direction, but St Thomas Division.' He scratched his head. 'That's a real cheap area, mostly blacks with some white trash, but they don't usually stay long - the white folks, I mean. How long ago? I live uptown a little, but never heard of any Limeys - pardon ma'am, I mean English, living round here.'

'That's all right, Limeys is fine,' said Molly, with a smile.

'Fifteen odd years, wouldn't you say, Moll?'

Molly kept her eyes intently on the policeman.

'No. Can't say I've heard of Limeys down there.'

'Said they had a camel-back,' said Molly hopefully, 'whatever that is.'

'That's like a shotgun with a room on top. I believe there is one down there. Not that many about now.' Gene moved off the fender and moved to the driver's door. The idea of leaving these two to wander made him uneasy. It was amazing they hadn't got into trouble already. 'Where y'all staying?'

'The Columns on St Charles. Do you know it?'

'Yeah, hop in. We'll drive past, and then I'll take you back. I was going that way.'

Molly and Bert hesitated.

'C'mon, I can't leave you here.'

'Are you arresting us, Constable?'

'Heck no. I can't force you, but it will be safer to come.'

They got in and Gene swung the car around. He slowed down and crept along St Thomas. There were some black kids kicking a ball in the road. They stopped their play and started to move away.

'There's your camel-back.'

He pointed at a long narrow building with a box perched on its rear end. It was shabby, and some of the clapboard cladding was missing. Gene lowered his window, cocked his head out and shouted at the kids.

'Hey, boy!' The boys glanced at each other, frightened. The tallest pointed to himself. 'Yeah, come here, boy.'

They picked up their ball, ready to flee. 'Y'all done nothing wrong that I knows of, boy. Just want to ask a question.'

Hesitantly they sidled up to the car and stood silently with downcast eyes.

'You know who lives in the camel-back, boy?' He addressed the tall one, who shook his head. 'Anyone living there, boy?' He nodded this time. 'Speak up, boy. Who?'

'Don't know, Sir. They's new folks. Them white, Sir.'

'How many, and how long have they lived there, boy?'

'Not long; coupla days.' The boy shrugged his shoulders. 'Man and woman and a girl. We never sees her, Sir.'

'Okay, you can go, boy. Keep out of trouble,' Gene barked.

The boys started to sidle away, still keeping an eye on the policeman. Molly leaned over the cop's shoulder.

'Thank you.' The boys took off as soon as she opened her mouth.

'Now, I'll take you home.'

'What's a shotgun, Officer?' asked Molly.

'Ways back, Ma'am, when folks were poor, and folks round here were always poor, they built one or two rooms. When they got more kids than they could handle, or got some money, they put another room on the back and so on until they reached the end of their lot. Said you could shoot straight through from the front door and out the back. Then they built up.' Gene pointed up to the sky. ''Cause most were cheaply built a lot have fallen down over the years and disappeared.' He glanced round. 'How long y'all been here?'

'Arrived this morning from Newark.'

'Are y'all thirsty?'

'A little.'

'Like doughnuts; American ones?'

'Are they different?'

'Probably. Com'on and I'll introduce y'all to the neighbourhood donut shop; makes real genuine Ny'awlins coffee. Not far from your hotel.'

26.

Danny had started to doze in the afternoon torpor. He was parked half a block away from the Barasitch's in a battered blue Chevy truck. The noisy Buick engine cranking over brought him out of his stupor. He started the truck, and followed as Lewis and Alice disappeared up First, towards Magazine. A little way up, a cop car was parked. The cop was leaning against the fender talking to an old white couple. Lewis took no notice, but Alice swivelled round in her seat and stared. He slapped her bare leg.

'What was that for?

'Don't ever stare at a cop like that; you'll draw attention.'

Alice found it hard not to check that her eyes hadn't fooled her. Seconds later Danny also passed the group. Something nagged at his mind, but for the life of him he could not fathom what it was. He glanced in the rear mirror quickly, then concentrated on following the Buick.

MacIntyre dropped them off at the hotel after a doughnut and coffee. Their room was mercifully cool and shady after the hot afternoon sun. They sat on the bed and spread the map to find where they had been. Molly rummaged in her bag and brought out her little address book.

'Right: I wonder where the detective's place is?'

'Moll; haven't you had enough excitement for one day?'

'We'll be a little more careful. If it starts to get rough, we'll turn back.'

'Haven't I heard that before?' he muttered,

'Ah, here we are. Danny Generve. Private Investigation Service. Corner of South Saratoga and Soniat. Uptown.'

He ran his thumb down the index in their map. 'F.3. We're in the same square.'

'You sure?'

'Yes.' He eyes travelled up St Charles. 'Only twelve blocks. Six stops on the streetcar and four blocks back.'

'It seems to get posher the further we go up the avenue, so it must be safe to walk.'

It was late afternoon when they left. The manager warned that it got dark between six and seven. As they reached the stop they saw a streetcar in the distance. It didn't take long to arrive. They sat on slatted wooden benches gazing out of the window at the passing gardens.

Soniat was a quiet, narrow street with tree roots lifting the concrete slabs making the paving uneven. Molly took Bert's arm as they walked down the shaded sidewalk; they soon became hot and sticky from the warm, humid air. After two blocks the trees became less frequent, the gardens less cared for and the paint on the clapboard houses peeling. The quietness was a little disturbing. Molly clung tighter to Bert.

'Would you believe it; not a stone's throw from St Charles Avenue?'

'If it gets much worse, we'll go back.' .

With hesitant steps they walked on. A cat sauntered out of a dusty yard, stopped and glared. Deciding they were no threat, it walked on. A brown bird with a fan-tail swooped down on the cat with a banshee scream. They both jumped; Molly's fingers dug hard into Bert's arm. The bird lifted away and circled back to swoop again. It let out another piercing squawk. The cat dashed under a car and stayed there.

'My Lord, what was that?'

'I don't know, just glad it's not mad at us,' muttered Bert.

Gaining their composure they cautiously walked on to the corner of Saratoga. Across the intersection was a shabby two-storey house, its veranda cluttered with junk, the ground-floor windows cracked, and one shuttered. Many of the clapboards had slipped, and insulation was spilling out like some old forgotten teddy bear. The upper floor was a slight improvement. One of the windows had a sign. They could just make out the name; 'Danny Generve, Private Investigator.' They weren't impressed.

'Well, we'd better go and see if he's in,' said Bert, guiding Molly to the front door. It was locked. He tried the doorbell twice, but there was no answer. 'Now this was a waste of time. We should have rung.'

'No it wasn't; at least we know what kind of place he's running.'

'It's not very prepossessing. Come on; let's get back to the hotel.'

Dusk was drawing in fast by the time they reached The Columns. It was buzzing with people. Bert, who had noticed a bar on the first floor, suggested they had a drink. The room had large windows that opened out onto the columns, giving a view of the street. Between the windows and the columns was a balcony with tables and chairs.

'Let's sit out there and watch the cars go by.'

Without waiting for a reply, Molly went and sat at a table. A waiter came to take their order.

'I've always wanted to try what Scarlett O'Hara had, but I can't remember what it's called.'

'Mint Julep, Ma'am; and you, Sir?'

Bert didn't know what to ask for. He was sure Molly's drink would be too fancy.

'A beer, please.' Then he remembered the American beers in the supermarket back home - not that he had ever tried one. 'I'll try a local brew.'

That'll be a Dixie. I think y'll like it.'

The bar hummed with murmured chatter while the fans whooshed slowly overhead. Intermittently a streetcar glided by with a whining whirr. The air was perfumed with the heady scent of the magnolias, and as they sat waiting for their drinks they were suddenly aware of a rising, chirping sound. The noise rose to a crescendo, before it passed and faded to nothing. The wave of sound happened several more times before the waiter returned with their drinks.

'Young man, what is that chirping sound we hear?' asked Molly.

'Ma'am, them's cicadas. One will start up, down the block, and slowly they'll all join in, then fade out again.'

'I think I'm going to enjoy going to sleep listening to that sound. Thank you.' The waiter left with a smile.

27.

Two hours after Alice had done her little show Arran Marx found her on the Net. The appearance worried him. With the Dancer twins searching for them it was the last thing Barasitch should have been doing. Arran's efforts to contact a group to snatch Alice had been met with a cold wall of silence. He wondered how Danny had fared. He rang him:

'Hi, Danny, got some bad news. The kid's back on the Net...'

'I suspected as much. I trailed Barasitch and the kid to a seedy joint the other side of the French Quarter. They were there for a couple of hours, and the kid came out crying.'

'I expect she did. It wasn't a pleasant watch. I downloaded it for evidence.'

'You want to be careful with that stuff.'

'I know; copied it onto disks, and not on my hard drive, and they're in a safe place.' Arran paused and pinched the bridge of his nose. 'I think the kid's in even more danger now she's back on line.'

'Yeah, I agree. How's the hunt for doing the snatch?'

'No luck so far. I was wondering how you'd fared?'

'Drawn a blank on that score, too, but I'll try again later today. It's pretty dodgy ground once we go past surveillance.'

'Sure,' Arran tapped his fingers on his desk as if that would relieve the tension. 'I'll call the grandparents with an update.'

'Yeah, you'd better. They need to be ready to upsticks at a moment's notice. I've a feeling things are going to move quickly when that happens.'

'Sure. Good luck.' Arran closed the call.

28.

Alice had the house to herself again. Once the enlargement of the hole was completed she had simply to smash through the boards. With the headboard tight up against her back, she kicked them out. They split; with another kick they swung out of sight. She had broken through – but only to the loft. Through tears of frustration, she nearly missed her mother coming home. She just managed to push the bed back and jump under the sheets with her clothes on. Tracey had had another awful night. With her face so badly bruised the punters had been thin. She cracked open the bedroom door to check on Alice. She was asleep.

Molly and Bert got up early and took a cab down to St Thomas. They circled the streets, scrutinising the kids going to school, but they didn't see Alice. They would come back in the afternoon and hope to spot her then. They had a slow breakfast back at the hotel, called Danny, who did not answer, and left a message on his machine. With nothing else to do they took a walk in Audubon Park. Sitting by a lake, they marvelled at a group of snap-turtles basking on a log that floated on the water.

Danny woke up late, so forgot to check his machine before hurrying off to St Thomas. He parked under a large mimosa tree, it's orchid-pink flowers falling like feathers onto the truck. The day was going to be long and hot.

The Barasitch household pulled itself out of the mire around lunchtime. Alice had been awake for hours, waiting to be released to yet another day of boredom and fear. She was depressed after the discovery of the night before. Tracey let her use the bathroom, but decided to make her go back up with her breakfast. She didn't want a reccurrence of yesterday. When Lewis finally rolled out of bed, it was no further than the couch. He slumped down and watched football reruns, shouting for beers and sandwiches. With so much running about she forgot to lock Alice's door.

29.

Danny was sucking on a bottle of lukewarm water when two large black Mercs rolled quietly up. The Dancer twins got out of the back of the first car. The driver stayed put. There were two men in the other car. They were told to check each side of the house and cover the back, while the twins climbed the steps to the front door.

'What the hell, that ain't no cavalry,' Danny murmured to himself. Alice was in there, but he could do nothing.

Lewis was still watching the television when Harry banged on the door. Tracey yelled and went to open it. She released the catch. The door swung violently back, knocking her to the floor. Lewis was taken by surprise as the Dancers swaggered in. They wore tight black leather gloves.

For all his unpreparedness, Lewis moved surprisingly swiftly, but not fast enough. Harry's foot caught him in the stomach and sent him sprawling back onto the couch. Before he could recover, Harvey had the muzzle of his gun pressed to his forehead. Harry dragged Tracey to her feet by her hair and shoved her down beside Lewis on the couch.

With the gun at his temple Lewis lifted his arms in submission. Harvey stepped sharply back so Lewis couldn't lash out with his feet, while Harry dusted his jacket and straightened his tie, then crouched behind the settee, level with Lewis's ear. Shaking his head and tutting, he leered at them.

'Lewis; you're a greedy, stupid bastard.' Harry's voice was level; a headmaster giving a pep-talk. 'You have taken something that don't belong to you.' Grabbing hold of a hank of Lewis's lank hair, he yanked back. Lewis gasped, but did not struggle. His Adam's Apple bobbed up and down as he gulped for air through his tightly stretched throat. He felt a sharp pain as the tip of a blade pricked his cheek.

'Lewis; where is the disk?' Harry glanced up - 'Shall I cut him, Harvey?' His brother's lips lifted. Lewis' eyes bulged with fear.

'Answer me, you motherfucker.' Harry bellowed into Lewis's ear, jerking on his hair at the same time. The knife scored a red line down his cheek. Lewis whimpered.

'I, I don't know what you're ta...' he tried to say, but the strain on his throat impeded him. Slowly, his hands moved up to his head.

'Keep your hands down.' Harry's voice was like honey. He relaxed his hold slightly. 'I'm waiting.'

'I don't know what you're talking about.' Lewis gasped.

'Do you know how I found you, Lewis? Do you?' Harry gave his brother another swift glance. 'Shall I tell him, Harvey? Shall I tell you, Lewis?' Lewis's eyes followed the wavering tip of the knife with mounting dread.

'One:' The knife stroked down Lewis's cheek, and blood oozed out in another bright slash. Lewis gave a sharp intake of breath, and quivered. 'You sold the car, instead of torching it. Greedy – greedy - greedy.

'Two:' The knife sliced out another line. Lewis, now shaking all over, could not stop from moaning. 'You put that fucking whore back on the street. And three:' Again the knife cut in. A wet patch appeared at Lewis's crotch. 'Hey, Harvey, Lewis wet himself!' They both laughed. 'You should have got rid of the kid, instead of putting her back on the Net, Lewis. But that's not what I'm worried about, is it? *Where is it, Lewis?*'

'I don't know what ...'

'Yeah, you said. You're getting boring, Lewis.' He let go of the hair and stood up, wiping the blood from his blade onto the back of the couch. He moved behind Tracey and round to her side. He brought the knife up to her face and tapped her on the tip of her nose. A little red spot appeared. 'Whore; where is it?'

'We - I don't know.' Tracey's voice was trembling with terror.

'Liar!' screamed Harry. He gave Harvey a slight nod.

Like ballet dancers, both men moved as one. Harvey stepped forward and stretched out his gun arm. As the muzzle touched Lewis's forehead, he squeezed the trigger.

Harry's arm looped over the top of Tracey's head. The knife came down and pulled straight across her throat. The gun shot seemed loud in such a small room. For a few seconds a bubbling sound came from Tracey.

The smell of cordite hung heavy in the room. Harry wiped his blade on the couch. The men moved through the house, searching as they went. They found the stairs. Harvey crept up and opened the door of Alice's room. It was empty. He tore at the drapes. The window was barred. A school book lay in the corner. Harvey went back down.

'The kid must be at school; the room's empty, but I found this.' Harvey threw the book to Harry, who opened it and read something on the inside of the cover. He dropped it to the floor and tapped on the window. The men in the garden swung round, their guns starting to level with it.

'Seen the kid?'

They shook their heads.

Harry waved his hand forward and they all met at the front of the house.

'We'll pick the kid up when she comes home from school.'

'Harry; what about the disk?'

'It's not here, Harvey. It won't matter with all of them dead.' He turned to the two men. 'You guys wait here. When the kid shows, snatch her; don't kill her. Once you've got her, burn the place down. And keep outta sight.'

He and Harvey drove away. The other car moved down the block and backed into a driveway.

Danny had been watching and waiting. He checked the time. They had been inside for close on thirty minutes, long enough to do a good search. It was smooth and slick, like the clothes they wore; totally professional. He had to admire it though he knew for sure that the place inside was pure carnage. But why were they waiting? Because they had not found the kid, though he was sure she was in there somewhere. Now he had to wait. He couldn't move and show himself.

When the door had crashed in Alice became immediately alert. She did not know why, but it sounded so different from Lewis's rages. The voices and the laughs that followed were neither Tracey's nor Lewis's. She peeped out of the window and seeing a man with a gun at the right side of the house she tried the door. It opened. Creeping down the stairs, she saw another guy on the opposite side and quickly retreated. Back in her room she soundlessly pulled back the bed enough to squeeze through the hole.

Once in the loft, she straddled the rafters, bent back through and pulled the bed back in place, shutting out the light. She crawled into the darkest corner and waited.

Alice actually cried when she heard the bark of the gun. The noise of their advance through the house to where she crouched set her trembling. The worst moment was when Harvey was moving around in her room, but she controlled herself, and waited. Time passed like a snail - then she heard him go back down the stairs, and the sound of cars driving away. Still she waited; hot, wet and sticky.

30

On returning from the park the Banks had rung Danny again, and again got his answering machine. After that it was an easy argument for Molly to win. They had the money; they would offer to buy Alice. That was what their savings were for. Reluctantly, Bert had agreed; on one condition. Molly was to stay in the cab with the money.

The cab cruised past the parked up-car and stopped outside the camelback. The door slowly opened, and Bert got out. The men staking the house stiffened, and Danny cursed. Who the hell was it? A nonce? Surely a nonce wasn't crazy enough to use a taxi?

Bert found the front door slightly ajar. He tapped gently, and it swung open. He staggered when he took in the scene, and clutched fearfully at the door frame. After some moments, he took a deep breath. Alice had to be somewhere in this house. He had to find out. Slowly, as in a dream, he crept from room to room until he came to the stairs. He mounted one step at a time, fearing what slaughter he would find behind the door at the top. He steeled himself to go through. It was empty.

Molly kept peering out of the cab window with increasing agitation. Finally she grabbed the door handle. The cabbie glanced round.

'Ma'am, your husband gave strict instructions that you were not to leave the cab. And I agree with him. It's too dangerous around here.'

Bert was about to leave Alice's room when the bed started to move. Standing stock still, he waited with bated breath. There was a scrabbling sound and Alice's head appeared. She gazed up at him, screamed and collapsed to the floor. Bert pulled her from behind the bed and lifted her in his arms. He was surprised how light she was; a little scrap of a thing. Gently whispering reassurances, he climbed back down the stairs. He hoped she wouldn't come round before he had her in the car. She came to at the bottom.

'Alice, love, it's Bert. Granddad.' Alice opened her eyes wide and struggled to push herself away, but he held on firmly. 'Hush, love, it's me - Bert. Alice; it's all right.'

With realisation, she crashed back into his chest and folded her arms tightly round his neck and sobbed.

'Child,' he gasped. 'Loosen up; you're strangling me.' Bert held the sobbing girl for several minutes, until he felt they needed to leave. He knew Molly would be going out of her mind. He pulled her away from his neck and gazed into her eyes. 'Alice, we need to go. You must understand. We need to hurry. Close your eyes and I'll carry you through.'

'They're dead,' she said, in a croaky but matter-of-fact voice. A statement, not a question.

'Yes, love. I'm sorry.'

'I'm not.'

'Hush, child. You don't know what you're saying.'

'I do. I want to see; to make sure.'

'Alice, it's terrible; something no-one needs to see. They are dead. That's all you need to know.'

'No. I need to see. I don't want to be scared anymore.'

Bert studied her for several moments until he realised she needed to see the reality. It was like saying goodbye at a graveside before carrying on living. He lowered her to the floor and stood up. She grabbed his hand tightly as they walked into the last room.

Her parents sat on the grubby couch like old crumbled guardians at the entrance to their lair. Empty beer cans lay at their feet. Alice let go of his hand and walked up to her mother.

'Good!'

Bert sucked in a breath noisily.

'Stop, child. She was your mother.'

Alice stared up at him with dark, soulful eyes.

'She wasn't my mom. Mom died years ago.' She moved and stood in front of Lewis. 'He killed her.'

She caught hold of a fine gold chain that hung about his neck and gave it a sharp tug. The chain broke and came free in her hand. She pulled it out from his shirt. On the end dangled several small coloured, plastic tabs. She put it in her pocket.

'Come.' He held out his hand again. Without a backward glance, they left the house.

Molly, waiting in the cab, was beside herself. She nearly fainted with relief when the familiar figure appeared with Alice, hand in hand at the door. The men in the car looked at each other. Danny, sitting tensely at the wheel of his truck, let out a breath of relief.

The cab door opened. Bert pushed Alice, and got in behind her.

'Where the hell..?'

'Quiet, Moll. Later. Driver - back to the hotel, please. As fast as you can.'

The cabby gunned the engine and drove off. The Dancers' henchmen's car rolled out onto the road and started to follow. The driver, accelerating, saw the cab take a right two blocks ahead of him. Out of the corner of his eye something blue came shooting out of a driveway, but it was too late.

Danny caught the tail end of the car as it drove by. He jerked hard on the wheel and swung their car round so it pointed in the opposite direction. Keeping his foot pressed hard to the floor, he kept on going. With a screeching of tearing metal he tore free and snaked down the road, fighting for control. On reaching the junction he followed the cab, but he had no illusions about catching up with it.

Cursing, the other driver tried to swing his car round. There was a screeching from the back, and a bang as a tyre burst. He cursed and jumped out. The rear end was a mess.

'We had better call and tell Harry,' said the driver. 'At least we've got the cab company and tag.' Tag ???

90

31.

Mr Ritter, the manager of the Columns hotel, stopped in front of Molly and Bert's bedroom door with some reticence. The telephone conversation had been rather strange. Many things passed through his mind. He had been in this business all his working life and nothing surprised him. Bert answered his sharp little knock.

'Come in, Mr Ritter.'

He quickly swept the room with his eyes. Nothing seemed amiss.

'I expect you're wondering what this is all about.' Ritter gave a jerk of his head.

'Please, sit down.' Bert offered him a chair and sat in the other. Molly was sitting on the edge of the bed, obviously anxious. 'Molly and me are not on holiday,' Bert said.

'Really. May I ask why you are here? Not that it's any of my business what our guests do during their stay.' His stiffness told them otherwise.

'I'm Molly's second husband. She has a grandchild. The thing is - the child was brought over here to live.'

'Really?'

'Yes. Today we were able to find her. You have to understand we had lost touch with her because her mother moved around,' Bert lied smoothly. 'The mother...' He paused and coughed. 'This is a bit unpleasant. We found out her mother is in prison - the stepfather is not taking care of the child as well as he should. As you can imagine, this is distressing to us both. We could not leave her there.'

'You mean she's here?'

'Yes.'

'Well; I'm not sure if this is proper.'

'We realised that, which is why we asked to speak with you. It is late now, and the British consulate is closed for the day. We would like to keep her here overnight.'

'That's impossible, Mr Banks. Do you have written consent, or any documentation?'

'Nothing.'

'I'm sorry, but I will have to ask you to take the child home.'

'We can't do that and all we're asking for is one night. She's very frightened. First thing in the morning, we'll go to the Consulate.'

'I can't allow this. How do I know you didn't kidnap her? You hear such terrible things.'

'Please, Mr Ritter. You must understand.'

'No. I'm adamant.'

'Alice!' called Molly.

The bathroom door opened, and Ritter watched as a slight child about the age of his own twelve year old came into the room and walked over to Molly. Her eyes never left the manager as she skirted past him.

'It's all right, Alice. Mr Ritter won't hurt you.' Molly put a hand on her shoulder and pulled Alice down onto the bed. 'Mr Ritter, the stepfather was ill-treating Alice. We could not leave her.'

'I'm sorry, Mrs Banks, but I only have your word for it.'

'Alice, dear; stand up and turn around.' The child implored Molly with pleading eyes. 'Come on, dear.' Alice stood, and turned. Molly took hold of the hem of her tee-shirt and raised it, revealing bruises and welts. 'I am begging, Mr Ritter. Please don't force us to take her back. She's not safe with him.'

Ritter stared open-mouthed at the thin, battered back.

'I don't know what to say. You should go to the police.'

'Can't you see the child's frightened?' interrupted Bert. 'They would put her in somewhere strange for the night, 'cause they have no time to arrange anything. She'll feel more secure with her grandmother and me.'

'I don't want to seem hard-hearted, but...'

'He fucks me as well,' said Alice, her dark watery eyes fixed on the manager.

'Alice; shush! Don't talk like that,' gasped Molly.

'But he does, Gran.' She buried her face in her grandmother's bosom. Molly's gaze levelled unflinchingly at the manager.

'Please Mr Ritter; for tonight, that's all? The child will sleep with me. Give Bert the room next door. If you had a child you'd know.'

He pondered over the situation. The kid was obviously frightened and needed nurture. Even one night in the city's Care home would be a trauma she needn't go through. He had that power.

'If you're ever asked, you didn't know,' suggested Bert. 'You can say you thought we had asked for an extra room because we had a falling out.'

'I'm not sure.' They could see he was wavering.

'We promise to sort it out in the morning. You can even do the 'phoning.'

'Alice…' Ritter spoke gently.

Molly pulled Alice away from her. 'Mr Ritter's speaking to you.' Molly slowly turned her round to face him.

'Alice, where do you live?'

'On First and St Thomas.'

'Do you know it?' asked Bert.

'No, but I know of it. Close to Chap-a-too-lis (Tchoupitoulas).

'Pardon?'

'It's the road that runs by the railroad and the levee.' Making up his mind he got up. 'Alice can stay one night. On three conditions: That she must stay in this room and not show herself and you must bring up food for her to eat (I mustn't involve my staff) - and at 9.00am you must all come to my office.'

'Certainly.' Bert got up, smiling, and held out his hand. 'Thank you, Mr Ritter.'

32.

The men had arrived back. Harry was beside himself with rage. Harvey stood quietly watching as his brother blustered around, cursing them. After a while he calmed down enough for Harvey to suggest they visit the cab company.

It was a small outfit with fewer than a dozen cars. A thousand bucks was handed over. It was that simple. The owner called the driver over the radio and asked where he had dropped off the old Limey couple with the kid. An hour later, Harvey booked into the Columns Hotel.

When Danny contacted the cab company a little later he was told they couldn't give out that information. He went back to his office and found the messages, but they'd forgotten to leave a number or the name of the Hotel. He rang Arran.

'Yo; what's happening, buddy?'

'The kid's been snatched. I think it's the old couple.'

'Well that's a relief. Send in what they owe - they left me with a couple grand which should cover it.'

'Did you know they were coming down here?'

'No, they told me nothing. Anyway we're off the hook; they'll go to their consulate and sort it out.'

'You don't understand; they're in danger.'

'What kind of danger?'

Danny told Arran about the Dancers and what had happened. After the thugs had had their car towed, Danny had gone back and entered the house.

'When I talked to the cab owner he wouldn't even oblige by telling me the cab driver's name.'

'So he's been paid off to keep stumm.'

'Which means the Dancers know their hotel.'

'I'll call their last hotel. Maybe they know.'

'Yeah, do that and get straight back to me.'

Arran had the same luck with the hotel that Danny had had with the cab owner. They couldn't hand out that sort of information to anyone without the Banks' permission. He

94

tried to explain, to no avail. In the end he got them to promise to contact the Banks with a message to ring Danny.

The timing of Arran's call was unfortunate; it was taken as shifts were changing and the woman who took over the desk put the request to one side to get on with what she thought to be more important business. It was almost midnight Newark time when she picked up the slip of paper and called the Columns Hotel.

Bert and Molly were saying goodnight when the call came through. With all the things that had happened, contacting Danny or Marx had slipped their minds. As far as they were concerned they had saved Alice and wouldn't need either man's services anymore. Their worry now was that once the police were told of the deaths of the parents things would get complicated, especially as they should have reported the killings immediately. As Bert succinctly put it.

'There's going to be hell up.'

'Mr Banks, this is the Renaissance Hotel, Newark. I have a message from a Mr Marx. He says you must contact Mr Generve immediately. You are all in danger.'

Bert waited for her to continue, but she stayed silent, waiting for a response.

'Is that it? Nothing else?'

'Yes, Mr Banks. That's what's written down here.'

'You didn't take the call?'

'No, Sir. A colleague on an earlier shift.'

'When was the call made?'

'Five to six our time. I'm sorry it took so long to be relayed to you, Sir.'

'Thank you, Miss.'

Bert replaced the phone and looked at Molly.

'What?'

'It seems this Danny Generve knows we have Alice. He says we're in danger and need to contact him immediately.' He glanced at his watch. 'That was six hours ago.'

'I shouldn't worry. Call him in the morning. It's a bit late to do it now.'

33.

Bert lay on the bed in the adjoining room. So far he had been unable to get to sleep. Images of the dead bodies on the couch kept constantly barraging his mind. The worry of sorting out all the problems next morning simply added to his anxiety. By two am he'd had enough; picked up the phone and called Danny's office, expecting to get the answer machine again. At least he could leave a number.

Danny was dozing when the call came. He jerked awake at Bert's voice and told him that they were in danger and must do exactly as he said: no debate. They must instantly pack small overnight bags. Any papers and money should be kept on their persons. (Luckily, Bert had forgotten to put his money belt back in the hotel safe). He also told Bert to wait for an hour, then phone his mobile number, which Bert wrote down. Arrangements must be made before he could give further instructions. Bert tried to ask a question, but was told there was no time. Danny cut the call.

He ran to his garage at the back of the house and from the rafters brought down a plastic Cab sign. This he clipped to the guttering of a dark, sleek Pontiac. Standing in the corner of the garage was a shrimping light, which he stowed in the trunk. At the press of a switch the garage shutters opened, the engine roared into life and he reversed out.

As he cruised down Carondelet, that ran parallel with St Charles, he started making calls. At Peniston he took a right for the avenue. At the corner a sedan was parked. He could make out the dark shapes of two men inside. He crossed the streetcar tracks and swung the car, cruising downtown a little way before turning back on himself at General Taylor. There was a similar car staked out on that corner, too. Whoever was doing the surveillance had the hotel sandwiched. Whichever way anyone tried to escape, they'd be upon them in a flash. Danny drove around a few more blocks, eventually arriving back across the street from the hotel, with both cars in view. He started dialling up cab companies. A few minutes later one arrived, flashed its lights and tooted its horn. He saw the men in both cars sit up, alerted. The cabby waited a minute, blew a hard blast on his horn and drove off. Five minutes later another came to a halt. It too, flashed its lights and tooted, merely to be frustrated and leave with an angry blast on its horn. For the next half-hour taxi after taxi arrived and left without passengers. Within that time Danny had got out of his car and fixed the shrimping light to his tow-hitch, aiming it backwards.

He got in and waited, watching the cabs come and go outside the hotel. He was ready. The phone rang. He switched onto hands-free and checked the clock on the dash. At least the Limey was punctual.

'Mr Banks, you keep a good watch.'

'Thank you.'

'Now listen. There are two cars staked out at each end of your block. Luckily, they won't be able to see you until you're on the sidewalk. Even so, y'all only have seconds to get into my car. No waiting politely. The girl, then the lady in the back, you in the front, and we're off; and I *mean* off! I suspect they have someone planted in the hotel – otherwise, why all the cars? Don't use the elevator. The girl, the lady, then you, in that order: hurry down the stairs, and keep close. Once by the door, wait for a taxi. If it gives two hoots of its horn a couple of seconds apart - it's me. When you're outside, come fast, but don't let the kid run ahead. As you hit the sidewalk the door will fly open. And mister, don't wait. Push the kid and your wife in, then yourself. I'll take care of the doors. Got it?'

'Yes.'

'How long do you think it will take for y'all to get down the stairs?'

'If you say 'go now', we would be at the front door in two minutes at the most.'

'If you have to run, drop those bags, okay?'

'Yes.'

'And mister, be as prompt as your call. Now get yourself ready to leave the room. When you are - tell me.'

Danny heard whispering, which went on for interminable minutes. The last of the ordered taxis left. He heard shuffling, and a few orders.

'We're ready.'

'Okay. Now don't over-rush, just be *fast*. Good luck. *Go*!'

Molly stood by the door clutching the handle, the catch already off. Her hand was on Alice's shoulder, waiting to push, her eyes fixed on Bert, her heart beating fast and her senses pitched so high that she heard Danny say 'Go'. Not waiting for the command, she had the door open with Alice half through it before she heard Bert's voice. The landing was not altogether dark. They moved fast and stealthily to the head of the stairs. Alice started down with Molly following. Bert grabbed the big ball on top of the newel post and was about to follow when a torch blazed.

'Stop!' growled Harvey Dancer.

They all froze. Bert could make out a shadowy figure behind the glare of the beam. The light caught the end of a pistol. It did not waver. The figure moved to the banister rail and glanced over.

'Move back from the stairs.' The voice was firm. It brooked no argument. 'Now you, lady, and the kid; come back up.'

Molly started up, and Alice followed. As Alice's waist came on a level with the floor above, she could see Harvey's feet the other side of the spindles. The gun waved above Molly's head, to motion her up the last step.

Alice raised her hand swiftly, and with all her might brought down Danny's knife. The blade drove through the leather shoe, twisted sideways slightly and slid between two bones, pierced the thin Italian sole and entered the floorboard. Harvey screamed, squeezed the trigger, and dropped the torch, simultaneously. The landing lit up with the sudden flash of gunfire. Molly swung her bag at Harvey's hand. The gun fell, clattering noisily down the stairs. Alice tugged at his other leg. He fell backwards and screamed again as his foot pulled further up the knife before the blade snapped. Molly started down the stairs again, pushing Alice before her. Holding to the newel post, Bert swung his foot into Harvey's crotch as he tried to rise. Harvey folded in agony.

By the time they had reached the front door the whole hotel was starting to stir. Outside, the road was empty.

34.

Bert pushed forward and tried the handle. It refused to budge. He noticed the key in the lock. The door rattled open. He stepped over the threshold, pulling Molly and Alice with him.

'Come on, we'll wait by the tree. Don't go any further.'

As they reached it, Danny came casually gliding to a halt and tooted the horn twice. He stretched across and opened the door. Alice and Molly were pushed in over the front seat to tumble onto the back. Bert literally rolled in, pulling a large holdall with him. Danny gunned the engine and the car tore away with screaming tyres. The force of the acceleration shut Bert's door with a bang. Everyone was tossed sideways as they screeched across in front of the stationary car and tore off down Peniston. A crash and a scream of metal came as the car on General Taylor gave chase and ripped the wing off the other, which had started to swing out from the curb.

'That should slow 'em. I thought I told you to wait at the door.'

'We couldn't. We woke the whole bloody hotel.'

'Bert; stop your swearing,' gasped Molly, between breaths. She was trying to put an atomiser to her mouth.

'Tell me later,' said an astonished Danny. 'Put on your belts.'

They were speeding up Peniston, not stopping at any junctions. At each crossroad a slight hump tossed them like corks on a rough sea. Danny checked his mirrors. The first car was not far behind, and he could see the headlights of the other a little further back. He wound both his and Bert's window down.

'Mister....'

'Bert!' shouted Molly, against the inrush of air.

'Put your hand up onto the roof gutter,' he continued, ignoring her. 'Feel around. You'll find a lever that holds the cab light on. Don't pull it till I say. Found it?'

'Hold on.' Bert's hand flapped about until he touched what he thought must be the lever. 'I think so. It's a flat piece of metal about an inch wide, with folded edges.'

'You got it. I'm going to slow up a bit, to let them catch up. When I count to three, pull down hard and let go.'

'Got it.'

The car slackened slightly. Alice was staring out of the rear screen. The headlights seemed to charge forwards, closing the gap. She dropped out of sight.

'Okay, mister. One. Two. Three.'

The plastic sign stayed where it was. They hit the cross section on Robertson and the thing became airborne. Alice peeped above the back seat again. The sign crashed into the windshield of the car behind; it went white. The headlights wavered as the driver desperately tried to hold to the road. It swerved again as he punched out the screen, mounted the sidewalk and took out a picket fence. Righting itself, his car came on again.

Danny killed the lights and swung a left on Clare and tore up the road in near darkness. The confusion caused by switching off gave them a couple of hundred more yards lead. Danny flipped the lights back on as he shot over Napoleon. As they reached the centre of the road they left the ground. Molly and Alice let out a scream. The car landed with a grinding crash, and sparks.

'Wow!' shouted Alice and peered between the men in front. 'Shiiit! We're going ninety, Gran,' she said, glancing excitedly at Molly.

'Oh me dear Lord,' exclaimed Molly, and closed her eyes. Her lips moved in a silent prayer.

At Nashville, Danny hung a right, and then a left onto Willow. The cars behind stuck to him like glue.

'These boys are good,' he shouted over the noise of the engine. 'Check your seat belts. Shit! We've picked up a cop.'

Alice peered back to see flashing blue and red lights and hear the wail of sirens.

'At least it's at the back. We're coming up to Carrollton Avenue. I'm going to have to slow; otherwise we won't survive the landing. Keep down in your seat and put your arms over your heads. We've got one block to go. I think it's time for Danny's little ol' surprise.'

He stretched to the dash and flicked a switch. Behind them, the road flooded with intense light. There was a screeching of tyres as the chasing drivers were blinded. Danny wound down all the windows.

The Pontiac shot out of Willow and mounted the steep camber on Carrollton. As they topped the rise the car became airborne, sailing over both streetcar tracks. The camber on the other side was as bad. The back wheels and tow bar hit the ground together. The end of the hitch snapped off and the light went with it, in a fantail of sparks. The front wheels came down with a bone-numbing jar. The windshield split, but didn't white out, but the rear screen exploded and disappeared, sucked out by the onrush of air.

The car behind came on, snaking out of control. It hit the camber sideways on and rolled several times, ending on its roof. As it reached the other side of the meridian it slid down the camber and into the front of a bookshop. The second car was able to swerve and miss it, before taking off. When it landed the windshield went white, but the co-driver punched it out. The unfortunate police car had not decreased its speed. It hit the camber at over ninety. The nose ploughed into the road and the front half of the car disintegrated.

The two remaining cars sped to the end of Willow, lifting on to two wheels as they zigzagged through the streets trying to get over to Oak and then onto the River Road. The cars stayed together, not much more than a hundred yards apart.

Danny held his speed. The vehicles seemed to be well-matched.

'Mister, I don't like the look of that screen. It could go anytime. Take off your shoe and use it to fist it if it goes. Do my side first, okay?' Danny shouted.

As Bert took off his shoe, Danny pressed his mobile. The sound of mush filled the car, but suddenly it cleared. A deep, resonant voice sang 'Yoh! Danny Boy. Can you hear me - can you hear me?'

'I'm here, Snowy!' shouted Danny.

'I'm glad you switched on, my coonass friend!'

'What are we going to do with my tail?'

'Okay. Hang the next right and let's give the mother behind you a scare!'

Seconds later Danny slowed suddenly and tugged at his wheel. They picked up speed as he entered the side road.

'Okay, that was neat. Now don't show off; next, take Claiborne and go on to Shrewsbury, then head back to the river. Start to slow down, so when you come out of Shrewsbury he's right behind you, maybe twenty yards.'

Danny swung out onto a wide highway. It was practically empty.

'Once you're on the home stretch,' said Snowy, 'start countin' down out loud. You cin come out of there at eighty and still keep to your tyres.'

'I'm on it!' shouted Danny as he headed for the river, the tyres squealing on the concrete road.

'Okay. Now keep your eyes straight ahead of you, if you don't want to be blinded: 'cause I'm gonna be lit up like the White House, and makin' all kinds of din. It's all clear, so come straight on out and take it wide. The mother will try to cut you off. Big mistake.' Snowy laughed. 'I hope he has a good insurance comp'ny, 'cause I'm gonna sue his sorry ass!'

Danny started counting. As they came up to the junction it seemed to grow light. They came out straight as a bullet. Bert glanced sideways. A huge tractor-truck was bearing down with every light blazing and horns blaring. The car behind took the corner sharper in order to cut Danny off and found it was right in the path of the juggernaut. The car crumpled under the onslaught as though the monster was trying to eat it. Then it was brushed aside, spinning until it hit the levee.

From Snowy's view behind the wheel of the truck, Danny's car disappeared below him. His reaction was to stand on the brakes. This slowed the vehicle enough to allow the skidding car behind Danny to slide in front of the oncoming vehicle, instead of its side. Snowy pressed on the gas and felt a jolt as his vehicle tried to mount the car. Braking again released the wreck and it spun off to the side, out of Snowy's line of sight.

'Whoo eeee...' came a triumphant whoop from the speakers. Danny glanced in his mirror and saw the carnage behind him.

'Thanks, Snowy.'

'My pleasure, man. I think that sonofabitch did me some damage. You're on your own, man. See y'all soon. Good luck, yo' old coonass.'

Danny slackened to a cruising speed and within minutes was on Jefferson Highway, heading for the Huey P. Long Bridge. They were dropping over the other side as the sun rose above the horizon. It bled a red swathe up the Mississippi.

35.

Radio New Orleans woke the city to the story of a fantastic high-speed car chase through sleeping Uptown -

-'*with the loss of a patrol car and two other wrecks, one as far out as the River Road. The patrolmen were slightly injured, but two men were hospitalised from the other car that rolled over. They are now in police custody.*

'*A car hit the levee, killing the driver, but there seemed to be some mystery about the passenger, who disappeared.*' The newsreader reported: '*The chase started from an Uptown hotel, and involved a mysterious cab. What that meant no-one from the police department would say.*

'*A man was taken from the hotel with injuries. He is helping with enquiries. Lieutenant Detective Usner is leading the investigation, and at this moment has issued a 'no-comment' bulletin.*'

Lieutenant Dwight Usner was in his fifties, slight of frame, with a thatch of dark brown hair. He was back in his office after three-and-a-half hours investigating what had happened at The Columns and in the Irish Channel. His arrival at the hotel had coincided with the departure of an ambulance carrying Harvey off to hospital. The place was in uproar. It seemed every guest in the hotel was up and demanding to know what had happened. The manager was running around like a headless chicken. He had come straight from his home, and was half-dressed.

Dwight calmed him down enough to get him to check that all guests were present, then made himself at home in the manager's office. Ritter brought the register and was dismissed. After several minutes with McCoy, the first officer on the scene, Dwight started to get a handle on what was going on.

Ritter burst back into his office, very agitated that three guests were missing. He told Dwight about the arrangement he had made with the Banks, constantly reiterating his qualms about their request. It now seemed that his suspicions were founded. They had kidnapped the child.

'What child?' exploded Dwight, who had listened patiently to Ritter for several minutes and could find no matching details in the register.

'That's what I've been trying to tell you, Lieutenant. This old English couple brought a young girl back to the hotel yesterday afternoon. They claimed she was their grandchild.'

'So why isn't she entered here?' The detective prodded a skinny finger at the register.

'Ah! I see what you mean. They asked me not to, until they had sorted out their affairs with the authorities today.'

'You know this is illegal, don't you?'

'It would be,' said Ritter, 'but if you open the top drawer of my desk you will find a loose register slip with the girl's name and address.'

Dwight pulled open the drawer and plucked out the slip and read it twice. He asked both McCoy and Ritter to leave and picked up the phone.

'Hello?'

'Marlene, Dwight here. You remember that enquiry that came through from the Feds in Newark a day or so ago? What was the name they were looking for?'

'Hang on, while I check it.' There was a pause; Dwight could hear the tapping of computer keys. 'Barasitch?'

'That's him. Lewis Barasitch. Nasty bastard, by all accounts. Thanks, Marlene.'

He tapped out a new number. Ringing his boss up in the early hours of the morning was as dangerous as tickling a cottonmouth under the chin.

'Hello?'

'Sorry to call you at this hour, Chief, but I think I've located Barasitch.'

'Barasitch who, for Christ sakes?'

'The APB the Feds have out. Came in a couple of days ago from Newark. I'll need the SWAT out.' Dwight heard a 'shit!' followed by the murmur of voices.

106

'What's the address?' He gave it. 'I'll be there as soon as I can. Don't start without me.'

'Sure, Chief.'

Dwight hit the buttons again to order out the SWAT team, as he shouted for McCoy. He poked his head round the door.

'Yeah, Dwight?'

'I've got to go downtown. Can you handle things here? Oh, and the guy in hospital with the knife in his foot - take him into custody.'

McCoy sent a young rookie to the hospital, and then set about questioning everyone at the hotel.

Dwight raced down to St Thomas Street, shouting orders to Control on his radio. The SWAT team had staked out the house and were waiting for him. Dawn had broken an hour before. The sky had lost its early morning colours. He was about to get out of the car when the radio squawked. It was to tell him that the car on the River Road had a dead driver inside. There may also have been a passenger, but there was no sign of anyone. This was becoming one of those days, he thought, and growing ever sourer by the second. He slammed the door as he walked away from his car. The Chief took another few minutes to arrive and give the order to rush the house.

Had the sight that confronted Dwight and his chief not been so bad the whole operation would have been an anti-climax. To compound the situation, the young officer sent to guard Harvey reported back that he'd disappeared after being treated. When his room was searched his suitcase was found to be empty. The Chief left in disgust, telling Dwight to handle everything. The detective was running around setting up murder enquiries, car-chase incidents, and investigating what had happened at the hotel. He'd also ordered an APB out for Bert, Molly, and the child. The paperwork was mounting. He needed to return to the office to get things under control.

36.

An hour after crossing the bridge Danny drove past a battered sign on the verge, declaring they were leaving the township of Berwick. A mile on, he turned down a dirt track leading to his mother's home. It appeared to be nothing more than a tin-roofed shack, sheltering under large, dark Live Oaks, their branches hung with festoons of Spanish moss. The front of the clapboard building was almost blank, with two small windows and a lathed door. Its paint, like the door and windows, was dark red.

'Well, I guess you folks are hungry?' he said, yanking on the handbrake.

'Before we go in, what should I do with this?' Bert pulled a large black pistol out of his pocket. He dangled it between thumb and forefinger, as if he might catch a disease.

'Well I'm damned, where did you get hold of that?'

'Remember me telling you about the man in the hotel? It's his. He dropped it on the stairs. As I was going down, I spotted it. I didn't want him using it on us.'

Danny took the piece and inspected it. He finally gave Bert a meaningful look.

'You don't know much about guns, do you, Bert?' Bert shook his head. 'This,' Danny pointed to a lever on the side, 'is the safety catch. It wasn't on. With all the jolting you're lucky it didn't blow a hole in your pants.' He pulled out the magazine and emptied the chamber before tucking it under his seat. 'Com'on, let's get sump'n t'eat.'

Inside it was dark and cool, smelling of spicy food.

'How about some service for poor hungry travellers?' Danny shouted.

There was a tinkling sound as a birdlike woman pushed aside a heavy beaded curtain. She shrieked, extending her hands in welcome and dashed towards them. Bert, Molly and Alice stood bemused - they could not understand a word she uttered. Danny bear-hugged her, lifting her off her feet, jabbering in the same language, which sounded like French.

The woman, in her sixties, pummelled Danny's back with tiny fists and screamed to be put down.

'Ducey, I'd like you to meet some English folk. Molly, Bert - this is Ducey!'

'And who is this?' asked Ducey.

'Alice, come here.' Alice left Molly's side. 'Meet my Ma; Miss Ducey.'

Ducey held out a fragile hand. 'Pleased to meet you, Alice.'

'And you, Ducey.'

'Miss, Alice, *Miss* Ducey.' He turned back to Ducey. 'Are you going to leave us to die of hunger, or should we go elsewhere?'

'You stop a-flusterin' me, Danny, and take our guests through to the conservatory while I put the coffee pot on. I suppose you didn't bring that Cafe Du-Monde you promised?'

'Sorry, Ducey, we left in a little bit of a hurry. Now off you go, whilst we all gits settled.' He gently pushed her shoulder. 'This way -' he beckoned the others.

They followed him through the beaded curtain, down a dimly lit corridor to a room full of plants. Chairs and table made an island amongst the foliage. A glass wall faced east and the faint, pinkish light of late dawn filtered in. Outside, where the trees crowded in close, it was still dark, but above their canopy the sky was pale and bright.

Molly sank down gratefully into a rattan chair that had been obscured by a giant fern.

'I'm glad to be motionless at last. I think me backside's bruised. If that's riding in a racing car, you can keep it.'

'It was a bit bouncy at times,' said Bert

'Bouncy; it was great!' enthused Alice, beaming at Danny. 'Did you see that car chasing us, Gramps? The truck ate it up.'

'Alice, whatever harm they wanted to do, they were still human beings, so have a thought,' said Molly sharply.

'Whatever you think, Molly. Those were the men who visited your daughter-in-law. I shouldn't pay them too much regard.' Danny smiled to take away any sting in his words.

Molly shivered and opened her mouth to speak, but Bert placed a hand on her shoulder.

'Danny's right. Without him, God knows what would have happened.' He turned to Danny. 'I don't think we have truly thanked you.'

Ducey waddled in, carrying a tray of coffee. The aroma mingled with the earthy smell of the room and seemed to bring life into Alice, sitting next to Danny. She took the tray from Ducey and started pouring the steaming liquid into cups.

'No cream in mine, Alice, and pass the sugar.' Danny stayed slumped in the corner of the two-seater sofa.

Alice held the cup out for him, then the sugar, the spoon poised in her hand.

'None for us. We need some sleep,' said Bert.

'Yes; coffee will keep me awake,' Molly agreed. 'That means you too, my girl.'

'Aw, Gran, I'm not sleepy.'

'Hush.'

'Why don't you and Bert rest up. I'll take care of Alice; she's still wound up. She'll drive y'all crazy if she sticks around here. Once I've grabbed a bite I've got to take the car over to Dee-Dee.'

'Are you sure, Danny?'

'Sure, Bert. She'll be no trouble.' He gave Alice a wink. 'Anyhow, I want her to meet, Dee-Dee.'

Ducey gave a low chuckle and sprang out of her chair. 'Alice is got herself a treat. Com'on Bert, Molly, I'll show y'all to your beds.'

37.

Dwight was still trying to pull the available facts together when, without a knock, his office door opened and two men walked in. He gazed up in surprise. One was in his late thirties and hung back, blocking the doorway. The other, smartly dressed in a suit, and with greying wings of hair, pulled up a chair and sat down. With measured slowness he put his hand into his breast pocket, brought out a leather wallet and tossed it on the desk in front of him. Dwight, opened it and studied the picture, then the visitor.

'How can I help you, Agent Fenwick?'

'By telling us what's been going on.'

'At this moment I don't know.'

'You've got two bodies...'

'Actual fact - three, and two seriously injured. What do you want?'

'NOPD were supposed to contact us when you found these people.' Fenwick threw two photos on the desk.

'Afraid I've been too busy.' Dwight gave the photos a cursory glance. 'They're two of the dead.' He wondered how they had heard about it and got down to the city so fast, but let it pass.

'I know. We need to visit the house and cover everything that's happened.'

'What gives you the damn right to barge in here, demanding...?'

'This does.'

Fenwick pushed a folded sheet of paper across the desk to him. Eyeing him speculatively, Dwight unfolded the paper and started to read.

'Before you ask, your boss has already read it. The instructions are quite plain, and before you get smart-assed, it also involves an alien - and a minor at that. To complete the picture, the US and British governments are involved. So is Interpol.'

'Why weren't we informed of this before?'

111

'It was a need-to-know basis.' Fenwick put a hand on the shoulder of the young man standing next to him. 'This is agent Smith. While you and I visit the house, he will sit here and read your reports.'

Dwight cast his eyes from the letter to the complacent smile on Fenwick's face. At that moment he could have ripped it off.

He got up and walked out of the room without a backward glance. 'Follow me.'

The house was cordoned off and crawling with Forensics. The bodies were gone. Where Tracey had sat the upholstery was blackened with her blood and red/grey splatters on the wall showed where Lewis's brains and blood had landed.

'I heard it resembled a slaughterhouse.'

'You could say that. Have you eaten yet?' asked Dwight.

'No. Why?'

'George, pass me the pictures.' An officer suited up in white handed some large photos to Dwight. He passed them to Fenwick .

'Like I said; a regular palace.' He whistled.

Dwight glared at him.

'Pros, don't you think?'

Dwight nodded and walked on into the next room. Everywhere was plastered with black grease.

'Have you been able to catalogue the prints yet?'

'No.'

'When will you know?' Fenwick persisted.

'The lab boys don't get started before nine. What's the time?'

Fenwick was about to answer when he realised Dwight had a watch of his own.

'Agent Fenwick,' said Dwight. 'I've been up for over five hours. When I have something, I'll let you know. What I don't like is having me and my office crowded. You Feds seem to know more than me, but it's on a need-to-know basis. Communication is a two-way street. Maybe if you free up some of the information I'll be able to tell you what might be significant.'

Fenwick studied Dwight for some moments.

'Okay, let's go through this place; then take me to a good breakfast joint. My call.'

They climbed the stairs to the stark attic, its bareness highlighted by sunlight streaming in. Two men were pulling the room slowly apart.

'What have you got, Will?'

A balding forensic officer by the window looked up.

'Not much, but it was well-lived in. It looks like the prints were mostly a kid's. Funny thing; there was some sexy underwear and drapes, cushions and things. It reminded me of a ho's room.'

Fenwick moved over to where Alice had hidden the knife. The skirting board was open.

'What's this?' he nudged it with his foot.

The other officer stopped his work.

'Some kind of hidey-hole. I think someone was kept prisoner up here.'

'What makes you think that?' Fenwick crouched to look into the loft space.

'Lots of things. Why the hole in the wall? That's new. There's a lot of dust behind and under the bed. The bars on the window, for another. They haven't been there long and there was a piss-pot in the corner, plus food.'

'Food?'

'Yeah; not your ordinary snacks, either, like candies and bars. We've found traces of potatoes, cabbage, rice, pizza crusts, that sort of thing. And the hole seems like someone was trying to escape. In the loft, right in the darkest corner, a child sat as though hiding.'

'A child?'

'Yeah, there're small foot and finger prints in the dust.

'Johnny, bring your camera over here.'

Will was kneeling under the window. Johnny handed him the camera. He started taking shots of the wallpaper.

'Hold the edge of the paper open.' The camera flashed. 'Perfect. Now let's see what we've got.'

Johnny was still holding the paper away from the wall. Will slid a pair of tweezers between the paper and the wall. He pulled out Danny's card and the folded twenty-dollar bill. With a gloved hand he held the card by its edges. The note dropped onto a plastic sheet.

'What is it?' asked Fenwick eagerly.

'A business card. Not very old. Should get some good prints off it.'

'Can I see it?' Dwight held a pair of tweezers.

'Sure.'

He studied the card.

'Mean anything?' asked Fenwick, as Dwight showed it to him.

'Yeah. Danny Generve was a cop here in the city some years back. Left under a cloud. Been on the edges of things ever since. Nothing proven.'

'A PI's card. I wonder how that got here.'

'Don't forget the twenty bucks.'

'Another stash?'

'Yeah, but this wasn't meant to be found. It's not like the skirting board. That was quite amateurish.'

'What you saying?' Fenwick frowned.

'Nothing, just a different feel.'

Dwight's mobile bleeped.

'Yeah?' Dwight pinched the bridge of his nose and concentrated, holding a monosyllabic conversation. Finally, he finished and looked at Fenwick. 'I think it's time for breakfast.'

38.

They sat in a seedy little hamburger joint on Magazine and Jefferson. The waitress chatted gaily with Dwight as they ordered.

'Seems to know you,' Fenwick observed.

'Yeah. I grew up in this neighbourhood, but it's changed a lot.' Fenwick looked around him. 'It's okay,' Dwight reassured him. 'We can talk freely. No-one will disturb us. Stella will make sure of that.'

'So what was the phone call?'

'What was Barasitch mixed up in?'

'Prostitution; kiddy pornography.'

'They were murdered because of that?'

Dwight picked up his burger and took a bite. Fenwick watched and waited. Dwight put down the burger and chewed, staring back at him.

'The way I see it, you can wait and get your information through the proper channels, or you can come clean,' he said, his mouth still full. 'Remember this is my city and I have lots of contacts, and that means help you can't call on without my co-operation.'

Dwight took another bite. They glared at each other, steely eye to steely eye. Fenwick was the first to relax his gaze and give a shrug of resignation.

'Child pornography. You know about the Internet?' Dwight paused in his chewing. 'There's a large amount on it and now organised crime has become involved.'

'And the killings?'

This time Fenwick nodded. 'We've been following it for over a year. The Barasitch's were involved. Small time, with the kid. The phone call - what was that about?'

'We took away some videos. They mainly with a naked kid doing nasty shit,' said Dwight.

'That figures. The PI. Tell me about him.'

'Oh, Danny... I don't think that's his game. I don't know how his card got there but it's sure odd. We'll pay him a visit after breakfast. You said governments were involved; us and the British?'

'Yes, but this must go no further. Not even to your boss.'

The men ate their food while Fenwick told him about the grandparents finding the site depicting Alice and reporting it to the police over in Britain.

'Their government is filing for repatriation of the mother and child, but when our people paid the Barasitch's a visit, they'd already vanished. Someone tipped them off. Who, we don't know, but it had to be someone on the inside. That person must be well-connected. The 'why' we can only suspect, but it must have been about the kid, or why would they risk trying to get her after killing the grownups, if she wasn't involved as well?'

'The old couple at the hotel. The Limeys. Are they the connection?'

'Well the whole thing started from Britain. So they're an obvious contender.'

'The old couple's name is Banks. Does that ring any bells?'

'Yes. The same as the grandparents.'

'Why didn't you inform us they were over here?'

'We didn't know, and it's only come together in the last few hours. The problem is, how did they know where to find the kid and who helped?'

'Danny?'

'Possibly. Have you finished?'

'Yeah.'

Both men got up from the table and left.

39

With the windows in the car wound right down, the wind through Alice's hair cooled her. It was the first time she had not felt hot and sticky since coming down South. She thought she would never get used to the hot, humid atmosphere. After a refreshing shower, she would be sweaty even as she tried to dry herself.

Every now and again she glanced at Danny, delighted to be on her own with him. His profile was silhouetted against the blue water beyond; dark hair curling over his collar, beneath a tatty straw Stetson. His jaw was shadowed with dark bristles and his long, slightly hooked nose gave him a predatory appearance, but not like those who had visited her. They had been mostly older, and always sweaty and slimy, even the skinny ones. She squeezed her eyelids tight, trying to shut the thoughts out. He stopped singing to the radio. Her eyes flicked open, and she found him regarding her.

'You okay?'

'Yeah.' It struggled out of her throat.

'When I have bad thoughts, I sing.' He started warbling again.

Alice sat watching him with wonder. She'd never met anyone quite like Danny. He didn't pry, yet he seemed to understand her without her saying a thing. She studied his hands lightly holding the steering wheel. She couldn't imagine him being rough. As the car went round a long, slow bend the wheel slid between his fingers as if he were gently caressing it. Her mother had used that word. Now it seemed nice, warm and - and Dannyish. When Lewis told her to do that, it had felt bad.

She came out of her thoughts and Danny was still there, the sun glistening on the dark hairs covering his bare arms. He was jostling to the music, which was some sort of country rock, but the voice was foreign and had a gummy, twangy catch to it.

'What's that?'

'What's what?'

'The music.'

'This is Cajun rock. You'll hear it all the time down here.'

'Why?'

'Don't you know nothin', chile?'

'Don't call me that,' she snapped.

'I'm sorree. I meant no never no min', Alice. This here,' - he swept his arm out of the window in a wide, sweeping arc - 'is Cajun country, and that there is a bayou.' He pointed to the stretch of water they were passing.

'And the funny language?'

'That ain't funny!' He put on an offended tone and seeing her mortified face, laughed. 'My cherie, it is French. Old French, and we round here are Old French people, from Acadia. We are Cajuns, my leetle Aleece.'

She chortled at the way his accent had deepened. The way he said 'My leetle Aleece.' So sing-songy, it seemed to wrap around her.

'Why you laugh? Am I so-o funnee?'

'Yes, when you say it like that.'

'But my cherie, I'm so mortified. I am deso-olate.'

She giggled. He tossed back his head and laughed. The wind caught his hat and swept it onto the back seat.

'You make fun, no? And now the wind joins in, too.'

'No. I like the way you speak. I like the way you say 'My leetle Aleece'. It's nice. So different from when…' Her eyes clouded.

'So serious for such a lovely day. Come; smile. Here is Dee-Dee's.'

He swung the car off the road and stopped before an old gas station. He got out and beckoned Alice to follow. At the side of the building a car lay dead on its axles. The rusty body seemed to droop in the heat. The hood was up and the engine compartment was empty. The windshield had gone; the rear window smashed. The interior looked forlorn, and the back seat was missing. Apart from a radio playing the song they had been listening to only a few moments before, the building seemed deserted.

Danny led the way round the car and through a side door. The interior was dimly lit and it took some moments for their eyes to adjust. Two short legs sheathed in greasy overalls stuck out from beneath a car tilted at a crazy angle. Danny put his finger to his lips, went over to the water cooler and poured some water into a plastic cup. He came back to the car, crouched down and gently peeled back a trouser leg to dribble some water onto the bared flesh. There was a yowl, a crash, and then a curse. Danny jumped back and sideways as the feet scrabbled for traction. The body pulled itself out from under the vehicle. His appearance reminded Alice of the fat character in an Asterix comic. Small-legged, with a ballooning body, he even had a droopy moustache.

He sat astonished, mouth agape, staring at the scrawny, giggling girl. Suddenly she realised that Danny had hidden himself.

'Who you?'

'I'm - I'm Alice.'

'Why you do that?'

'It wasn't me.'

He got to his feet and started towards her.

'What you mean?' he shouted, in the same patois as Ducey. Alice took a step backwards and came up against a wall. 'I could have been 'urt! I bumped my 'ead.' He pointed a greasy finger to a graze on his forehead. 'I could 'ave knocked myself out.'

'With a head as thick as yours - no chance.'

He swung round, a growl emitting from his throat.

'Generve; I should have known.' He rushed to Danny and putting his arms around him, picked him up.

'Put me down, you greasy coonass.'

'Not until you beg forrrgiveness!' he roared, with laughter in his voice.

'Not on your life, you Hicksville grease-monkey.'

'Not on your life is it, you city slickaire? Let's see what a little oil will do.'

With Danny still crushed between his arms and belly, he waddled over to an open drum.

119

'Dee-Dee, don't. Okay; put me down. I give in.'

'Not enough; you city bum.'

'I'm sorry! Now put me down.'

Dee-Dee suddenly released his grip. Danny's feet landed with a squelch and he nearly lost his footing.

'Careful, my friend; you will sleep up one day.'

Alice started gurgling, rather like a drain. Both men looked at her.

'Alice; this is Dee-Dee.'

Dee-Dee ceremoniously wiped his hands on his overalls, took hers, and drew one to his lips.

'Mademoiselle. Enchanté.'

Alice giggled again.

'Don't be deceived. Dee-Dee's a rogue; no gentleman.'

'Hi, *Mister* Dee-Dee.' She remembered local etiquette.

'To my friends, plain Dee-Dee will do, though I would expect someone with such beauty to have more taste than to be found in the companee of such a villain.'

'Dee-Dee, behave. She is spoken for. Now come; down to business.' Danny put an arm round his shoulder and walked him to the door. 'I rode the old girl a little hard this morning. I need you to check it over.'

'Danny, I keep telling you, there are many speeds between stop and verrroom.' Dee-Dee shot out his hand as he said 'verrroom'.

'I'm sorree, but I had no option. I was being chased.'

'That wouldn't have been through Uptown in the early hours of the morning?'

'Shit: how do you know?'

'Hush. A lady's present.' Dee-Dee tutted. 'Two cars and a cop bit the dust.'

'Damn. Who told you?'

'Ah. I have many spies.' He wagged a finger. 'The whole of N'Yawlins knows by now.'

'Have the cops been round?'

'No, my friend. Your secret is safe with me. It was on the radio. I thought at the time some mad fool must have gotten drunk. Now, let's see my poor baby.'

Dee-Dee walked around Danny's car, shaking his head and cursing at intervals.

'Drive it round the back and up on the ramp.'

The car hung in the air as Dee-Dee inspected beneath it. He came out shaking his head.

'Shit, man. What did you try to do? Fly?'

'Yeah, it was great.' said Alice, beaming.

'I crossed Carrollton a little fast. You know what the camber's like. We took off and it lost me the trailer-hitch and rear screen.'

'You nearly lost more than that.'

'How long, Dee-Dee?'

'You serious?'

'Yeah.'

'Not today. Maybe tomorrow. There's a crack in the sump, and you nearly tore the rear axle mountings out. It's a wonder you made it this far.'

'I slowed down once I was over the Huey. I need to get back to N'Yawlins.'

'Pick up a lift.'

'No. I can wait a day if you make it early morning.'

'I'll try. No promises.'

'Okay. Can I use your skiff? I want to take the scenic route back to Ducey's.'

'Sure, it's down by the landing.'

40.

It was almost eleven o'clock when Dwight ushered Fenwick back into his office. Smith, shirtsleeves rolled up, was studying a file. Others Dwight did not recognise were spread on the desk together with a legal pad covered in notes.

'How's it going?' enquired Fenwick.

'Nearly finished,' Smith said, as he studied a report.

Dwight beckoned to a young woman. 'Any messages?'

'Yeah; on your desk.'

He started lifting corners of files. He burped.

'Nothing like a good breakfast.' He patted his stomach.

Smith stopped reading and watched with amusement as Dwight continued searching through the clutter. Finally giving up, he scratched his head.

'Is there food and coffee coming?' asked Smith.

'No. You didn't ask,' retorted Dwight.

'Is this what you're looking for?' The agent picked up some message slips from the windowsill at his side.

'Yeah.' Dwight snatched and waved them at Smith. 'Why didn't you give these to me in the first place?'

'You didn't...'

Dwight waved a dismissive hand at him.

'Yeah. I know. Didn't ask you.'

Fenwick sighed. 'Can you stop needling each other?'

Dwight grabbed the telephone as it rang.

'Yeah. - Yeah. - APB. Yeah, I'm interested. - Yeah. He's here now? - Send him up. Thanks.'

He sat back in his chair, staring at the ceiling, drumming his fingers on the desk. He smiled at the two agents.

'What is it?' Fenwick asked impatiently.

'A patrol officer has something on the old couple. Maybe nothing, maybe...' he left the word hanging.

He picked up his phone and pressed a series of numbers. 'I want to speak with Arnold. Yeah, I'll hang on.'

There was a knock on the door. It was the patrolman.

'Sir?'

'Yeah?'

'Patrol Officer MacIntyre, Sir!'

'Come in.' Dwight held up his hand before the officer could speak, and curled himself around the telephone.

'Arnold. Good morning. Yeah, I know it's all ASAP, but could you do me a favour?' He paused to listen, then continued. 'Sure, but this may be really important or it may be a red herring, so I want to get it out the way. The PI.card; can you analyse the prints on it and any around where it was found. See if they match with an ex-cop of the same name.' He paused again. 'Yeah; left a few years back, with Arran Marx. Great buddies. Both left under a cloud. I think Marx is in Newark, but Danny stayed. Thanks. I owe you.'

Dwight put down the phone and looked at MacIntyre.

'What have you got, Mac?'

'The APB, Sir. Came out this morning. The old couple from the hotel on St Charles. I gave the Limeys a lift two days ago. Can I ask, Sir? Has this got anything to do with the killings on First and St Thomas?' MacIntyre paused.

'Go on.'

'You wouldn't have a picture, Sir?'

'No.' Dwight looked at Fenwick enquiringly, who shook his head.

MacIntyre licked his lips and looked at the two suits nervously.

'It's alright, Mac. They're part of the investigation team. Tell me about the people you picked up.'

'They were English, in their late sixties. She was small and tubby and a bit breathless and he, maybe older, was tall and thin, with a mustache. They said they were staying at the Columns. I dropped 'em off there after we went to the donut house on Prytania, by the hospital.' He looked down at a pad in his hand. 'They said their name was Banks; Bert and Molly.' He paused to gauge if what he said had any significance.

'Carry on. We're listening. Why did you pick them up?'

He quickly told him what had happened. Dwight frowned all through the report.

'How did you know about the killings?'

123

'I heard about an incident in a camel-back near First and Tchoupitoulas. It got me wondering, so I drove by to check it out. When I got there the whole road was cordoned off. That and the APB, - well, you can gather the rest.'

'Did they mention anything about a kid?'

'No, Sir. Some black kids playing ball in the street said two white adults and a girl.'

'Thanks, Mac. I needn't warn you not to pass this on -'

'Sure, Sir.'

'Especially to the press,' added Fenwick. MacIntyre looked offended.

'Make out your report. If I'm not here give it to Jack Washington.'

'Yessir.'

'Thanks again.'

MacIntyre left.

'Well, that seems to tie in neatly, but doesn't give us anything we don't already know.' He sat thinking. 'I wonder...' He picked up the phone.

'Jack, I want you to ring the cabbies; find any who have driven English passengers around the murder area in the last two days. Ring Ritter at the hotel; ask if he ordered any cabs for the Banks couple. If he didn't, ask him which firms the hotel uses.'

He put the phone down. It immediately rang again.

'Yeah?' Whatever the caller was saying made Dwight's brow crease. The two agents exchanged glances.

'What about what lamp?'

The conversation carried on for some moments, the two agents looking on in silence as Dwight wrote down numbers and an address. He pressed the bar on the phone and re-dialled.

'Cajun Coastal Chandeliers.' The voice had a slow, French-American drawl.

'Yeah; can I speak to the manager?'

'Mr Lapitte is the owner. Will you hold, or I can take your number and call you back?'

'No. I'll hold.'

Fenwick leant over the desk.

'What's happening?' Dwight looked up, then waved his hand.

'Lapitte here.'

'Hello, Sir. This is Lieutenant Usner, N'Yawlins Police department. I have a 2000 watt shrimper lamp that was supplied by you. If I give you the serial number, is there any way you can link it to an owner?'

'It should be possible.'

'How long would this take?' he enquired briskly.

There was a slight pause.

'Maybe a day or two,' Lapitte said cautiously.

'Shit; can't you do it any faster?'

'Monsieur, we are not in the city. We don't have everything on computers.' The voice was distinctly frosty.

'Sorry. I could send someone down to go through your books for you?'

'Not without a warrant, Monsieur. Please give me the number and I will do my best.'

Dwight gave it and hung up. He got up from the desk and walked to the window, mumbling to himself.

'Are you going to enlighten us?' asked Fenwick. He looked at Smith, who shrugged.

'Shut up. I'm thinking. Cajun, Cajun,' he repeated to himself, snapped his fingers together and picked up the phone again. 'Records? I need a Danny Generve's records. Now. Yeah, he was a cop. I don't know; some years back. Thanks. I'll send someone to get it.' He slammed down the phone, giving the two men a triumphant smile.

'What?' asked Fenwick.

125

41.

Alice sat in the middle of the boat, watching Danny manoeuvre it through the sluggish current of a small channel flanked on either side by tall reeds. The small outboard growled complainingly. They had been travelling for over an hour and it felt to her that they were intruding into a silent world with watchful eyes. Gone were the trees, and the Spanish moss.

A few miles back they had passed through a grove of ancient cypress trunks; gaunt, leafless giants of another time. Weathered and sentinel-like, they made her think of a dock full of old-fashioned sailing-ships, striped to the mast. Brown, ungainly birds sat on stubby branches, then sprang away, dropping down near the water's surface, wing-tips clipping it in silver slashes as they struggled to lift their heavy bodies into the turgid air. Zigzag necks held their heads proud above their bodies as they gained height and flew away over tall reeds - the same reeds that now hemmed in the skiff.

Alice turned quizzically to Danny.

'They're pelicans,' he told her.

She watched until they'd flown out of sight. 'They're really strange-looking. Are they rare?'

'Yeah. They're being reintroduced, but still you don't see that many. Louisiana is called the Pelican State. We had to get 'em back.'

'Were there a lot at one time?'

'Yeah, millions; but even when I was a boy they were thinning out.'

'Hunting?'

'No. Sure we did, but that wasn't the cause. This whole area is fed by the Mississippi, which brought down dirt off the rich mid-west farm lands, silting all around here creating what is known as the Delta. This whole area is the fish hatchery for the Gulf and beyond. About thirty-forty years back insecticides, DDT and the likes, floated along with the farmers' dirt. It got into the food chain and the poor old pelican, being fond of fish, ate it all up.'

To Alice, they were lost in a forest of stalks. The boat nudged aside great clumps of reeds. One large stand blocked their passage, and Alice moved forward to push it away with her hands.

'Don't do that!' Danny shouted sharply to her. 'Use the pole in the bottom of the boat. Cottonmouths live in the reeds.'

'Cotton Mouths?'

'Snakes. They're deadly.'

She pushed the pole into the base of the reeds and made a passage. The sun had grown hot and heavy above. Bubbles of stinking gas popped up around the boat as they floated by. Alice watched the reeds pull in behind, hiding where they had been. It was as though they were in an island surrounded by brown, murky water and the world and city lost and gone forever. The sound of unseen wildlife was the only sign that they were not alone.

The reeds suddenly parted and they slipped out into a wide open channel. The sweaty heat vanished as a cooling, salty breeze blew it away. Danny opened up the motor and they sped alongside the reed beds, skipping over the choppy current. A loud blast on a horn from behind made Alice jump. They both watched as a large shrimping boat bore down upon them like a winged beast, with its nets hung high on rigging each side. As it closed, the engine cut, and it slowly drifted towards their skiff.

The bows of the boat slipped by and Alice looked up into the pale netting that passed high over her. As the shadow of the nets passed, a small man appeared and flung a coil of rope over the side. It fell with a 'thunk' into the bottom of their skiff, in front of Alice. She grabbed it, and the skiff was pulled in beside the boat.

Agilely, the man swung over the gunwales and dropped gently down in front of her, quickly taking the rope and tying it fast to the bows of the skiff. A young boy leaned over and stretched out his hands. She looked back anxiously to Danny who was now standing in the stern, having cut their motor.

'Go ahead.'

She took the boy's hands, scrambled up over the gunwales and onto the deck. Danny and the small man followed. The young lad undid the rope and walked the skiff to stern, paying it out a little before tying it fast again.

Danny put a hand on Alice's shoulder and steered her towards the wheelhouse. She felt the vibration of the engine through her feet. The rhythm changed, and the boat started to move forward. Another small man behind the wheel turned and gave a toothy grin as they entered. He sported a large walrus moustache which matched his extremely bushy eyebrows, over which hung a black, floppy cap. Leaving the wheel, he came over and hugged Danny.

'Who is the little one?' he asked, standing back and gazing down at Alice.

'Philippe, this is Alice. She and her folks are staying at Ducey's.'

'And, my friend, what are you doing so far from home?'

'Had to take my car to Dee-Dee, so I borrowed his skiff to give Alice a tour of Cajun country.'

'Ah!' He beamed at Alice, 'And what you've seen so far, you like?' Alice smiled coyly. 'That is good, and tonight you are invited to see us Cajuns dance! Philippe Junior, there is my grandson and will teach you the two-step, yes?'

The young boy had taken over the wheel. Now he lowered his eyes shyly.

'Maybe she doesn't like, grandpa.'

'Thank you, Mr Philippe. I would like.'

'Good.' He gave a slight bow and glanced at Danny.

'I will drop you at the head-cut. It is pleasant down through Dumont's Ditch to Ducey's.'

Alice settled herself once more in the middle of the skiff. Danny sat cradling the burbling outboard. Philippe leaned over the side and handed the girl a large paper sack.

128

'Give this to Miss Ducey from Monsieur Philippe. Also - I claim from her the first dance tonight.'

He laughed and pulled the rope free, and the skiff fell back as the shrimper's engines roared into life. Their little craft bobbed in the wash. Danny opened up the engine and swung it into a narrow passage of water. Soon, they were hemmed in by a tunnel of trees. It was both dark and cool, but a blazing hole of light shimmered ahead. They passed out of the green cavern to find themselves on an open stretch of water.

'There,' shouted Danny, pointing ahead to a house on the far bank. 'That's Ducey's place.'

Alice held a hand above her eyes, shielding them from the glare. The house seemed no bigger than a matchbox, sitting slightly lower than the road which ran behind it, a straight line on the horizon.

'Is that the road we came on?'

'Yeah. It's part of the levee. Do you want a go?'

'Sure.'

Alice scrambled back, holding tightly to the gunwales as the craft rocked. With a pink, sweaty face she reached the stern and plonked herself down next to him. He let go of the tiller and the engine died to a muted cough.

'Hold the tiller and twist the hand grip.'

Nervously she held it and twisted. The skiff surged forward, and then slumped as she let go. She tried again. This time they moved gently, gradually picking up speed. She giggled with glee.

'That's it; now start to take it in a circle, slowly.'

Bert came out of the house when he heard the drone of the outboard. Molly was still resting. He ambled down to the wooden jetty at the water's edge and stood watching the antics of a boat slowly circling and coming closer. He could make out Alice in the stern, next to Danny. As they came in Danny took over the tiller and Alice got up and went forward into the prow. Her face lit up with laughter as she threw

Bert a rope. He caught it, and pulled. As the boat touched the dock she leapt up, took the rope from him and tied it fast.

'It looks like you two have had a good time.'

'It was great,' she said breathlessly. 'Danny! - the bag.'

'Here.' He handed it over. 'Now go give those to Ducey, and be sure to pass on the message as well.' He chuckled.

'We've been invited to a dance.'

With that she turned tail and ran towards the house, cradling the bag in her arms. The men stood on the dock watching her go.

'She's a great kid.'

'Yes, but, extremely damaged.'

Danny studied him for a moment.

'Who wouldn't be, after what she's been through?'

'Yes,' he sighed. 'I believe you saw Alice before we got her out?'

'Ducey has been talking. What has she said?'

'Not much. Molly got upset, but I think I should know. It will help the social workers when we get her back home.'

'Sure. I've written it all down.'

From the bedroom Molly watched them. She had been disturbed by Alice calling for Miss Ducey. The two men walked along the edge of the bayou, deep in conversation. When she entered the kitchen, Alice was chatting with Ducey. Molly sat down heavily on a chair next to the girl.

'Hi,Gran. We've been invited to a dance tonight. What did you call it, Miss Ducey?'

'A Fais-do-do.'

'And Miss Ducey has already got a partner.'

'Hush child, ya'll be telling the world next. Anyways, nothing more than one dance.' Ducey giggled.

'Come on, Miss Ducey, you were really pleased when I told you what Monsieur Philippe said, and what he sent you.' Alice touched the bag on the table, which had fallen on its side. Shrimp had spilled out over the table top.

'My goodness, I've never seen prawns so big.'

'Them's shrump,' corrected Ducey emphatically. 'But I must say they a good size. Have you seen Danny?'

'Yes. Down by the water talking to Bert.'

'We'll call 'em shortly, but now I'm going to show you how to cook these Cajun-style. We'll have 'em for lunch.'

Danny had finished telling Bert about Alice's ordeal in the camel-back when she appeared at the door of the house. She waved, sprang off the steps and ran down towards the two men, skittering over the ground like a young colt. Light and fast; not flattening even a blade of grass.

42.

Lapitte was still frowning an hour after Dwight's call. It annoyed him that the city boys thought they owned the place. Come down and go through his books? He snorted. Still a little worried at his lie he brought up a database on his computer and entered the serial number. He lifted the phone and tapped out Ducey's number. Danny answered.

'Yeah?' His mouth was full of shrimp.

'Ah, glad I found you, Danny. Jacques Lapitte here.'

'Hi, Jacques! What can I do for you?'

'Nothing, mon ami. It's what I can do for you. It seems you left your shrimp lamp behind.' Lapitte paused, as Danny cursed.'A Lieutenant Usner of N'Yawlins Police Department has called asking if I know who the owner might be.'

'How did he trace me?'

'He hasn't yet. He doesn't know. It had my company's name on it and a serial number. That's how I traced you, from my records.'

'So did you give him my name?'

'No. I told him I would look it up. I gave the impression that I didn't have a computer; and 'it could take days'. Lapitte chuckled.

'How long can you give me?'

'Danny; answer me this. Has it got anything to do with what's on the radio?'

'Yeah.'

'Is it anything to do with drugs?'

'No. Trust me. I can't tell you about it, but it's important the cops don't come out here.'

'Can I talk to Ducey?'

'Sure.' Danny called her to the phone.

She took it hesitantly.

'Hi, Jacques?'

'Hi, Ducey. Can you tell me what's going on?'

Danny shook his head at her raised eyebrow.

'Jacques, all I can say is it's important to stall the police.'

'But I need more than that,' Jacques pleaded.

'Trust me. Are you coming to the dance tonight?'

'Sure, but...'

'Wait till then. We'll talk; and I need you to meet some folk.'

'Okay. 'Til this evening. 'Bye, Ducey.'

Bert looked at Danny with concern.

'What's wrong?'

'It seems the cops have traced the shrimping lamp to my suppliers, but I think Jacques will stall them. The problem is the guy running the investigation.'

'Why?'

'He's a detective called Usner. He's good, and if my name gets connected, it won't take him long to come knocking.'

Danny phoned his answering machine and heard a familiar voice he couldn't place.

'Danny, this is Mac. I'm not sure if it's important, but I think we should talk. I'll be by a phone after six. Here's the number.'

Danny shook his head. 'Mac. Mac who?' he wondered aloud. He knew several Macs, but he didn't recognise the voice. No matter; it would have to wait till six. He looked at the clock. Four hours away. There was plenty to do.

'What's wrong, Danny?' He came out of his reverie to find Bert beside him.

'I'm not happy. A guy named Mac left a message'

'Know him?'

'I'm not sure, but whoever it is, he needed to speak with me confidentially. He wouldn't leave anything else on the machine.' He thought for a moment and came to a decision. 'I want y'all to get some more sleep.'

'I'm not tired,' protested Alice.

'You'll do as you're told, child.' Danny rounded sharply.

Alice stood stock still, her mouth open with shock. Tears started to well up in her eyes. She fled out of the room.

'Hell. I didn't mean to speak to her like that.'

'That's all right,' said Bert. 'She'll get over it. Molly, go and sort her out and put her to bed. Give her one of Ducey's pills if she can't sleep.'

Molly nodded, and moved to the door.

'Molly, tell her I'm sorry. Don't take one yourself, but put everything you need in a bag before you get some rest. We may need to flit at a moment's notice. We can't afford to leave anything behind that is important.'

Danny got a couple of beers out of the fridge and touched Bert's arm.

'Let's go and sit outside. We need to talk.'

They sat on the steps in front of the conservatory, looking at the water. Danny offered a beer. Bert shook his head.

'Go on. It goes down well after shrimp. Anyway, it will keep you cool.' After a few minutes while both gazed out over the water, Danny spoke.

'Bert, I think I'll need to get ya'll to Arran. It's not safe down here. I must go back to N'Yawlins to arrange things. I don't think you can stay here much longer, but you'll be safe for the moment. All I ask is; if I tell you to do something - you do it. Okay?'

'Yes, but-'

'No buts, Bert. Y'all do it, is that clear?'

Bert nodded.

'Good. Now I'm going to get you new ID's, clothes, the lot. Sometimes I'm not going to be about and I'll need to send you on to people you don't know. You're not to worry. If you're uncertain who they are, ask 'em 'What does Danny like best?' Got it?

'What does Danny like best?'

'That's right. If the answer is not 'Ducey's shrimp' - run. Do anything you need, but get out.'

He pulled a card from his shirt pocket. 'Here; memorise this number. If you find yourselves on your own, call it. It's Arran's, but it's only for emergencies. He will know what to do; okay?'

'Yes.' Bert studied the card, turning it over several times.

'Another thing. Do you have much cash on you?'

'Yes. Do you need some?'

'It would help. Things are going to start costing. What can you spare?'

Bert unbuttoned his shirt and pulled out the money belt.

'There's twelve thousand in here,' he said, holding it up, 'and I've got a card too. I can draw another fifteen on that.'

'No, give me two grand for now. You keep the rest safe. I'll ask for more when I need to. Now *listen;* don't *ever* use plastic, even if you're stuck for money. Steal if you have to.'

'Why?'

'It's a bit complicated, but trust me; you can be traced when you withdraw money. Lastly; I'll be sending you to someone who'll teach you to use that pistol.'

'Danny, I don't want to sound ungrateful, but it's against my principles to use a gun.'

'Thought you might say that. This is an unusual situation. The men you're up against won't have those scruples if they find Alice, or Molly, or all three of you. Think it over. Now go and rest.'

43.

Dwight was leafing through Danny's record. Fenwick was in a corner bringing Smith up to speed, especially about Danny's business card. Suddenly Dwight slapped the file.

'Got it.'

Smith and Fenwick stopped and joined him as he went to a wall map. .

'There!' His finger stabbed, not quite covering the town of Morgan City. It moved and stabbed again, no more than a centimetre away. 'And here - Danny Generve's mother - not more than five miles further on.'

'You think he's there?' asked Fenwick cautiously.

'I don't know, but I feel it.' He stabbed his finger again to emphasise the point.

'May be he was never in the room,' protested Fenwick.

Dwight looked at his watch. 'We'll wait till two-thirty, then we'll make another visit to his office. If he's not there we'll go straight on out. It will take three hours to get there.'

'Why wait?'

Dwight looked at Smith. 'Because if I can I prefer to go calling with more than a gut feeling.'

Two-thirty passed with no call from Forensic about the fingerprints. They were treading water. Dwight was loath to wait. He picked up the phone and called the switchboard.

'Marlene, I'm going to put my 'phone back through the board. If Arnold calls, patch him through to my car.'

'Sure, hon.'

He stood up, dragging his coat from the back of his chair as he went. The others followed. Marching down a corridor with offices buzzing on both sides he suddenly stopped dead. Smith and Fenwick nearly collided with him as he pushed himself back past them. A woman in her early fifties, glasses perched on the end of her nose, was tapping away at a computer.

'Beth.' Pale blue eyes stared over the top of her half-moon lenses.

'Hi, Dwight. What can I do for you?'

'If a company is on the internet, can you find it without an address?'

'Sure. You got a name?'

'Yeah, and it's local. Well, Louisiana. Fishing industry.'

He gave her the details. In seconds flat the company's name came up with a website.

'Shit. The bastard was lying,' he said to Fenwick. 'Beth; can you get business details like names of clients? You know; who bought what, and when?'

'Hacking, you mean. That's illegal.'

Dwight shrugged. 'Worth a try,' he said as an apology.

'I said it was illegal. I didn't say I couldn't do it.' She gave him a wink. 'Give me some details. I'll go down to the basement. We've got a machine hooked up to a private line that's routed through New Hampton in Maryland. If I get caught, I'll crash their system. It'll take days to sort it out unless they have a wizard, and even then they won't know what we were looking for.'

'God bless you. Remind me to take you out for a meal.'

'Shoo! How many times have I heard that?' Beth said scornfully.

'Well if he don't, I will, Beth,' said Fenwick with a smile.

'I might take you up on that, stranger.'

The men hung around the doorway.

'Well. What are you waiting for?'

'How long is it going to take, Beth?' Dwight's voice held hope.

'Hell! I'm not a miracle worker. I don't know. I'll call your office when it's done.'

'They'll patch you to my car. 'Bye, Beth.'

He left in a rush, the others half-running in pursuit.

Halfway to St Charles Avenue Arnold came through on the phone. They had found Danny's prints on the wallpaper hiding the card and the twenty dollar bill. Both his and one other. They were small; probably a child's.

'Bingo,' muttered Fenwick with a chuckle.

Danny's office looked deserted when they got there. No-one answered their knocks. Dwight drew from his breast pocket a set of skeleton keys. He looked up and down the street, and after a few fumbles the door opened.

'Chief, I'll stay down by the car. There's no call for all of us cluttering up the place,' volunteered Smith.

'Right,' said Fenwick. 'Give a toot if anyone turns up.'

'No one's going to; he's out in Cajun country. We won't be long,' said Dwight gruffly.

'I'll follow you up. I need to take a leak.'

'Take your time. From the smell of it, it's in back.'

As Dwight climbed heavily up the stairs, Smith closed the street door behind him and got back into the car. He glanced up at the window. There was no sign of Usner. He knew Fenwick would keep out of sight. He pulled out his cell 'phone.

Harvey had a heavily bandaged foot propped up on a chair. He was playing solitaire. Harry was wearing a hole in the carpet and cursing under his breath. His face was badly bruised and he was walking stiffly, as though he wore a corset. When the phone rang beside his brother Harry stopped and stretched out his hand. Harvey put the cards down and passed it over.

'Yeah?'

'They're out in Cajun country. Got a pen?'

'Hang on.' Harry clicked his fingers at his brother. 'Pen, paper,' he hissed. 'Okay, what have you got?'

Harry scribbled fast.

'Got that?'

'Yeah.'

'We're going there now, so use a chopper. Oh. Harry.'

'Yeah?'

'Don't fuck up this time.' The phone went dead.

44.

The office was cramped and hot. A real mess. Dwight went through the desk methodically, leaving no sign of disturbance. The filing cabinet was locked. He fiddled with his keys again. When Fenwick came into the office he noticed the light flashing on the answerphone. He pressed the button. A whispered voice came over the speaker. Dwight stopped flicking through files, listened hard and cursed.

'That's the bastard patrol cop. Replay it.'

'Danny, this is Mac. I'm not sure if it's important, but I think we should talk. I'll be by a phone after six. Here's the number.'

'Take down that number. Better still, there's a blank tape in the drawer. We'll take that one. When this is over I'll have his ass.' He looked at his watch. 'Shit, it's gone three. If Danny has already got that message, he'll be talking to him before we get there and he'll be gone. Let's get out of here.'

They clattered down the stairs and into the street, running to the car. They yanked the doors open violently and tumbled in, startling a dozing Smith. Dwight gunned the engine and jammed it into "drive". The car shot forward as he flicked a switch. A siren whined and they saw the blue flash of their beacon gantry lights in the windshields of parked cars.

'What's up?' asked a bemused Smith.

'That patrol cop we had in the office this morning was trying to get a message to our friend Danny.'

'Shit!'

'Exactly.' Dwight grabbed the microphone from the dash. 'Marlene: Come in, Marlene.'

'Hello! Is that you, Dwight? What's the racket? Going to an accident or something?'

'Yeah; something. I need to talk to Jack Washington.'

'Hold on.'

Seconds ticked by. The radio stayed silent. They were now on South Carrollton, racing towards the Huey P. Long Bridge.

'Dwight! Jack here.'

'Jack. Get hold of Patrolman MacIntyre and throw him in a cell. Don't let him near a phone till you hear from me.'

'Why?'

'Obstruction of police enquiries. Hold him.'

'Okay.'

He put down the microphone and concentrated on driving through the thickening afternoon traffic.

The Dancers didn't exactly rush to their car; they were in no fit state. Their driver, a stranger to New Orleans, made the big mistake of going through the business district instead of around it and it took a whole hour to get untangled and head for the heliport on the lakefront.

Because they had not thought of warning their pilot, the chopper had to be refuelled. The brothers were not happy by the time they were in the air. It was a quarter to five. The pilot said it would take less than an hour. He threw a map onto the chart table and told them to find the place.

Dwight got the next call when they were on the bridge. It was gone four.

'Dwight; Arnold here.'

Yeah, Arnold. What have you got?'

'You know the guy who disappeared from the hospital - the one with the knife in his foot? Left an empty case in his room.'

'Yeah.'

'Found a couple of clear prints. Otherwise very clean, very careful. Belong to a guy called Stenato, alias Harvey Dancer. Twin called Harry, and links to the mob.'

At the name Dancer, Smith and Fenwick let out a 'shit'. Dwight looked in his rear mirror.

'Thanks, Arnold, the suits will fill in the rest.' He gave a sigh. 'Fenwick, you've been holding out on me.'

'Not at all, Dwight.'

'Are you going to come clean, or am I going to turn this car around and you can tell me at the office - everything you've got on this case?'

140

'No, we can talk while you drive to Danny's.'

'No, we don't talk. *You* talk, mister,' he bellowed.

Fenwick looked visibly shaken.

'What do you want to know?'

'Everything; but first - who are the Dancers?'

'Right. The Dancers are twins. Harry, who seems to be boss, is a psychopath, and Harvey is the quiet brother who doesn't hardly open his mouth. He's actually far cleverer than Harry. Cold-blooded about sums them both up. They're hit men and very good. They clean up for the mob. It's said that when they kill they become artists, dancing around their victims like doing a ballet, hence 'Dancer twins'. The work on Barasitch and wife has their hallmark.'

'So you guessed they were involved this morning, you bastard?'

'I've been following this case for nine months and every time we get close bodies fall at our feet and the trail goes cold. It's amazing that the old couple and the kid got away. Generve must be either lucky or resourceful. The injured men and the one dead in the other car all worked for the twins.'

'What you said this morning about Barasitch getting away the first time. Is it...?'

'I don't know,' snapped Fenwick. His tone made Dwight cut to the mirror. There was a warning in the agent's eyes.

'So that's the twins. Now tell me the whole story.'

'I told you everything else this morning.'

Again Dwight glanced in the mirror. The expression in Fenwick's eyes was now pleading; pleading for him to stop. The guy did not want to talk and he had the feeling it was not because of him. His focus shifted to Smith, who was sitting back as if dozing; but there was a tension about him as though he was keyed up. He knew then that Fenwick didn't trust his partner. The radio came alive. It was Jack.

'Dwight; MacIntyre has finished duty for the day. We can't find him. What do you want me to do?'

'Go to his home and drag him out. Wait! Here's the number he left. Check it out.' Dwight looked at his watch.

It was quarter past five. 'Jack, you haven't got long. He's expecting a call from Danny at six.' He hooked up the mike.

'The sign says thirty miles to Morgan City. How long do you think it'll take?'

In answer, Fenwick felt a surge of power as Dwight pushed his foot to the floor. Ten minutes later, had they looked up to their right they would have seen a helicopter.

45

Danny had been resting on his bed for the last hour. He could not stop making lists in his head, and speculating on what could / could not happen. His watch said another forty-five minutes to go. Sighing deeply, he swung his feet off the bed and walked through into the lounge, where Ducey was watching her favourite talk programme. .

She glanced up. 'Restless?'

'Yeah, it's no good - can't stop my brain from whirling.'

'I'll get you some coffee.' She rose and made for the kitchen. 'Why don't you try that number now? He might be there.'

'Worth a try, I suppose.' He said it without much conviction.

He tapped out the number. The phone rang three times and was picked up. He could hear music and laughter before a voice asked 'Yeah?'

'Is Mac there?'

'Who's calling?'

'Danny.'

'Hold on.' He heard a shout for Mac, and after a few seconds the phone was picked up again. 'No pal, he's expected soon.'

'Can I leave a message?'

'Sure.'

'Tell him Danny called. He can reach me on 503-886657. Got that?'

'Yeah.'

The barman had no sooner hung up when the phone rang again.

'Yeah.'

'Is Mac there?'

He sighed. This was getting to be a joke.

'Who wants to know?'

'Oh - Just a friend.'

'The answer is 'no'.'

'Hey, where am I calling to? Sounds like a bar.'

143

The phone went dead. Jack Washington cursed, and called exchange for a trace. It wouldn't take long to find out.

The barman redialled Danny's number. It was picked up instantly.

'Yeah?'

'Is that Danny?'

'Yeah. Is that you, Mac?'

'No. Listen. I don't know if it was a coincidence or what, but someone else has been asking for Mac since you called. He wouldn't give his name and he wanted to know where this phone was at. The number he was calling from was the police department, but not Traffic.'

'How do you know?'

'I've got this little ol' screen telling me.'

'So you knew my number?'

'Sure. It's a precaution; no offence meant.'

'None taken. Grateful you called back. I'll give you my mobile number.'

After he had finished, Danny wandered over to the window and looked out upon the placid water, but noticed nothing. He was deciding.

'Coffee, Danny.'

'No time for coffee. Get the others up.'

He went back to his bedroom and threw some things into a dirty old sports bag. When he returned, Bert was carrying Alice in through another door.

'The poor child is tuckered out.'

'Yeah. That and the sleeping pill. Take her to the boat. I'll be there in a moment.'

'I'll need to get my bag.'

'Don't worry about that; I'll pick it up. You get to the boat.'

Bert pushed through the screen door and stepped down onto the path. Danny went to Molly. Ducey was helping her with one of the bags.

'Here, give me those. You get to the boat, Molly. I'll be with you in a minute.'

She turned to thank Ducey.

'There's no time, Molly. You'll be seeing her later anyways. Now, Ducey, I don't know what's happening, but if the police are coming the others might know about this place too. It won't be safe here. Don't pack anything, but get in the car and drive over to Jacques'. I'll see you at the dance; okay?' He reached the door, but she made no move to leave. 'Ducey - go *now*. I mean it. I won't start the boat until I see you in your car. I'll lock the screen door. You lock the front.'

'But Danny -'

'No buts, Ma.' He leaned forward, planted a peck on her cheek, and left.

The engine was running when Danny got there. He sat down at the tiller and held onto the jetty. Bert had already undone the rope. He was watching the house.

They saw Ducey's car move up onto the road and drive towards Berwick. He let go, and twisted the throttle. The front end lifted up and they slid away from the dock. No more than halfway across, Danny heard the distinctive clatter of a chopper. It came slowly along the edge of the bayou, searching the shoreline.

'Bert, take the tiller. Molly - hand me my bag! 'Head it straight on out, Bert. Don't deviate. They're not looking for a boat, so let's be bold.'

He pulled out a battered pair of binoculars and put them to his eyes.

'Well, they're not cops. Lucky for us they're looking landward. At least Ducey's away.'

46.

The helicopter hovering in front of the house slowly descended onto the grass by the jetty. Two figures in dark suits got out, but the pilot stayed with the chopper. The rotors had sagged, but still circled slowly. Danny watched them walk up to the house. One was limping badly.

'The two mothers who gave Alice's house a visit. One is limping badly. Alice would be pleased to know that, if she were awake.'

'Good,' said a sleepy voice at the prow of the skiff.

Danny's lip lifted as he watched Harry put his foot to the door. It sprang open and they disappeared inside. He knew they wouldn't be long.

'Bert; see that dark area by the clump of trees over there?' Danny pointed ahead. 'Like a black hole.'

'Yes.'

'That's a channel. Make straight for it. Let me know when we're close. I'm going to keep an eye on our friends.'

'Fair enough.' He twisted harder on the throttle grip.

Back at the house Harry and Harvey silently moved through the rooms, guns in hand. Harry put his hand lightly on the coffee pot. He took it away quickly.

'It's just been made,' he whispered warningly.

Where Molly and Bert had rested was a complete shambles. Harvey burrowed through the odd assortment of things that Molly had dumped on the bed when they repacked. He picked up an airline ticket. It had fallen to the floor unnoticed in her haste.

'They've been here.' He handed it to Harry.

'Yeah, from Britain. A return ticket. Huh!' He gave a twisted smile as he pocketed it. 'She won't be needing it.' He looked at his watch. 'We haven't much time. Let's see what else we can find.'

They left the bedroom and swiftly searched on, finding the little room that Ducey used as an office. A photo of an oldish woman standing proudly in front of a gleaming Oldsmobile sat on the top of a filing cabinet. Harry opened the top drawer and leafed through the files, stopping at car insurance. He pulled out several certificates going back through the years. He lifted the most recent and put it in his pocket.

'Come on, let's get out of here.'

As an afterthought he grabbed the picture of Ducey. They had reached the chopper when they heard the distant wail of sirens.

'Here comes the cavalry.'

The Dancers jumped in. Harry patted the pilot on the shoulder, lifted his thumb skyward, and motioned across the bayou. The helicopter lifted off and moved straight out over the water. They were nearing the centre when Dwight drove down the track to the front of the house, which blocked his view of the disappearing machine.

The skiff was no more than a hundred yards from the channel when the Dancers reappeared from the house. Danny offered Bert the binoculars.

'I'll take over. We need to get under cover. Take a good look at those men; you need to know your enemy.'

'Do you think they found anything?'

Danny gave Bert a knowing nod. Molly took the glasses and had a long look. Alice nudged her impatiently.

'Let's have a go.'

When she finally was given them, she caught a fleeting glimpse of the men before they ducked into the chopper. It took off and came straight out.

'Danny!' she screamed, 'they're coming for us!'

Danny looked over his shoulder. 'Shit! Get down on the floor; and you, Bert.'

He looked at the dark hole of the channel and back at the chopper, which was catching up fast. He twisted hard on the throttle. There was no more speed to be had. It seemed that the skiff was creeping too slowly towards their refuge. They could feel the throb of the machine bearing down; it was almost on top of them. Their boat entered the channel, the low, overhanging branches catching at Danny's hair. The thwack of the rotors beat down on the canopy above, and it was gone, the sound bleeding away. He cut the engine and they slowly glided into the bank.

'It's okay. You can get up. I don't think we were spotted. If we were, they didn't twig it was us. Let's wait awhile and listen out.'

It was utterly quiet in the dark channel. Nothing seemed to move, except for the skiff, shifting with the current, and the gurgle of water passing the hull, and Molly's gasping breath. They had survived yet again. Suddenly there was a shrill beep, and they all jumped. Danny pulled the mobile from his jacket pocket.

'Yeah?'

'Mac here, Danny. Don't know where you are, but get the hell out of there.'

'Thanks, Mac; we have. Oh - Mac?'

'Yeah?'

'Which Mac are you?'

'MacIntyre Mac.'

'Enlighten me more.'

'Gene MacIntyre from Laurel and General Pershing Patrol. Got me now?'

'Sure. Thanks again, Gene. We got out in the nick of time, but it wasn't cops who came visiting. All the same, thanks.'

'You sure? Well, expect Old Usner. He's on your case.'

'How did he find out about me?'

'Had to see him about some Brits I gave a lift to. There's an APB out on an old couple -and a kid.'

'They're with me now.'

'That figures. I was in his office while he was on the phone. He'd found a card, I assume one of yours, in the house where two bodies were found. Started talking about your friend Arran Marx in Newark and mentioned the name Danny in the same breath. It had to be you. Store my mobile number; that's what I'm speaking on.'

Danny pressed 'store'.

'The guy who answered the 'phone said someone else had asked for you, but wouldn't leave their name.'

148

'I know. That's disturbing.'

'Well, watch your back. There's some nasty bastards out there. I'll call you tomorrow.'

Danny pocketed the phone, then looked up into the canopy. The chopper had not come back.

'Danny?'

'Quiet, Alice. Can't you see Danny's thinking?'

'It's alright, Molly. What is it, Alice?'

'Before we got under cover I saw flashing blue lights up on the road behind the house.'

He gently nudged the skiff to the entrance of the channel.

'Someone hold onto the branches. We don't want the current to take us back out.'

He moved forward in the boat, taking the binoculars from Alice as he passed. He scanned the horizon. Usner and Fenwick came into focus.

47.

After getting out of the car and banging on the front door, Usner had walked round to the back of the house. The helicopter, no more than a dot above the trees on the far side of the bayou, soon disappeared. Finding the back screen door flapping, he had entered. After the search, Fenwick and Dwight stood on the top step, looking out over the water.

'What do you think?' asked Dwight.

'They were here; the clothes in the back were English.'

'I agree. MacIntyre got through. Wait 'til I get his ass.'

'Can I suggest something, Dwight?'

The cop looked speculatively at him. 'What?'

'If you haven't picked up MacIntyre yet, let him run free?' Dwight opened his mouth to object, but Fenwick raised his hand. 'Let's say he warned Generve. So he's got his trust. Generve will need to get back into the city and he'll want to know what you cops are doing. Who better?'

A sly smile slowly spread across Dwight's face.

'Shit; we've got to warn off Jack.'

He jumped off the step and ran back to the car.

Jack was a block away from the bar, moving in slow traffic. At that moment he spotted Mac coming out.

'Leave him,' shouted Usner, over the intercom. 'He's already done the damage.'

'Shit, Dwight, what you talkin' 'bout? I got him cold.'

'No,. Let him walk free. We can get him later. I've got the evidence. I don't want him to smell you.'

'Shit.'

Dwight heard a bang as Jack bashed the microphone onto the steering wheel in frustration.

'Are you coming back tonight?'

'Not sure,' said Dwight. 'I'll pay the local cops a visit, but they'll be tight as an alligator's ass. Danny's gone to ground and the locals won't want to help us city boys. We'll have to wait till he surfaces. I'll call you.'

48.

Dusk was falling and the cicadas were all starting to chatter when they nosed out of the other end of the channel. Molly looked all around. The place seemed alive with strange creatures, mostly eager to bite, claw or sting. It felt hostile; remote.

'Alice, are you still awake?'

'Yeah, Danny.'

'I need my flashlight; it's in my sports bag.'

'Got it.'

'Great. Switch it on and hold it in front of you.'

'It's not that dark. Can't you see?'

'Sure, but we don't want to be run down.'

Alice looked around her. The bank was cloaked in dark shadows. She could only make out trees, standing like black, leaning columns, the Spanish moss now dark swags dripping close to the water. She let out a little gasp.

'What is it, dear?'

'I thought I saw some eyes, Nan.'

'That's possible,' said Danny. 'There're several species of nocturnal animals around, but it's probably a house cat.'

'That croaking,' asked Bert. 'Anything in particular?'

'Yeah, an old bull frog.' There was a splash near to the bank. 'That could be anything from a snap-turtle to an alligator.'

Molly snatched her hands off the gunwale which she had been holding with white knuckles, and put them firmly in her lap. There was a solid bump on the hull. She let out a squeak.

'It's a log, Molly.' He didn't want to fluster her too much and bring on another attack. Bert chuckled to himself.

'You can stop your laughing, Bert Banks. I don't like boat travel at the best of times,' she snorted. 'At least I didn't leave nail marks in the armrest on the aeroplane.'

Alice giggled. 'And you can be quiet, young lady.' Molly clipped the top of her head.

'I didn't say a thing,' protested Alice, her head ducking away from any more.

'You didn't have to; your shoulders were going up and down like a Jack in the box.'

'It won't be long now, Molly; a couple more minutes.'

They rounded a bend and the creek opened out into a natural pool. On the far side sat two large shrimpers, their rigging lit up with strings of little lights. They were moored to a dock and behind it was the open mouth of a large shed. Floodlight washed out of it. Men were busy moving large crates from it to a truck.

'Is this Monsieur Philippe's?'

'Yeah. Get that rope ready. When we touch, jump up and tie us fast, Alice.'

She stood up in the prow, and as it gently touched the dock she scrambled up and pulled the skiff along to a post and tied it tightly to the worn wood. A figure separated itself from the working group and came along the dock, wiping his hands on his overalls. Alice was taking a bag from Molly.

'Hi, Alice, let me take that.' Philippe took the bag, placed it on the wooden slats of the dock, then held out his hand towards Molly. 'You must be Madame Molly. May I?'

Molly took his hand, stood up and wobbled. The skiff rocked, and with her free hand she grabbed out blindly at the slatted wood of the dock.

'It ees safe, Madame. Take your time; that's eet. Now step up. Don't worry; the boat may rock but eet ain't goin' nowhere,' he soothed. 'Weve been expecting you for some time.'

'You've heard from Ducey?' Relief filled Danny's voice.

'Sure. She phoned from Jacques'; said she'll see you at Guidry's.' Philippe picked up both bags before Bert realised.

'Let me take those.'

'No, Monsieur Bert, you are my guests. So what kept you, mon ami?' he asked Danny.

'I decided to sit it out in the channel until dusk in case they flew over again. We got out in the nick of time.'

'So the police came visiting?'

'Yeah, but it wasn't cops nearly caught us, but someone else. They came in a chopper and flew out over the water.'

'Do you think they will come looking?'

'I'd like to think not, but I'm not counting. I'm certain they would have found something in the house. They'll know our friends here were in there. They're pros.'

Philippe frowned. 'Tonight you must stay with us.'

They came to a brightly lit house. The grandson, Philippe Junior, held the door open. His face lit up when he saw Alice and he shyly stepped aside for her to enter. In the kitchen a woman in her early thirties with long, dark hair was preparing food. She cleaned her hands and was introduced as young Philippe's mother.

'So you are Alice. I sure have heard a lot about you,' she said, with a sparkle in her eyes, 'from Philippe.' Alice looked at the boy, who reddened.

'She means my grandfather.'

Alice smirked. 'Sure.'

His mother looked beyond the girl as the door opened again. 'Danny!' she said, her eyes sparkling with excitement.

Alice felt herself go cold.

'Hi, Marie.' He kissed her on both cheeks while Alice stood stoically watching. 'You comin' to the dance tonight?'

'Yes, but first we'll eat. Food is about ready. Will you show our guests to the bathroom, Philippe?' Marie's hand still lingered on Danny's arm. She gave it a tug. 'Come and help me with the table.'

Alice stood watching Marie take Danny away, her hand still on his arm. She jumped as young Philippe touched her.

'C'm-on.' Reluctantly, she followed.

When she returned, a long table had been laid and set in the centre of the room. Bert and Molly were seated on one side, and on the other Danny and young Philippe had taken the centre two chairs. Alice ignored Philippe's offer of the chair next to him and instead sat by Danny with a triumphant smile. Marie came from the cooker bearing a big pot.

'Oh! Alice, I thought you might like to sit by Philippe.'

'I'm okay here, thanks.' She gazed innocently at Marie.

'Alice, go and sit by Philippe,' said Molly sternly.

'I'm okay here,' she said stubbornly.

'It's no matter,' said Marie, who put down the pot heavily and rushed back to the stove.

A moment later Philippe senior and three other men came in and sat down. Philippe sat next to Alice at the head of the table. He bent towards her and rested a gentle hand on her wrist.

'You are honoured. Marie always sits next to me.' Alice reddened.

'That's nice of her.' Molly treated her granddaughter to an old-fashioned look as the food was served amidst a lot of chatter. Marie carried the empty pots away and a hush fell on the table as they waited for her to sit. Alice picked up her fork and set to eat. She had raised it to her mouth when Philippe senior gently touched her arm.

'Child, we always give grace before we eat.'

'Sorry.'

She reddened, and dropped her fork with a clatter onto her plate, as though it had burnt her. He bowed his head and mumbled a few words, then picked up a shrimp, shelling it so fast that Alice could not see how he did it. He popped it into his mouth with relish. Alice looked down at her plate. A mound of shrimp stared back with black, beady eyes.

'I've been thinking, Danny. If those men, or the police did not return to N'Yawlins, I could make a few discreet phone calls.'

'I agree, but I think it should be me. If you made them and someone talked they would be around here damn quick.'

'You have a point, my friend, but there are some I can trust. My brother's son-in-law works for the heliport in Morgan City. I imagine they would land there . No stranger would risk setting down on the side of the road.'

'I wouldn't think these city boys would. One, at least, wouldn't want to walk far.'

'How come?'

'I watched through my binoculars; one had a definite limp.'

'Yeah, I saw him, too. He'll think twice before he holds us up again!' said Alice, boastfully.

'Why's that?' The younger Philippe looked across Danny to Alice with wonder.

'I spiked him in the foot with Danny's knife.'

'You're kidding.'

'I'm not,' retorted Alice proudly.

'Wow!'

'Let's hope there is no next time,' piped in Molly, who did not altogether like Alice's boastful relish.

'Let's pray so, Madame, because next time they will be more cautious and so more dangerous.'

'Yes; it seems they were expecting a couple, and a child with no experience of violence.' Marie finished speaking blithely, picked up some dirty plates and took them to the sink. Alice glowered, and Molly gave her a knowing smile. She leant over and patted her hand.

'You did very well, but you should not boast about hurting someone, dear.'

Alice fell silent. She knew her grandmother was thanking her, but she did not like the way it came out. It felt like she should not have done it at all. Philippe got up from the table, and the others started to move.

'No; please stay. Marie has made dessert. I must make these phone calls. You had better come too, Danny.'

49.

As soon as the helicopter landed at Morgan City, Harry and Harvey took a taxi with the pilot to find a hotel. On the way into town they stopped at a garage and tried to hire a car, but were told it was too late and everywhere would be shut. Harry pointed out that there were plenty of cars on the forecourt. Protests of the cars being for sale broke no ice. Harvey drew out his wallet and laid out five hundred dollars. The owner didn't need any other encouragement when he noticed the gun in his shoulder holster. After dropping the pilot at the hotel and telling him to book some rooms the men went back to Ducey's place.

It was dark when they rolled quietly off the road and parked up round the side of the house. Harry wandered back to the road and with a satisfying grunt turned back and joined Harvey at the broken door.

'Okay?'

'Sure. We can't be seen from the road.'

They carefully entered and went straight to the bedroom where Molly and Bert had slept. Methodically, they searched every inch, but learned nothing new. The room that Alice had slept in had nothing to indicate her stay, except that the bed had been left unmade. In Ducey's they found a photo they presumed to be of Danny. In his room they became meticulous, finding many references to his old life in NOPD, and business related to his present work. What files he kept there gave the number of his mobile and the make and registration of his cars. Sitting on Danny's bed, Harry phoned their contacts in New Orleans, whilst Harvey, saying 'The hub of any woman's home is the kitchen', set about rifling it.

He was about to give this up as futile when he glanced at a calendar hanging askew on the wall. Being irritated by the asymmetry of it, he stretched out a hand to put it straight. There, in bold black writing, within the box of that very day, was *'Dance at Guidry's with Philippe.'* Harry lifted his head as Harvey's shadow fell across him.

'You finished?' He was bored, and also hungry.

Harvey ignored his question.

'I think I've found something.' He threw the calendar onto his lap.

'Could be worth a try. We can ask around. If it's a friend's place it might be difficult.' Harry looked happy for the first time that day.

'If it were friends, would she have written 'Dance at Guidry's?' Sounds more like a place for a date. Can't be many dance places around with that name.'

'Yeah, I think you're right. C'mon, let's get out of here before we push our luck. I need to get me some food.'

50.

Dwight, Fenwick and Smith called in at the sheriff's office. He wasn't too pleased to find not only a New Orleans cop prowling around his neck of the woods without his knowledge, but two Feds as well. He listened patiently to what Dwight told him, but would do nothing until the morning, and then no more than 'I'll ask around.'

Fenwick started to press him, bringing the full force of the agency to bear. The sheriff cursed them for bullying tactics by an outsider organisation. As long as the suspicion regarding Ducey Generve was because of something her son might be involved with it would wait till morning.

Smith reported that clothes that were obviously British had been found on the premises. Dwight closed his eyes and waited for the wrath of his country cousin to descend.

Two hours later, after being made to write separate reports on what had gone on at Ducey Generve's, the three men left. They had orders not to come back without papers from the courts, and were assured that no action would be taken in the morning until Dwight's boss had spoken with him. Also, if they didn't go back to New Orleans that night they'd spend a night in a cell; one that would inevitably fill up with drunken rowdies, it being a Friday night. Dwight drove back to the city with the muted agents, both relegated to the back seat of the car. They knew better than to talk to him. He kept muttering under his breath about stupid idiots who couldn't put their brains in gear when they opened their mouths. But even he got tired of it and drove the rest of the way in silence.

Luck was with Danny. Philippe's brother's son-in-law had been at the heliport when Harry and Harvey got into the taxi, which also happened to be driven by a friend of his. The taxi driver reported back that the men had stopped at Duke's garage and hired a dark green saloon. Ten minutes later he had seen the two, without the pilot, drive off in the direction of Ducey's place.

Ducey's second cousin was janitor at the sheriff's office. He said that a big row had blown up with three cops from New Orleans, now furiously scribbling reports. The sheriff had even told the janitor that he was going to send their sorry asses back to the city, where they belonged.

Danny was loath to miss that night's dance. There would be people he wanted to see. His problem: he didn't want to leave Molly, Bert or Alice behind. Philippe thought nothing could possibly happen at Guidry's if they took them along, as no one would know that they or Ducey were going, and it would be safer in a crowd.

Alice moaned that she could not go as her only clothes were too dirty. Marie rang a friend who had a daughter the same age and size, to ask if she'd lend some. Alice was shown a wardrobe and told to take her pick. Molly was scandalised at the skimpiness of the dress Alice chose, but the girl explained that she couldn't offend the lender, even if she didn't have much taste. Molly wasn't totally convinced, but said no more.

51.

It was already dark when they left, in a large car driven by Marie. Philippe Senior said he would be along later.

Like many roadside bars in Southern country states, it was unprepossessing from the outside, and did not seem large enough for a dance. A neon sign flashed spasmodically above the door. It announced 'Guidry's Friendly Lounge'.

The very small bar was almost empty. When they entered everyone went quiet and looked at the newcomers curiously.

Marie opened a door to one side. Sound swelled out, similar to that Alice had heard on the radio earlier that day. Danny ushered them through and then ordered drinks, acknowledging two men sitting on stools either side of him.

'Who's your friends?' asked the barmaid.

'Come through and I'll introduce you, Lureline. Have you seen Bruno?'

'Not yet. Should be in later.' She stacked beers on a tray and pushed it towards him. 'Go on through. I'll come bring your order in a minute.'

He joined the others in a surprisingly large hall with a large stage. Tables and chairs lined three sides, leaving the middle as open floor. His party were sitting around a table near to the band, which included a very small boy sawing vigorously away at a fiddle.

Danny traversed the floor, dodging dancing couples, and placed the tray full of cans on the table. Molly and Bert suppressed surprise at the lack of glasses. When in Rome...

'I got the kids coke.'

Alice pouted.

'Well, this is a surprise,' said Molly, looking around her. 'Who would have thought all this was here?'

'Yeah, well, Guidry's is famous hereabouts. Tonight's Old Time Dancing. Cajun Rock on Saturday and the rest of the week. Hope you can dance, Molly?' Danny asked, his eyes twinkling.

'I'll have a go. Bert's the one to get up.' She gave a naughty giggle.

'Give over, woman. She's talking a load of nonsense.'

'We'll get you both up. Here, have a beer!' He passed each a can.

The music finished. Bert was aware of someone standing next to him - a diminutive elderly man sporting an enormous whiskery moustache. The stranger gave a slow bow.

'Monsieur, may I dance with your wife?'

'You'd best ask her.'

'No, Monsieur; not without your permission.'

'If Molly wants to, it's okay by me.'

He bowed again smartly, and walking round the table to Molly, he bowed yet again.

'Madame Mollee?' She looked up, startled. 'Would you geeve me the pleasure of the next dance?'

'I, I don't know how to...' She looked pleadingly at Bert, who gave the little Cajun an encouraging wink and shot a wicked beam to Molly. The band started a slow waltz.

'Madame, I will show.Yes?' He held out an expectant hand. Alice giggled and Molly shot her a withering glance.

'Yes. Why not?'

Although the steps were a little different, Molly found it easier than she'd thought, and soon the pair were circling round the floor amongst the other dancers. The little Cajun seemed swamped by Molly's bulk, which made Alice smirk. Bert was talking to Philippe junior when he became aware of the barmaid setting down another round of drinks.

'Excuse me; who ordered these?'

'Pierre, Monsieur.'

'Who is Pierre?'

'The one dancing with your wife.'

Bert lifted his can as he caught the dancer's eye. The Cajun gave a twitch of his lips, and swung a somewhat breathless Molly into yet another circuit of the floor. When the dance had finished she arrived back panting slightly, to be greeted by Ducey, who had arrived with Jacques Lapitte and his wife.

'Where's Philippe?' asked Ducey in a whisper.

'I don't know. He didn't come in the car with us.'

161

'Oh.'

Danny came up behind her and clamped hands onto her shoulders, which made her jump.

'Don't worry, Ducey,' he whispered in her ear. 'He's bringing his launch.'

'Why?'

'I'll tell you. Come, we need to talk.'

He drew her away from the crowd and told her what had happened since she had left her house. By the time he'd reassured her that he was having the house checked by Dee-Dee, who would secure it before coming on to the dance, Philippe and Dee-Dee turned up. The latter actually danced with Alice, who, when the number had finished, came back laughing at something he had told her. When Danny asked what the joke was, they both exploded again, tears streaming from their eyes.

Food had been placed at the back of the hall and was now ceremoniously uncovered. The music stopped and everyone made a bee-line for the serious part of the evening: Eating.

'What are those?' asked Molly, intrigued by what looked like halves of knobby green pears, filled with something of a vivid red.

'Stuffed Merlitons,' said Marie. 'They're a special kind of squash stuffed with devilled crab. Go on- try. They good.'
Bert could not be persuaded, and chose a safe old sausage sandwich instead. He gasped and choked on the first bite.

'My God! What's in it?' he croaked.

All the locals around him collapsed with laughter.

'It's our Cajun Hot Sausage. We like the cayenne in our party food. Sobers us up - '

'- so we can drink some more!'

Danny gradually pulled a group of men away and they discreetly went through into a back room. Their meeting had been going on for a few minutes when the door opened and Bert poked his head round. Danny stopped talking; the other men looked at him.

'You better come in, Bert, seeing's it concerns ya'll.'

'Thanks.'

Philippe offered his seat to Bert.

'Most of you have met Bert.' Danny paused. 'I know, Bert, you think this is your business, but once those boys came into this neck of the woods it became ours, too. All of us aroun' here.' Everyone grunted agreement. 'We cain't go to the police without giving you up, which everyone knows ain't on the cards, so we have to protect ourselves.' Danny paused to let it sink in. 'First, ya'll need to know that these boys are dangerous and not beyond killing, so those who don't want to get mixed up in this should leave now. No-one will think the worse.' He paused again. No-one got up. 'Right: let's get to business. First; by now they know everything they need about me and Ducey. She cain't go back to the house until this is all over.'

'She'll stay with me and Louise.'

'Thanks, Jacques. I need to get back to N'Yawlins and prepare for getting these folks out of the country.'

'How long'll that take, Danny?' asked the shrimper captain.

'Hopefully, four or five days, Philippe. What you got in mind?'

'They can crew with me for that time, and I could bring them into the city with the catch.'

Suddenly Danny's mobile bleeped. He pulled it out and peered at the screen. He didn't recognise the number.

'Yeah?' he asked cautiously.

'Is that Danny Generve?'

'Who wants to know?'

'Enjoying the dance, Danny?' The Northern voice ended in a laugh.

Danny pressed the mute button. 'It's our boys. They know we're here, which means they're somewhere close.' Several men stood up and went to the door. 'Wait. That's what they want, like throwing a firework in the middle of a bunch of animals.' He held up his hand and released the mute button. 'What do you want?'

'The kid.'

'I suggest you're in the wrong neck of the woods to make demands.'

There was a long pause. 'I think we need to talk.'

'The last time you talked two people were found dead.'

'Well, you can't stay there all night.'

Danny gave a chuckle.

'You don't know how we Cajuns can party!' He switched the mobile off and placed it in his pocket. 'We need to get the folks onto Philippe's launch, but we can't do that until we know where these loons are. I reckon there're no more than three, they prob'ly left the flyer back at the motel. If it's just the two they'll be stretched to cover back and front.'

'There's one way to find out,' said Dee-Dee.

'And how do you propose to do that?'

'Go out there, get in my car and drive away.'

'What do you expect you can do when someone stops you with a gun, or more to the point, with a bullet?'

'I reckon they'll want to ask questions before they start shooting.'

'It's risky, Dee-Dee.'

'They'll let me get to my truck before stopping me. That's all I need.'

'I don't know.'

'D'y' have anything better in mind, Danny?'

'No I don't, but...'

Dee-Dee scraped his chair back and got up. 'That's all I needed to know.' He put his hand in his pocket and brought out a silver tube and placed it between his lips. Danny recognised the dog whistle, and gave a knowing smile.

Before Dee-Dee went out into the dark he picked up a bottle of beer, put his large thumb over the neck, and gave it a sharp shake. Once he had closed the door behind him it took him several seconds before he could make out anything. He stood swaying, trying to hear through the constant chirping of cicadas and night noises. To his left the slight sound of gravel grated. Good, he thought. At least it was the opposite side of him to his truck. Lifting the bottle to his mouth he took a pretend swig and staggered blindly forward.

Once he stumbled into a car, cursed, took another gulp of beer and staggered on. Finally he found the truck and as he reached out, fumbling with his keys for the lock, he heard the gravel shift behind him. Grunting, he slowly started to turn, staggered and fell back against the car parked by his side. As he lifted the bottle to take another swig he heard a click by his head. As if in a daze he faced the sound. The tip of his nose was a fraction away from the muzzle of a gun. His eyes opened wide and fearful, trying to focus beyond the revolver.

'Where's the kid?'

Dee-Dee staggered back, teetered and fell against the side of his wagon. Harvey moved with a limp towards him and held the muzzle hard against his cheek.

'Where's the kid?'

'You want money?' Dee-Dee slurred, struggled for his pockets and dropped his keys. 'My keys.'

'Fuck the keys.'

Dee-Dee staggered backwards, sliding along the side of the truck and felt his hip hit the door handle. A few feet more, he thought, and with his tongue pushed the shiny tube into position between his lips. Harvey followed him, trying to keep the barrel pressed against his face. He was starting to have doubts. Maybe he was just a drunk after all. This guy was too uncoordinated. Dee-Dee took another step until his back came up against his wing mirror. His hope was that Harvey would follow him, until he was adjacent to the driver's window.

Harvey was getting seriously agitated at the reaction of this drunken hick and grabbed at Dee-Dee's collar with his other hand and brought his face close.

'Where's the fuckin'...'

To his amazement he saw a silver tube slide out of Dee-Dee's mouth and his cheeks ballooned. There was a breathy sound and Harvey felt more than saw a dark shape crash into the side window by his face. His reaction was to turn his head towards the flying shadow and pull the gun round to fend off the attack. Dee-Dee brought up his hand with the beer bottle and released his thumb. The pent-up beer gushed out and upwards in a thick jet. At the same moment Harvey felt a searing pain travel from his groin like an express train. He opened his mouth to scream, but instead it became flooded with beer. Choking, his body crumpled around the pain. Blackness descended as Dee-Dee's ham of a fist slammed onto the back of his neck. Dee-Dee puffed out his cheeks again and the creature stopped its onslaught on the window and subsided to the floor.

52

Harvey came to with everything dark around him. He made to move but found it impossible. He felt hot breath from behind him and turned his head. There came a deep, rumbling growl.

'I shouldn't do that mister, if I were you. You likely have your face ripped off.'

Dee-Dee had been sitting patiently waiting for him to revive. Now he pressed the buttons on his mobile.

'Yo-ho, Danny, it's me. I'm parked down the road from y'all with one of the turkeys trussed up.' There was a replied mutter that Harvey couldn't make out. 'Hang on, I'll ask.' He took the phone from his ear. 'How many are you back there?'

'Fuck off.' Immediately a growl started up behind him, and he shrunk away.

'I shouldn't do that. Now there are two ways we can do this - the easy way or the painful way. Do you want a hole in the other foot? This time I'll use a screwdriver, and it ain't too clean.'

'Only one.'

'I don't believe you.'

Dee-Dee curled his chubby hand round a large screwdriver and bent forward and placed the tip on Harvey's good foot and raised his hand to slam it down on the handle. Harvey found that his legs were strapped to the seat and he couldn't move it away.

'I'm telling the truth.' He started to scream, but it changed into a whimper as the dog growled again.

'Duchess doesn't like noisy people. Remember; if you're lying you get the screw-driver *and* my dog.'

'There's only one,' he whispered.

'Danny - he says there's his brother - that's all. I'm inclined to believe him.' He prodded Harvey in the shoulder with his finger. 'What's his phone number?'

'Go to hell.'

Dee-Dee pressed down with his heel on Harvey's bad foot. Harvey screamed.

'He left the 'phone in the car.' Dee-Dee pressed harder. '987 000555.'

'Did you get that, Danny? Now mister, where's your car parked?'

'It's under some trees on the bar side of the road by the car park entrance.'

'Is that the truth?' Harvey nodded. 'I think the truth is still working, Danny. Yeah, sure. I'll hang on.' He held the phone close and idly looked at the man trussed with tape. Harvey eyed him back nervously. Suddenly Dee-Dee grabbed a roll of wide silver tape, tore some off and stuck it over his mouth.

'You'd better be right, or I'll be very angry, and so will Duchess here.' On cue, the dog growled. There was a murmur from the phone. Dee-Dee put it to his ear. 'Yeah, Danny. - You sure? Okay.' He closed the connection.

Dee-Dee then pressed out the number Harvey had given him. It rang four times before it was answered.

'Shit, Harvey,' Harry whispered. 'What do you want?'

Dee-Dee switched it off again and studied his watch. After a few minutes he pressed the re-dial. This time it rang twice.

'Fuck sake, Harvey!' Harry's voice was still a whisper.

'Are you Harvey's bro?' asked Dee-Dee cheerfully.

'Who the fuck?' There was a distinct snap of a twig.

'Hey, man, I shouldn't go stumbling about in the brush. You never know what you might tread on. Them 'gators are real mean.'

'Who the fuck is this?'

'Shit, man, you're making enough noise to waken the dead.'

'Where's Harvey?'

Dee-Dee bent towards Harvey, caught hold of the tape and yanked it hard. Harvey screamed. Dee-Dee looked at the tape with surprise.

'Shit, Harvey, I didn't mean to take your *mus*tache. Now tell that asshole to get into his car and go back home or you will become like ole J.C. Two holes in the feet and hands.' He shoved the phone in Harvey's face.

'Harry, get the fuck out of there. They're a load of madmen.'

Dee-Dee switched the phone off, and started the engine. He slid the truck into gear and slowly moved forward. They came off the verge and drove without lights along the road back to the bar. The edge of the road was barely visible. A hundred yards ahead a wash of light lay across the road. Into this ran a figure which stooped and yanked at something darker under the trees. A small light came on, showing that it was a car. The figure scrambled in, the light went out and the tail-lights came on.

Dee-Dee put his foot to the floor and switched his headlights full on. The engine roared and the truck lurched forward, gaining on the parked car. Suddenly from under the back wheels of the car came clouds of smoke and the tail end snaked as it came onto the road. Dee-Dee kept his foot to the floor and for good measure pressed his hand to the horn. Harvey's eyes widened as the truck bore down on the panicking Harry. The car in front gave a jolt and the rear wheels flew out from under it and swung off the road. The car dropped down and slid on in a blaze of sparks. Dee-Dee's truck caught up and tore into it, spinning it around and pushing it into a ditch.

'Shit, that was fun!' shouted Dee-Dee, when they had come to a standstill. 'I've heard about it, but I've never seen it done.'

Harvey watched as some figures appeared around the car and pulled a dazed Harry out from behind the wheel.

53

Taped together, the two brothers were dumped outside their hotel room and told to leave as soon as they could get the pilot out of bed.

'I don't think Quick-Buck-Duke is going to be hiring out any more cars in a hurry,' said Dee-Dee.

The wrecked car was sitting in the centre of the car lot. The rear axle stuck out through the windscreen.

'He'll probably ask you to put it right,' chuckled Danny.

'And that's a fact,' said Dee-Dee, and slapped Danny's leg. 'What happened with the old folks and the girl?'

'Once Harry had high-tailed it back to the car, Philippe took 'em out the back way and onto his launch.'

'You want dropping off at Philippe's?'

'Yeah. Marie's taken the car.'

'Tell me what happened after I left.'

'We watched you go to the car,' said Danny. 'You hadn't taken more than a few steps when Harvey crept out of the shadows, but there was no sign of Harry. We guessed he was round the back. That's when the Thierry boys shot out through the front. I got the rest of the lads to stand at all the windows and waited for you to call.

'The band stopped playing and we all listened for you to contact Harry. He was only a few yards from the back door; we heard him cuss. When you called him again he started stumbling about. What we didn't know was what our boys were up to. Hitching the fishing hawser to the tree and the car's rear axle was pure genius. A few of us piled out into the car park when Harry took off and watched you charge down on him with all lights blazing. He must've thought Old Nick was after him. He floored it! Well, you saw the rest.'

'Yeah, a sight never to be forgotten.' Dee-Dee let go of the steering wheel and slapped his hands together. 'Ver-boommm...'

Both men roared with laughter.

54.

Bert and Molly were still up with Philippe when the two friends walked through the door with cans of beer in their hands. Their laughter crumbled like the ashes of a dying fire when they saw the three sombre faces watching them silently from the kitchen table.

'Why aren't ya'll in bed?' asked Danny.

'We needed to talk to you about the arrangements.' said Bert. 'We don't want to seem ungrateful, but we're concerned about Alice. You and all these folk have been very kind and it seems it has brought danger into your very homes, but Molly and me need to know what's happening. This is all very confusing and downright bloody frightening.'

Molly tutted. 'Watch your language, Bert.'

'I'm sorry. It's like – well; since finding Alice we haven't caught breath.'

Danny pulled out a chair and sat down. He held the eyes of each in turn.

'I'm sorry. Things have happened so fast.' He paused and looked around the room. 'Where's Alice?'

'When Dee-Dee's truck hit that car she thought he was hurt, and she became hysterical. For all her resilience she is a very frightened child. The quicker we get her home the better.' Molly stopped and looked at Bert. 'Tell 'em Bert, about when her mother was murdered.'

'She had to walk through the room where her mother and stepfather had both been slaughtered. She stopped in front of 'em; wouldn't go any further until she'd had a good look. I've seen some sights in my time but this was the worst; there was blood everywhere.'

Danny put his hand to his brow and shook his head.

'Poor baby,' said Dee-Dee mournfully. 'That shouldn't happen to anyone. She's a kid.'

'But with the attention she receives from you men, and what that monster put her through, she thinks she's a woman when she's not. You must take more care!' Molly looked around pleadingly. 'You're good men, I know, and mean

171

nothing but good for her. You treat her like a princess. It would break her to see any of you hurt.'

Danny stretched out his hand, took hold of Molly's and squeezed it. Looking earnestly into her eyes, he spoke.

'Molly, we will take more care, but you must trust us. I don't think you realise what danger y'all are in. I brought you here because these are trustworthy people and I needed to hide you. The folks round here will close up tighter than an oyster shell when needed.' His eyes flitted to Philippe. 'We have ta make y'all disappear until I can arrange things, and the easiest way is to keep you on the move. When you come back to N'Yawlins no-one must recognise you.'

Molly bent towards him.

'And when will that be?'

'About three day's time, but I need to go back tomorrow.' He looked at his watch. 'I mean today. I can't explain everything because things might change. Alice and ya'll will be safe as long as you trust the people I send you to.' Danny smiled. 'Sometimes that might be hard, but you must try.'

Molly glanced at Bert who shifted uncomfortably.

'And you have to understand us, Danny. This is all very strange for us: we're not used to this.'

'I know, Bert. Believe me, nor am I.' Danny frowned. 'Someone wants Alice dead; she's met or seen someone very powerful. We can try and find out - or we can run like mad, away from this devil. I think it safer to run.'

Bert gave a deep sigh, and bowed his head. Molly's eyes, full of concern, saught Danny's. They all stayed motionless for some time. The silence was broken by Philippe.

'I think Danny is right.' He paused. 'All of you will come with me. They will be looking for an older couple with a child. Even in such a tight community as ours someone will talk.'

Molly nudged Bert's hand which still lay on the table. He raised his head. 'Alright; we'll do as you want, but do take care of yourself, Danny.'

'Don't worry. I mean to.'

55.

Danny was not quite sure what had woken him. The house was quiet and the night air still and heavy, the cicadas whirring. He felt something touch his shoulder and heard his name whispered. He turned in his bed and saw a shadowy shape standing over him. He started.

'Alice?'

'Danny, I can't sleep,' she whined.

Now fully awake, he pulled himself up into a sitting position, the sheet slipping from him and baring his chest.

'Can I get in?'

'No, peanut, you can't.'

As he looked at her, his eyes becoming accustomed to the gloom, he watched as in a dream as she slipped the over-large shirt off her shoulders and let it fall to the floor. The dim light coming into the room caught her budding breasts, boyish flanks and the whisper of hair at the vee of her legs. She bent forward and kissed him on the lips. He felt the tug of the sheet as she started to lift it. He slammed his hand down hard, pulling it out of her grip.

'No, Alice! Put your shirt on!'

'Danny, I'm scared. I had a bad dream.' She sobbed, then stammered on. 'I saw you - you with those men, but you weren't moving. I wanted to hug you but I couldn't. I wanted to love you.' Again she bent forward and crushed her mouth into his, fiercely. He stayed stiff and unyielding. She pulled away and looked steadily into his eyes.

'Don't you want to love me?'

He felt her eyes search him, pinning him into immobility like an animal before a spotlight. His dry mouth felt scratchy as he started to speak.

'I do love you, but...'

The sheet started to slide from under his hand. Coming to his senses he grabbed at it and pulled it firmly back out of her grasp.

'No, Alice. Pick up your shirt, put it on and go back to your room.'

His voice betrayed his emotion and a stupid thought flashed through his mind. He hadn't felt so out of his depth since he had made his first hesitant steps into manhood. With widening eyes he watched as she stepped back and started to stroke her hands over her body, one pushing and pressing a breast, the other wandering over her flat belly down to her crotch. She tilted her head, and looked from under her eyebrows.

'Don't you want me, Danny?' she asked huskily, and pouted, coquettishly.

If he had not felt so shaken by what she was doing he would have laughed at the parody. As it was he could see that this was not Alice, but a child trying to get what she wanted the only way she knew how.

'Alice.' This time his voice was steady. 'Pick up that shirt. Put it on - and go to bed.'

She groaned, and carried on stroking herself, undulating her body. He sighed and bent over the edge of the bed to retrieve the garment that lay like a white circle around her tiny feet, the sheet sliding over his hip. Alice stepped sideways; he thought, to move away from him, but too late he felt her press her undeveloped breasts into his shoulder and a hand stroke the small of his back and onto his hip, snaking downward under the sheet. He nearly toppled out of the bed as he withdrew the hand steadying himself to grab at hers to stop her touching him. His head banged on the floor, preventing him from sliding further. She giggled and pulled to remove her hand, but he held on firmly, fearing she would make another grab at him. She bent and bit his shoulder. His face jerked round, colliding with her crotch. The smell of cheap perfume and her own arousal invaded him. She giggled again and grabbed his penis. She gave a throaty chuckle.

'You do love me,' she said with glee and pressed herself harder onto his face. He relaxed his hand and she started to rub him, smothering his shoulder with kisses and holding his head into her. 'I love you, Danny, I love you.'

174

Deep down within he roared with panic, and with all the strength in his abdomen he pulled himself, with Alice on top of him, upright. She flew off him and landed on the other side of the bed. As quick as a cat she scrabbled back, but he caught her arms and pinned them to her side.

'Stop!' He whispered sharply in her ear.

She stopped pushing and looking into his panicked face. All she saw there was anger. Her shoulders slumped and she crumpled into a torrent of crying, once more a frightened little girl. Carefully, he pulled the shirt over her shoulders and wrapped it around her.

'You don't love me,' she sobbed.

'Not like that, Alice. No.'

Tears streamed down her face and sobbing wracked her body, making her tremble. Slowly he held her to him, gently rocking and patting her head.

'Hush now, little one.' His eyes smarted for her pain. Fuck those bastards who had ruined her, he cursed silently.

A little time passed and as her sobbing diminished she lifted her tear-stained face.

'Danny?'

'Yes.'

'Why don't you love me?' She gave a little croaked sob.

'Oh, little Missy, I do love you, but not that way,' he said gently, as he stroked her hair. 'You don't need that from me. Now go to sleep.'

With that she dropped her head onto his chest. He waited some minutes in the darkness. Thinking how his body had started to react, he felt ashamed. He put her from him, stood up and wrapped the sheet round his nakedness. For some time he stood over her, aware of her frailty, curled up like a baby, defenceless. Picking her up he took her back to her room and laid her down, tenderly covering the little woman-child.

On the bedside table he noticed the gold chain with the plastic tabs attached. He picked it up. He wasn't sure what it was, but he'd seen something similar in a computer mag. The latest gadget.

'Alice, Alice.' He shook her gently until she became awake. 'Where did you get these from?'

'They belonged to Lewis,' she said sleepily. 'I took it from him; he'd said it was an insurance policy.'

'Can I have them?'

'Why?'

'I don't know, but I think it could be important.'

'Sure. Can I go to sleep now?'

'Yes,' he whispered, and left the room.

In the darkness between the two bedrooms he felt a hand touch his arm. It made him jump.

'You're a good guy, Danny Generve.'

He stood silent, unable to speak. He felt the warmth of her body as she bent into him. Her hand groped and found his and felt the chain and tabs.

'What's that?'

'Something Alice had. I've taken it for safe keeping.'

'Is it something to do with the mess she's in?'

'I don't know.'

She squeezed his hand and moved away; he followed. By the bed she reached up and removed the winding-sheet from his shoulder and dropped it to the ground.

'Get into bed,' she whispered.

She lifted the bed-sheet and he lay back watching her as she dropped it back over him, covering his groin. He felt the early dawn chill lie on his skin, but he made no attempt to cover himself.

Taking the hem of her night-gown she slowly lifted it over her head, revealing first her flared hips, then the dark clump of hair and her slightly rounded belly. Finally, he studied her woman's heavy breasts, nipples sharply outlined, so different from the child's. Her head reappeared from the billow of cloth and she smiled. Climbing onto the bed she moved over him and kissed his chest. There was no cheap perfume now, just the smell of herself. She slipped flat down by his side and pulled the sheet up. Her hand moved down on to his stomach and he started to respond. He buried his head in her breasts and held her tightly. With a butterfly's touch, her fingers moved over his body.

'Marie?'

'Yes?'

'I started to react to her.'

'It's no wonder.'

'What do you mean?'

'Christ, Danny; she may be little more than a child, but she has had more experiences than most women, poor thing.'

'But...'

'For Christ's sake, you're not a monk. Danny: you didn't do anything! Now shut up, lay back and close your eyes. Relax and enjoy.'

'Marie?'

'What?'

'Thanks for not barging in.'

He saw the corners of her lips lift. 'Now shut up.'

She started chasing her fluttering fingers down his body with nibbling kisses.

'Marie?'

'What now?' she sighed with exasperation

'Do that again. It felt great.'

They both giggled.

56

Fenwick met Dwight in the breakfast bar on Magazine Street. The morning rush-hour traffic sped past the window, but neither noticed it.

'So are we going back out there?' asked Fenwick.

'What's the point? Even if he takes them down through Texas to the border, he'll still have to come back here first.'

'Why do you think that? Surely he could arrange to take them on from where they are.'

'Several reasons.' Dwight paused, raising his eyebrows meaningfuly. 'I went back into his place last night.'

'You've been busy. Why didn't you let me know?'

'Because it's illegal, and the fewer people involved the better. Anyhow, I had a hunch and I wanted to try it out.'

'What was that?'

'I wanted to find his passport.'

'And did you?'

'Yeah; also got his mobile number and his card accounts. Plus I found out he has another car and that was gone. If he uses his mobile, his plastic, or crosses into Texas, we'll know where he's going.'

'If you give me the details I can get the plastic and the mobile monitored.'

Dwight shook his head.

'Why not, for God's sake?'

'Until I know what you guys are about it's on a need-to-know basis. Anyhow, I can monitor it all myself.' Dwight leaned back in his chair and studied Fenwick for a few seconds.

'What?' asked Fenwick, mystified and annoyed.

'Nothing. This mess is tying itself into more knots than a 'ho's stocking.' Dwight remembered vividly the late night phone call he'd had from the sheriff out at Bayou Teche County. It seemed Danny had other visitors there from the big city; two men who'd left the area quickly in a helicopter.

How they had found out about him was difficult to imagine, unless someone in the department had been talking.

Only Fenwick, Smith and himself had known of Danny's connection and where he could possibly be. Further enquiries revealed that the brothers had arrived in the area at the same time as themselves. It was too much of a coincidence.

'I believe Danny will need to bring these people back to town. We shall be waiting.' He decided not to mention another theory he had, which was that Danny would try to get to New Jersey. His old buddy Arran Marx would probably have contacts in Canada. Barasitch had come from there so it was logical to think the tracing had started from the same place. 'We've got another problem.'

'What's that?'

'Gene MacIntyre has disappeared.'

'Shit, that's all we need.' Fenwick slammed his cup down on the table. The breakfast bar went quiet as people turned to stare. 'When did you find out?'

'Moments before you got here. He was supposed to be on duty this morning.'

'So he overslept.'

'No. His wife said he left to go on duty, and Stella here,' – he flitted his eyes towards the woman talking to a customer - 'gave him breakfast. He always comes here. It seems he was visited by a couple of men and they left together - didn't even finish his food. And before you ask, they don't fit the Dancer Brothers, but that don't mean much.'

57

It was late morning when Danny rode down towards his office in a black Honda Eleven Hundred Super-Blackbird. He had been in the city for a few hours and had made contact with MacIntyre before the cop had gone on duty. After talking to Gene he'd gone downtown to the French Quarter. He needed to arrange new identities and a few other things he couldn't do over the phone before going back to his place.

He drove the powerful bike without hesitation, up into a driveway across the road from the office. The neighbours were already away at work. He dismounted, and swiftly approached the front door. Within a few seconds he was in. Anyone watching would have assumed he owned the place. He placed his helmet on the ground as he passed to the stairs. The front bedroom door was open; he dropped to the floor and crawled to the window. It was on a level with his office.

As he peered over the sill the top of his desk could be seen, with the telephone sitting squarely in the middle. It was not the usual place for either the phone or the desk. Pulling a mobile from his pocket, he rang Gene. Suddenly a shadow flashed across the office window.

'Shit,' he cursed and switched off the phone.

He watched as the shadow flashed back. He slumped back against the wall under the window in deep thought. .

Tapping out Gene's number again, he waited for it to be answered.

'Hi, Gene it's me.'

'Hi Danny.' He answered with a gasp.

'Can you meet me at my place in thirty minutes?'

There was silence; the mute button had been pressed. Danny tapped his office number into his neighbour's phone. It started to ring. The mute button was released and he could hear Gene's stertorous breath, and above it his own ringing phone. He slammed down the handset and instantly the ringing phone stopped.

Gene spoke; 'Sure, Danny.'

'Oh, Gene, you still there?'

'Yeah.'

'Tell those mother-fucking killers you got with you at my place that I want to talk to them.' There was a flurry of noise, and then another voice spoke.

'Yeah?'

'You want the kid?'

'Yeah.'

'Go fuck yourself.'

'Listen to this, smartass.' There were two loud shots. The phone went dead.

From the window across the street came two gun flashes. He started to get up, but stopped. It was no good rushing in there. Gene was already dead. After a minute the men came out of his house, looked up and down the street then walked off, disappearing around the corner.

He let himself out by the kitchen door, clambered over the back fence and into the neighbouring yard. From the corner of that house he watched the men get into a car. He recognised Harry. They drove off.

He waited five minutes before he entered his own house and quickly climbed the stairs. As he opened the office door he gagged on the smell of gas. He put his hand over his nose and mouth and saw Gene slumped in a chair, blood dripping from his hands. They were mangled. Poor bastard! He understood now why Gene had set him up. 'It's okay, fella,' he whispered, 'I'll get those mothers.'

The door to his kitchen was open wide. As he went into the room he didn't notice a lit candle sitting on top of a filing cabinet. He checked the cooker; saw the taps were wide open and threw himself at the window as the top floor of the house disintegrated around him.

Harry watched with a smile as the fireball rose into the sky, then tapped his driver on the shoulder. As the car moved off he relaxed back into his seat in gleeful satisfaction. It couldn't have been better! Danny had been in the centre of the house when it blew.

58.

Dwight leaned against his car, gawping at the smouldering wreck. He felt a tap on his arm. It was Fenwick, still inside.

'What you waiting for?'

'To see what they come up with.' He was watching the firemen sift through the ruins. One stepped through two upright smouldering posts - what had once been the front door. He came over to Dwight, who pushed himself upright.

'What you got, Jamie?'

'A body, and before you ask, it's in a mess. It'll take some time to make an ID and that would be easier with a head. D'you want to see?'

'Sure.' Dwight trailed after him, into the smoking pile. 'What caused the explosion?'

'A cooker. All the taps are open.'

He looked at the tangled mess in the corner. The smell of burned flesh was almost overwhelming.

'You can make sense out of that?'

'Just about, but it's still a theory just now. Conclusions might change, but I doubt it.' They stopped. 'Here's what's left of the cadaver.'

A blackened trunk, with part of a thigh, was lying before Dwight, all clothing completely burnt off. He shook his head and turned away to trudge out of the building and back to Fenwick.

'Bad.'

It was more a statement than a question.

'You could say that. Well, if it's Danny, we need to get back to the bayous and find those people. The news will break pretty fast. I think we'll go by chopper this time.' He got into the car and started the engine.

59.

The sheriff of Bayou Teche was waiting in his car as the helicopter touched down. This time his greeting was less abrasive.

'You boys don't give up, do you?'

'What we're looking for this time is a bit different.'

'Yeah,' said the sheriff. 'And who's looking for Danny's killers? 'cause you ain't going to find them out here!'

'You've heard, then?'

'Yeah; it's all over the bayous. Danny was a popular guy in these parts, so you ain't gonna get a skeeter's scream from no-one.' He spat in the dust at Fenwick's feet.

Or any help out of you, either, thought Dwight.

'I s'pose you want to meet Miss Ducey?'

'You s'pose right.'

The sheriff opened the door of the car.

'Y'all better get in. I'll take you to her.'

Mrs Lapitte showed the men into a darkened room. Ducey was slumped in a chair, staring blankly at a television in the corner of the room. The screen flickered with images but there was no sound. Dwight and the other two men stood on the threshold of the room, staring at her.

'I'll leave you alone,' whispered Mrs Lapitte.

'Thanks.'

She moved quietly away pulling the door shut behind her. Still they waited; silent, uncertain.

'You com' 'bout my boy.' The statement sounded flat and dead above the hum of the television. She didn't look up.

'Yes, Mrs Generve.' Dwight moved toward her. 'I'm Detective Usner. May I sit down?'

Ducey slowly turned her head until her eyes were locked with his.

'Sure,' she said finally. After a long scrutiny of Dwight she shifted her gaze to the other men before moving back to the silent action on the television.

Dwight sat across from her. 'This here's Mr Fenwick and Mr Smith. They're with a government agency.'

Ducey ignored the two men and spoke to Dwight.

'What do you want? Danny's dead. That's all I know.' She stared bleakly at him.

'We don't know that; not for certain.'

'What do you mean? Sheriff's been round and told me that Danny's place had blown up, and his body was found.'

'Sure, but it hasn't been identified yet.'

'You mean it could be someone else?' A little hope seeped into her voice.

'The problem is - the explosion was so bad that he - the body - is not recognisable. Even the normal dental check can't be done.' He clucked sympathetically.

'What do you mean?'

There was a silence. Dwight gulped audibly, before saying 'There is no head. We can't find it. Sorry, Ma'am.'

Ducey gasped and held her head in her hands, rocking backwards and forwards, making short gurgling noises. After a while she stopped, and became quiet. 'If you don't know who it is then what are you doin' here? Cain't you leave me to my grievin'?''

'We need to ask some questions about the people he brought to your house.'

'What people would they be?'

'Mrs Generve; we know he brought out an older man and woman, and a child – here, to your house. We searched it last night and found evidence of their stay.' Dwight sought her eyes. 'We need to talk to these people because we don't think that Danny's possible death was an accident.'

'They wouldn't do such a thing.'

'Sure; but the people chasing them would.'

'What, those boys they chased out last nigh...' It was out before she had realised. Bending her head away from him, she hid her face.

'What happened last night?' The voice was Smith's. It was sharp and hard, and what filtered through to Ducey was– Northern.

She jerked her head up at the new voice and frowned. So did the others. Dwight gave a sharp shake of his head to stop Smith going further. He looked back to Ducey and leant forward. Taking her hands between both his, he squeezed gently. She gazed at him before turning away again.

'Mrs Generve, there is so much we need to know if we're to find these people and stop this from going further. Let me briefly tell you what we do know: That Danny has been helping an old couple and a child and they're hiding somewhere out here: That the old people are English and came to New Orleans to find their grandchild. We know the mother and her husband were into nasty things and were using the kid.

'The mother and husband were brutally murdered, but for some reason the girl survived. We think we know who did the killings, but we don't have any proof.

'Somehow the grandparents found her and took her to their hotel. We now know that one of the killers was already waiting inside. They escaped with Danny's help and were chased through Uptown N.O. before escaping out here. Now your son is possibly dead. We believe the same killers had something to do with it - and I know you can help us.' He paused to let it sink in. 'What we don't know is the reason they are searching for the little girl.' His voice ended gently.

'What do you want to know?'

'Why haven't the English couple come to us?'

'I don't know.' She looked mystified. 'Danny said they couldn't; it wasn't even safe to go to the police. He was trying to help. I didn't need to know more.'

Dwight glanced sharply at Fenwick, who gave a shrug.

'Why couldn't they come to us?'

'He didn't say and I didn't ask.'

'Where are they now?'

'Went back with Danny early this morning. Wasn't safe here any longer.'

Dwight sighed. 'You sure?'

Ducey kept quiet. She couldn't trust her voice.

'Did you see the men who were chased out last night?'

'No, the menfolk took care of it.'

'We need to talk to your menfolk.'

Ducey stayed silent.

'Your people won't get into trouble, but they must've got darn close and can identify the killers.' He squeezed her hands again. 'Help us find Danny's killers.'

Something held him back from mentioning their real quarry. Ducey stared long and hard at Dwight, till he thought 'She won't break'.

'You might talk to Dee-Dee. He and Danny are - were, good friends. He's got a garage back-aways. You with the sheriff?' Dwight nodded. 'He'll know where to find him.'

'Thanks, Mrs Generve.' He had noticed the 'were' good friends. 'Hold up now; the body may not be Danny's.'

'It is,' she said bleakly. 'I know it. I feel it here.' She crushed her clenched fist into her left breast.

'Can I have your permission to take something personal of his?'

'Why?'

'We need a DNA sample to verify whether it is Danny or not.'

Ducey scrutinised Dwight. 'When you mean personal, do you mean clothes?'

'Yes. Preferably something he's worn recently.'

'You'll find some in the laundry basket; I didn't have time to wash 'em. You'll tell me as soon as you know?'

'You'll be the first.'

60.

Dee-Dee was under Danny's car when the phone rang. At first he let it ring until he couldn't stand it any more. He dragged himself out from under, rubbed his greasy hands on his overalls and picked up the 'phone. It was Mrs Lapitte. She told him about the visit to Ducey and how she had mentioned his name.

He got back under the car and waited. No more than twenty minutes passed until the sheriff shouted his name and walked into the garage, the other three following. He stopped by Dee-Dee's feet, which where poking out.

'Dee-Dee, I 'spect you know I was bringing some people to see you.'

'Yep. What do they want?'

'You know about Danny?'

'Yep. I know about Danny.' There was a sound of tapping as though he had decided to carry on working.

'Dee-Dee; I ain't going to carry on a conversation with your feet, and neither is this officer, so will you come out?'

'Nope. Tell him to come under.'

The sheriff gave Dwight a shrug.

'He hasn't said he won't talk to you; all he's done is choose where he wants to do it. I don't think he's breaking the law, so if you want to chat...' He held his hands out as if to say "it's beyond my control."

Dee-Dee's voice came from beneath the car: 'Tell him he can lie on the skid-board; it's leaning against the wall.'

Dwight sighed and lying down on the board, pulled himself under. Dee-Dee was still tapping with his hammer. Fenwick and Smith got close on the other side of Dee-Dee and crouched down to hear what he was saying. Suddenly, a jet of oil came out from under the car and landed on Smith's shoes. He swore, and both men jumped back and stood up. The sheriff moved back to the door to hide his amusement.

'It seems Dee-Dee don't like you listenin',' he muttered under his breath.

Dee-Dee kept up the tapping.

'Good. The Suits don't like getting dirty,' he whispered.

'Okay, stop the racket and let's talk.'

'Danny said not to trust anyone, but that you were straight.'

'You talked to Danny today?'

'No. Wadja think? Yesterday.'

'Where's the old couple and the child?'

'Back in N'Yawlins. Danny took 'em back.'

'Do you know where in New Orleans they could be?'

'Nope; I didn't know Danny's business.'

Dwight put his hand in his pocket and struggled awkwardly to pull out some pictures.

'They're the boys who came visitin' us last night.'

'I heard you had some fun.'

'Sure did.' The smile died on his face before it really started. 'I wish we'd fed 'em to the 'gators! We will if they come out here agin. They're damn killers.'

'So do you know who they are? Who sent 'em?'

'Danny said they're called the Dancer Twins, 'cos of their method of doin' business.'

'Then how did Danny get himself caught, if he knew about them?'

'He said he had to go back and pick something up, but he thought he could do it without being noticed. Said he was more worried about you cops than those thugs. There was something that Danny said that keeps nagging at the back of my mind.'

'What's that?'

'How come they found out he was involved, and knew where to come? He knew you found his calling card in the kid's bedroom, but there was nothing to link him to her as far as those hoods knew.'

'Maybe they traced him through the car plates. They did chase him right through Uptown.'

'That's stupid. He was riding on fake plates at the time.'

'Yeah, I thought as much. Maybe we got careless and they followed us.'

'Nope, that's not it, because they got here before you. They dropped in on Ducey's house and then flew off again moments before you arrived.'

'What do you mean, flew off again?'

'Helicopter, Lieutenant. We traced their flight back to N'Yawlins, but couldn't get no further, jist like someone didn't want us to know. After leaving the house they flew back to Morgan City and started asking questions. They taxied into town to find a hotel, but before they got there they stopped and hired a car.'

'You seem to know a lot about their movements.'

'Let's say we're one big happy family out here.'

'So you went in and roughed them up.'

'No. They found out where we were meeting and gave us a surprise, but not as big a surprise as they got.'

'Yeah, I can imagine, if Danny had anything to do with it.' Both men chuckled.

Dee-Dee pulled a slip of paper out of his pocket and gave it to Dwight.

'The chopper's number is written down, plus the pilot's name and the time it left N'Yawlins.'

'Thanks.' Dwight grabbed hold of the chassis to slide out, but he felt himself being held back.

'There is something else Danny would want me to tell you.' Dwight frowned. 'The reason why neither he nor the old people went to you is that someone somewhere seems always to find out what is happening whenever it concerns the kid: like immediately. Danny was trying to find a way to bring Alice in without jeopardising her safety. He thinks someone big somewhere has a lot to lose and it's got to do with that Internet shit the kid was used for. He took them back to find the reason; otherwise they'd be halfway to Mexico by now.'

61.

They had finished their lunch and Dwight was sipping his coffee. He looked speculatively over the rim at Fenwick.

'What?' Fenwick frowned.

'I don't know. I got this feeling Danny went back alone and left the old folks and the kid behind.'

'Why do you think that?'

'Well, what would you do? We're on his tail and so are the Dancers. He's got to get back to the city to find out what's going on, and quickly.'

'So how do we set about a local search?'

They all gazed at the sheriff, who was leaning against the door.

'You ain't got a hope in hell. They're probably in another county by now, being passed along,' he muttered.

'We still got that APB out on them.'

'Are you crazy? I haven't got enough men. Within five minutes of me sending out a call they'll know the search is on again. People 'roun' here don't use just roads to get around on. neither. There's miles of waterway out there.' He shook his head. 'Shit, I could board a boat out there and not need to step back on dry land until I got to the middle of Ohio.'

Dwight glanced at Fenwick.

'If anyone knows where they are, it will be Dee-Dee.'

'So?' Fenwick raised his eyebrows.

'We put agent Smith to tail him.'

'Mister, you are crazy!' shouted the sheriff. 'That guy will stick out like a nun in a brothel.'

'I know, but it will make Dee-Dee cautious; slow him down; give us time to get a grip on things. Everything's been goin' way too fast. They've got us chasing our tails.'

'So I'm supposed to sit in a car outside his garage and follow him when he goes out,' Smith commented sourly.

'Yeah.'

The sheriff took a sharp intake of breath, decided he didn't want anything to do with it, and left the room.

'And what will you two be doing while I'm shadowing our friendly greaseball?'

'We'll be back in New Orleans, busy detecting,' Dwight said in a bland tone.

On the way back to the chopper, Fenwick turned to Dwight.

'How long do you think before Dee-Dee shakes off his tail?'

Dwight pursed his lips. 'Not long.'

'So why did you set him up?'

'The same reason you let me have him.'

'Meaning?'

'How is it that when we find a trail the Dancers get there before us? By the time we got here they'd beaten us to it.'

'There's one thing knowing, and another proving.'

'I need a breathing space, and from what you didn't say last night, so do you.'

Fenwick said nothing; but stared musingly out at the scenery. A minute passed before he opened his mouth again.

'Have you thought that an out-of-sight Mr Smith could cause some trouble?'

'Not much harm out here, - except phone his buddies.'

'I don't think so.' Dwight glanced at Fenwick in surprise. The agent drew out a mobile phone and they both laughed.

'How did you get that?'

'When we both tried to get through the door together.'

Dwight shook his head in disbelief, then a thought struck him.

'Sheriff, can you make sure he obtains another mobile?'

'Sure.'

'I appreciate that. Could you go one better?'

'What's that?'

'I'm sure you know your friendly mobile dealer. Get details of the purchase; name, number,account.' The sheriff gavea nod. 'Thanks, it's been good doing business with you.'

62.

With a gesture of disgust Smith threw the phone onto the seat next to him. He had made four calls in the last hour and no-one had answered. What was going on? The sun had been beating down on the car roof for what seemed an eternity and he was sweating like a pig. The mechanic was still inside his garage and didn't seem likely to leave soon.

It was a shock when Dee-Dee appeared in the doorway, staring across at him. He took a slug on a bottle of coke, gave a wave and sauntered over with a grin plastered over his face. When he reached the car he crouched down until his eyes were on a level with Smith's.

'I hear you have to keep a watch on me and follow wherever I go.' He squinted up at the sun. 'Shit, it's hot out here.' He rolled the dewed bottle of coke across his forehead. 'Mister, why don't you find a tree to shade under and have a shut-eye? I'm not leaving till five and that's three hours from now.' At that he got up and walked away. The mother, thought Smith, the bastard's trying to goad me. He slumped down in the seat and accepted that he was in for a long, hot wait.

Nearly two hours had passed and Smith was feeling decidedly groggy from all the heat. His head ached like hell. The side doors of the garage slid open with a clang and the car that Dee-Dee had been working on rolled out on to the forecourt. With a sudden cloud of dust from the back wheels and roar of throaty engine, the car came up onto the road and sped away.

'Shit,' shouted Smith. He sat up quickly and started his engine, to rush after the disappearing car. It was not hard to follow its dust; fine stuff that stuck to his forehead like flies to a tack strip. Suddenly Smith shot out into clear air, to find the dust trail had gone off at right-angles on itself. He cursed again, swung round and headed back after it. The road was no more than a track and the dirt-cloud even denser. He had been going for about a mile or so and had decreased his speed when the track became smoother and the air slightly clearer. He started to accelerate. He hit a ramp.

A main road ran immediately across his path. He jammed on his brakes and came to a screeching, sliding halt on the other side of the road. In front of him was water. It started right below him and it stretched as far as he could see. To his left, Dee-Dee's car was disappearing into the distance. He swung doggedly back onto the road and gave chase again. At least there was no dust now. Perhaps that ape thought he had shaken him off. He would show him.

There had been no turnings for ten minutes and he started to feel he recognised the place when Dee-Dee's garage came into view. The car was on the forecourt with the hood up. Dee-Dee's big bottom and legs were all that could be seen of him. The rest of him was under the hood. Smith drove onto the forecourt and rolled to a halt by the side of the car. He stuck his head out of the window.

'What the fuck did you do that for?' he shouted.

Slowly Dee-Dee emerged from under the hood and studied him perplexedly.

'What do you mean, mister?' he asked innocently.

'Charging off like a crazy...'

'Oh, that! I was test-running the car. Always do it after a service.'

'You nearly got me killed.'

'What? You mean you followed me?' Dee-Dee slapped his thigh and gave a belly laugh. 'Sheeit, no wonder you look so dusty. Hell, I told you I wouldn't be leaving before five.' Still bubbling with laughter he popped his head back under the hood, ignoring Smith's glare. He couldn't have been more eloquent; he had no time for idiots. Smith decided he wasn't going to win, and turned off his engine. At least he could get out of the car and stretch his legs.

'Do you have a coke machine?' he asked.

'No.' It was more of a mumble coming from under the hood. 'But if you want one, they're in the chiller inside.'

'Thanks.'

Smith wandered through the large open doors into the cooler air of the dim workshop. Odd bits and relics of long-gone automobiles hung from every beam, covered in a thick coat of dust and linked together by festoons of cobwebs. He ambled around, trying to guess which model this belonged to and what long sleek ghost that had come from, until he forgot what he had come in for. He heard Dee-Dee shuffling behind him. A coke bottle was thrust in his face. He took it, nodding his thanks.

Dee-Dee raised his own bottle to his mouth, clamped his teeth down hard on the cap, and gave a sharp twist. There was a hiss, and without withdrawing the bottle from his mouth he spat the metal cap out. Smith looked at his own bottle in dismay. It still had the cap securely on.

'Do you have a bottle-opener?'

'Use your teeth, mister; that's what they're for.'

'I paid a lot to keep these teeth the way they are.'

Dee-Dee stuck out his hand, took the bottle and raised it to his mouth.

'What a pussy,' he muttered, and gave the bottle a sharp twist. The cap ejected out of his mouth and landed at Smith's feet. Dee-Dee handed back the bottle and moved through the clutter of his garage, staring up at the pieces of the past. 'This is my art gallery,' he said proudly. 'You can look, but don't touch. We'll be going soon.'

Smith's new phone started to bleep in his pocket. He pulled it out and put it to his ear.

'Yeah?'

'Hi, Smith; it's Harry here. You ain't doing any good out there, you asshole.'

The phone went dead. Smith stared at it in disbelief. He jerked round as a hand fell on his shoulder.

'You ready, mister? It's time for me to go.'

Dee-Dee offered a lift in his car, but the agent said he would follow. The Cajun gave a Gallic shrug and said 'You can take me, instead. Same difference.'

Smith wanted to refuse. He knew there would be a catch, but he was unwilling to be Dee-Dee's passenger, as it would

194

be too easy for him to be stranded. What really worried him was that phone call, and how the Dancers had his number. While he was out here kicking his heels it would be impossible to find answers, and he had no idea what Fenwick and Usner were up to. He was also trying to work out how he'd lost his phone. Still and all, although inconvenient, it had not taken long to replace it.

They had been travelling no more than a few minutes when Dee-Dee asked Smith to pull over. He'd been expecting something of the sort and was prepared. His gun was ready to hand under his seat, and he knew the Cajun did not know about it, so he stopped. They came to a halt by a small jetty. At the end of it was Dee-Dee's boat that Danny had borrowed the day before.

'What now?' asked Smith.

'Nothing, mister. Thanks for the lift!' At that Dee-Dee got out and started down the jetty towards his boat. Smith swung out and raced after him.

'Wait. Where are you going?'

'For a boat ride.'

'You can't do that.'

'Wanna bet?'

Smith put his hand to his holster. It was empty. In the rush to follow Dee-Dee he had left his gun under his seat. He raced back to the car and scrabbled for it, but it was gone.

Dee-Dee's shout made him turn. He stood at the end of the jetty holding something up in his hand. 'Is this what you're looking for?' He spun round and tossed the gun far out into the water. 'Goodbye, Yankee!' He dropped down into the boat and started the motor. It coughed into life and sped away into the dying day.

In a little over an hour it would be dark. Smith decided to go back and search the garage. There was sure to be an address book or something in the poky office. It took him a second or two to free the padlock. Inside, the place was dim, but Smith could still see that the car the mechanic had been working on all day had gone. He had watched him drive it into the workshop and lock the door before climbing in and

folks are still out in Cajun country. They will need to come back into the city, either separately or all together. My guess is separately. When I don't know; but again I think Danny Generve came back here to get false papers, and that would take a couple of days. So; tomorrow I want you on to all of your contacts and pick up any whispers from the street.' He stopped, scrutinising the faces around him.They all looked as tired as he felt. 'Go home and get some sleep. There will be two officers monitoring things here so leave contact numbers if you go out this evening. If anything comes up I want to get on to it straight away.'

Slowly the room emptied, leaving Dwight and Fenwick alone. Fenwick handed over a slip of paper. Dwight glanced at it and chuckled.

'Our suspicions were right. The Dancers have been in touch with him. What do you want to do?'

'Nothing. It seems he's been locked up for breaking and entering. I'm sure those hicks can hold on to him for a couple days, and by then things should be sorted out.'

'Yeah, keep him on ice until we have time to deal with him.' Dwight went to the window and watched lights of evening traffic surge through the crowded streets and away into the distance. 'Well; I'm off home. Can I give you a lift?'

64.

It was dark and the moon was yet to rise. Dee-Dee kept the boat to the middle of the channel. The purring engine, which he held steady, left an unbroken white ribbon of wake that disappeared into the darkness behind him. He opened the ice-chest and pulled out a beer. Sam, who could always be relied on to help him out had done good; a po'boy stuck out of the chest as well. Dee-Dee settled back. There was a long way to go; he'd eat that later. When he came to the busy areas he put on his lights, so he didn't get run down. He kept away from the bank where watchers could spot him, and so his passage through a darkening world went unnoticed. After leaving Smith on the jetty he had at first headed west, but doubled back once the agent had got into his car and driven off back to the garage.

He had been so certain that Smith would break in that he had not waited for proof before calling the cops. Well, he'd said he thought someone had been hanging about all day, casing the joint. Sam had snuck in and taken Danny's car as soon as Smith and he had left, so it would have been a surprise to Smith to now find the place empty. The test drive had been interesting, too. He had waited on the levee road for Smith to shoot up off the track. The guy had good reactions to have stopped the car from going into the water on the other side. He had not relied on shaking him off, and was glad he had arranged with Sam to come and move his boat upstream. He wondered how long it would take for Smith to extract himself from jail. Hopefully, a day or two. It all depended on whether Smith did his city-boy act.

Dee-Dee pressed on, the remorseless drone of the engine unchanging for hour after hour. He was making for his uncle's place out at Grand Isle, but his journey would only end when he boarded the shrimper.

65.

Dwight got out of his car. Behind him the red sun was sinking below the trees. He was glad to see lights on all over the house. His son's music was blaring out of an open window on the second floor and he could hear the two girls arguing in back. He shook his head, glad things were normal here. The door opened and Donny's girlfriend came out.

'Hi! Mr Usner.'

'Hi, Sharon. Not staying?'

'No, I've got to get home. See ya.'

'Yeah.'

He watched her walk down the block. Donny should have walked her home. 'Kids,' he thought and going inside, he called out. No one seemed to hear. He walked on through, opened the fridge and took out a beer. Fran, her back towards him, was shouting at the girls. He went over and snaked an arm around her waist. She jumped.

'Hi, you startled me!' She turned and gave him a peck on the cheek. 'Y'all home for the night?'

'Hope so. Got any food ready?'

'No, the kids have already eaten, but it won't take long. Why doncha take a shower?'

'Sure, but I'll drink this first.' He raised the can of beer. 'I met Sharon at the front door. Shouldn't Donny be walking her home?' Fran let the flyscreen close on the girls' row. He gave his wife a kiss and went to find his son.

After chiding Donny he went into the bathroom and stripped off and got under the shower. It was not until a little later when he was emptying his pockets of money that he found the slip of paper that Fenwick had given him showing Smith's communication with the Dancer twins. There was a list of four attempted numbers; none to New Orleans, and none had been connected. Under these was the known number of the Dancers, but it was *to* Smith not from him. Dwight thought it strange. Perhaps he'd contacted them first from a land phone. It didn't make sense. He picked up his own phone and called a friend in Washington.

Dwight sat over dirty dishes talking with his wife, the house now quieter with the sound of the television and Donny's music at a more reasonable level. Fran got up and started to clear the table. Dwight caught hold of her hand.

'Why don't you go up and get ready for bed? Let me clear these things and stack the washer. I'll lock up. I won't be long.'

'Okay. Promise.'

'Sure.'

The kitchen took minutes to straighten and Dwight had switched off the yard light when he heard someone call his name. He saw a shadow flit across the dark corner of the yard. He opened the door.

'Who's there?' His voice was no more than a whisper, he wasn't sure why.

The figure came further into the yard, and the wash from the kitchen light caught his face.

'Usner, we need to talk.'

Dwight never did get his early night, but by the early hours of the morning what his visitor had told him had been acted on. The friend from Washington had been back on the phone and things were starting to clarify in Dwight's mind. He had always thought this case was strange. His contact couldn't give him much; only that it had ramifications that crossed international borders. There were whispers that it had to do with powerful people; also children, porn and the Internet.

There seemed to be a desperate search by the underworld, with tentacles that spread into government circles – and all for that kid. He also confirmed that Smith was with the bureau and had been working on exotic cases for the last couple of years. As for Fenwick; he wasn't sure where he came in. Where he came *from* was a mystery. There was a note of caution in his contact's voice, and Dwight realised that the fewer people who discovered what he knew, the better. Those he didn't know or trust needed to be kept at arm's length, but how to do it without arousing suspicion?

66.

The sun was also going down over the shrimper, which was gliding slowly a mile out in Terrebonne Bay. It was a gaudy sun, tinting the underbellies of the clouds to a rosy hue and the sea to a copper-toned mirror. Philippe slowed the motors till the boat was just making way. He held the wheel with one hand and leant against the open window of the wheelhouse, watching the progress of a small boat heading their way. A couple of hundred yards from the shrimper and the captain could hear the putter of its engine. Alice heard it too, and went forward. It dawned on her that the figure in the boat was familiar. Suddenly she twisted round.

'Philippe, it's Dee-Dee!' she shouted excitedly.

'Yeah. Get ready to throw him a rope.'

As the large Cajun hauled himself over the side, Alice sprang forward and clasped him round the neck, hugging him and dragging him onto the deck.

'Stop pulling, Alice,' he gasped, as he clung to the gunwale to stay on his feet.

'Dee-Dee, it's so good to see you.'

'And y'all, my little princess.'

'Why have you come?'

'To travel into N'Yawlins. Where're Molly and Bert?'

'Down below. Something's wrong, ain't it? I mean, that wasn't the plan.'

'Well no, little one, but things have changed.'

'What things?'

'Many things. Danny won't be able to make it.'

'What's wrong with Danny?'

'Well, nothing...' Dee-Dee tried to turn his face away, but she read his distress.

'Something's wrong; wrong with Danny!' She stood stiffly, glaring at him, and trembling. Her face drained of all colour, and when she spoke her voice was strangely hard and old. 'He's dead, ain't he?'

Their eyes met and Dee-Dee watched her face crumple.

'Yes, Princess; Danny's dead.'

She leapt at him, her arms flailing into his immense bulk. Her knotted hands pummelled him as he tried to hold her. Molly and Bert appeared, ran over and pulled her off him.

'Alice - what are you doing?'

'Danny's dead!' she screamed.

'Surely not?' Bert cut to Dee-Dee.

'I wish it wasn't true.'

Alice sagged and collapsed into a sobbing heap at his feet. Bert moved to pick her up, but Dee-Dee stooped and gently lifted her like a baby. He went forward past the wheelhouse to sit down cradling her. Nets hung all around them, creating a little sheltered tent.

'Hush, my little princess, you're breaking my heart,' he croaked. She continued to sob as he rocked her to and fro, tutting and clucking at her. With his huge hands he smoothed her hair. Philippe came forward; after some time he coughed.

'It's true about Danny?' Dee-Dee just looked at him with glistening eyes. 'I heard about it at lunchtime, but kept it from them. I couldn't believe it.' Philippe regarded him, uncertain what else to do or say. He shuffled from one foot to the other, threading his hat round and round in his hands. 'I was relieved when you called. We go back now?'

'No, Philippe. Danny instructed me to go on if anything happened to him. Can you lift my skiff on to the boat?'

'Sure, you stay here. Little Philippe and I can cope.'

As the dusk deepened, the old deckhand and the boy winched the skiff aboard. Alice did not stir in Dee-Dee's arms as the boat's engine took on a deeper note and the shrimper moved faster into the approaching darkness, away from land. His arm went numb and he cautiously tried to move it. She lifted her face from his chest and her eyes flashed, like a cat rudely disturbed from sleep. He caught his breath.

'Did you love Danny, Dee-Dee?'

'Yes,' his voice caught. 'Most people loved Danny.'

'I loved Danny, Dee-Dee...' she broke into tears that ran freely down her face. He hugged her tightly and they both cried together.

'I know; and he loved you, princess,' he choked out between gasps.

Later, when all except the throb of the engine was quiet, Dee-Dee carried Alice down into the cabin and laid her on a bunk. He pulled the curtain across it. Little Philippe lay in the other bunk, his wide dark eyes watching him. Dee-Dee stretched out his hand and mussed the boy's hair. 'You keep a watch over her.'

With serious eyes, he nodded. Dee-Dee smiled and left for the wheel-house. The three adults turned as they heard the door slide open.

'How's Alice?' asked Molly, who couldn't help noticing that Dee-Dee's eyes were bloodshot. 'I should go to her.'

'She's asleep. Let's hope she stays that way till morning.'

'And what do you want me to do now?' asked Philippe.

'Same as you agreed with Danny.'

'Sure. One problem, though. Where do we drop you when we reach N'Yawlins?'

'You know the jetties right before you reach Algiers point?'

'The ones off Patterson?' Dee-Dee gave a nod. 'Yeah. But be careful. Some are in a pretty dangerous state.'

'Don't worry.' He turned away from the captain. 'Bert, Molly: we need to talk. You excuse me, Philippe?'

'Sure.' He watched all three leave and walk to the nets.

'How did it happen?' ask Bert

'His place in N'Yawlins was blown up and an unidentified body has been found.'

'Danny's body? Poor Ducey,' murmured Molly.

'It was too badly mutilated by the explosion to be recognisable, but it's Danny. Who else could it be?'

'You said 'blown up'. That suggests it's not an accident.'

'Who knows? The police are saying it was a gas leak. They're treating it as suicide.' Dee-Dee sniffed hard. 'After you went to bed, two nights ago, Danny and me talked. We laid down some plans. He left instructions for everyone to follow if anything should happen to him and I know how he planned to get y'all in and out of N'Yawlins. He gave me numbers to ring, and the contacts are ready for you. Danny had organised most of it before he was killed.'

Bert put his hand on the Cajun's shoulder.

'No. We can't. We must go to the police. You've all done too much for us already.'

'Danny thought you might say that. He insisted you must wait, and do it in Canada, far from the people you've stayed with; otherwise you'll put us all in danger.'

'How come?'

'I will not give up Alice; Danny made me swear to that. If she is taken into custody she will be dead within the week; most likely earlier.'

'You cannot do this!' snapped Molly.

'You can't stop me. If you raise the alarm that I have her, those others will find us first. Like that's been the pattern. Each time the police get close those killers beat 'em to it. I'm not as clever as Danny: *And even Danny was not clever enough, it seems.'* Dee-Dee paused; sucked in a deep breath. 'If you give yourselves up here your enemies'll threaten *our* friends - to find out where Alice is. They'll certainly try to grab y'all. No; *I know* Danny was right; ya'll git to Canada.'

'Danny seems to have had it all covered.'

'I think so, Bert. Except for himself. Let us help you. Don't waste what Danny has done for you, and all he's given up. As soon as I heard about that I called Arran Marx in Newark. He's coming down to take over. He said he'd get to N'Yawlins before nightfall, so he'll be there waiting for you. I need to know what you're going to decide.'

Bert studied Dee-Dee. It was strange, but he felt more affinity with the large Cajun than most, if not all his own countrymen. These bayou people were the *real deal*: good right through.

'In England we call this blackmail,' Molly said sharply.

'Strange as it seems, so do we.' Dee-Dee gave her a lopsided grin.

67

Dwight was already in the incident room when the other officers started to arrive. Fenwick appeared a few minutes before the meeting started. He chatted and joked with several of the men as the room became crowded.

'Morning y'all!' shouted Dwight. 'Can I have some silence?' Murmurs of response rippled round the room, tailing off to nothing. 'Since last night things have taken a leap forward. Another body was found a few gardens away.' Fenwick looked up sharply. 'It seems that the blast had thrown it clear out of the building. This, I've been told, can happen if the person is at a window when the blast happens. The body has been identified as Danny Generve, although his front has been torn away in the blast. Luckily, his I.D. was found in his back pocket.' Dwight paused, and held up a plastic bag which contained a leather wallet. 'We also now know the identity of the first body.' He paused for effect. 'A head was also found. One of our own; Gene MacIntyre.'

With this the room erupted. It took some minutes before Dwight could bring order to the assembled officers.

'His wife has been informed, and has taken it badly. As yet, we don't know when the funeral will be, but everyone will be told as soon as we hear. This leaves some questions to be answered; the connection between MacIntyre and Generve being top of the list.' He paused again, and waited for the significance to penetrate. 'So apart from your other enquiries, this needs to be attended to as well. A list of what I want from each officer is pinned up on the duties roster. Thank you, everyone; and good hunting.'

Dwight jerked his head for Fenwick to follow, and walked out of the room before any of the officers could throw more questions. Fenwick squeezed past some men who had stood crowding the doorway, and ran after him. By the time Fenwick reached Usner's office he was sitting at his desk. Fenwick stood breathlessly, seething with anger.

'Are you going to tell me what's going on?' he growled through clenched teeth. 'I thought we had an agreement.'

'Calm down, Fenwick. This all developed late last night. It was very messy, and to be honest there wasn't a damn lot you could have done. So I left you to sleep.' He held up a blue file. 'It's all in here. Photos, reports; the lot.'

He threw it towards Fenwick, who caught it and sat down without a word. After several minutes he closed it and tossed it back onto Usner's desk.

'I still think you should have called and warned me. I felt a right dick in there.' He yanked a thumb over his shoulder.

Dwight sighed. 'I'm sorry. I was so tired when I got up this morning, I clean forgot.' They stared challengingly at each other for some moments. 'C'mon, let me buy you breakfast and we can talk.'

The usual clientele were in the diner. They waved to Stella behind the counter and sat at an empty table near the back. Dwight put his hand on Fenwick's wrist.

'My call.' He raised his hand to the room. 'Two large ones, Stella, and can we have some coffee now?'

She scribbled their order down, hung it on the Lazy Susan and started pouring the coffee.

'Don't see you for ages, Dwight - now it's three days in a row.' She gave him a smile.

'You know how it is.'

'Sure. Did you find him?'

'Who?'

'Mac. You were asking me about him yesterday. He went off with those guys, remember? I told you.'

'Would you recognise them again?'

'No, not really. I was pretty busy. They all left together, but I told you that yesterday.'

'Would you look at some photos?'

'Sure. Is Mac still missing?'

Dwight's eyes clouded and he shook his head. 'No. He's dead.'

'Jesus, Mary and Joseph.' She promptly put the coffee pot down on the table and crossed herself. 'You mean - murdered?'

'I can't say at the moment and I'd sure appreciate it if you kept it to yourself. About these photos?'

'Sure, but there ain't no point. They had their backs to me.' She moved away, then turned back. 'I can tell you who would be able to; and he knew Mac.'

'Who?'

'Georgie Brody.'

'That old derelict still about?'

'Yeah. He was sitting straight behind Mac. With their backs to me, they were facing him straight on.'

'Where does he live?'

'Your guess is as good as mine. He moves from one doss-house to another. Could be anywhere, and he's already been in to eat.'

'Breakfast?'

'No, his evening meal.' Dwight frowned. 'He works nights as a watchman. He'll be crashed out by now. I won't see him till the morning.'

'Do you know where he works?'

'Yeah, that big building site up on Tchoupatoulis by the old grain elevators, but he doesn't start till ten. If you go round there at that time of the night you'll scare the hell out of him. He comes in faithfully every day to eat. I don't think his place has any facilities. No more than a shack, I believe, with cold water.'

'Well; it's pretty urgent, Stella.'

'All I know is, it's probably downtown near the docks somewhere, and you know how big an area that is, and all the places he could kip down in. If you go down there and start asking for him he'll more likely get the wrong idea and disappear. As soon as he comes in tomorrow morning I'll give you a call. He's here by seven-thirty like clockwork.'

'Dwight; that might be best, you know,' said Fenwick. 'There're lots of other lines to follow and if I'm thinking what you're thinking, those boys aren't about to leave town. We can still be building a case.'

'Yeah, perhaps you're right.' Dwight pulled a card out of his pocket and wrote a number on the back and handed it to Stella. 'This'll get me at home, hon. Be sure not to forget.'

''Course I won't. Now let me get you your breakfast.'

As she walked away he filled Fenwick in on the night's events, even to waking the doc to do an urgent autopsy on Danny's body.

'I'd like to see that stiff.'

'What's the point, Fenwick? He took it full in the front. It was a mess. We were lucky he carried his wallet in his back pocket. He was blown out the window. They found glass in him.' Fenwick grimaced. 'If he hadn't landed on his back we wouldn't have found that; most of his clothes were burnt off. It was under his ass, where his jeans didn't get burnt.'

Fenwick whistled through his teeth. 'That must have been some explosion - and you found the head.'

'Yeah, quite close to Danny's body. It was because of the head that we found Danny. Believe it or not, there wasn't much damage to the head; hardly a scratch.'

'Is that so? Who found it?'

'The poor woman who lived in the house where Danny landed. She'll be having nightmares for some time.'

'How come?'

'I told you. This body and the head were not found till late last night. The garden is quite secluded, with trees, and the corpse landed on the roof; so when the officers searched the garden earlier that day they found nothing.'

'Was the head on the roof, too?'

'No, it had got caught up in the branches of a tree. The woman and her husband got back late last night. Went up to prepare for bed. She'd taken a shower and was drying herself when she realised there was a face staring at her through the window. The poor bitch nearly had heart failure. They took her to hospital.'

Fenwick giggled, shamefacedly. 'You must admit it sounds funny when you tell it.'

'Yeah, suppose it does. Ah, great; here comes breakfast.'

209

68.

Dwight slumped down into his seat behind the wheel of his car. Another day over. Rain drummed on the roof and slashed in front of the windscreen, closing him in. It was dark and he could see little but pools of water on the tarmac, gleaming wetly from the lights of the hangar. A throbbing clatter came from above as a chopper came in to land. His visitor had arrived. Two minutes later a figure dashed towards his car and bent down to peer in through the partially opened window.

'Get in.'

Smith opened the door and slid into the seat.

'Damn, but it's nasty out there.' He rubbed his hands.

'Yeah, it's the kind of weather we need for tonight.' Dwight glanced at the agent. 'Good to see you again.'

'Thank God you had a contact in Washington; otherwise I doubt I would have got out before Thanksgiving.'

'My pleasure.' Dwight raised the window and started the engine. 'I've heard stories where people have disappeared altogether out there. They're a bit of a law unto themselves.'

'I can believe it. Those boys sure don't muck about. I didn't get five yards out of that garage before I was spread-eagled on the ground with a gun at my temple.'

'Well, they don't trust city boys! I'd better fill you in with what we're doing. I might be totally wrong, but I could think of no other way to find out, so I set up a little charade.'

Dwight cut across town as he told Smith the set-up. It took him twenty minutes before he turned onto a rough roadway that led towards the river. The car rocked violently as he drove over rail tracks. The ground ahead was fenced off. The compound inside was a building site, most of it still down to foundations, and further back the area was laid to waste with a couple of old grain elevators. The site itself was huge, and went as far as the levee. On the other side flowed the Mississippi.

Dwight stopped at a barbed-wire gate. Smith swung the gates wide open for the car. As he closed them he followed it into an area with great stacks of building blocks. Dwight backed in between the stacks, facing the way they had come. He got out, opened the trunk and pulled out a tarpaulin. The two of them pulled it over the car and placed a number of blocks to hold it down.

Dwight leaned across the hood and cut two slits into the cover, in line with the windshield. Both men got back into the car and waited.

'I think you could have made those holes a little larger,' grumbled Smith.

'Maybe, but I don't want to make it too obvious. I think we can see all we need.'

Smith checked his watch.

'So now we wait?'

'Yeah, I'm afraid so.' Dwight removed his revolver and placed it on the dashboard. He pressed a button on the side of his seat, and it fell back. 'Give me a shout about nine-thirty.'

'Gee, thanks.' Smith peered through one of the peepholes. 'Usner?'

'What?'

'What made you check up on me?'

'I found it strange it was you who got the call from the Dancers, and not the other way round. I suppose you could have called the twins earlier on a land-line, but as soon as you had your new mobile you started to call a Washington number, so it didn't make sense to be so cautious about calling those two.'

'Okay, I understand that, but how did you link me with the Special Unit?'

'Well, first I checked the Dancers' line to see who had called. There was one, using a mobile, immediately before the brothers rang you. The call had been made here in the city. I checked the number and was given a name and an address in Washington. My friend up there dug some more and found the name and address didn't exist. I reckoned that neither of the Dancer boys would go to all that trouble, and who else do I know from Washington that is here in the city?

'I got back and gave my buddy the numbers you'd been ringing. He got the run-around for some time,though someone picked up my name; I had a mysterious phone call asking a whole load of strange questions. Your name came up as Cleared for Special Duties. After that I traced you to the county jailhouse, which wasn't easy. Now you're here'.

'Yeah. So who set me up? Fenwick?'

'We both did, and you haven't told me how you got thrown into jail.'

'Don't ask. That Cajun asshole set me up real good.' Dwight couldn't help a little chuckle. 'And you can stop laughing! Bastard led me a real dance. Nearly had me drive into the bayou at one point. At least he made sure I didn't have a gun on me when I got cornered by the cops. They were so twitchy I'm sure they would have blown me away.'

'Quite possibly if that had happened, no-one would have found you. Now explain all this cloak-and-dagger stuff.'

'How much have you been told?'

'Not much; only that Fenwick was being watched.'

'Yeah, but that's not the half of it. My people have been investigating child porn and prostitution for nearly two years and every time we seem to get close the whole thing blows up in our face.

'We've traced it back to Washington several times, but every time we seem near to finding the leak it goes dead on us. All we know is that this racket is being run by people high up in government circles. Not one person - there's a whole lot called 'The Group'. They use kids to entertain politicians, visiting dignitaries and world shakers. It's a setup for blackmail. For what purpose we're not sure, but we think it's mainly political leverage. It's been said that the dirt reaches up to the White House.'

'You mean the President?'

'This we're not sure about, but there are other powerful folk up there apart from him. For some months the leads dried up, but two weeks ago an inquiry came through the New York office about this kid we're trying to track now. Unfortunately, someone in Washington got to hear about it before we did. By the time we got geared up and contacted the New Jersey Police the kid and the parents had vanished - less than three days before the police got there. We finally traced 'em down here, but because police had got involved we couldn't stop Washington interfering as well, without rousing suspicions. Somehow the Dancers got here first.'

'But so did Danny. Whisked the kid and her grandparents away from under their noses. - Tell me, how are these Dancers involved?' asked Dwight.

'They're old-fashioned hit-men; hired to clean up the mess and plug the hole. They nearly succeeded, but then Generve got involved. The Dancers had not been expecting a loner to come sneaking in - that's why he surprised them. He got away with it once, but as we all know, he paid for it in the end.' Smith paused, and peered out through his ragged spy-hole. 'Now those Limeys and the kid are on their own, with a few well-meaning people playing pass-the-parcel. It's a pity we haven't got a few more leads to their whereabouts. Surely Danny's records were'nt all destroyed?'

'No, and I've got people going through it all with a fine tooth comb, but I don't hold out much hope. Cajun Country is another world.'

'Don't I know it. Isn't there anything else we can do?'

'No.' Dwight shook his head and sighed. 'All we can do is to stop our own leak and wait.'

'Wait for what?'

'Believe it or not, they have to come to me. I can get messages out to the people in the swamps and my message is to come on in. It's their one chance. I've been in contact with the British consul. He told me the old pair have been in touch. They're coming back into the city in a day or two.'

'So that leaves Fenwick as a problem.'

'Yeah; he must be nailed first to make it safe.'

'Tell me something; what made you set this thing up tonight?'

213

'Once I knew you were clean, it had to be Fenwick, so I fed him a line with a little help from a friend, and Georgie was born. My friend passed on enough details for Fenwick to fix Georgie's whereabouts for ten tonight.'

'They say the simplest plans are the best.' Smith illuminated the dial on his watch. 'It's not nine-thirty yet. I think I'll risk a piss. I won't be a second.'

'Be careful. They might already be out there. Keep to the shadows. Don't let yourself get silhouetted.'

Dwight lay back thinking over what they had discussed. After some minutes he leaned forward and squinted through the hole in the tarpaulin. Nothing. Smith was taking his time for a piss. He heard a car engine coming up towards the gates, its headlights bouncing up and down as it advanced along the rutted road. Dwight started his engine. The lights steadied as the newcomer reached the gates.

A silhouette made by the glare of the lights passed in front of the tarpaulin and stopped. It was moving as though lining itself up on the car. Instinct drove Dwight to flatten himself across the passenger seat. Four holes punctured the windshield just above the steering wheel. Had he not moved he would have received four bullets in his chest.

Dwight jammed the stick into drive and floored the throttle. The car lurched forward, tearing out from under the tarpaulin. Still keeping down, he grabbed the wheel to keep the car straight. Out of the side window he saw Smith flinging himself to the ground.

'Smith, you bastard!' shouted Dwight.

The car was going right for the front gate; Dwight dared a quick glance above the dash. On the other side of the gates another car was parked, with it's headlights on. He yanked the wheel to the right and drove away from the gate and headed towards the levee. Glancing over his shoulder, he saw the other car crash through the gate and give chase. The car's headlights came full on and as they swung in behind Dwight the lights caught the shadowy figure of Smith to the side of him, raising his arm. Two holes appeared in the side window and he felt a burn in his shoulder. He was hit.

Jamming his foot hard to the floor he rocketed through the chain-link fence, ripping out several panels. There were screams of tearing metal as the fencing wound round the front wheels. Suddenly both tyres burst and the car nosed into the soft ground at the bottom of the levee.

Dwight shouldered the door open and fell out onto the slippery, wet grass. He did not need to turn to know that they were close behind. He staggered upright and started up the levee. As he reached the top he felt something slam into his back, spinning and pushing him over to sprawl and slide down the other side towards the water's edge. The breath was driven out of him as he came hard up against a marker post. Winded, he lay struggling to gain his breath. He pulled out a small tape recorder. 'It's Smith, it's both of them,' he whispered into the machine.

He plunged it deep into the grass at the base of the post, and started to crawl away. From his other pocket he pulled out a mobile and pressed out some numbers. Instantly it was answered.

'Yeah?'

'Listen! Come down to the old grain elevators and go up onto the levee. Find the river marker post. At its base is a tape recorder. Don't...' Blood bubbled through his lips and he spluttered and gagged. 'Don't trust anyone, not Fenwick or Smith. You were right. I should have listened. Get them out. Get them to Canada. Right?'

'What's going on, Usner?'

'Come now! Don't wait.'

Again Dwight had to pause to catch breath. He knew he had to get as far away from the marker as possible, and started to drag his body over the wet grass. There was a sharp report from a gun and he let out a scream that turned into a bubbly whimper. He was still too close to the post. The sound of a tinny voice came from the mobile in his hand.

'What the hell is happening? Usner! Speak to me; are you okay?'

'No, I'm flying without wings.' He stopped speaking.

A pair of Italian shoes stepped into view. He rolled onto his side and looked up. Smith was behind a gun aimed at his head. Dwight couldn't remember if he had named the voice on the phone. He hoped not.

'Fuck you,' he gasped out, his eyes burning into Smith.

A bright flash of light spat at him. He didn't hear the bang. Smith bent down and felt for a pulse. Dwight was dead. He eased the mobile from the inert hand and put it to his ear. There was the sound of breathing.

'Who is this?'

'Fuck you; motherfucker.'

The phone went dead. He shrugged and flung it into the turgid swirling currents of the Mississippi. Fenwick came over the top of the levee. He leaned against the marker post, breathing hard.

'Dead?' asked Fenwick.

'Sure.'

'Did you get Usner to talk?'

'What d'ya think, Fenwick?' Smith sneered triumphantly.

'Good. Now let's get out of here.'

69.

The motorbike came from Uptown. It kept below the skyline of the levee. As it drew closer to the grain elevators it slowed, then stopped. The rider dismounted and keeping low, crept carefully to the top of the steep bank, all the while studying the ground.

Immediately below was Dwight's car. The building site was all in darkness. The car looked forlorn, stuck at the bottom of the bank, its nose embedded in the soft earth. The rider, staying low, slid down. The hood was still warm to the touch; the smell of hot metal overwhelming. The interior was empty. The man (there was no mistaking his gender) climbed back up the levee and disappeared over the top. Still low to the ground, he raised the visor of his helmet and scanned the land before him. Slightly to his left was a darker hump in the night-black grass. A yard or so further on a tall post stuck out of the bank.

He made his way cautiously, constantly checking all around, but nothing stirred. The hump became a body. Dwight's face was staring blankly at the fast-fleeting clouds. His eyes had taken on the dullness of death; the skin had a sheen of dampness. The rider took his gauntlets off and pressed the back of one hand to the dead detective's cheek. The skin was already cool. He closed Dwight's eyes and his fingers became covered in blood that had leaked from a tiny hole above the eyebrows and seeped onto the eyelids. He wiped his fingers in the wet grass, got to his feet and moved to the post. The grass around it was wet, but he touched something hard. He pocketed it and ran back to the bike. Police sirens sounded in the distance. The engine coughed into life. He pulled the machine upright, turned it around and drove off.

217

70

Smith was lounging on a low sofa with a stiff drink in his hand. Fenwick sipped his by the bar. The Dancers were on the other side; Harvey on a stool to take the weight from his foot.

'So you're certain they're coming in?' asked Harry.

'Didn't I say so? The thing we must make sure of is they don't connect Usner's death with the cop covering their case.'

'How do we do that?' asked Fenwick.

'Inform the guy who takes over from Usner that he needs to keep the name alive as far as the British consulate is concerned,' Smith said glibly.

'So we keep it out of the newspapers. I doubt the Consul and Usner ever met - and everyone gets a cold once in a while.' Fenwick emptied his drink down his throat in one gulp, and started crunching the ice.

Harry smiled. 'So you feed the guy the right information and the kid and the geriatrics get directed to us.'

'Wrong, Harry; just the kid. We don't want an international incident. Too many questions would be asked by too many people in high places.'

Smith said, 'We bring them into open ground and you pick the kid off from a distance. After that you can pack up and go home.'

He sighted his forefinger at Harry and cocked his thumb. 'Bang, she falls down dead. Simple.' He laughed, and Fenwick chuckled. Harry and Harvey exchanged glances.

'Who's gonna do the shooting?' Harvey's face showed no humour. 'You clowns think we're gonna expose ourselves like that? You must be outta your minds. This ain't the friggin' movies.'

Fenwick crunched on an ice cube. 'If you and your brother had done your job properly and not let the kid slip through your fingers there wouldn't have been any exposure for anyone.'

'Do you think we liked putting *our* heads on the line?' growled Smith. He got up, swirling his tumbler, making the ice clink. He moved over to Harvey. 'We exposed ourselves to get this information, so don't screw up this time!' He slammed the glass down on the bar counter by Harvey's elbow. It shattered. Spirit splashed out over Harvey's sleeve. 'Now look what you've made me do,' Smith said quietly, as he brushed the liquid off Harvey. He was chuckling and smiling, but his eyes were as cold as the ice left melting on the bar top.

Fenwick moved towards the bar.

'Calm down, Smith. This won't get us anywhere.' He stopped in front of his agitated colleague, gently patted him on the shoulder and turned to Harvey. 'Are you saying you're not going to do the job anymore? Is that what you're saying, Harvey?' 'Hey, man,' Harry said nervously. 'That's not what Harvey said! We're marked, is all; we have to be careful.'

'Okay, I understand, so let's talk.' Fenwick's tone was placatory.

'Alright, what do you suggest?' asked Harvey.

'We don't know when they're coming in, or how, or where. Not yet, but when we do I think we can manipulate it to our advantage. So let's leave the worrying for the moment. The 'how' is simple. Once we know when and where they're going to arrive, Harvey here can pick the kid off from a safe distance. We can convince whoever takes over that they must be brought in as soon as possible.' He knew he had everyone's attention, and continued: 'With Usner dead we'll make sure they rely on us more, and remember that with Generve out of the picture the others will be in a state of confusion. We'll tell whoever takes charge that he must convince the consul to persuade them to come in soon as possible.'

'Remember what Usner said: - it was a matter of time,' added Smith

Fenwick's mobile phone bleeped. 'Yeah?' He listened for a few seconds, then put his hand up to stop any talking in the room. '*Usner?* Are you sure? Hell, where are you? I'll get Smith. We're on our way.' He stopped and listened again. 'Sure. We'll find it. Who's taking over? You, McCoy? Great. Couldn't have anyone better. Okay. See you soon.' He pocketed the phone.

'We'll finish this conversation later. Come on, Smith, we can't keep a dead man waiting.' Both men laughed.

71

Ralph McCoy tiredly got into his car and sat there silently for a moment, watching his men scour the ground for clues. Smith and Fenwick had been a great help. He was glad they were there. Things would get done right, he was certain. Taking a deep breath, he started the car. The next couple of hours were not going to be pleasant. On the way to Usner's house he called his wife and told her not to wait up.

He had met Fran a few times at police socials. Outside of work the couple kept to themselves. He recalled something Dwight had once said; work was work and family was family; the two never mixed well.

As he stood on the Usner's porch he could see in her face that she guessed something was wrong. That old dark cloak of fear that hung over all cops' wives was draping her shoulders. She opened the door wide and asked him in. The house was quiet. They went through to the unbearably bright kitchen. He could see by the way the muscles in her face twitched that she was trying to form questions.

'Fran. Sit down,' Ralph said gently, pulling out a chair.

'Yes.' Her voice trembled, while her eyes moved everywhere except to meet his. 'I think I'd better.' She slumped heavily down.

Ralph took hold of her hands. Their eyes met and held.

'There's been a shooting. Dwight is dead.' His own voice sounded blank and hard to him.

It was as though with those words the tensed, trembling limbs went slack and she sagged forward into him. At first he thought she had fainted, but he felt a fierce pain as she started to sob and clawed her nails into the palm of his hand. He stayed holding her, the pain from her nails throbbing. Finally, she pushed away and put her hands up to her wet face. A sad hint of a smile lifted the corners of her mouth.

'I must look a mess!'

'Understandable, so don't worry about it. Can I get you anything? A drink?'

'Yes; would you make a coffee?'

'Sure. Do you want anything in it?'

'No thanks. Dwight and I never drank much, so I don't think I'll start now.'

'I'm going to call the doctor.' He picked up the phone.

'There's no need.'

'What would Dwight do if he was in my position now?' He didn't wait for an answer. When he had finished the call he turned back to her. 'The doctor won't be long. Do you have family close by?'

'Yes, dial hatch-four, it's a speed number to my sister.'

Ralph busied himself at the sink. Without glancing her way, and trying to sound casual, he asked the question foremost in his mind since finding Dwight's body.

'Do you know who Dwight was meeting tonight?'

'No. I thought he was with you. Ralph, what happened?'

The question he had dreaded now surfaced. He moved the coffee pot over to the boiling kettle.

'Let me make the drink and we'll sit down and I'll tell you everything.'

The half-emptied coffee pot was cooling rapidly by the time he had finished.

'Ralph - you asked me a question - about who Dwight was meeting? Are you trying to tell me he didn't leave notes in his diary?'

'No, I had that checked as soon as I heard about his death.' He put his hand up slightly to stop a question forming on her lips. 'But that isn't as unusual as it seems, especially on a case like this. He may have been going to meet with an informant, and those people you don't share around the office.'

'What, not even with you?'

'This case is a bit special. He's been escorting a couple of Feds around. They've stuck to him like glue.' He paused, and rubbed his chin. 'That was, until yesterday, when there was just one, the eldest. I don't know what happened to the other. I assumed he was in Washington, but he turned up here tonight. Dwight had put me in charge of liaison, to try and hold the group together. I didn't even see him leave.'

He made a clucking sound as though he was pondering something mysterious. 'Has anything out of the norm happened in the last couple of days? Did he say or do anything unusual?'

Fran stared blankly out of the window into the blackness beyond. She frowned.

'There is something, isn't there?' The excitement caught in his voice.

'Last night Dwight had a visitor.'

'Go on.'

'It was late; the children were in bed and Dwight told me to go up. I heard the back door screen go; Dwight called out. The bathroom is above the yard. I left the light off and looked out. The security light came on and I saw this guy wearing leathers and a helmet. Dwight went down into the yard. I could see the back of his head, but didn't hear what he said. The man lifted his visor; whoever it was, Dwight recognised him.'

'Are you sure it was a man?'

'I assumed it was from the way he moved.'

'Did you see the face?'

'No, it was hidden from me. Dwight dragged him into the shadows at the bottom of the yard, as though he didn't want anyone to see what was going on.' Fran studied her hands. 'That guy's got something to do with his death, hasn't he?' The last sentence sounded between a plea and a scream.

'I don't know, Fran. We found some fresh motorcycle tracks near Dwight's body, though the scene around him doesn't make sense. As I've said, he was chased up onto the levee. His car had crashed below it.'

'I want to see him.'

'Of course.' There was a ring at the front door. Ralph got up. 'That will be the doctor, or your sister.'

She shivered. 'I feel very cold.'

'That's shock. I won't be a moment.' He went through to answer the door. She heard some murmured talk and guessed it was her sister.

72.

It was gone three am before Ralph reached home. The neighbourhood was as silent as the grave. Even the cicadas were quiet. The humid air had that early-morning chill about it that clawed its way to the bone. He walked up the path to his front door, head down, deep in thought. A figure detached itself from the shadowed shrubbery.

'Ralphy...'

Ralph spun on his heels, his right hand reaching for his revolver.

'Slow down, man.' The figure had a helmet on, but he held up his hands. 'We need to talk.'

'Who the hell are you?'

'A long-lost buddy.' He gave a chuckle, and lifted his visor. 'I have something for you to listen to.'

'You'd better come in, but for God's sake don't make a noise. My wife and kids will be asleep. I'd like to keep it that way.'

They entered the house and Ralph guided his visitor into the den before going to the kitchen to pull some beers from the fridge. Returning, Ralph threw a can to his guest before dropping into a deep chair. A low table stood between them. A small tape recorder now stood on it. His visitor switched it on. It whirred for a few moments. Dwight Usner's voice sounded tinny, coming from the small speaker.

'Hi, Ralphy! If you're listening to this, I'm probably dead. This whole case has been one crazy mother. Has had us chasing our tails, so for the time it takes this tape to run I want you to put everything out of your mind and listen.'

The tape hissed for a second. 'For some reason we always seem to find ourselves last in the queue. That started me thinking; then last night I had a visitor.'

That was the night before,' interjected the rider on the opposite side of the table.

'You?' asked Ralph. He nodded, and put a finger to his lips. The tape was still running.

'He brought me information that makes real sense, so I set up a trap. I figured that one of the Feds was a leak. The problem was - which one? Smith, who we left out in the bayous, or Fenwick? Seeing I had Fenwick with me I fed him a story about a witness to the men who picked up MacIntyre, and where that person could be found. That was tonight. I led him on to think I would wait until morning to see him, as it would be easier. After my visitor had gone I rang someone in Washington and found out that Smith was genuine and Fenwick was under surveillance, but nothing could be proved. He'd been seconded into Smith's investigation from somewhere, but no one would be specific. I found out where Smith was and had him brought in by chopper, unbeknownst to Fenwick.

'I knew that the Feds were holding something back and that either or both would know what that was. I felt sure they thought I was holding out too, so I decided that if I showed Smith I trusted him - and not Fenwick, he might be encouraged to give me some information, especially if he thought it might make me talk. So Ralphy, listen: this, I hope, is it.'

There was more tape hiss for several moments and then a rhythmic clatter that went on for some time.

'I think it's the sound of a helicopter...'

Ralph grunted. There was the whine of an electric window.

'Get in.' It was Dwight's voice.

'Damn, but it's nasty out there.'

'That's Smith's voice isn't it?' asked Ralph.

'Yeah.'

The two of them went on listening intently, forgetting their beers. They heard Smith leave the car to have a piss and for several minutes all they could hear was Dwight's breathing. Four loud bangs went off. Ralph jumped.

'Gun shots. Did you see Dwight's windshield?'

'Of course.'

There was a roar from an engine, which turned into a scream. A tearing and then a rumbling sound. 'Smith, you bastard!' Dwight's voice came clear above the noise.

'It was Smith all along. Shit.' Ralph shook his head in disbelief. -

A scream of wheels, as though the car was going round a tight corner. The next two shots were not as loud, but both listeners knew immediately from his howl of pain that Dwight had been hit. The engine was gunned harder. The screech of the chain-link fence being ripped out set their teeth on edge. The popping sound of tyres bursting was insignificant against all the other noise. When the car came to a halt, Dwight's laboured breathing seemed to be the only sound they could hear. It was shocking. The noise he made scrambling out of the car and up the levee was so compelling that McCoy leant forward over the tape machine.

When it came, the shot that caught Dwight in the back was no more than a sharp crack. There was a grunt and an expulsion of air, and a sudden crash to the ground, followed by a slithering noise that made Ralph close his eyes. Dwight gave a groan, and except for his stertorous breathing all other sounds stopped for a moment.

'It's Smith, Ralphy. It's fucking Smith. Promise to nail the bastard!' The voice was a hoarse whisper. There was a grating sound.

'I think that's the sound when he hid the machine.'

'Hid it?'

'Yeah, it wasn't on him when I found him.'

'Listen.' Dwight's voice continued: 'Come down to the old grain elevators. On the river side of the levee you'll see a marker post. At its base you'll find a tape recorder. Don't...'

'That was Dwight talking to me on the mobile.' Over the top of the visitor's voice Ralph could hear Dwight's spluttering gasps.

'Don't trust anyone, not Fenwick or Smith. You were right; I should have listened. Get them out - get them to Canada.' There was a pause. 'Come *now*! Don't wait...'

They could hear Dwight moving again. There was a sharp report from a gun and Usner's scream. 'No; I'm flying without wings.'

'Jesus,' swore Ralph.

'Fuck you!' The final shot made the speaker rattle. There was a long pause. 'Who is this?'

'That's Smith talking into the mobile to me,' said the rider.

'Oh.'

They heard someone else join Smith. He was breathing particularly hard.

'Dead?'

'That's Fenwick's voice.'

'Both of them,' said McCoy in disbelief.

'That's right.'

'Did you get Usner to talk?' Fenwick asked.

'What do you think?' The voice had a sneer to it.

'Good. Now let's get out of here.'

The recording picked up the sound of the men walking away. Soon afterwards, the tape stopped.

'The bastards!' fumed Ralph, shaking his head to rid his eyes of tears. 'The mother-fucking bastards.' He went to the window. Dimly, in the east, the sky was lightening and the stars were starting to fade. He pulled out his mobile.

'Who are you ringing?' the rider behind him asked suspiciously.

'Dempsey.'

'I see; and you're going to let Chief Dempsey listen to the tape, then go out there and bust their asses?'

'Too right! What the fuck do you think I'm going to do?'

'Use your brain. Dwight seemed to suspect you had one, otherwise why would he leave you the message?'

'I can't hide this.'

'No one's telling you to, but bust the two you can see - and you'll never know who takes their place.'

'What do you suggest?'

'I think it will suggest itself. Dempsey will most likely put you in charge. When that happens, act the innocent lamb and they'll help you form a plan.'

'You think they have one?'

'Sure. All they're interested in is getting the kid, and Dwight told Smith that he was in touch with the British consulate.'

'But why didn't he tell me? It seems Dwight didn't trust anyone. He played everything close to the chest.'

'You'll take over tomorrow. Let Fenwick and Smith help!'

'But...'

'No buts, Ralphy; otherwise you'll follow Dwight. Your strength is that you know who they are but they don't know about this tape. The fewer who do, the safer you'll be. You can't trust anyone.'

'So what do you plan for the kid?'

'We do what was always planned.'

'And what's that?'

'First find out what your 'friends' want to do. After you know that I'll let you into some secrets. All I'll tell you now is that we knew things could go wrong, so we made arrangements for the family to carry on without either of us.'

'Are you going to meet the kid?'

'No. Other friends will do that. I'm their shadow; and no-one but you and two others know I exist. While it stays that way the kid and her grandparents will be safe.'

'You mean none of them know about this?'

'No; and they mustn't. They must act innocently.'

'So what has been organised?'

His visitor shook his head. 'No more until we find out what your buddies the Feds want to do. We don't want you accidentally giving something away. Your own safety lies in knowing just enough and no more.'

'I don't know if I can look those murdering bastards in the eye.'

'You will.'

73.

Chief Dempsey came into the crowded room, Ralph and Fenwick at his side. The officers present were starting to show the strain of working too many long hours. Several of the younger men crowded around Smith, asking him questions. Ralph realised that his men had now accepted the two Feds as their own. Slowly the talk dwindled. Ralph coughed.

'Thank you, Lieutenant McCoy,' Dempsey's voice boomed. 'You know why I'm here. Last night Lieutenant Detective Usner was brutally murdered.' He paused for effect. 'We don't know why at this moment, but we feel sure it's to do with this case. It seems, from what he told Agent Fenwick, that Dwight was going to meet an informant. Whether it was a setup, or they'd followed and murdered him after his meeting, we don't know. Whatever the score, there seems to be a motorcyclist involved. I want you out on the streets talking to your contacts, showing a high profile.

I'm passing the case to Lieutenant Detective McCoy, and I would also like to add that the FBI is still playing a major role. Thank you for listening. Good luck.' Dempsey patted Ralph on the shoulder and left the room.

'Relax, everyone.' There was a noticeable sigh. 'Yes: I want a higher profile on the streets, but not from all of you. I have posted your duties. Any queries - come to my office; otherwise get on with your jobs.' Fenwick bent forward and whispered in Ralph's ear. 'One more thing. There will be a collection going round with information about the funeral. Thanks, everyone. Do your best for Dwight.'

Ralph stepped past the men in front of him and went back to his office, Fenwick following. Smith chatted for a little while before excusing himself. Ralph and Fenwick were talking when Smith entered the office.

'I don't understand, Mr Fenwick. He was staking the place out?'

'At first we thought he must have been chased there, because he was certainly trying to escape up over the levee, but it doesn't make sense.'

'What doesn't?'

Smith posited: 'If he was chased into the site, and presumably he was still in the car at that time, why are tyre marks going towards the gate from the stack of blocks?'

'So what was he there for?' asked McCoy.

'We're not sure, but we think it had to do with meeting the kid. We know he had made contact with the British Consul, and...'

'What? Here in the city?'

They both looked at him in wonderment.

'You mean he didn't tell you?' asked Smith. 'It's in his notes, here.' He bent over Ralph's shoulder and leafed through some papers on his desk. He stopped and stared at Fenwick. 'It's gone.'

'Shit,' cursed Fenwick. 'The Consul spoke to him on the phone yesterday. He'd had contact with the Banks'. Dwight was excited because he had convinced the consul that they needed to come to him.' Fenwick placed a fatherly hand on McCoy's shoulder. 'Don't worry; I'll get on to it right away.' He picked up the phone.

McCoy said 'Hold on. First; you tell me everything that you know - and that means everything that is missing, as well. You're supposed to be helping me; not running things.'

'You're right, Lieutenant. I'm sorry. I got carried away.' Fenwick sounded contrite.

Smith smiled behind McCoy's back. He would be no problem.

74.

It seemed that Fenwick and Smith could do no wrong. They convinced McCoy to visit the British Consul in person. He had not left his office more than three minutes when the phone rang. It was answered by Fenwick.

'Fenwick here.'

'Can I speak to Detective Usner?' The voice had a slow drawl.

'Who's calling, Sir?'

'This is Sheriff Fourgge, from Morgan City.'

'From where?'

'Out by Bayou Teche.'

'I remember, Sheriff. How are you? Can I help?'

'Yeah; get me Usner.'

'Sheriff, have you not heard the news about the cop-killing last night?'

'Yeah. You people up in the city seem bent on murdering each other.'

'Well, we're trying to keep a lid on it at the moment, but the cop in question was Usner. We'd be obliged if you didn't spread it around.'

'Sheeet.' There was a slight pause. 'So who's in charge?'

'A Lieutenant McCoy, but he's out at the moment; that's why you came straight through to me. I'm still on the case and using Usner's office, so can I be of help?'

'Maybe I should leave a message for McCoy.'

'Sure; or you can tell me and I will pass it on to him.'

'Okay. After what happened to Danny, I asked around about the British couple and the girl.'

'Why are you telling us now? You couldn't be less helpful before.'

'Well, I'm sorry, but you guys came out here as though it belonged to you, but after what's happened I don't want any more folks getting hurt around here.'

'Okay; so what have you got?'

231

'They stayed out at Philippe Boucher's place, the night Danny sent those hoods packing.' The sheriff gave a chuckle. 'The next day they were gone.'

'So where did they go?'

'I can't be sure, but I can make a good guess.'

'What's that?' Fenwick gave a sigh. He was starting to get fed up with the sheriff's long-windedness.

'Well, Philippe also left early that morning in one of his shrimping boats and I bet they're out there with him.'

'Where is 'there', Sheriff?' Fenwick asked tensely.

'Out in the gulf, around the shrimp beds. He'll be sailing back in either tomorrow or the next day.'

'And where will that be, Sheriff?'

Smith noticed Fenwick had sat up straight and tense.

'N'Yawlins. Where d'ya think?'

'Do you know where in New Orleans?' Fenwick could hardly contain his excitement.

'Sure. Everyone knows where; down at the packing wharves. There are wharves below the French Quarter on the N'Yawlins side of the river.'

'Do they know when a particular boat will be arriving?'

'Sure, but I wouldn't ask around down there; they'll get to hear about it. Your best bet is to ask the coastguards. Once they enter the channel - and there are three main ones, they can tell you when that boat will be arriving, within fifteen minutes.'

'Could they stop off anywhere else on the way up?'

'Sure, but you can have your own boat running up at the same time.' The sheriff gave a sigh of exasperation. 'Mr Fenwick, I'm a busy man. You give that information to McCoy; he'll know what to do and who to contact.'

'Yeah, of course. Sorry to waste your time.'

'That's okay, Mr Fenwick.'

'Oh; one more thing, Sheriff.'

'What's that?' Fenwick could hear the irritation in his voice again.

'Would you know the name of the boat?'

'You knocked that clean out of my head with those damn-fool questions. It's either the Marie or Philippe Junior.'

'Thanks, Sheriff.'

'My pleasure, Mr Fenwick.'

Fenwick leant back in his chair, chuckling to himself. Smith was studying him quizzically.

'We've got 'em cold and McCoy knows nothing about it.'

'You sure? Couldn't the sheriff check back?'

'What for? In an hour we'll send an email saying 'Thank you - signed McCoy.' He'll glance at it and delete it, thinking it's all been passed along.'

Fenwick got up.

'Come on, we've got work to do.'

75

Throughout the morning the nets were out and the crew pulling in the shrimp. They were out of sight of land, but they had the company of four other boats and a wheeling flock of birds. Alice and Molly sat in the prow away from the gear.

'Nan.'

'What, Alice?'

'Do you think there could be a mistake?'

'About Danny?' Molly gazed softly into Alice's eyes. 'I don't think so, my love.'

She watched as her granddaughter sagged deeper in her chair. There was nothing she could do to shield her from this pain. Alice gave a sniff.

'I asked Danny to love me the night before we left.'

'Of course he loved you, Alice.'

'You don't understand; I asked him to have sex.' Molly stayed mute, not wanting to say the wrong thing.

'But he wouldn't,' Alice sighed. 'I wish he had.'

'Well, I for one am glad he didn't. He's a grown man and you're just a child.'

'I'm not a child. I have periods.' She stood up and glared down angrily at Molly. 'Anyway, not long ago girls my age were marrying men as old as Danny's; it wasn't wrong then. And it's not like I'm a virgin. I've fucked lots of times. At least I *wanted* to do it with Danny.'

Before Molly could say anything, Alice fled aft. Staring after her, Molly's eyes filled with tears. She slumped back, not knowing what to do, lost in sorrow that her little girl had been through too much. Once the box had been opened there was no going back. A shadow cut across her, shielding the sun. It was Bert. He knelt down and patted her hand.

'Are you all right, Moll?'

'No, I'm not.' She took a handkerchief from her sleeve and blotted her eyes.

'I saw Alice below in tears. Do you want to talk about it?'

'Oh Bert, how are we going to cope?' She looked into his eyes. 'Do you know what she's told me?'

'No, I can't imagine. With a normal girl her age I could have a good guess, but Alice isn't normal for her age. Do you want to tell me?'

'Oh, I don't know, I feel out of my depth.'

'Well, join the club. I've been out of my depth since we boarded that bloody plane.'

'You shouldn't swear, Bert Banks.' She lightly tapped his leg. 'Alice told me she offered herself to Danny the other night.'

'You sure?' Bert frowned.

'Of course I'm sure. She said 'to love him in bed'. He compressed his lips and shook his head. 'It's alright; it seems Danny refused her.'

'Thank goodness for that. So what did you say?'

'I said I was glad he had, him being the age he was and she a child.'

'I bet she had something to say about that.'

'Yes, that one aint short of an answer.'

'Seems to take after someone else I know.' He chuckled.

'Are you going to keep interrupting me or shall I tell you what she said?' She paused, and he didn't attempt to say anything else. 'She said it wasn't that long ago that girls her age were married to men Danny's age. She said that it wasn't as if she were a virgin.' Molly nudged him and whispered the last part - 'She said *that* word.'

'What word?' he asked, confused.

'Oh Bert, don't be so dense. She said '......!' she mouthed.

'Woman, I don't know what you're on about.'

'*She said 'fucked'* Molly hissed. She caught his smile and gave him a playful slap. 'You knew what I meant all the time!'

'Yes Moll, I knew. We both suspected it before we came here; that's what forced us to get on that bloody plane. Yes, it's shameful what's happened to her, but let's not make her ashamed of herself. She is an unhappy victim caught in an adult maelstrom.'

'Bert, I'm not sure if I can do it. She takes my breath away with her talk. It's too wide a gap.'

'I know; but you've got to leap that gap to bring her back. You can't expect her to come to you.' His eyes traced the criss-cross lines of netting that lay strewn on the decking. 'No one else can do it. I can help, but it's you she trusts. Maybe she'll never trust men, I don't know, but she needs to trust someone who will listen to her and not make her ashamed.'

'It's too much, Bert.'

'I know. We'll take it a little at a time.' He hugged her. 'Come on; let me make you a cuppa.'

'I don't know, Bert Banks.' She wagged a finger at him. 'You think all the world's ills can be cured by a cup of tea.'

'No I don't; well, not all of them...' He went aft.

Molly sat pondering on what he had said, idly looking northwards over the water, which was flat as a millpond. To the right, another boat was fishing. The white specks of birds wheeled around the craft. Squinting, she thought she could make out the crew on the decks. Something made her gaze above the wheeling birds and a little to the right. A black speck was stationary for a moment, then veered off to the east and hovered over another craft. A gut feeling told her it was searching for Alice. She got up and ran aft, calling to Dee-Dee. He stepped down from the wheel-house.

'It's okay, Molly, I've seen it. Go below and tell Bert and Alice to stay hidden.'

'Is it the police?'

'I don't think so. Don't worry; I've been expecting something like this for some time.'

'You knew they were coming?'

'No. Now stop your questions and go below. Remember what I told y'all.'

'Of course I will.' She hurried past him and climbed down into the cabin to join the others.

76.

Dee-Dee picked up a pair of binoculars and swept the horizon until he came to the boat to the east. He raised the glasses, his field of vision gliding smoothly past the mob of birds above the boat until he had the black speck framed.

'As we thought, Philippe, it's a helicopter and it's inspecting the boats. It will come to us soon.'

'Dee-Dee, you must cover your skiff and you must also hide. They mustn't know you're here.'

Some minutes passed before they heard the thwack of the chopper flying overhead. It circled the boat several times before it lost interest and flew back towards land.

A few moments later little Philippe's head appeared above the hold.

'It's safe for you to come up, but grandpa says keep near the hatch in case it comes back.'

When they got back on deck Philippe Snr. poked his head out of the wheelhouse. 'Bert, Dee-Dee, come in here. I think you were right, Dee-Dee, they were searching for us. Once they located our name they headed back to N'Yawlins.'

'How do you know it was for us?' asked Bert.

'Simple,' said Philippe. 'If they weren't looking for the boat they would have gone on to the other two shrimpers to the west of us, but they didn't.' Keeping his hand on the wheel, he turned. 'What do you want me to do, Dee-Dee?'

'What we've planned; nothing else. What time are you pulling up the nets to set out for the South Pass?'

'When do you want to approach N'Yawlins?'

'An hour after dark.'

'Hold the wheel for me, Bert.'

Philippe moved over to his chart table. Dee-Dee came behind him and looked over his shoulder. The captain's stubby finger prodded the paper. 'We're about here. Dark is 18.30 to 1900 hours. It will take two hours to get to the mouth of the South Pass, another four up to N'Yawlins. To get us in about twenty hundred hours we need to leave in two hours' time.'

'What time will it be when we get into the skiff to drop off at the Algiers wharf?'

'It will be dark, but I can take you to the wharf before going to the dock.'

'I think when we get near to the wharf we'll have company. We must act as though we don't know we're expected.' Dee-Dee pulled out a mobile phone.

'Hi Snowy; it's me. Yeah, we had our visitors; they know we're on our way.' He paused, and listened. 'Yeah, about eight. We'll be leaving a little before that. Can you lay on some transport? Sure; I can hang on.' Dee-Dee tapped his foot. 'Yeah, that's great; four of us. Sure, I'll let you know if we have company before we arrive. Be seeing you.' Dee-Dee snapped the phone closed, and pocketed it. 'Don't look so worried, Bert. It'll work out okay. You'll see.' He rested his large hand on Bert's shoulder. 'I think it's about time I showed you how to use that gun.'

'Do you think it's necessary?'

'If Danny said you had to, you have to. No argument. Ain't that what he said?'

77

Harry put down the phone and grinned at Fenwick, but there was no warmth in his eyes.

'It seems they've located the boat.'

'Did they spot the kid?'

'No, but we didn't expect to.'

'How far out are they?' asked a small guy who captained a fast charter boat.

'About two hours from the South Pass.'

'Why don't we go out there and blow the boat out of the water?'

Harry looked at Smith and shook his head as though he could not believe what he'd heard.

'Two reasons, Smartass. One, they would have a mayday out before we could get close; and second, they're amongst a small fleet and what's the betting they all come in together?'

'Give me the phone.' The small guy held out his hand, and Harry threw it to him. 'I have a friend on the wharf.' He pressed out some numbers and waited.

'Hi, Dave. Jeff here. Tell me, you expecting any shrimpers in today?' He paused, and listened. 'Five. Yeah. What time? Early evening? Great. It'll be after dark? They do? Thanks.' He tossed the phone back to Harry. 'Thanks.'

'That's them. The chopper counted five including the Marie.'

'Yeah, but if I were him, I'd try to unload at another wharf; somewhere lonely,' said Jeff.

'When?'

'After dark.'

'That makes sense.' Fenwick paused, and thought for a second. 'Where could they get off?'

Jeff pondered the question for a moment. 'Don't know; could be anywhere on the river. There are so many small wharves, you couldn't cover 'em all.'

'So what would you do? Follow in your fancy boat - and if they dock before the downtown wharf you go in and shoot 'em up?' Smith asked humourlessly.

'Something like that, Smith, but not so crude.'

'What then?' asked Harry.

'I could pick the fleet up where the South Pass joins the river and follow behind, right up to the city.' Jeff was enjoying the attention.

'They'll see you.'

'Sure, but we'll be a noisy fishing party. They'll not be sure what we are. Once we reach Venice...'

'Where's that?'

'Got a map?'

'Yeah; over here.' Harvey opened up a large-scale map.

'Let's see. Here's Venice.' Jeff pointed. 'You could have a car to keep level with us up into the city, and have another on the other side at Bohemia. If they stop off we can have someone waiting on either side.'

'But surely they'll have friends waiting, too?'

'Sure, but they won't be expecting anyone to be coming from behind. They'll be concerned to get away from us out on the river.' Jeff looked around to see if anyone disagreed.

'I think you're right. How long will it take you to get downriver?'

'About two hours or so.'

'Okay. Get going. We'll organise the cars. Call us once you see them. Can you pick Harry and me up at the Venice wharf?' Jeff gave a curt nod. Fenwick slapped him on the back. 'Smith will see you out.'

78

It was four in the afternoon when the first shrimp-boat nosed its way into the South Pass. It took ten minutes for all five boats to sail into the channel to the Mississippi and within the hour they were passing Venice on their port side. They overtook a noisy party in a white launch which slowly lagged behind, until it was only just in view.

The shrimpers sailed in single file, the Marie in their midst. Slowly they crept up the Mississippi, against its sluggish current, the light starting to fade as they passed Bohemia on their right. Through the rigging of the boats Alice watched the sky darken to mulberry hues. One by one the boats switched on their navigation lights, except for the boat party, who were now quiet and moving stealthily closer.

Dee-Dee was with Philippe in the wheel-house when the Marie got called from the last boat in the line.

'Catfish to Marie; come in.'

Philippe calmly picked up the mike and pressed the transmit button.

'Marie to Catfish, over.'

'Philippe; remember the noisy fishing party we passed at Venice? We've been keeping an eye on 'em. At first they seemed to drop way back, but they've been holding steady with us ever since Bohemia. When we put our nav lights on I also switched on the radar. Now it seems they're starting to catch up with us - and they're not showing their nav lights. Over.'

'Thanks, Jean. Keep me posted.' Philippe put the mike back in its holder. 'What do you make of that, Dee-Dee?'

'I'd say that's our tail.'

'You don't think they'll try to board us?'

'No, I don't think so; they're too out in the open here, and they would be scared of being rammed.' Dee-Dee stared out through the screen. 'Can these boats go a little faster, Philippe?'

'Sure, but that boat can outrun us if it wants to.'

'I wasn't thinking of outrunning it. If the two boats behind us dropped half a knot while the rest of us increase our speed, they would be quite a way behind by the time we got to Algiers.'

'Yeah, that would work - and if we switch off our rear navigation lights that would confuse the bastards further,' suggested Phillipe. 'I'd wait until we got to English Turn: by then it will be good and dark. They won't realise how far ahead we are until we're close to dropping you off.'

'Will the other boats go along with it?'

'Sure, I'll fix it up.'

Dee-Dee left the wheel-house with a couple of deckhands as Philippe started to organise the little fleet. They moved his skiff into position for lowering into the water when the time came. Bert watched as they tied the skiff to the swing-boom.

'Dee-Dee, I've been thinking. Were you expecting to take us all off whilst the boat was moving?'

'Sure; nothing easier.'

'It won't work. Molly found it difficult enough getting into the thing when it was from a dock and we weren't moving.'

'I thought of that. Once the boat's in the water, we'll rig a seat onto the boom and lower Molly down.'

'That might work, but don't tell her until you're ready to do it; don't give her time to worry.' Dee-Dee gave a wink.

79

Since dusk Jeff Wilkes had slowly crept up till he was no more than thirty yards behind the last shrimper. As they came to English Turn the right-hand corner cut off a view of the forward boats. He would be relieved when he got to the left-hand bend at Caernarvon, when he'd get a clear view of them all again.

As they came to this last bend a large tanker was on the curve, going down-river. It took to the centre, forcing all the boats over. For ten more agonising minutes all but the last shrimper were out of sight. He cursed, knowing he would not get another good line of sight until the tanker had passed. Another obstacle was the working light that swung at the rear of the last boat. It made it difficult to see anything beyond. He cut a glance at Fenwick, who stood next to him peering anxiously ahead.

'Can't you overtake?' Fenwick asked.

'No. If we do it now they will know who we are, and God knows what they'll try. Probably squeeze us into the tanker. That's what I'd do.'

'Maybe they know who we are. That lamp is killing our night-vision.'

'I doubt it. It's a pain, but it's a work light. Can't you see someone's working up there? Maybe a winch is jammed.'

A chuckle came from behind.

'You'll have to be patient, Fenwick. Come and sit down. You're making the captain nervous.'

Fenwick knew Harry was right and stepped back.

'If we go in too soon,' said Wilkes, 'they'll know we've guessed they're coming into dock.'

Philippe stuck his head out of the wheelhouse and waved to Dee-Dee. The boat was shrouded in darkness; the only illumination the wash from the city lights. It enabled him and the two deckhands to swing the skiff out and lower it into the water.

For such a large man, Dee-Dee jumped lightly down into the boat, quickly bending over the outboard and starting it. By the time he turned round the crew had released the harness and were fitting a seat to the boom. He cupped his hand over his mouth to shout. A horn blasted from behind and kept on blasting. Swinging round he saw that both shrimpers were way over the other side of the river and perilously close to colliding with an outgoing barge. At what seemed like the last moment the leading shrimper, followed by the other, swung back out of its way. Philippe hung out of the wheelhouse again and bellowed:

'They know we're trying to do something; they're manoeuvring to overtake. Alice!' He shouted, 'Jump down into the boat.'

Alice hesitated, and watched as Molly was being cajoled into the seat, her eyes as big as saucers with fear.

'Do as you're told girl...' Before she could utter another word the boom gave a jerk and lifted Molly off the deck. She let out a shriek as they swung her out over the water. With the practice of years, the crew lowered Molly into the centre of the skiff. With a light bump that had her rolling out of the seat, it was lifted out of the way. Bert helped Alice down, then gave a backward glance and waved to Philippe. He dropped his hands onto the gunwale, climbed over, and disappeared from sight.

Alice released the prow rope as Bert's feet touched the bottom and Dee-Dee gunned the engine. The outboard roared, and they swept out and away from the shrimper, towards the left bank. Alice laughed as Bert was taken off-balance and toppled, landing with his backside in a pool of water next to Molly, who was clutching for dear life to both sides of the boat. Her eyes were closed tight and her lips moved in a silent prayer.

Alice saw a flash of light stab out from the darkness ahead and pointed, an excited grin spreading over her face. It flashed again.

'I see it!' shouted Dee-Dee. The skiff swung towards it.

As they neared Chalmette and the river straightened, Jeff Wilkes became concerned. He could only see two sets of navigation lights. He nosed the boat further out but the craft in front seemed to be moving to block his view.

'Shit!' he cursed.

'What's up?' Fenwick started to get out of his seat.

'I think they know who we are.'

Jeff gunned the engine and swung out even further into the channel. The prow of the boat lifted sharply as it shot forward and to the left of the shrimper, to overtake it. Unprepared, Fenwick fell back, missed his seat and slammed hard against the cabin door. It burst open and he toppled out and slid across the open deck, coming up hard against the stern. It knocked the breath out of him, leaving him half-stunned.

An arc-welder lit up as the boat moved out and gained speed to overtake the shrimper. The swinging lamp had been a nuisance, but nothing like this. The arc-light was blinding. Their launch nosed past the stern of the shrimper and the light was no longer a problem, but Wilkes' night-sight was destroyed for the moment. Before he could recover completely, the shrimper beside him dropped its net boom over the water. The nets hanging from it became a curtain that would snare the launch. It pushed them further over to the other side of the river. The curtain of nets swung up out of the way as Wilkes gunned his launch forward. The next shrimper had its nets down as well, but they now knew that the Cajuns would not risk damaging their equipment.

The shrimpers' manoeuvres had created a wall of boats that forced the launch across into the downriver channel. Blindly, Wilkes bore down on the second shrimper, which with its nets down, was forcing him further into the oncoming channel. Fenwick came to, and managed to claw his way back up the sloping deck, grabbing hold of the door-jamb to pull himself into the cabin.

'What the hell happened?'

Jeff glanced over his shoulder. The shrimper lifted its nets as a horn blast split the air. Fenwick's eyes widened and Harry shot out of his seat to grab the wheel.

'Jesus Christ, look out!'

Wilkes turned back in horror. 'Shit!'

The shrimpers were peeling away to their right to give way to the barge, but there was no room for the launch. He spun the wheel hard to port as the blunt prow drove towards them like a huge battering ram. Harry was thrown hard against the right side of the cabin; Fenwick lost his grip on the door-jamb and slid back across the outer deck, while Wilkes managed to stay on his feet.

As the boat cleared the barge he tried to spin the wheel back. The craft tilted the opposite way as it sharply straightened up. Harry became airborne, and was flung back across the cabin. In a desperate grab to save himself he caught hold of Jeff, tearing his hands away from the wheel. They both ended against the other side of the cabin with a solid thud. They heard a scream cut off as Fenwick was also tossed to the other side of the deck.

The wheel span back to centre. The boat straightened up and drove its full length up onto a wharf. The engine roared out of control. Wilkes staggered up and pushed the throttle back. The boat settled and creaked. The sound of gurgling water came from beneath his feet. His head sank over the wheel, and he lashed out with his foot.

'Fuck.'

Harry and Fenwick staggered to their feet as Wilkes raised his head, tears welling in his eyes.

'Look, Fenwick.' Harry pointed.

They all watched as Dee-Dee's skiff, now silhouetted by the city lights, made for the shore.

'Where are they going?' asked Fenwick.

'One of the Algiers wharves.'

Fenwick pulled out his mobile and pressed one button. Immediately, it was answered.

'Miller, Fenwick here. Now listen up; they are making for one of the Algiers wharves.' He paused and listened. 'Which one, Wilkes?'

'I think it's the first one. Yes; did you see that light flash? Tell him he can reach it on Patterson. Which road they on?'

'Did you get that?' Again he listened. 'Newton Avenue.'

'If they take a right on Thayer it'll get 'em straight there.'

'Did you hear that? And watch your step; they're being met.'

Harry tapped them on the shoulders. 'I think we should get off this wreck before it sinks.'

They had managed to leap onto a stable part of the wharf when there was a grinding sound, followed by a sharp bang. A piling that had been part of the wharf came up through the floorboards of the cabin. The boat settled lower in the water. Harry and Fenwick started walking towards the bank, leaving Jeff to watch the death of his pride and joy. Fenwick gave Harry his mobile.

'Harvey; they're not coming. Get the hell out of there. Send the car to Patterson in Algiers. We'll be waiting.'

80.

The first shrimp boat was pulling into the wharf as Harvey pocketed his mobile. He tapped Smith on the shoulder.

'They've left the boat. We'd better be gone.'

'Shit,' Smith swore.

Harvey dismantled his rifle and stored it back into its soft shoulder-case. Smith was still peering over the gable-end of the warehouse roof when he felt another tap on his shoulder. He pushed himself away from the edge and stooping low, followed the dark figure of Harvey to the back of the warehouse. They scuttled down the steel inspection ladder that ended with a drop of ten feet into a dirty, stinking alley. Smith had gone first so that Harvey could pass his rifle to him before also dropping to the ground. Harvey gained his feet when a searchlight came on, scorching the area of any hiding place.

'Stop where you are, Smith. Drop the case.'

Smith glanced at Harvey and started to lower it to the ground.

'I said - drop it, now!'

It clattered to the ground. Harvey winced.

'Okay! Both of you: Hands in the air and lean facing the side of the building. *Now* - legs apart as far as they can go.'

As they followed the order they heard several feet running towards them, then felt hands swiftly frisk their clothes. Both were relieved of their hand-guns, and Harvey of a flick knife.

'They're clean, Mac.'

'Okay. Cuff 'em.'

Ralph picked up the gun case. He unzipped it, pulled the rifle partly out and whistled.

'Nice; but there are no deer around here, and didn't they ever tell you, Smith, not to drop a thing like this? You can damage it!' Several of the police officers chuckled.

'Bastard! I want to see a lawyer,' growled the twin.

'Shut the fuck up.' McCoy glared into Harvey's eyes. 'Take him down to the precinct and read him his rights, and don't let him talk to anyone until I get back.'

As they moved the men out Ralph put his hand on Smith's shoulder and faced him. 'I've been waiting for this for some time.'

'Suck my dick,' sneered Smith.

Suddenly the agent was on the floor coughing and spluttering, clutching at his crotch.

'When I've finished with you there won't be anything to suck. Take him away.'

McCoy walked out of the alleyway, flanked by five uniformed officers. He went to his squad car and opened the back door.

'Mr Cardew; will you come with me? The boat will be docking soon.'

The 'Marie' came gently to rest against the dock. Ropes were thrown and tied, holding it against the current. Philippe cut the engine, switched on all the deck lights and left the wheelhouse. He watched as his crew set to unloading the catch. Lt McCoy, Mr Cardew and the five cops walked out into the pool of light beside the shrimper.

'Captain Boucher?'

Philippe swung on his heels to gaze down. A man was holding out a badge. 'I'm Lieutenant McCoy, and this is Mr Cardew from the British Consulate. I believe you have some British subjects on board.'

'No, Lieutenant, you're mistaken.'

'May we come aboard?'

'Be my guest, Lieutenant, but watch your step.'

McCoy had been about to step aboard, but he hesitated. 'Why?'

'We've been shrimping; the deck is very slippery.'

81.

As they came up to the wharf Dee-Dee cut the engine, to glide in to rest with a slight bump. Alice sprang out, a rope in her hand. She fastened it to a ring that was fixed to the decking. She looked around but couldn't see a soul, only hear the cough of an engine start up. The hard glow of red and white reversing lights sprang into life and an SUV reversed towards them. It screeched to a halt; the driver jumped down. She could hardly make him out; that was, until he smiled. Gleaming white teeth lit up his black face.

'Hi! I'm Snowy. I believe we've met briefly before.'

'I don't remember.'

''Cause you wuz tryin' ta git outta N'Yawlins at the time. Someone was chasing ya'll ass. I kinda got in their way.'

Alice grinned. 'Yeah, I remember. Your name had me thinking of someone different.' Snowy slapped his thigh and laughed.

'Can you help get Nan out?'

Snowy knelt down at the edge of the dock and shot out a hand to Molly. She hesitated.

'Nan; grab his hand!'

Trembling, Molly got to her feet while Dee-Dee and Alice held the boat steady.

Once Molly was on dry land the men handed up the baggage, which Alice packed into the open back of the truck. Molly scrambled into the rear seat and waited for the others to join her. This was all a little too much for her. She searched for her atomiser.

The truck was spacious, with plenty of room for everyone. Dee-Dee took the front passenger seat. Alice made a comment about some people taking up more room than others and got a slap from Molly, but Dee-Dee laughed.

'Hell, Alice, at least I travel in comfort.'

'Everyone - git ya seat-belts on, 'cuss I think we may git comp'ny.' Snowy slammed his door.

He shoved the stick into drive, the wheels span, and the truck shot forward towards an alley between two blacked-out buildings.   From the other end appeared two pairs of headlights.

'Hell! Sooner than I thought. Hold on.'

Snowy swung the steering wheel hard.   The tyres squealed and Molly squeaked.   The headlights picked up buildings, disused equipment, derelict cranes and the skeletal remains of old boats, and then a gaping hole in the side of a warehouse wall. The truck shot towards it.   There was a squeal of tyres from behind and the interior of the truck was lit by the lights of chasing cars.   As they penetrated the building their headlights pierced the darkness before them. The following vehicles held tightly behind as they snaked through the old building.

'Wotcha reckon? They dunno this place?' asked Snowy.

'Probably not,' answered Dee-Dee.

They came out through another gap, into an open area. To their right the lights of the French Quarter were reflected in the river.   The SUV swerved, and again they were engulfed by another hole, the wall of the building flashing perilously close to their left. On the other side were yachts, propped up on wooden legs. An opening appeared ahead. At the last moment Snowy swerved to the right and smashed through two stanchions holding the last boat. Alice peered back through the rear screen and saw the yacht shudder, and slowly start to topple. The first car was beneath it, but managed to get clear before it crashed across the gap. The toppled boat yawed sideways as the last car tore into it. A fireball spewed out of the warehouse entrance and lit up the area for a few seconds.

'At least it got one, Snowy.'

He glanced in the rear mirror and caught Alice's eyes. 'One's not enough, girl. There's a hatchet in back under your bags. Move your fanny and fetch it out.'

Without answering, she released her seatbelt and foraged for the hatchet. As the wagon went over a bump, she let out a scream and disappeared behind the back seat. There was a scrambling sound and she reappeared, hatchet in hand.

'Got it.'

'Pass it to Dee-Dee, girl.'

'My name's Alice,' she replied tartly.

'Yeah, I know, girl.'

She nudged Bert, who took the hatchet from her, not once taking his eyes off the road ahead. He passed it on to the Cajun.

'Dee-Dee, I'm gonna take us back to the river's edge, then down onto the wharf. As I hang a right I'll slow enough for you to jump out. Got that?' Dee-Dee gave a grunt, beads of sweat glistening on his forehead. 'Take the hatchet and go to the floating wharf. It's held on either side by two rope hawsers. Cut the down-river one and wait for me to come round on it. When I blow my horn cut through the other hawser. Hopefully, with the thrust of the wheels and the current of the river, there should be a gap by the time they get there.'

'And if not?' asked Bert.

'We don't ask them sort of questions. They bad luck, mister. Now girl, get back in your seat and belt up.'

Alice started to climb back. Seconds later she was flying again, this time into the back of the driver's seat as Snowy braked suddenly.

'Now, Dee-Dee. Jump man; jump!'

There was a rush of cold air and Dee-Dee was gone. The wagon swung right and the passenger door shut with a bang as it straightened up.

'Are you belted up, girl?'

'Give me a chance; you didn't warn me you were going to brake. And stop calling me girl.'

'Sorry, girl. Now hurry; they catching up. We gonna take a sharp left. Now!'

The tyres screeched and they were going sideways along the concrete wharf. He gunned the engine and it shot forward towards the water. There was a crash as the back end smashed into a post which tied the floating wharf to the concrete dock. They clattered along the boarded wharf. At its end they turned up-river. They felt, rather than saw the chasing vehicle start along after them.

Alice was disconcerted by the sensation of travelling on a narrow boarded causeway with water flashing by on either side. It lurched and swayed as they crossed from one floating section to the next.

They entered the last stretch, and headed back towards the bank. Alice caught sight of Dee-Dee in the headlights, his arms raised over his head.

'Wait for it, wait for it,' came a chant from the front seat. 'Now!'

The horn blew and Dee-Dee's arms fell, rose, and fell again. The truck came roaring up onto the concrete, its back wheels spinning before they bit and shot forward.

With the end released from its ties, the wharf bucked and swayed. The current caught it and floated it away from the concrete dock. The driver of the chasing car stood on his brakes, but on the slippery wood his vehicle slid towards the end, slowly going sideways. One back wheel came off and the unbalanced wharf tilted to one side, making the car slide further, until it tipped right up and it slipped sideways into the water.

82.

McCoy slammed his fist onto the table. Smith sat stoically staring at the wall beyond the lieutenant.

'For the last time, where is Fenwick?'

'How the hell should I know?'

McCoy straightened up. 'Okay, have it your way. Turn on the tape again, Bernie.' The young cop by the tape machine flicked the switch. 'Agent Andrew Smith of the Federal Bureau of Investigation, Washington Sector: I charge you with the murder of Police Lieutenant Dwight Usner on the night of May the fourteenth.'

Smith shot out of his chair.

'I had nothing to do with that...'

'Sit down, Smith!' McCoy screamed. 'To continue: - and to conspire with one, Harvey Dancer, to obstruct the police in apprehending two British subjects and a minor, one Alice Jones, who is wanted to help police with their enquiries into the murders of Tracey & Lewis Barasitch. Anything you say will be taken down and may be used against you in a court of law.'

'I want to see my lawyer.'

'All in good time, Smith.' McCoy went to the door and opened it. 'Sergeant; lock him down.'

Harry put down the phone. 'It seems the cops have arrested Harvey and Smith.'

Fenwick peered down into his glass of whiskey and swirled it around. He took a deep slug and pulled out his mobile to contact Brevison. The phone rang several times before it was picked up.

'Fenwick, where the hell are you?' Brevison shouted.

'In New Orleans. The cops have arrested Smith.'

'Yes, I know; and one of the twins. There is also a warrant out for your arrest. What the hell did you think you were doing?'

'What you asked; getting the kid.'

'And where is she right now?'

'I don't know. Our people were sent to intercept them, but they fouled it up.'

'No; you fouled up. I suppose they're with the police now.'

'No, they landed in a place called Algiers. It's a section of New Orleans. They could even be out of the city by now. The Cajuns don't trust the cops...'

'If that's the case, I think they'll try to go north,' interrupted Brevison, 'and meet up with a guy called Arran Marx. Ever heard of him?'

'Yeah, another ex-cop. I think he's an old friend of Danny Generve. The name has been bandied about. That's all I know.'

'Well, he works out of New Jersey, doing the same as Generve. We've checked him out but he's not at home. We now know the grandparents went to him first to find the girl. Some of our people are watching out for him to turn up.'

83.

Ralph McCoy flicked the cigarette out of the window. He was parked on Lakeshore Drive, facing Lake Pontchartrain. He glanced at his watch and decided he would wait a few more minutes. A single light showed in his rear mirror. A deep roar rapidly diminished as the powerful motorbike dropped down through the gears. It came to a stop by his car door. The engine died. A leather-clad figure raised his visor.

'You're late,' muttered McCoy.

'Making sure you haven't been tailed.'

'So where are they?'

'Safe. Did you get everyone?'

'Yeah;' but McCoy hesitated.

The rider pressed the starter button; the engine came to life. 'If you're going to lie, McCoy, I'm off!'

'Okay. We only caught Smith and Harvey.' The engine died. 'Fenwick and Harry were not with them.'

'That's because they were following the boat up-river.'

'That's what I wanted to do, but you said no.'

'I told you; two's company. You would have made it a crowd. Harry and Fenwick have gone to ground. I'll let you know when I hear something.'

'What about the kid and the couple?'

'No deal, Ralphy. Anyway, as you saw, they didn't come in after all.'

'That's bullshit, and you know it. They came in at Algiers.' McCoy lit another cigarette. 'You played me as a decoy. You had no intention of bringing them to the wharf.'

The biker chuckled. 'What would you have done in my case? Danny's been taken out of the picture and you've lost Usner. Find and arrest the other two and we'll talk again.' He started the bike.

'How will I contact you to tell you we've caught them?'

'I'll know.' The rider slammed down his visor, kicked the bike into gear and roared off.

84.

Harry and Fenwick were still free by the time Smith and Harvey were taken to court later that morning. The hearing on Smith took no more than five minutes and McCoy had him held in custody awaiting further investigation. McCoy stayed for Harvey's hearing while Smith was taken out through the basement car park back to his cell. He never made it. They found his police escorts coughing their guts up from a couple of smoke bombs and Smith with a neat hole through his forehead. When the security cameras were checked the video tape was missing. The security guard was getting over a sore head.

Harvey's hearing took longer than Smith's. His expensive lawyer fought hard and had him freed on bail. The charge of attempted murder was not enough to hold him, and there was no provable link as yet to the Barasitch killings. McCoy watched from the courthouse door with mounting frustration as Harvey jauntily walked down the steps to the street below. He never reached the sidewalk alive. His head caught a sniper's bullet.

Two hours later McCoy was standing in an uptown apartment staring down at the bodies of Fenwick and Harry Dancer. They were riddled with gunshot wounds. They had been dead for some time.

Before McCoy could get away from the reek of cordite and blood that hung in the apartment, his mobile buzzed.

'Yeah.'

'Do you think it's safe now, Ralphy?'

'How the hell did you know?'

'It doesn't matter how I know; answer the question.'

'I'll get extra people in and we'll use a safe house.'

'Hell, Ralphy; wake up. Who will you protect them from; - *whom?*'

There was a pause.

'You still there?' asked Ralph

'Just about. You have not answered my question. Who are the people to watch out for? What're their names?'

'How the fuck would I know?' screamed McCoy.

'Precisely. At least, before, we knew their identities. Now there are watchers in the shadows.'

'Let me meet the kid.'

'Can't do that. At the moment they're all safe - and I aim to keep it that way.'

'I want to talk to the girl; see if I can work out what all this is about.'

'It's more than your life's worth, believe me, Ralphy. I know what it's all about - and it goes deep into Government. I'll tell you somethin' for nothin'. It scares the bejeezus out of me.'

'We can work something out.'

'Goodbye, McCoy.'

'Don't hang...' McCoy stared at the phone. It was dead. They were gone and he had more bodies on his hands than he knew what to do with.

85

Alice chomped on gum as she leaned against the side of the window and watched a transvestite walk up and down Dumain in the French Quarter. Two blocks away the tourists trailed by in an unending stream. Her hair had been bleached and cropped with a streak of magenta trailing out towards the back. Her eyebrows and lashes had also been bleached and now she sported a nose stud and four rings in her left ear and two in her right. Her breast had been strapped and she now resembled a scrawny young boy. She was wearing a Marilyn Manson tee-shirt, tight jeans and well-worn Nikes.

'Get away from the window, Alice.'

'Don't call me that, Gladys. I'm Toby! I don't think gramps likes the way I look.'

Molly squirmed. She wasn't sure he had been happy about her own makeover either, and she still didn't feel comfortable with her hair. It had been fuzzed and coloured a silver-mauve. The butterfly-framed glasses felt top-heavy, and the light blue Banlon slacks were tight. She stared down at her hands. The nails winked back at her with a silver-pink sheen that did not quite match her blouse.

'Do you want some gum?' asked Alice.

'No, Toby. I don't want any gum. It sticks up my dentures.'

'You should practice. You must be in character; that's what Jerry said.'

'Yes, until I open my mouth. Then my disguise - what is it he said?'

'Shot to hell. Well, you'll have to practice keeping your mouth shut.' Alice smirked.

'That's enough cheek from you, young lady.'

'No, Gladys; young *man*.' Alice huffed a fake sigh. She was having fun. 'Dee-Dee said we need to melt into the background;it's too dangerous being English at the moment.'

'I wonder how long Bert will be?'

'Hey, Gladys, you must stop calling us by our real names! He's Bubba.'

'Oh! Stuff and nonsense.'

Bert was in the next room, and if Dee-Dee had not been sitting there with him he would not have let the two men do what they had. They peered over his shoulder as he was grimacing at the mirror. For the last two hours, since finishing with Molly, they had been sorting him out, as they put it.

'Whad'ya think, Girl?'

Jerry studied Bert for a few moments and shook his head.

'I don't think there's much more we can do.' He paused, and appraised Bert with pursed lips. 'I'll tell you something, Girl, if he treats me nice, I think I've found myself a sweet old sugar-daddy.' Bert winced.

'That's it!' He struggled up from the chair and tore the hairdressing cape from around his neck. 'I've had enough of you two ....' He struggled for a few moments. 'You two people!' he finished weakly.

'What do you think, Jerry? He nearly said queers!'

'I know, Girl, and after all we done for him.' Jerry swooned into the chair they had been using, and his boyfriend flapped around him. 'And to think he could have taken you away from me.'

Bert swivelled round, contrite.

'I'm sorry, you two. I - I didn't mean to be nasty and all that. It's, well, I'm not used to all this.'

Jerry sprang out of the chair.

'That's all right, Bubba, don't mind me. I think it's the menopause. Now get out of those pants; they're so English!'

Bert cast around for help from Dee-Dee, who merely shrugged his shoulders.

'Come on. No messing,' said Jerry ,who pulled out some trousers from a wardrobe.

'It's not like we're not all men here!' said Girl coquettishly, and giggled. 'We've seen it all before.'

Bert slowly pulled down his trousers. Girl shouted an 'Oh My!' and Bert yanked them up again.

'Come on, Bubba, she's only fooling with you. Now stop it, Girl, or I'll ask you to leave.' Dee-Dee was chuckling quietly to himself in the corner. Jerry rounded on him. 'And you can behave as well, or we might start on you next.'

'The hell you will! I ain't havin' no queen messin' with me.'

'Do you want some help, boys?' Bert grinned.

'Hey, who's side you on, Bert?'

'I'm fooling with you, as they say.' Both men laughed.

Bert had pulled on the jacket and a hat was placed on his head when Alice opened the door. Her mouth dropped open.

'Holy shit!'

'Alice - don't you use that language.' Molly came to the door and clamped a hand to her mouth. 'Oh, my God.'

'Hi, Bubba. You look finger-lickin' good.' Alice giggled.

Bert stood, not quite sure how to hold himself; a little bit self-conscious. He wore a white suit with a black string bow tucked under a silver-white pointed goatee. The hair poking out below the wide-brimmed white hat was the colour of his beard.

'What do you think, Moll?'

'People will think we're a couple of Charlies. We won't fool anyone.'

'That's where Danny would say you're wrong.' Jerry dried his hands and threw the towel into the chair. 'The last time I saw Danny we talked about what we could do. We both thought no-one but a pair of stupid American tourists would walk around like you're dressed up, and the last thing those people chasing you are searching for are outlandish American tourists.'

Bert and Molly seemed dubious.

'But nobody goes around like this, do they?' asked Bert.

'Some do, and people give 'em no-never-mind.'

'Dee-Dee; someone wants you on the phone,' Alice interrupted. 'In here.'

He went through to the other room, pushing the door to behind him. Alice, leaning against the door jamb, nudged the door open again with the heel of her Nike.

261

'Hi, how are you?' Dee-Dee paused. 'Yeah, sure I can come. We can't move until we have the papers for the old folks. Sure, they'll be here by dark, then we can get going. Have you sorted the wheels? Yep; that sounds about right; big and old. Bert is not sure he'll be able to cope with driving on the wrong side of the road, as he puts it, but the Girls says they can deal with that. And it's not like he'll need to drive through the city. We'll keep mostly to the country roads.' Dee-Dee paused, and glanced at the door. 'I think there are some ears listening to me. See you soon,' he whispered.

Alice heard the pause in the conversation. She crossed the room quickly and managed to sit in the chair that Bert had used to have his hair cut. She was smiling at Girl when Dee-Dee pulled the door sharply open.

'I gotta go out.'

Everyone turned to him.

'Anything wrong?' asked Bert.

'No. I just find it difficult to stay indoors like this. I won't be long.'

86

Alice went to her bedroom and shrugged on her denim jacket and grabbed some money that Bert had left on the dressing table. She glanced out of the window and watched Dee-Dee cross the courtyard that separated the apartment block from the street. Instead of going through the wrought iron gate he hid behind a clump of elephant-ears. He stayed there for several minutes before going out into the street. As the gate closed behind him, Alice sneaked out and down the stairs. She peered out through the gate and saw him disappear round a corner.

She followed him carefully for ten minutes, weaving in and out of doorways, until he came to Decatur Street and flagged down a cab. It drove off towards uptown. Alice ran to the street. Cursing under her breath she waved at a passing cab, which ignored her. She put her fingers into her mouth and let out a piercing whistle. A cab screeched to a halt. She ran and flung herself in before the driver could protest.

'Follow that cab, mister!' She pointed through the windshield at the disappearing vehicle.

The cabby shook his head and opened his mouth, but before he could utter a word she slapped a twenty-dollar bill on the top of the seat.

'Hurry, mister, or you'll lose it.'

'Sure.'

Dee-Dee got out on Camp and Foucher. He climbed the steps to an exquisite small shotgun with a Classical Greek Revival facade. He did not notice Alice get out further down the street..

She hid behind a large azalea bush that was shedding its last flamboyant orange blooms and peered at the front of the house, wondering who Dee-Dee might be meeting. She stayed hidden, debating what to do. A neighbour stepped onto their porch, forcing her either to retreat or creep into the garden. Dashing into the driveway she crouched down behind a powerful black motorbike. She brought her hand close to the shiny exhaust and snatched it away again. It was red-hot, and must have been driven shortly before Dee-Dee had arrived.

Even to her inexperienced mind this was a meeting place for a group of people, but it was the bike that intrigued her. Danny had said something that nagged at the back of her mind. After some hard thinking it came back to her. It had been the first time she'd met him in the top room of the camel-back. She'd been scared, and wanted to go with him. He'd promised that when he came back to set her free he would take her far away on his big black bike. Surely it couldn't be... Danny was dead! Dee-Dee had told her so. He'd cried with her and held her till she had slept and since then had never left her for a moment; excepting now.

As she calmed herself, she became aware of voices from a window a little above and beyond her. She moved towards it, but it was still too high to see in.

'Com'on, man, I'm not leaving Alice. Wherever she goes, I'm going too.'

'Dee-Dee, you can't'. The voice was not one that Alice recognised. 'You'll stick out like Jesse Jackson at a Klan convention. We don't know who is going to be hunting them now that the others are gone. Some big shot is looking for the kid; someone with much more clout than even we suspected. You don't get rid of good operatives unless they leave you very exposed. They were executed swiftly and with precision. No; you'll endanger everything.'

'I understand that, but I promised Alice I wouldn't leave her. You don't know how fragile she is! When I told her about Danny...' Dee-Dee's voice stopped and there was silence from the room.

'Maybe he could go with Snowy,' a voice whispered. It sounded gaspy, as though the owner was in pain.

Alice, craning to listen, did not sense her danger until she was grabbed around the chest and a hand clamped over her mouth. The large hand spread, fully covering her breasts in an iron grip and as she struggled, she was crushed harder into the body behind her. She was lifted from her feet and carried into a dim kitchen at the back of the house.

'Arran, come and help,' shouted the man holding her.

A leather-clad stranger came through an inner door, followed by Dee-Dee.

'I caught this kid snooping round the side by the window.'

'Alice! It's okay, Jake, you can let her go.'

'She?'

Alice sunk her teeth into his hand and Jake yanked it away with a gasp of pain. He still held on as she tried to wriggle out of his grasp.

'Get your filthy hands off my tits!'

He let go as though he had hold of a snake.

'Shit, kid. You don't call those tits.'

Alice rounded on him and glowered at his toothless grin.

'Fuck off, you dirty old bastard!'

'Stop, Alice, or I'll tell Molly! Jake's a friend and this is Arran, Danny's partner.'

'Who else is in that room?'

She jerked her head at the closed door beyond Dee-Dee. He shot Arran a look.

'You heard Jake's voice.'

'He may be a friend but he ain't Superman.'

Alice brushed him aside and was through the door like lightning. She saw over by the window, the silhouette of a man in a wheelchair

'Danny!' She sprang forward, but Arran caught her.

'Steady, girl; you'll hurt him.'

Danny moved his head. The hair on the side and back had burned away, and his ear was a scrumpled piece of bacon rind. He lifted his hands from under a rug. They were both bandaged and one arm was encased in plaster.

'Do you want to see more?' gasped Danny.

Alice shook her head, tears glistening in her eyes. 'What happened?' She turned sharply to Dee-Dee. 'Why did you lie to me?'

'He didn't, Alice. He didn't know until he came here.'
Arran moved over and crouched down by her. 'Only we in
this room know, and it must be kept that way for Danny's
and other peoples' safety. Do you understand?'

Alice nodded, and gazed doe-eyed at Danny. 'What
happened, Danny?' Her voice was no more than a whisper.

'I got hurt when they blew up my office.' Danny's voice
came in gasps and pain clouded his eyes. He beckoned as
tears rolled down her cheeks. 'Come here.'

He raised a bandaged hand and wiped away a tear.

'It's okay, Alice. I'll be all right; you'll see. Now let's
have a good look at you.' He met Dee-Dee's eyes and
chuckled. 'You sure this ain't a boy?'

'Well, I didn't find any tits,' laughed Jake.

'That's 'cos of this.' Alice lifted up her tee-shirt. Her
chest was tightly bound with a wide bandage.

'The Girls have done a good job. Now, Alice, not a
word: Promise; and you must do *everything* you're told.'

87

Alice had eaten with the men and afterwards sat in the corner watching the television while the others sat around a table trying to plan the journey through the States. After a time, Danny became tired and beckoned her over. For some minutes neither acknowledged the other. Alice picked up the remote and the screen went blank.

'You didn't want to watch?' she asked

'No.'

'Does it hurt much?'

'When I laugh.' Danny chuckled, but his grey face showed the pain.

'How did it happen, Danny? You promised me to be careful.'

'Yes, I remember. I suppose I got too close.' His eyes watered as he remembered that morning. 'I watched as they murdered an old friend in my office. When I went to see if I could help him they had set the place to blow. I was lucky.'

'Lucky. You kidding me?'

'It depends on whether you want to be dead or alive. I might be a mess now, but a year on you won't know it had happened. Believe me, I was lucky.

'I realised a second or so before the place blew, and dived for the window. It simply blew me through; the glass must have gone just before I hit it. I have no wounds from that. The explosion knocked me out before I landed, so I must have been pretty relaxed; also, a tree cushioned my fall.'

'You make it sound a doddle,' said Dee-Dee dryly. Danny did his best to shrug, then resumed:

'I woke up to hear sirens, and for some reason I knew I had to hide. I crawled under the house two doors away. From there, I went from house to house until I was at the furthest end of the block.' He paused, and gave several deep gasps before resuming: 'It took some time, 'cause I kept blacking out. Miraculously, my mobile still worked. Jake came and fetched me. He got onto Arran, who dropped everything and flew down. He picked up my bike, and met with Usner.'

'Who's Usner?'

'He was the cop who was dealing with your case; the one who got murdered.'

'Murdered?'

'Shit.' Danny swore over his stupidity. Of course; she wouldn't have known. 'That's another story.' He looked drawn and exhausted.

Arran butted in. 'Let me tell it. Usner found an old John Doe that no-one knew. He'd been burnt up in a car wreck by some thugs. The cop put Danny's name on the body. How he did it, I don't know. He must have had good friends down at the morgue.'

'What about the other body?' asked Jake. 'Someone must be missing that.'

'Sure, but stiffs are coming and going all the time. So a John Doe went missing. It's happened before, and no one is going to worry too much: It's not like he was the mayor.' He laughed.

'Don't they have to report accidents that go into a hospital? What about Danny, then?'

'I haven't been to hospital,' said Danny. 'Jake's a doctor, though from the way he dresses, you wouldn't guess.'

At the sound of his name Jake came over. 'You taking my name in vain?'

'No,' said Alice, in wonder. 'Are you really a doctor?'

'Was, Alice, was. Got struck off twenty years back, before abortion was made legal. Tried to help a poor kid not much older than you. Instead of the parents being relieved, they sued. The rest is history.' He went back to talk with Dee-Dee and Arran.

'What are you going to do when we leave?' Alice asked.

'Jake will take me back to Ducey, and he'll stay with me until there's no more need.' Danny leant towards Alice and whispered, 'He'll get fattened up, and he 'likes' Ducey, so between him and Philippe they'll all drive me mad. The house will become filled with flowers and Ducey will drift around with a dopey, moon-struck face.' Alice giggled.

Arran looked up from what he was studying. 'Having fun, you two?'

'So what's the plan?' Danny asked.

Arran drew his chair round. 'Leaving in the morning if the papers come through as promised.'

'They will. Angel has never let me down yet,' said Danny.

'We have an old Cutlass for Bert and Molly. Jerry and Girl will take them out to Slidell later tonight. I'll be taking the panelled truck and you, Alice, will be coming with me; we can bunk up in that. Dee-Dee will ride shotgun with Snowy in the back-up truck. Alice can stay here with us tonight.'

'But -'

'It's okay, Alice. Your folks know you are here. Dee-Dee called and told everybody the plan.' Arran thought for a moment. 'Alice, we need to know more about what happened to you in New Jersey.'

Alice's face darkened. She turned her head away and pressed the remote. The TV blared out. It started to skip through the channels, getting faster.

'I want to go back to Nan; now.'

Danny jerked his head, and the men left one by one and went into the kitchen. He watched the back of her head. She sat stiff-backed, defiantly staring at the changing screen.

'Alice; if you carry on doing that, you'll break Jake's television.' Still the screen flashed on. 'Alice: We *need* to know.'

'Why?'

'If I'd realised how bad these people are I would not have involved so many of my friends.' Still she didn't budge. He sighed. 'Alice - see what's happened to me...'

She suddenly stood up, her eyes so full of tears she couldn't see; her cheeks red and wet, her lips trembling.

'I'm sorry, Danny.' She drew in a deep breath, put a hand to her eyes and brushed the tears away. With lips still quivering, she tried to smile bravely. 'I better go.'

Danny gazed into her little face and wondering at her courage, he sadly shook his head. 'Alice, you can't.'

'You going to stop me?' she asked through gritted teeth.

'No. Nor will the others. You'll be out on the streets alone.' He closed his eyes. He knew he was being brutal, but he had to be, to be kind.

'They'll find you out there and they'll kill you,' Dee-Dee said from behind her, cutting through the tension.

Alice swung round. 'I don't care. It will be all over...'

Dee-Dee interrupted her again.

'They'll *kill* you, Alice. They'll *kill* you, my little princess, for something you know about; and when they've done that they will come and kill us, because they will think we know as well.'

'I'll say you don't know nothing,' she said stubbornly.

'Even if you get the chance to say anything before they kill you they won't believe you.' Dee-Dee carried on remorselessly as Alice stood there, shaking and crying. 'They'll come for Molly and Bert...'

Stop, she mouthed: 'For Ducey and Philippe;' he said, 'for Jake; for Arran, for me.'

He looked down at Danny, placing a large hand on the push-bar of the wheelchair, and then, staring directly at Alice: '- and for Danny, who you thought was dead.'

'Stop!' shouted Danny, but Dee-Dee had said it.

Alice screamed piercingly for several seconds, and collapsed onto Danny. He grunted and held her. Dee-Dee jumped forward to lift her from him, but she put her arms around his legs and held on tight.

'Stop, Dee-Dee. You're hurting me, man.' he gasped.

'Sorry, Danny.'

'Leave us.'

'Alice: I'm so sorry.'

'It's okay, Dee-Dee. Leave us. We'll be okay.'

Dee-Dee backed out of the room. Danny gritted his teeth and waited a few minutes until he couldn't bear the pain any more.

'Alice,' he gasped. 'You're hurting me; please let go.'

She relaxed, slid off his lap, buried her face in his legs and sobbed.

'It's all my fault. I'm so sorry, Danny.'

Danny stretched out a bandaged hand and laid it on her head.

'Shush, my little one. It's not your fault. That doesn't belong to you.' They sat there, her sobs slowly diminishing; his swollen hand on her head. It was dark outside. That was all he could register.

The outside was always dark, he thought.

He didn't know how long they sat there, but he had to start asking her.

'Alice: We really have to know *everything*.'

'Okay.'

'Do you want a drink?' She nodded. 'Get a coke. It's out in the fridge. Go fetch it, and bring me a beer. Ask everyone to come in.'

'But Danny - I only want to tell you.'

'Better they hear too. They might ask questions I don't think of.'

88.

The offices of the Washington Bureau were practically empty. On the third floor, Brevison was working at his desk, reading the latest report. He couldn't believe it; these people had slipped through his net - and his team were supposed to be the professionals. His fingers drummed on the desk-top.

Liquidating two of his top agents in the manner he had would cause questions. Only success in the mission would subdue his critics. If the child, or worse, copies of the stolen disk, came to the media attention, no amount of cover-up would protect him. His masters would distance themselves. He'd be left to hang out for the vultures to pick his bones.

He leaned back and closed his eyes. It was no use worrying; it would come good in its own time. In the old days it had been different; easier. If you couldn't do it one way, you found another angle to try. These days, break one rule and that was it. He shrugged at the irony. If they hadn't been offering those 'special services' to turn certain diplomats they wouldn't be in this mess now.

Three years' work was now in jeopardy and it would put the government in a hell of a position. They would lose their conduits into some really sensitive countries. The US would get slaughtered by the world press. With terrorism confounding the leading powers, America could not afford to alienate anybody. The British would never trust them again; corrupting, and using blackmail - and on their politicians.

The problem was - did the kid know? Could she put it together? All that was needed was for her to see one face she recognised and the rest would fall into place.

Thank God most of the people she had met had been faceless men: the ones you never saw; the real influences behind the decision makers. It all came down to - where was that disk, and would it die with her as Fenwick had thought? With a weary sigh he lifted up his phone.

'Andrews; I know it is late, but I need you to track someone down urgently. No - I don't know their name. Stop asking questions and listen.'

272

89.

The sky was mostly grey, but several dull rose smears brightened the eastern horizon as a mud-spattered white panelled truck left the Irish Channel. It crossed Magazine Street and got itself lost in the myriad tiny roads until it came out below the crossing of Carrollton and Claiborne. It's passenger snuggled low in the seat, and dozed.

'Alice, wake up,' Arran said to her as they were leaving New Orleans behind.
'What?'
She woke with a start. The sun had broken through the cloud cover and poured in through the side window, warming her face and relinquishing its hold on the rim of the water as she sat up and stared all around her. There was water everywhere, except for the white concrete strip that ran straight ahead and back towards the city they were leaving behind, hung over with a bruise-purple mantle; a still-slumbering place lying low at the water's edge.
'Where are we?'
'Lake Pontchartrain Causeway. About halfway across. Twelve miles behind and the same in front.' They flashed by a signpost. 'We're now in Saint Tammany Parish.'
'Shit!'
A sailboat appeared from under the road a little way ahead. A wind caught and billowed the sails, veering it further away as it slowly moved back towards the city, becoming merely a triangular white shape on the water.
'Where are we going?'
'Up into Mississippi. We'll keep to the old road as long as we can, so it's going to be slow.'
'When do we meet up with Bert and Nan?'
'In under an hour. We'll breakfast with them at a truck-stop.'
'Will Dee-Dee be there?'
'Yeah. Bert's getting his American driving lesson right now with The Girls. Dee-Dee will go out with Snowy.'

'So when will The Girls leave Nan and Bert?'

'After they've had breakfast.'

'We going in a convoy?'

'No. The plan is for us to not be seen as travelling together. Sometimes we'll be in front and Snowy behind, sometimes in reverse. We'll never be far apart, though, and always in close contact.'

'So where's the truck-stop?'

'A little place called Bogalusa on the Mississippi border.'

'Bogalusa.' She said the name several times, as though she were savouring it. The sound was like a thing you could eat and taste. She smiled to herself. 'Sounds like a sausage.'

Bogalusa was small, not much more than a crossroads. As they neared it shabby houses peeked out from behind stands of dogwood and myrtle. It was a rundown sort of place. The trees gave way to a gas station, workshops and stores, their fronts cluttered with barrels and farm implements. Outside one frontage was the obligatory bench for a couple of old boys to sit and watch the world go by. The truck stop was a large area of uneven ground just short of the crossroads. It was full of heavy haulage vehicles and an odd assortment of beaten-up cars. A shack-like building plastered with signs was in back of the lot, proclaiming itself 'Lurline's Place'. Whether it was full was hard to see; the windows were so steamed up. Arran climbed out of the truck, leaned against the fender and casually checked around.

'Come on, Toby, let's go eat. They're all here, but remember what I said. We don't know 'em - and remember, you're a boy! Put your cap on and swagger a little.'

The place was full of sounds, smells, smoke and people. They took a bench at the back of the room and waited for the busty peroxide blonde to squeeze past other tables to take their order.

'Hi; what can I get y'all?'

'I'll take a coke and one of ya large breakfasts.'

Alice's head went back down as she studied the dog-eared menu, but her eyes were elsewhere. She spotted Bert and Molly in the corner next to the counter, their backs towards her. Dee-Dee was on the opposite side of the room, staring out of the window. He turned his head and glanced around aimlessly. His eyes cut in her direction, hesitating fractionally on her face before moving on without a trace of recognition. Pressing her hands each side of her on the bench, she wanted to jump up and shout 'Hey, Dee-Dee, over here!' Arran pressed his large hand on hers. He gave a slight shake of the head.

90.

They were finishing their meal when the door opened and the room became quiet. Arran cut a glance across to Dee-Dee who had a view of the door. He jerked his head in that direction and gave it a slight shake before lowering his eyes and continuing with his meal. Alice wondered why the people behind had stopped talking, and turned to see before Arran could stop her. She quickly spun back round.

'Arran, there are some cops and they're looking for someone,' she whispered.

'Keep eating.'

They both concentrated on what was left on their plates. A shadow fell over them. From the corner of Arran's eye he spied the characteristic dark trousers by the side of their table. A night-stick hung from a heavy belt, along with a revolver and cuffs. He raised his head and looked straight into the cop's eyes.

'You driving that white panelled truck out there?'

'Sure. What's the problem?'

The officer ignored the question. 'Let's see your licence.' Arran pulled it out. 'Is he with you?' The cop indicated Alice.

'Yeah, he's my son.'

'Let's see his i.d. as well.' Arran put out his hand and Alice gave him her card.

The cop looked at it, and handed both back.

'Where y'all making for?'

'Forrest.'

'What you carryin' in back?'

'Our home.' The cop stayed silent, as though debating what to do. Arran sighed. 'Gotta problem with that, officer?'

'Yeah. It looks to me like your truck is overloaded. I think we should go outside and take us a look.'

'Okay.' Arran shrugged. 'Toby, you stay here. Order me some more coffee. I won't be long.'

'The kid better come too.' Arran stiffened at the suggestion.

'What for, officer?'

'Bring the kid.' His tone stopped all argument.

'Dad; I need to go for a shit.'

'Later, kid. I don't want to be going into no wood chasing your ass.'

As they walked across to the truck, a familiar figure got out of the back of the cop car.

'Hi, Ralphy.'

The detective didn't even smile. 'Let's go round the back and look like we're inspecting your load.'

Arran undid the lock and rolled up the shutters. The back had hardly anything in it. A large crate was tied to the side, and in one corner were slung two holdalls and sleeping bags.

'Not much of a home, mister.'

'Who's your friend, Ralphy?'

'Cousin. It's okay, you can trust him. And this, I presume, is Alice.'

Alice looked sullenly at him. 'You going to take me away?'

'I should; but no. I think that would give us more trouble down here than a bunch of Mardi Gras' put together.'

'What do you want, Ralphy?' asked Arran.

'We need to talk, and I got someone you need to meet, but not here. Are the old couple in there?'

Arran pondered the question for a few moments. He decided it would be better if the cops didn't have to yank them out as well.

'Yeah. You want to meet them, too?' McCoy nodded. 'Don't go in. I'll give them a call. We can meet at their car.'

'Just tell them to drive up the road two miles 'til they see a sign to a turkey farm on the right. They're to drive down to a big barn and wait.'

91

Dust billowed about Bert as he got out of the car. The barn was flanked by fifteen buildings like long scout-huts. Each roof wore a series of metal cowling vents, and from these came the squabbling of thousands of turkeys, but it was the smell that grabbed him by the throat. He'd never experienced anything worse. Three sleek, powerful-looking vehicles with windows of black mirror-glass were parked up close to one of the sheds.

He leaned back against his seat and watched as a cop car came down the track. Arran and Alice jumped out of the truck and ambled over before the other car had stopped rolling to a halt.

'It's okay, Bert.' Arran leaned against the car. 'They don't know about Dee-Dee and Snowy.'

'I'll go and help Molly out of the car. I'll tell her to keep mum.'

'Mum?'

'Quiet.'

'Yeah, you do that.'

Ralph walked over, offering his hand to the English pair.

'This way, everybody.' His cousin opened one door of the shed. Inside were six men sitting around a large trestle table. One rose and walked over.

'Hello, Arran.'

'Hi, Menkin.' His eyes wandered over the assembled crew before settling back on Ralphy. 'Having a party? What's the FBI doing here?'

'Believe it or not, you need them.'

'I believe everybody who needs to be here is here,' said Menkin. 'Shall we sit down?'

Chairs creaked as everyone settled themselves. Molly, Bert and Alice huddled around Arran in a worried knot.

'How did you find us, Ralphy?'

'A little bit of luck and a lot of hanging around. I felt sure y'all were still in town. There were whispers that someone was paying over the odds for a bunch of papers in a

hurry. I knew it wouldn't take long and then you'd be gone.'
He studied their faces.

'We're still listening. Go on,' said Arran.

'We discounted Mexico when y'all returned from the
bayous. So that left you with three routes out.' He waved
his arm at the silent men sitting round the bottom end of the
table. 'We covered all of them. As it happened, I chose
your route.'

'Congratulations, Ralphy. So what now; are you going to
throw us all in jail?'

'No. I said not at Lurline's. Anyway, I doubt if we could
guarantee your safety. Also, I want the bastard who started
it as much as you do.'

'So where does Menkin come into it?'

'I want the same as Ralph,' said Menkin. 'There might
not be much love lost between us, but I don't like what's
been going on. Usner was my brother-in-law.'

'Okay; so you got a score to settle. I don't actually give a
shit,' said Arran.

Menkin started to rise. 'You cold-blooded bastard. Usner
left a wife and two kids.'

'Hey, I didn't invite you here.'

'Both of you - cool it,' said McCoy

'I'm here because the bureau got infiltrated,' enunciated
Menkin carefully, his face red and sweaty.

'Crap...'

For the first time in minutes there was a stunned silence.

'Alice!' Molly rounded on the girl. 'I've told you before;
I don't like to hear you swear.'

'But Nan, it *is* crap.'

'Alice: Don't you dare.' Molly faltered, as she felt a
hand on her arm.

'You may not like to hear her swear, but I think we
should listen to what she has to say,' said Bert gently. 'It is
her life, after all. Go on, Alice.'

'I, I...' She stopped, and looked round the table. Every
eye was upon her.

'Yes Alice, we're listening:' McCoy said intently.

'Shit; you all are trying to cover your asses. Where were the cops or FBI when I needed them? And when they did come, trouble found me first. If it hadn't been for Danny, I wouldn't be here now. I'd be dead, and look what's happened to him…' She trailed off into silence. Everyone seemed to take a deep breath. Swiftly she turned on Menkin. 'So when you started your stuff, Mister, I thought - Sheeet!'

'Out of the mouths of babes,' quoted Bert.

Menkin looked sheepish.

Suddenly Molly spoke. 'Well, Mr ahh…?'

'Detective McCoy, Ma'am.'

'Well, Detective, I don't know what you intend to do, but with the help of Mr Marx here, Bert and me intend to take our Alice home; and that's home, *England*. So do you mean to help or hinder us?' Her eyes didn't blink as they moved onto each cop.

'So what's it to be, Detective?' Bert leaned back in his chair and folded his arms in deliberate, challenging way. 'Molly has spoken, and she wants an answer.'

McCoy looked desperately around him. 'This wasn't supposed to be confrontational.'

'Really; well you need to work out what you want, Son.' McCoy cut a sharp glance at Bert, and raised a hand.

'Look, mister; we need as much help as we can get. But it's no good you saying - "You do this, you do that, or else."'

Bert glanced at Alice. 'What was it Girl said yesterday, Alice?'

Her lip lifted in a sneer. 'That's a crock of shit!'

McCoy visibly winced.

Arran Marx interposed: 'I think what the gentleman is saying, Ralphy, is – "What do you want and what can you do for us?"'.

'Now stop this.' Ralph stood up. 'You're not in a position to demand, here. I could still sling y'all in jail.'

'Sheeet…' drawled Alice again. McCoy opened his mouth, but Bert beat him to it.

'Well, with New Orleans City Police record so far, we'll be dead within the hour and our solicitor back home will be quite happy to take instructions.'

'Yes; he'll sue your sorry ass!' said Molly proudly.

'Nan: where did you get that?' Alice sounded shocked.

'Oh, television. A coloured person said it in one of those violent cop movies they make here. It sounded good at the time.' She gave a chuckle.

There was a cough. It was the man in dark sunglasses sitting silently next to Menkin. He'd not been introduced.

'Ma'am, Sir. I'm Haskins from Washington D.C., seconded from the FBI to a special governmental committee. No one knows I'm here but a select few. The infiltration of the Bureau that Mr Menkin spoke of started in Washington. That is why they've been able to circumvent whatever we've been trying to do. We need Alice's assistance. In return, we'll help you cross into Canada.'

'What's your guarantee for her co-operation?'

'We think we know why Alice is being pursued, but we don't have the proof. It's in our best interests to keep Alice alive, and also get her out of the country.'

'To ensure Damage Control,' Arran commented cynically. His eyes locked with Haskins, who shrugged.

'Sure, it's in everyone's best interest. Once we have the proof we can round people up and Alice will be out of danger.'

Arran turned to Alice. 'Danny mentioned to me the morning he died that Lewis had an insurance policy. What was that??'

'I'm not sure, but it was on some memory-sticks. Lewis once said he knew people who would pay a lot of money to get their hands on them, and others would pay even more for them not to exist.'

'And where are they, Alice?'

'I don't know. Danny took them; but he got blown up, didn't he?'

For a second, Haskins' shoulders slumped.

'Someone getting hold of a copy was always their fear. That's why they're seeking Alice.' He looked directly at the girl. 'My dear, do you remember anything about the parties, where they were held, what people were present?'

At the mention of the parties Alice's eyes darted round the table at the men in their suits. The only time she had mentioned the parties was the night before to Danny, Dee-Dee and Arran.

'Only a woman my mum's age. She took us into a big room and told us what to do. We never spoke to the men and they never spoke to us.'

'What about the house, Alice?'

'No. It took forever to get there, and it was always dark when we reached it.'

She looked down at her hands, and tears started to dribble down her face. Haskins sighed, stood up and turned to face Molly's wordless outrage, before pleadingly addressing Bert:

'I'm sorry. I had to ask.'

'That's all right, sir. It's your job.'

Molly put an arm around Alice. 'Come on, dear, let's go for a walk; get some fresh air. That's all right, isn't it, Detective?'

'Sure, we've got a lot of talking to do with Mr Marx.'

'Does that mean you don't need me?' asked Bert hopefully. 'I could do with stretching me legs.'

Ralph nodded his head.

'Right. What do you want to know, and more to the point, how can you help?' asked Arran.

'We're going to escort you to Washington,' said Haskins.

Shaking, Alice ran out of the barn. Molly and Bert rushed after her.

'You might as well shoot her now, Haskins,' Arran said dryly, watching her disappear through the door.

'We'll get her there safely.'

'Even if you did, which I doubt, how long will it take once she's there for someone to get at her?'

92

Once outside, Alice looked round the corner of the barn. She found no one standing guard over the cars, and smiled.

'Nan, Bert; keep a lookout,' she whispered.

'What are you doing, child?'

'Look, Nan; you don't trust that bozo in there, do you?'

'Well; he seems very nice.'

'Oh, Nan; he's creepy. I don't, and I'm not going to hang around to find out. So keep watch.'

Alice sauntered over to the three cars parked in front of the barn. She dropped to the ground and crawled under the first one, then did the same to the others.

'That should do it. Now for the other cop car.' She strolled over to McCoy's and disappeared under it. When she reappeared again, she waved Bert and Molly over to the Cutlass.

'Nan, get in back; and Bert, get comfortable, but don't start her up until I come back.'

'Alice, we can't leave like this!'

'I think we must, Moll; but what about Arran, Alice?'

'He'll be okay. Didn't Danny say if we don't trust someone to run like hell?' Bert nodded, remembering Danny's warning on the steps of Ducey's house.

'I won't be long,' she said, and racing over to the white panel van, reached in and grabbed the map stuck behind the visor; ran back, scrambled into the Cutlass and closed the door quietly.

'Start her up. Let's get goin'.'

The engine caught instantly. The wheels spun on the loose dirt, found traction, and jerked away. As they came to Ralph's car, Alice held up her hand.

'Slow down.'

She wound down the window, lit a whole box of matches and threw it onto a wet patch seeping out from under the car. There was a sudden "whoosh!" The ground blossomed into flames.

'Let's go.'

'Oh, my goodness: Alice - what *have* you done? That poor man's car.'

'If McCoy wasn't sure whether you trusted him, he knows now,' chortled Bert.

There was an explosion that rocked the car. The men in the barn had been so concentrated on how they were to get Alice to Washington they had not missed the little family. That was - everyone except Arran. The explosion was like shoving a stick into a hornet's nest. Everyone rushed out; some to give chase. The fire had spread across the track. It meant driving through flames.

When they got to the other side, they found their own vehicles' back-ends were on fire. Arran, alone in the barn, got up from the table. All had left their mobiles. He gathered them up and walked out of the barn and over to the van. When he beeped his horn for the men to jump out of his way they realised what was happening and that, sadly, it was too late. Two cars with their tails on fire drove off the road and into a stand of maize, the drivers desperately trying to put the fires out.

The police never found the panel van. Jerry and Girl had waited back in Bogalusa, where they had delivered Bert and Molly earlier that morning. Now they drove them to Crossroads, a small place a couple of miles further on. They left Alice and the Banks to climb up into Snowy's truck and hide in the sleeping area until they were the far side of Hattiesburg. Jerry and Girl took the Cutlass and met Arran. They drove back to New Orleans in both vehicles, leaving Arran to catch the others up on the motorbike, which had been hidden under the large crate in the back of the van.

The motorbike joined Snowy at Meridian. Once the convoy had crossed into Alabama they found a small truck park for lunch. Their vehicle was hauling two containers. In the front of the first was a small doorway. The space inside was adapted for cooking and sleeping.

'Well, it seems we needed the back-up plan after all, though it's a bit of a tight squeeze with me along.' Dee-Dee patted his stomach.

'Yes, it's a pity we had to lose the car and panel van so early on in the journey,' said Arran, 'but it should keep everyone confused for at least a day or two.'

'So - is McCoy one of them?

'No, Bert. He was doing his job. At least now that we've left he'll be able to clear up the mess made by those people.' Arran looked at his watch.

'Shouldn't we get going?' asked Molly anxiously.

'Yes, in a little while; but first, you will be pleased to hear, Molly, you can all get out of those clothes and wash that stuff out of your hair.' The men got up and moved to the door. 'Be as quick as you can. We've a long way to go.'

The three came out looking very different. The men were closing the large double doors of the rear container.

'Where's the bike?' asked Alice.

'In there.' Arran jerked his head to the back of the trailer. 'We're all going to travel as a happy family.'

'I wanted a ride on it.' She sulked.

'Not this time.' He put an arm round her shoulder. 'Come on. We've wasted enough time already.'

93

Brevison's day was one of constant frustration. He had pulled those watching Arran's place once Haskins had confirmed his whereabouts down in New Orleans. How that agent had been picked was a bit of a mystery, but as Haskins didn't know what was going on it didn't matter that much.

They now knew the vehicles being used, although the highway patrols had yet to find them. The quarry were probably holed up, waiting for night before moving on. At least that would slow their progress, he thought with grim satisfaction. The firing of Haskins' car had provoked questions from certain quarters he'd rather not hear from. More and more people were getting to learn about the search for Alice. He started making notes. With everything slowed down he would have time to get things in place before they reached the Canadian border. He felt certain they would keep to back roads. He scanned a map pinned to the wall. His finger traced three possible routes; one direct, the others meandering. He had at least two days; hopefully three. He relaxed a little. Probably the latter. The phone on his desk brought him out of his reverie.

'Brevison here.'

'Mr Brevison,' drawled a lazy voice. 'This is Brian Johns of the New York Times.' He closed his eyes; thought - what the hell does he want?

'Yes?'

'Can you confirm that the violent murder of a couple in New Orleans is connected to an ongoing investigation with a paedophile ring up here? And...' the voice drawled on, '-that the Bureau are investigating government connections ?'

'Who the hell's been feeding you such nonsense?'

'Mr Brevison - are you sure? In four days time, I have been reliably informed, I will be supplied with undeniable evidence that high-level members of the government are connected to this ring.'

'No comment.' Brevison slammed the phone down.

So, it was going to be four days before they reached New York and the press. Just *one* pressman? Were there more? No, the phone would have been ringing off the hook. That was a good sign. They were a bunch of amateurs after all, but the really best break was - it would take four days! He clapped his hands with glee. At least tonight he could sleep easy. In the morning he would get Andrews on to tracing the mobile phone Marx was using; maybe get a position.

94

Alice sat back and relaxed. They had eaten, and she felt slightly sleepy. The air-brakes gasped as Snowy released them. She peered down from her perch on the driver's bed at the thin spiral of hair on the crown of Dee-Dee's head.

The cab trembled as the truck moved forward. It roared, quietened for a second as the gear was changed and gave a jolt as the power bit in and bore them forward. She knew for certain that they were finally off, taking her home. She leaned sideways and lifted her lips to Molly's ear.

'Nan, I know this sounds silly...' She paused, suddenly shy. 'I know we've been travelling all morning, but it's only now that I really feel we're going home.'

Molly smiled and laid a hand on her granddaughter's and squeezed it gently.

'I know what you mean, dear. That's how I feel.' She shouted joyfully over the roar of the engine –

'We're going *home!*'

Bert's head jerked up from his chest, where it had slumped. 'Wha-what?'

'I said; 'We're going home'.'

''Course we're going home - are you daft or something?'

The back bench of the cab was a little above the front seats, and curtained off. Arran ruled that these be kept drawn as they could take no chances. Bert sat directly behind Snowy the driver and had already sagged against the side of the cab, dozing. Molly was in the middle, sitting bolt upright.

Nervous tension had her constantly knitting her hands together on her lap. Alice faced a small gap between the curtain and the cab wall and for a while squinted out through it, watching the verge flash by.

The breeze from the open window in front wafted in, keeping the skirts of the curtain in a constant dance. A sweet, cloying smell of magnolia smuggled itself in and curled around her, then the draught sucked it off and away. Someone in front lit a cigarette, and it invaded every corner.

The men's voices kept up a soft rumble broken by laughter, the thing that identified each.

Alice moved her head and looked at Bert. He was fast asleep, his mouth hanging open. Molly still sat straight, but with eyes closed. Her head kept jerking forward. The nervous hands had ceased their mindless work; just twitched from time to time, as though still dreaming of knitting.

Music began to play; music that scrolled images Alice would never forget. She smiled and closed her eyes. When Dee-Dee started to sing she was back in Danny's car, his head silhouetted against the blue water beyond, a tatty straw Stetson perched on his head, and under it his dark hair curling over his collar. She could still hear the thwack of the tyres as they went over the seams in the concrete road. She opened her eyes to find herself back in the cab, but the sounds of tyres on highway carried on. They blurred with the miles - thwack, thwack, until the monotony of it drew down her eyelids and she was lowered into a warm sleep.

Her lids flickered open and the rosy light of evening shone in. She was disorientated before she realised that she was now lying on her side with her head resting on Molly's legs. She listened to the men in front talking to each other. They had evidently changed drivers, for Snowy was now lightly snoring. Arran was at the wheel. The curtains did not quite meet the top of the seats in front, giving Alice a better view than before.**

They seemed to be travelling through a wide, open valley with hills on either side. A large red sun hovered above the horizon in the west. The straight road ahead faded into a blue haze as the truck rumbled forward, neither losing nor gaining on the vehicle ahead. A large billboard seemed to come towards them slowly, then flashed by.

'Not long to Chattanooga now, Dee-Dee.' Arran looked at his watch. 'Once we pass it I must stop and make a call to New York.'

'Why don't you use the mobile?'

'No; they can trace it; far safer to use a payphone.'

'What did the billboard say?' asked Alice.

Dee-Dee turned. 'Hi, princess; thought you were asleep.'

'I was.'

'That was the State sign. We're now in Georgia.'

'Didn't you say we're not far from Chattanooga?' asked Bert. 'I thought it was in Tennessee.'

'It is,' shouted Arran. 'We'll be crossing into Tennessee in a few minutes, and within half an hour we'll be stopping.'

'How y'all doing back there?' asked Dee-Dee. 'Haven't heard a squeak out of y'all since before Birmingham. Is Molly awake?'

'She is.'

'Not long now, Ma'am. Then you can stretch your legs.'

They pulled into a large truck stop several miles north of Chattanooga. Arran drove away from the lights, far from any other truck. He parked under some trees, keeping the passenger door on the farthest side.

'Wake Snowy, Dee-Dee. Right, folks, you can get out and have a walkabout, but keep out of the pool of lights and away from the other trucks. We'll get the back open so we can make some food. If anyone comes snooping, especially cops, hide in the back.' Arran looked at his watch again. 'I've got to make this call. Be back in a little while.'

He opened the door and jumped down. He was silhouetted against floodlights as he walked over to a Seventy-Nine. The air was humid, scented with the perfume of dogwood and magnolia. Molly and Alice disappeared off behind the trees while the men stood around talking and moving their limbs.

'How are we doing?' asked Bert.

'Not bad,' said Snowy, and took a deep pull on his cigarette. 'We lost a lot of time this morning, but we knew we might. Now we're about on schedule.'

'That was very worrying, wasn't it?'

'Yeah, but now they're chasing ghost vehicles, though if we break down it will be difficult. Still an' all, I think we come out the best.' He scuffed out the cigarette.

'How the hell did he know where to find us?'

Dee-Dee coughed. 'Because we told him.'

'What?' Bert stared at him.

'Well; not actually told him personally. We kinda made sure he would hear about it.'

'Wasn't that a bit risky?'

'Yeah, Bert. But on the other hand - no.' Snowy climbed into the container.

'Why the hell didn't you tell us?'

'We couldn't tell you,' said Dee-Dee. 'You wouldn't have reacted properly. We relied on your reaction to lull the cops into a sense of security.'

'Well, I'll be blowed. But why did you need to do that?'

'Look, Bert; we didn't know how much he knew. We were dealing with some very unreliable people to get your papers. We also needed to know what the new agents looked like, and we had to let on that we were on our way.'

'I don't understand.'

'Bert, if you had to drive all the way up, how long would it take you?'

'Oh.'

'That's right. They think that the two vehicles are coming and that we know they've identified them so that forces us to travel at night; which they'll calculate to take about four days. Instead, we have all three drivers in one vehicle they can't know about. We'll be in New York by mid-afternoon tomorrow.'

'You cunning buggers.'

'I take it that's a compliment. Yeah, we're quite proud.'

'So which of you thought up that little scheme?' demanded Molly as she walked out of the darkness. 'I nearly had kittens back at that turkey farm.'

'Sorry about that. I was explaining it to Bert. If you'd known about our leetle scheme you would have reacted differently. Danny thought it best.'

'But Danny is dead -' said a stunned Bert.

'No, he's not. He was badly injured - but no; not dead.'

Molly was furious. 'You mean to say you told us he was dead when he wasn't?'

'Dee-Dee's fault. He didn't know until last night.'

Bert laughed. 'You must admit, Moll; these fellas have got everyone running round in circles, and to tell the truth, if they can get us home I don't care what subterfuge they use.'

'What do we do when we get to New York? I thought we were going to try and cross the border into Canada?' asked Molly.

'I don't know that part of the plan yet,' said Dee Dee apologetically. 'I'll leave that to Danny and Arran to work out. All I know is that a journalist is involved.'

Snowy poked his head out. 'Food's ready, you guys.'

95.

Brian Johns was sitting on a stool in his favourite bar. He had a Miller in his hand and was watching a game of pool. It was becoming a minor battle as young reporters fought it out. The balls sounded like rifle-cracks as they ricocheted off each other and slammed into the pockets. He felt a tap on his shoulder and turned; the barman put his hand to his ear and told him he had a call. He sauntered over to the phone at the end of the bar.

'Yeah?'

'Mr Johns; Arran Marx here. How y'all doing up there?'

'Okay. Where are you?'

'Let's say we're making good time.'

Johns looked at his watch. 'When d'ya think ya'll be with us?'

'Sometime tomorrow. Late afternoon, maybe. Can you be by this phone tomorrow at nine a.m.?'

'Sure. But why don't you call my mobile? You've got my number?'

'This way is safer, I assure you. So you'll be there?'

'Yeah, I'll take a hair of the dog.'

'Have you found out anything yet?'

'I've asked a few discreet questions in certain quarters, but no nibble so far. Also talked with someone in the FBI who owes me a favour.'

'Be careful, man. Watch your back.'

'Don't worry. I'm meeting the contact tonight.'

'I mean it. These people are serious; they've silenced their own people to keep this quiet.'

'Sounds like a great story.' He gave a chuckle.

'Speak to you in the morning.' Arran put down the phone with misgivings. Johns wasn't taking this at all seriously enough.

When they got going again, it was after nine. Although they could have stayed in the container, Bert and Molly didn't like the idea of travelling in a box, and now it was dark the

293

curtain could be opened. Arran gave up his seat so Alice could sit in front, and in no time at all he was asleep. She sat between the two other men with a huge grin on her face.

After Knoxville the road became quieter, with mainly convoys of trucks. The oncoming traffic was very sparse, which helped with the night-sight. At midnight the moon came out from behind the clouds and coated the landscape with a silver sheen. The eastern skyline was humped up in a series of ranges, low and dark.

'What mountains are those over there?' asked Bert.

'That's the Appalachian range, and those in the middle are the Great Smokies.'

'The Great Smoky Mountains. The same as the music?' asked Bert, entranced by the name.

'If you mean Smokey Mountain Breakdown, yeah.'

For long stretches of time there was silence but for the continuing low, even throb of the engine. People yawned, squirmed in their seats and tried to sleep. Even Alice found her eyes closing, jerking her head back each time it fell forward onto her chest. Four hours later they crossed into Virginia. Dee-Dee left the highway for a country road.

They stopped for a little while to drink and stretch their legs, then they rested. Bert, Molly and Alice were persuaded to lay out on the bunks in the back. Once the truck was on the road again they soon fell asleep. Dee-Dee, bunked up on the back shelf of the cab, was soon snoring deeply.

It was gone eight o'clock in the morning when they stopped at Staunton. Arran was pleased to be on schedule. He felt they would be rolling into New York by late afternoon. They cooked and ate some food in the container, leaving the door open to change the air. Rain had started in the middle of the last stint of their journey, and now it had settled into a misty, dreary morning. Standing by the door and looking out at the low clouds, Arran said

'I think it will clear when we get out of these hills.' He checked his watch. 'I've got to make another phone call - it'll take about half an hour. After that we'll get on our way.'

'Why don't you use your mobile?' asked Bert.

'No. By now they must know all the phones I own, and they'll be monitored. If I should use any they will be able to trace us within a few feet from where I'm standing. At the moment I'm hoping they believe we're further back down the road and are now hiding out during daylight hours.' He left the doorway and dropped down to the ground. 'Dee-Dee, get everyone ready for us to roll when I get back.' He walked off to a building on the far side of the truck stop.

96.

The girl behind the bar picked up the phone. She gave a shout but no one owned up to the call.

'Sorry mister, he isn't here.' She was about to hang up when a colleague of Johns' shouted from the other end of the bar.

'Jan, is that for Brian?'

'Yeah.' He held out his hand. 'Hold up, mister. I think there's a friend of his wants to speak with you.'

She placed the phone on the bar. Arran, on the other end, stayed listening. A lot of things were going through his mind; none good. Finally it was picked up.

'Yeah?'

'I need to speak with Brian Johns.'

'You haven't heard?'

'Heard what?'

'He's dead, man.'

It stopped Arran in his tracks. 'You kidding me?'

'No, man.'

'When?'

'Late last night.'

'How?'

'A friggin' mugger. He was shot. It goes on all the time. This city is shit.'

'Thanks.'

'Hey, are you a contact or something? If you've got a story, maybe I can help. I'm doing Brian's obituary.'

'You know him?'

'Sure, I've worked alongside Brian for the last five years.'

'Do you know what he was working on?'

'Lots of things, but nothing earth shattering...'

Arran caught the pause in the reporter's voice.

'What?'

'He said something real interesting had come to him in the last few days.'

'But you don't know what?'

'No; though thinking about it now it had to be something dirty.'

'Howdya make that out?'

'Anything of real interest will be dirty – or maybe involve the government. I'd stake a month's salary on it.'

'And now he's dead,' Arran said blandly.

'Yeah, bit of a coincidence.'

'You think so?'

'Give me your number. I'll do some digging back at the office.'

'You don't want this story, man.'

'Why the hell not?'

''Cause you'll end up the same way. Dead.'

Arran looked across to the truck. He needed to hurry. The place was filling with more vehicles: time to move on.

The journey to Hagerstown was uneventful. Arran stayed in the container. He needed time and solitude to think, to plan. It was clear to him and to Danny that they had to lure their pursuers out into the open. They had no chance of finding them by any other means. After an hour of planning, he laid back. It was going to be a long, stressful day. He would need all the energy he could muster. He felt he had just closed his eyes when Dee-Dee shook him awake.

When he climbed out of the container the rain and mist had gone, and although the sun was out there was a sharp wind. The truck was tucked into a corner away from other vehicles in yet another gas station. The group was keeping a low profile.

It was time to exchange ideas with Danny and then call Tom, a buddy of his in New York. Pulling Dee-Dee and Snowy away, he asked for the motorbike to be ready when he got back.

'You're going ahead of us?' queried Dee-Dee.

'No. The journalist we were to meet has been murdered.'

'So there's not going to be any media coverage?'

'We can't risk it.' He glanced over his shoulder to make certain that Molly, Bert and Alice weren't close. 'These

297

people seem to be able to cover their tracks and it will be far easier for me to do what's needed without having to worry about you guys.'

Snowy looked down at his shoes for a moment, then lifted his gaze to Arran.

'You're going to make a false trail, aren't you?'

'Yeah. Whatever happens, *you've* got to get to the border. If I don't get in contact, assume the worst and smuggle them across with a bunch of tourists.' He dipped his hand in his pocket,bringing out a slip of paper. 'Here's a contact on the other side. He'll get you all to Toronto.'

97

Arran was tightening the chinstrap on his helmet when he felt a tap on his shoulder.

'I need a word,' said Bert.

'What's the problem?'

'I'm not sure I understand why our plans have changed. I thought we were going to meet up with a journalist in New York.'

'We had to change that.'

'But Danny was convinced that Alice would only be safe once this was out in the open. That's what Dee-Dee said.'

'Yeah, I know what he said, but since then it's become too dangerous.'

'So what's with the motor bike? Are you planning to ride ahead of us?'

'No; something has happened that makes it imperative they think *you are* going to New York, while instead, you make a dash for the border.'

'Is this all necessary?'

'I think so. When we don't turn up soon, they'll start checking routes to Canada. If they think you're still on your way to New York they will relax a bit. Enough, I hope, to get you across at Buffalo as visitors.'

'You're going to act as decoy.' Bert stood staring at Arran. 'Won't that be dangerous?'

'Not the way I do it. No.'

'And how do we get into Canada?'

'Dee-Dee will handle that.'

'Then this might be goodbye.' Bert held out a hand. 'Thanks for all your help, and good luck.'

They shook hard. Arran started the bike, shifted it into gear and moved off.

Two hours after leaving the truck, Arran left Interstate 81 and joined 78. The others would also leave the Interstate to use route 15. They were heading northwards to freedom, whilst he was making directly for the heart of danger - New York.

His phone sat on the gas tank inside a clear plastic pocket. It started to ring. He pressed a button.

'Hi, Tom, how's it going?' he said into the mike fitted in his helmet.

'Okay. Everything in order as asked. How 'bout you?'

'On 78; five, ten minutes. Traffic not bad and making good progress. At least the weather's cleared up. Should be with you in three hours or so.'

'Okay, I'll keep in touch.'

'Sure, be hearing from you.' The phone went dead.

Tom, a large black guy, walked over to a street bin and chucked away the recently stolen mobile phone he'd used to contact Arran.

98

Andrews called Brevison's office. The call was re-routed to a hotel room overlooking Central Park. A large, heavy-set man picked up the phone.

'Yeah?'

'Mr Brevison, please.'

'Hold on.' He handed the phone to Brevison.

'Yeah?'

'Andrews here, Sir. Marx is using his mobile again.'

'Good. Where are they?'

'They're on 78 and heading your way.'

'Are you sure? They weren't suppose to get that far for at least another day.'

'Certain, Sir. He mentioned they were on the interstate and I was also able to track both phones.'

'They're moving faster than we thought they would. Did you get a line on who he was talking to?'

'Yeah, a Mrs Warburg, from the Bronx, but the call was made from Coney Island.'

'Were you able to listen in?'

'No. Too fast.'

'Okay, give me the address. Let me know if he goes on air again.'

Brevison put the phone down and scribbled the address on a pad, handing it to the thickset man.

'Get it staked out.'

He walked over to a map lying on a table in front of the window. He looked out onto the park. It was a warm day and the joggers were out, sweating their way around the pathways. Looking back at the map, he shook his head. It didn't make sense.

The bike gently vibrated under Arran as the engine purred, keeping to an even note. He kept it dead on the speed limit. The last thing he wanted was to be stopped by a traffic cop. If his licence was reported in, he was sure it would be picked up straight away. It was one thing for them to know he was

on his way into the city; it was another to know how. He
also hoped they would think he was bringing everyone with
him. It was the only way to coax them from the shadows.
With Tom using stolen phones he hoped the operatives
would be spread thin throughout the city. It would make it
difficult to recall everyone at a moment's notice.

His phone bleeped again. He frowned. It was a bit early
for Tom. He pressed the switch.

'Yeah?' he answered cautiously.

'Mr Marx. I see you're answering your phone again. We
need to talk.'

'Who are you?'

'Let's just say a friend.'

'Oh, yeah; prove it.'

'Listen; your phone is already being monitored. It won't
take long to patch in and listen to us. I'm going to give you a
number. Get to a payphone and call it as soon as you can.'

Arran pulled into a service area a few miles on and rode
round the back of a Dunkin' Donut and parked up by the
phone booth.

'Mr Marx, that was fast.'

'Leave out the crap. Who are you?'

'The name's unimportant, but we have something in
common.'

'No name, no game.'

'Look, Mr Marx, the kid and the old couple don't have
many friends, but they have lots of enemies stacking up.
They can't afford to let any of you keep that material. This
thing reaches too high.' The voice paused.

'I'm still listening, and you haven't told me anything I
didn't know. You still haven't convinced me.'

'I know who's after you.' The caller let it hang like a
hook.

'So who is it, and what does he want?'

'He wants what Barasitch stole from the Group. We
think it must be film or photographs, and we want it.'

'Sure you do; then you pick us off at your leisure. No,
Mister, unless you give me a name I'm about to hang up.'

'No, don't do that, Marx. I'm from a unit called 'The Internal Investigation Agency of the FBI. Let's meet?'

'No deal. What's the head honcho's name, or I hang up.'

'I'll give you it when we meet.'

'No deal. Goodbye, Mister.'

'No; don't. The name's Brevison and he's staying at The Bristol on Central Park.'

'Thanks. See you around.'

'Hey, slow down. You tied up a true agent down there. My name's Hinge. We need each other more than you know. Call McCoy. Then get back to me.'

'I'll think about it.' Arran put the hand set back on its hook. He straddled his bike and waited. It wasn't long before his mobile rang.

'Tom?'

'Yeah. How's it going?'

'Okay. Can you get to the bar in ten, fifteen minutes? I need to talk to you and get you to check some names out.'

'Sure, I'm on my way.' Tom dumped another mobile.

99

Brevison paced up and down. The light outside was fading. Most of his agents were out scouring the city for elusive callers to Marx. He was starting to get low on men. Hinge's call had worried him. It had come from an unknown source outside his hotel. He looked at his watch for the umpteenth time. They had to be getting close to the city.

The phone rang again.

'Sir; Marx is getting careless.'

'Really? Where is he now?'

'Just past Springfield, still on Route 78, but not for long.'

'What do you mean?'

'He stayed on the phone too long. I was able to listen in.'

'Would they have known you were listening?'

'No. Not the way we did it. Anyway, the static created by his vehicle would cover any interference we made. It's not like physically tapping into a landline. We shared a signal, like turning on a radio.'

'Good. Can you play it over the phone?'

'Sure, hold on.' The phone seemed to go dead, then after some squawks Arran's voice came over, loud and clear.

'Hi, Tom; within an hour we'll be in. I'll get 'em settled, then I'll bring the disk. Where are you; the warehouse?'

'Yeah. When do you expect to be able to come?'

'Not before eleven. Must get everyone to the safe house, ready for the media circus tomorrow. Johns been in touch?'

'No, but don't worry. Knowing him, he'll be beavering away getting background material. That's the way he works. We'll give him a call when we're together and arrange a meet.'

'Better cut this before they get a bead on us. See you.' The transmission was cut.

'Were you able to get bearings?' asked Brevison.

'Yes, Sir. I can give you the street, and the building. It's not a good neighbourhood. No wonder he didn't want to take those people with him.'

Brevison looked at his watch. 'Give me the address!'

100.

The motel was a little rundown, on the edge of a small town, but no-one was concerned; everyone glad to stop travelling, they climbed down from the truck. Dee-Dee nudged Alice.

'Pick up your bag, princess. Can you manage mine, Bert?'

'Of course. Aren't you coming in?'

'In a little while. I needta give Snowy a hand parking up. You're booked in under Friend.' Bert scooped up both bags.

'Friend?'

'Yes. Gladys and Denis Friend. Same as your papers.'

Alice started chortling at the face Molly made

'If you ask me, Danny could have picked nicer names. And you can stop your sniggering.'

With her bag slung over her shoulder, Alice pushed through the door and wandered up to the reception. It was a hole in the door; beyond it a small, cramped office. She turned to see if the others were following. Bert was struggling with the two bags and trying to shoulder the door open. Molly was behind him and couldn't stretch past to hold it for him. They were both getting flustered.

'You need to sign in, Gramps.'

The meal was a quiet affair at a diner a block away. They were all tired, and looking forward to a decent bed. Alice played with her food as she listened to Dee-Dee and Snowy telling Bert and Molly what had been arranged. She nudged Molly.

'Can I have the key, Nan? I want to go to bed.'

'I'll come with you.'

'You don't have to. It's not far. I'll be alright.'

'You sure, dear? Let me finish my coffee and I'll take you.'

'It's okay, Nan. It's safe around here. Don't worry.'

Molly glanced at Bert, who shook his head. Dee-Dee caught the signal.

'I'll walk Alice back to her room, Molly. Once she's there, she'll be safe.'

They walked back slowly, Alice sullen.

'You must forgive them, my little princess.'

'They treat me like a kid.'

'I know, and to them you are.' He raised his hand to stop her moans. 'You've been through a lot, but so have they, and they're a lot older than you. It will take Molly and Bert some time to get used to things. You might not have liked the shit that happened to you, but at least you've had time to get used to it, even if it ain't normal. They're still virgins in your world.' He started to chuckle and Alice, infected with his humour, laughed and slapped his arm.

'You are silly sometimes, Dee-Dee.'

He opened the door to the motel and guided her to her room.

'Now I'm going back. You sure you'll be okay?'

'Yeah.'

'We shouldn't be long.' He leaned forward, and holding Alice's head between his huge hands, he kissed her forehead. 'Good night, my little princess.'

'Good night, Dee-Dee.'

The door closed behind her and as she moved across the room she dropped her coat to the floor. She undressed, and except for her panties slipped naked into bed. With the light out, she closed her eyes and waited for sleep.

Tiredness washed over her in waves. Her muscles ached from the long periods of sitting in the truck, but hard as she might, sleep eluded her. Opening her eyes wide, she stared at the closet-mirrored door. Images squirmed inside her head. Molly and Bert's door was ajar, and their bathroom light on. It reflected in the mirror like an empty slot. She clamped her eyes shut and the empty slot filled again with things she didn't want to remember; things that made her skin crawl.

She could bear it no longer and got up and went to the toilet, catching a glimpse of herself in the mirror above the basin. A child's face stared back. She looked so small; but she felt so old, so afraid. Tears dribbled down her cheek.

'Oh, Danny,' she whispered. 'Why won't they go away?'

She gulped down a mouthful of water, rubbed her face dry with a towel, wandered back into the darkened room and over to the open door. She peeked in. They weren't there; of course they weren't. She would have heard them.

Clothes spilled out of the holdall at the foot of the bed. They lay limp and worn. The room was a little larger than her own, with another door leading off. She padded over and turned the knob. Dee-Dee's bedroom lay beyond, in semi-darkness. The light from Molly and Bert's bathroom was enough.

His room was tidy. Had it not been for a holdall in the corner and his jacket lying on the bed, no-one would have known anyone was staying. She poked around the room before sitting on the bed and picking up the jacket. It smelled of Dee-Dee. She put it on and lay down and curled up. Drawing her knees in close, she shut her eyes.

A late guest walked down the corridor and put his electronic key into the slot and rattled Dee-Dee's door handle. Alice's eyes flicked open. She wasn't sure how long she had slept - seconds, minutes, hours? She pushed herself upright and looked around. The bedrooms were still empty, but she felt uneasy. The door handle rattled again and there was a thump as if someone had slammed their shoulder into the door.

Alice fled back to her own room and carefully easing open the door, peered out into the corridor. A man with his back to her was still trying to get into Dee-Dee's room. He reminded her of the killers she'd seen in the garden of the camelback – dark suited. As noiselessly as possible, she slipped out and ran down the corridor away from the intruder. She crashed out through the front doors of the motel and disappeared into the darkness.

101

Once away from the lights, she stumbled along the verge and onto the road. A speeding truck sped past, so close that the force of its passage flung her to the ground. She lay there, crying, stuck, not knowing what to do. A shiver ran through her. Apart from her panties all she had on was Dee-Dee's coat. Even her feet were bare. Something hard was digging into her ribs. She rolled over and felt the ground, but it was smooth. She patted the jacket and brought out Dee-Dee's phone. Like a gift, the thought came to her. Danny would know what to do.

The number was easy. She had looked at his card for so long, hoping he'd come back to that dingy room, it was printed indelibly in her brain. In the dark it took time to find the right button, but once the panel lit up, she was able to dial the number quickly. The phone rang and rang, till Alice was frightened no-one would answer. Five more rings and she'd hang up. Five rings went by. She closed her eyes. 'Five more,' she said out loud. 'Then I'll ha...'

'Yeah?' It was Ducey. Alice opened her eyes.

'Ducey; it's me: it's Alice. I need to speak to Danny.'

'Alice - you can't. He's asleep.'

'Please. I must. I need to talk to him. It's important.'

'I don't know. He's been in pain all day; the Doc gave him some pills he said would knock out a horse, and the Doc's gone off for the night.'

'Please, Ducey, you must wake Danny. *They're* here and no one knows it.'

'Who, Alice? Calm down. You're not making sense. Oh, hell; stop crying, stay calm and I'll see what I can do.'

Danny clawed his way through layers of stuffing. The closer he came to the surface, the more intense was the pain.

'Danny, honey. Wake up. Wake up!' Ducey bent over him, fearful to touch him. 'Danny: *Alice* needs you. *Please* wakeup!'

Alice needed him was all he heard. The surface was close, but so was the pain: *but Alice needed him*. He finally broke through the last vestiges of the drug to raw agony, and sweat poured off him, leaving him chilled.

He opened his eyes. Ducey's face was no more than an inch away from his.

'Thank God. Danny; Alice needs to talk to you.'

He closed his eyes and took a couple of deep breaths. 'Danny - it's.' He lifted his hand.

'Wait. It's the pain. Tell her to hold on.'

'Alice,' she whispered. 'Hold on. He's just awake. He'll speak with you in a moment.'

She could hear the girl gulping air. Danny nodded that he was ready. She held the phone by his good ear. A shudder of pain tore through him, but he took another deep breath and opened his cracked lips.

'Alice…'

'Danny, oh Danny; they're here! They were trying to get into our rooms. You must help me.'

'Alice, stop.'

'No; you must listen - they're here!'

'Who? Alice, you're not making sense.' Danny gasped as another wave of pain sliced through him like forked lightening, taking his breath away. He slumped back into the bed.

'Listen, Danny. Please,' she sobbed. 'They found us and they don't know.'

'Alice!' shouted Ducey. 'You must listen to Danny and answer his questions - otherwise he can't help you.'

'Ducey, he must help.'

'You must calm down. Danny is in great pain. This is hard for him. Now take a deep breath.' She waited as she heard Alice breathe deeply several times.

'Right, where are you?'

'At a motel.'

'And where is that, Alice?'

'I don't know. Arran arranged it.'

'She's at the motel that Arran arranged,' Ducey relayed. 'Are you in the room, Alice?'

'No. I ran away.'

'So where are you?'

'On the highway.'

Danny suddenly beckoned for the phone and she placed it close to his ear again.

'Alice,' he asked. 'Where are the others?'

'In a restaurant. I was tired and they were talking plans so I went back to my room.'

'Alice, why didn't you go back to the restaurant?'

It was the first time she had thought about it. 'I don't know, I was scared.'

'You must go and find them; Dee-Dee will know what to do.'

'Okay. I'm sorry, Danny.'

'Good girl. Now don't worry, everything will be alright, you'll see. Off you go and good luck.'

'Bye.' She paused. 'Danny, I love you.'

'I love you too, girl. Oh - what phone are you using?'

'Dee-Dee's. Why?'

'Does it have a number on it? Can you read it out?'

She read out the number on the LED display.

'Alice, listen carefully. Get back as quickly as you can. Run. Go straight to Dee-Dee and tell him what you've done. Tell him I said you must leave right away. You've blown your position; tell him that.'

'I'm sorry, Danny.' She started to cry.

'Alice, there's no time to cry! Run girl, now. Do you understand?'

'Yeah,' she said weakly.

'Good, now go.' He switched the phone off and closed his eyes.

Ducey stood over him, waiting. 'What has the child done, Danny?'

'I'm certain they'll be monitoring everyone's phone.'

'But surely they won't be monitoring yours. They think you're dead.'

'But they'll monitor Dee-Dee's.'

'Is that bad?'

'Yes. They can locate where the signal came from, and the longer you're on, the more accurate they can get, like within feet of where you're standing. Worst of all, if you stay talking long enough they can even listen in.'

'You mean they'll know it was Alice, and that she's not in New York.'

'I'm afraid so. What's the time?'

'It's half-ten.'

'Get me the house phone. I need to talk to Arran and that mightn't be easy.'

102

Arran and Tom were on the roof of an old building overlooking the warehouse he had set as a trap. Brevison had yet to arrive. It had gone eleven.

'I don't like this, Tom. Something's gone wrong.' He started to get up, but Tom caught his arm and yanked him down.

'Wait. Someone's moving down there.'

From the side of the building a tall figure walked into the open area, awash with security floodlights. The killing ground. Tom lifted the rifle above the parapet.

'Shall I take him out?'

'No. Wait. There's something familiar about him.'

At that moment the figure stopped, raised his hands above his head and turned slowly right around.

'Marx. - Brevison's not coming. He's already left New York. They've located Alice.'

Arran stared at the figure in stunned silence.

'It could be a trap,' cautioned Tom.

'I've got this horrible feeling that it isn't.'

'Marx; we're wasting time. Ring Danny. She called him from outside Dansville.'

Arran buried his head in his arms. 'Shit.'

'We can help, but we must have the disks. We'll get them all across the border.'

Arran stood up. 'I'm up here, Haskins. Where is Hinge?'

Haskins swung round at the voice, lowering his arms. 'In a helicopter ten blocks away, waiting for you. Come down. I'll call him in.'

Arran came out onto the killing ground as the helicopter came in to land. Tom had stayed behind to cover Marx's back. Hinge was in his forties and look like he belonged behind a desk. He put out his hand.

'Mr Marx, it seems you *do* need our help.'

Instead of shaking the proffered hand he slapped the memory sticks into it.

'Thank you. I assume they're copies?'

'You assume right. How do you know they've traced Alice?'

'Alice used Generve's mobile.'

'Why did Dee-Dee let her do that?'

Hinge gave a shrug.

'Unfortunately, I was unable to stop the information getting to Brevison. Once he knew Alice wasn't in New York he realised this was a trap. Out of interest; how were you going to deal with fifteen well-trained agents?'

'Once they found the warehouse empty they'd think it safe to search. We were going to blow it up. Anyone left we'd pick off.'

'How the hell were you going to do that?'

'The place has fuel drums all over, set with small charges.'

'Not subtle; but yes, I think it would have worked. Even Brevison would not have expected such massive overkill. I hope your buddy is going to clear it up before he leaves?'

'Of course.'

'I think we should go, don't you?'

They were a hundred feet up and a block away when Tom cleared the warehouse of explosives. The chopper rocked from the shock wave. Arran smiled across at Hinge.

'As promised, my friend has got rid of the explosives.'

'That's one way of doing it,' he said wryly.

103.

Molly sat nervously on the edge of the bed whilst Bert wore a patch in the carpet.

'Oh, Bert; do stop pacing up and down.'

'I'm worried, Molly.'

'I know. So am I. Now come and sit down and hold me.'

He heaved a sigh, lowered his weary body next to her, and held her tight.

'Where is that blessed girl?'

'Hush. Dee-Dee will find her.'

Suddenly there was a disturbance out in the hall and the door swung wildly open. Alice stood on the threshold, breathless and wild-eyed.

'Where's Dee-Dee?' she gasped, between breaths. 'I need Dee-Dee.'

'Alice, where have you been?' Molly struggled off the bed.

'I need to see Dee-Dee. It's important.'

'He's out looking for you.'

'Alice.' Bert stood up. 'Both he and Snowy are out there somewhere. Now, you stay with Molly.'

'But you don't understand. We've got to leave. Danny said so.'

'Danny?' Bert looked confounded. 'Alice; Danny's in New Orleans, love.'

'I know!' screamed Alice.

'Molly, take care of Alice.'

'You don't understand! I spoke to him!' But she was talking to an empty doorway. Bert was gone.

'Alice, come and sit down. Tell me what has happened.'

'I called Danny on Dee-Dee's phone.'

'That was naughty, Alice.'

'I know.' Alice's eyes were darting round the room like a hunted animal.

'What did Danny have to say?'

'He said I've blown our position. I don't really know what he meant, but he said I must tell Dee-Dee at once.'

'What else did he say?'

'He said we must leave immediately.'

'Well, while we wait for Dee-Dee, you get some clothes on and I'll pack again.' She gave a deep sigh. 'Come on.'

Snowy and Dee-Dee got back before Bert. Reluctantly, Alice told them what she had done.

'How long ago did you call him?'

'I don't know.'

Dee-Dee looked perplexed.

'Alice has been back about fifteen minutes, so not more than half an hour since, I would think.'

'Can't you call Arran, Dee-Dee?' asked Snowy. 'It seems the damage has been done.'

'No; that'll help pin-point us. At least Alice made the call away from the motel. They won't know how we came, and it will take a little time to find out.' Dee-Dee rubbed his chin, in thought. 'Bring the truck to the front, Snowy. We'll make a big show of leaving that way, then we'll transfer to Danny's car once we're out of town.'

'Yeah, that should cause some confusion. I'll go get it. Have the bags ready.'

It had taken no more than ten minutes preparing to travel. Bert had returned and climbed up into the cab without any argument.

It took Brevison another hour before he got to the town.

104.

The noise in the helicopter was such that Marx and Hinge had to shout to hold a conversation.

'How long will it take to get to Buffalo?'

Hinge leaned forward and asked the pilot.

'It will be around one when we arrive. Is that where you want to go?'

'No, but it's close. I'm hoping Dee-Dee is using plan 'B'.'

'We can call and arrange a meeting.'

'Won't that give Brevison an advantage? Surely he's ahead of us?'

'Yes. Air Traffic Control said he will reach Dansville by midnight.'

Arran looked at his watch. 'That's in half an hour.'

'We've pulled Andrews.'

'Andrews?'

'He's in Monitoring: He's been feeding information to Brevison. Without that, Brevison's blind and we're safe to call your friends.'

'What about his men? How many are there?'

'He's on his own, with just a pilot. The rest are back in New York. My people are rounding them up as we speak.'

'So you don't know where he is.'

'Don't worry; I have several agents at each of the border cross-points.'

Arran pulled out his phone and touched out Dee-Dee's number. It was answered immediately.

'Hi, Dee-Dee, it's Arran here. Where are you?' There was a pause. 'It's okay; we're not being monitored.'

'It's good to hear you. We're parked up outside of Aurora. What do we do now?'

'Is Snowy with you?'

'No. He's gone back home, calling everyone he can think of, to confuse the trail.'

Arran smiled. 'I'll give him a call and tell him he can stop. We'll be with you at about one.'

'What about the others?'

316

'They're being taken care of, don't worry. Give me your exact position and I'll get some friendlies to watch over you.'

In the confines of Danny's car it was cramped and uncomfortable. They had cracked open the windows to stop the windshield misting.

'Well,' said Bert, looking around. 'I didn't expect to end up in this thing again.'

'Last time I rode in it I got a bruised backside,' moaned Molly

'From what Arran said I don't think we'll be chasing round the countryside anymore,' said Dee-Dee, looking over his shoulder. Alice touched his leg and pointed. 'Hold up; someone's coming.'

He bent forward and turned the ignition key. The engine caught. A car swung into the lot, drove to the centre, and stopped. The lights died and a figure got out.

'Hold on, folks. It might be one of the friendlies, but put your seat-belts on in case.'

A figure started to walk over to their car. Dee-Dee wound down his window. The stranger got within ten feet.

'That's far enough, mister. What do you want?'

'I'm here with the compliments of Mr Marx. I'll park over there, Sir.' He pointed to the far side of the lot. 'Two other cars are on their way. I was the closest.'

Dee-Dee visibly relaxed. 'Great. Thanks.'

'That was a bit worrying,' said Bert. He could still feel the weight of the gun in his pocket – the gun that Danny had given back to him.

One o'clock had come and gone when they heard the clatter of the helicopter, and saw the landing lights as it came in over the tops of the trees. It hovered for some moments before dropping slowly to the ground. As the dust cleared two figures leapt out, and crouching, ran towards them. The machine lifted away and disappeared back over the trees.

'I hate those things,' shouted Hinge.

Everyone got out of the car and grouped round the two new arrivals.

317

'Bert, Molly; this is agent Hinge, FBI.'

'Pleased to meet you Sir, Ma'am.'

And this-' Dee-Dee, his hand on her shoulder, gently moved her in front of the agent - 'is Alice.'

'We've finally met. You're a very brave girl.' Alice gave him a straight, hard stare. 'Well,' he said, looking around him, not sure what to say next. 'I think we better get going. You can travel in my cars; it'll be more comfortable.'

'I think we'll stay with Dee-Dee. I expect we'll be saying good bye to him soon,' said Bert.

'I'll travel with you, Hinge. I'm sure we don't need the others to wrap up the business,' said Arran.

Hinge waved to the cars that had stayed silent on the perimeter of the parking lot.

105.

It was a quiet journey into Buffalo. Bert and Molly sat in the back, exhaustedly holding each others' hands. Alice stared despondently out of the window.

'Soon be over,' muttered Dee-Dee.

'Are you coming with us?' asked Alice.

'No, princess. I'll go back with Arran.'

'I'll miss you, Dee-Dee.'

'Me too, princess. Maybe when everything is sorted you'll come back and visit us.'

'Can I?' she asked hopefully.

'Sure. You can stay at Miss Ducey's.'

They followed the sleek agents' cars into the forecourt of a large building. "US Border Control" was blazoned above the entrance. A set of wide glass doors slid open as they approached. Inside, they were shown to a large room where they were greeted by a group of people seated round a table. Hinge introduced everyone.

The Secretary to the British Ambassador got up and shook hands.

'This won't take long. We need some signatures, then you'll pass freely into Canada. Our people are waiting in Toronto to sort you out and get you back to England. Can I have your passports?'

Bert undid his shirt and pulled them out from his money-belt.

'We don't have one for Alice.'

'That's already being taken care of.'

They walked over to Arran and Dee-Dee.

'Do you have any more copies? Because this is the time to hand them over,' said Hinge firmly. 'They're of too delicate a nature to be allowed out of the country.'

Arran gestured to Bert. 'He has a set.'

Hinge held out his hand.

Bert hesitated, then asked, 'What about Arran, Dee-Dee and Danny?'

'We won't be pressing charges, if that's what you're worried about.'

'I was thinking more of protection.'

'I have that all covered. The copies, please.'

Bert pulled his hand out of his pocket and dropped the memory sticks into Hinge's hand. He smiled, and put them in his pocket. Alice barged past him and dumped her holdall on the table.

'Mr Hinge.' She turned to the agent and held out her hand. 'I'd like to thank you for all your help.'

'My pleasure, Alice.'

'Even if it *was* late in coming.' She picked up the holdall and walked away.

Brevison peered through binoculars to watch the convoy reach the Peace Bridge. They stopped at the entrance, then one of the large sedans pulled away and started to cross. He dropped the glasses and walked back to a waiting car.

Alice, tears running down her cheeks, looked out of the rear window and waved. A large figure stood alone in the centre of the road and lifted his hand. The sky behind him was streaked blood-red.

'Goodbye, Dee-Dee,' she whispered, then leaned over the front passenger seat. 'Gramps.'

'Yes, Alice?'

'I got you a present.' She held up the three plastic memory sticks that Hinge had put in his pocket.

'How the Dickens did you get those?'

'It fell out of his pocket.'

They passed under the welcoming banner to Canada.

106.

Niagara had been left many miles behind. The stretched-sedan was cruising quietly through banks of dark pine, and the road behind was swallowed in a haze of empty loneliness.

Bert and Molly were slumped exhaustedly in the back, while Alice sat chatting to the driver. She had swapped seats soon after entering Canada. The road some hundred yards in front erupted in a cloud of spurting dust which rushed to meet the car. Alice yelled, grabbed the wheel and tugged it towards her. The driver fought, in consternation. A thud came from the front of the car and the windshield starred. Blood exploded over everyone. Through screams, she did not know whose (perhaps they were her own) she yanked on the wheel, trying to keep to the road. The car slowly mounted the verge and struck a small tree. It stopped dead.

Alice hit the door and rolled out. She tore at the back door, screaming for the others to do the same. Bert sprang out and rolled into the middle of the road. He got up and ran back to Molly, struggling with her seat-belt, her hands flustered with panic. He leaned across to help. The sound of a chopper, getting louder, made him look up. He saw the machine straighten up over the road and charge back at them above the dark alleyway of trees. He stepped away from the car and stood stock-still in the middle of the road, facing the oncoming machine. From his pocket he drew the heavy revolver. With both hands he raised it, sighting along the barrel as Dee-Dee had instructed him - and waited.

The bullets started tearing up the road several hundred yards from him, and wove a zigzag stream of dust towards him. He squeezed the trigger and felt it kick; again, and again, and again. Suddenly something hit him like a truck and threw him across the road like a leaf, landing him hard on his back. He still had hold of the gun as the dark shadow of the chopper ran over him. Opening his eyes he saw the underbelly of the beast and let off two more rounds. Then lost consciousness.

Brevison sat at the edge of the open side door of the chopper, his mouth lifted into a shark's grimace. On the road ahead he saw the car skewed up onto the verge. A dark figure got up from the road and ran back towards it; then stopped and turned, facing the helicopter and standing stock-still. Brevison pressed the trigger and the machine gun came alive in his hands. The bullets ran ahead of him, snaking towards the figure. They connected, and like a puppet, it lifted and was flung backwards. Then the machine was over it. A sharp crack was audible over the clatter of the engine.

He looked across to the pilot, who fell over the controls. The craft tilted and veered sharply away from the road. Brevison tried to scramble forward, but the force of the turn held him tight to his seat. Out of the window he could see the tops of trees, standing up like spears. One came into view and blocked out all the others.

Molly stumbled out of the limo and ran to Bert with a shriek, Alice not far behind. She sank over his body, sobbing, while Alice stopped and looked down, helpless. There was a crashing of branches, and an explosion. Both air and ground vibrated with the noise.

'Our driver's dead,' said Alice, matter-of-factly, 'but I think the car is alright. Gran: We must get Gramps to hospital. Help me move the driver onto the passenger seat.'

Molly moved as in a dream. With a struggle, Alice backed the car onto the road. They stretched Bert across the back seat and Molly squeezed in beside him. Alice glanced over the back of hers and seeing the pallor on Bert's face, gritted her teeth and put her foot on the gas. After a while she got the hang of it and kept the car mostly to her side of the road. She scowled with concentration; there were just the two pedals to contend with; "Stop" and "Go". As long as she kept the speed down, she'd be okay.

'How's Gramps?' She asked it without looking

'Get a bloody move on - and get us to a hospital, Alice.' Through tears she whispered, 'I'm not going to let the daft bugger die on me!'

Bert moaned as if in agreement.

Epilogue
Bert's Last Word.

He awoke in a dimly-lit room. His tongue was stuck to the roof of his mouth. He heard a snort beside him. Twisting his head, he found Molly sitting dozing. Beyond her Alice lay on a couch. He put his hand out to touch Molly's knee, but there was a tube strapped to his wrist by tapes. Molly gave another loud snort, and opened her eyes.

'Bert! You're awake.'

'Don't be daft, woman. I always sleep with my eyes open,' he croaked. 'How's Alice?'

'She's okay.'

'Good.'

'I'd better get a nurse.'

'Molly.' He gripped her wrist. 'Before you go, tell me: Did I hear you swear?'

Lightning Source UK Ltd.
Milton Keynes UK
UKOW04f1926081213

222592UK00001B/9/P